ON WINGED GOSSAMER

New Earth Chronicles – Book 3

A Novel by
VICTORIA LEHRER

ON WINGED GOSSAMER
New Earth Chronicles ~ Book 3
Copyright © 2020 by Victoria Lehrer

All rights reserved. No part of this book may be used or reproduced in any manner whatsoever, without written permission, except in the case of brief quotations embedded in articles and reviews. For more information, please contact publisher at Publisher@EvolvedPub.com.

FIRST EDITION SOFTCOVER
ISBN: 1622533747
ISBN-13: 978-1-62253-374-9

Editor: Becky Stephens
Cover Artist: Richard Tran
Interior Designer: Lane Diamond

www.EvolvedPub.com
Evolved Publishing LLC
Butler, Wisconsin, USA

On Winged Gossamer is a work of fiction. All names, characters, places, and incidents are the product of the author's imagination, or are used fictitiously. Any resemblance to actual events or persons, living or dead, is entirely coincidental.

Printed in Book Antiqua font.

BOOKS BY VICTORIA LEHRER

NEW EARTH CHRONICLES
Book 1: *The Augur's View*
Book 2: *The Triskelion*
Book 3: *On Winged Gossamer*
Book 4: *Tall-ah Earth*

INTRODUCTION

Whereas one or two human protagonists usually take the lead in a drama, the Sovereignty Movement takes center stage in the *New Earth Chronicles*. To save the survivors of Solar Flash from a totalitarian takeover, several people including warriors and visionaries, reluctant heroes, people who contribute in quiet and small ways, and even an antagonist or two, serve as the supporting cast. The Sovereignty Movement pushes, pulls, and sometimes drags the participants through defeats and victories. It changes them, molds them, you might say, and causes them to access inner resources. From unsuspected depths, they mine character strengths such as courage, ingenuity and understanding—whatever is needed to move the movement along. Together, this cast of protagonists and antagonists, in turn, influence the Sovereignty Movement, ultimately alerting others to rise up and face down oppressive forces that underestimate the power for change of the sleeping giant underfoot.

LIST OF CHARACTERS, TERMS, AND LOCATIONS

LEADING CHARACTERS

Dora d'Arc – Daughter of Peter d'Arc, Governor General of Sector 10; dedicated to the Sovereignty Movement; married to Rolf Scholtz; loves Caellum Nichols.

Caellum Nichols – Leads Sovereignty Movement in Transtopia; loves Dora.

Doctor Monroe – Medical doctor who helps the Sovereignty Movement.

Raymond Muñoz – Co-founder of Gaia's Gardens.

Elise Muñoz – Co-founder of Gaia's Gardens.

Charles Scholtz – Imperial Governor of Sector 10; resides at the Imperial Ritz in Transtopia.

Rolf Scholtz – Son of Charles Scholtz; married to Dora.
Biate – Self-proclaimed queen; resides at New Denver Airport.
Nathan Abelt – Spy and pilot serving Charles Scholtz.
Eena Bergemeister – Leader and chief strategist for Sovereignty Movement with mixed ancestry (father is a defected landlord; mother is Native American); augur pilot bonded with Cesla.
Matoskah (Grandfather) – Lakota elder whose name means 'White Bear' in Sioux language; resides on Thunderbird Mountain.
Gavin – Runner from township; augur pilot bonded with Phoenix.

LEADING CHARACTERS FROM BOOKS 1-2 OF THE "NEW EARTH CHRONICLES"

Eena Bergemeister – Leader of Sovereignty Movement with mixed ancestry (father is a defected landlord; mother is Native American); augur pilot bonded with Cesla.
Matoskah (Grandfather) – Lakota elder whose name means 'White Bear' in Sioux language; resides on Thunderbird Mountain.
Gavin – Runner from Township; augur pilot bonded with Phoenix.
Doctor Monroe – Medical doctor.

SUPPORTING CHARACTERS

Yanniv Lebedev – Military Police lieutenant.
Adair – Creates the mural in Cedarhenge; mother of Shaun.
Leslie – Scientist; creates free energy devices; works on holograph device
Cosima – Apprentice of Matoskah.
Professor Neil – Resides in Techno City; teaches history at the university.
Peter d'Arc – Governor General of Sector 10; resides in Techno City.
Chas – Three Mountains farmer of Japanese descent; Eena's love interest.
Rigel – Resides in Three Mountains; of African American descent.
Shaun – Son of Adair and Achmed Scholtz.
Achmed – Oldest son of Charles Scholtz; scientist; father of Shaun.
Emory – Soldier and ornithologist stationed in Three Mountains Valley.
Raiel – Runs an enlightened school for children; close friend of Matoskah.
Anaya – Erathan who now resides in Erath, the inner Earth city.

TERMS & LOCATIONS

Solar Flash – A solar flare that has destroyed the grid and caused destructive storms on Earth; necessitates a start over for surviving humanity.

Plasma Field – Solar System-wide phenomenon connected to Solar Flash; Restores genes switched off by Annunaki visitors to Earth thousands of years ago. These genes foster independence and awakening to the deceptions of the landlords.

Landlords – Progeny of an Annunaki bloodline which presumes the right to rule the world.

SEI – Social Engineering Initiative, an organization under the landlords to keep the 'workers' in-line.

Sector 10 – Extends from Northern New Mexico including the townships and Techno City, the former Farmington, and through Western Colorado including Transtopia, the former Colorado Springs.

Townships – Towns of people conscripted by the U.A. military to build stacked units to live in. The people are forbidden to leave the townships at will.

Runners – Escapees from townships.

Retrievers – Sent in cars with rebuilt engines to capture runners.

Three Mountains – Quartz Mountain, Blue Lake Mountain and Thunderbird Mountain.

Three Mountains Community – A community of runners from townships and the Lakota elder, Matoskah.

U.A. – Union of the Americas, a totalitarian regime that has replaced all nations in the North American and South American continents.

SuperRos – Biate's robot warriors.

SynRo – Human/robot synthetic; cyborg.

Mu – An ancient landmass in the South Pacific (remnants include Hawaii and Micronesia), now underneath the ocean; a remnant on the verge of being submerged 40,000 B.C. is accessible through a portal on Quartz Mountain.

Runners – People who escape landlord/SEI tyranny in townships.

Rovers – People displaced by Solar Flash, violent storms and destructions. Most are families looking for a new place to settle. A minority are armed renegades.

Interludes   I

Chimed notes floated from the balcony, and sunlight streamed through an open window toward the tapered fingers that rested on Caellum's chest, insinuating a promise that such beatitude would shower all his and Dora's awakenings. That he was alive to clasp the hand that had waved him away from base camp three months back and to share the secret that their child gestated in her womb strengthened the promise of unremitting happiness. The breeze from the ceiling fan lifted strands of hair as he brushed away the dark and shining veil to admire her beauty in repose, and as his eyes caressed her, he synced his exhale with her soft breath and pulled her close. Beneath the whir of the fan, his heart drummed his devotion, while the impression lingered that every morning of their lives, chimed notes would float through the window and sunlight would stream just so—and for these blissful moments of their renewed embrace, he cherished the lie.

Caellum waited over an hour—after another round of lovemaking and showers—to speak the truth. Ensconced in the breakfast nook; their plates scraped clean as they sipped their second cup of tea, he voiced what must be said. "I can't stay here at the Imperial Ritz one floor below Charles the SynAnn, I mean the imperial governor. No, Charles the Terrible."

"But no one other than Rolf or Shaun ever comes to my door."

"Am I to remain inside this apartment like a pet dog?"

With an irritating whine a gust of wind tossed the window curtains against the table.

"Of course not. There's an elevator."

"And risk social engineering minions recognizing me?"

"What about the stairs?"

"It's not that I wouldn't climb the fifteen-story stairwell to be with you...."

"We can move to a lower floor."

"And publicize my presence each time I cross the foyer of the Imperial Ritz?"

"We can live on the third floor, below SEI residents. You can ride the elevator between there and the basement."

"Still...."

The wind and flaps of fabric paused, and Dora fanned the dampness from her neck.

"I know." Resignation subdued her tone. "I'm grasping at straws. You can't live anywhere near this building."

The day after their stunning victory; the day after his life was saved; the day after their ecstatic night together, despondency settled between them.

"Or this city." A stricken look followed Dora's declaration.

In the oppressive heat, Caellum willed the air to stir between them.

"But we agreed that the sovereignty movement needs a push." Dora's addendum echoed yesterday's sentiment.

"Or an assassin." Though Caellum's words floated like softly chimed notes, her look of abhorrence unsettled him.

Defensiveness charged his rebuttal. "Charles the SynAnn's not a human being."

"But he's sentient, alive."

"With plans to replace humankind with cyborgs."

"You can't kill someone for intentions."

"He's declared war on humanity — our humanity."

"Thanks to you, we fired the first volley against a nanite invasion — and won the battle."

"One shot from the gun that's hidden under your mattress...." Caellum left and returned with a gun, "A well-aimed shot from this would end this takeover that has grown exponentially more hostile since the arrival of Charles the Terrible."

"More likely, trigger martial law with SEI ministers in command." Abruptly, Dora left the room.

Through the doorway one eye of Cal's vacant stare challenged Caellum's exasperation. Originally, he had placed his dummy look-alike in their bedroom.

"I treasure Cal as a lifesaver as you do," Dora had said, "but during our lovemaking, even a dummy's stare unnerves me."

So Cal, who had hanged from the noose in Caellum's stead, ended up on the living room sofa—a reminder of his human look-alike's brush with execution and, thanks to the dummy, escape.

Their argument hung in the stagnant air until Dora returned with a small fan, and the renewed breeze dispersed the tension between them.

Above the gun Caellum's open hand invited feminine fingers to slide across his palm. "We were discussing my lodging."

Her hand moved to clasp his. "Give me three days."

Caellum thrust his fingers between Dora's and flipped their hands palm to palm to bring her fingertips to his lips and kiss them one by one. "I'll give you as many days as you need."

On reflection, that they would always wake up together immersed in chimed notes and sunshine was a lie. Already restlessness, the urge to do more than skulk about in the dark, the urge to expand the perimeter of his knowledge of the post-Solar Flash world, the urge to vanquish the landlord stranglehold, wedged a tiny crack in this idyllic interlude. But as long as the love between them remained true, he could live with the forces that would separate them.

Emory's urge to expand his knowledge of the giant birds brought him to the summit of Quartz Mountain in the middle of the night and to this predicament. Seeking a large nest, he carried his gun along for protection, but didn't expect to have to use it. Poised to leap, the snapping, growling wolf, its snout wrinkled to expose deadly fangs, faced the man. His hand shaking, Emory pulled the trigger and stepped back. When he tripped and fell, silence sliced through the gun report, and the wolf disappeared.

His skin stippling in response to an envelope of cool moist air, Emory lay on his back. In the heavy atmosphere the effluvia of decaying vegetation afflicted his nostrils. Worse still, the flashlight beam, rather than shedding light on his confusion, illuminated a wall of stone that challenged his recall of falling through open space. Above the rock barricade that shouldn't be there, the tree line touched a patch of stars as distant as the air was close, their twinkles enigmatic, indifferent to his growing panic. He had to get out of here, wherever 'here' was. What just happened?

A new reason for alarm assailed him as he shined his flashlight on his surroundings, and his heart pounded in protest against the alien silence. The trees were all wrong. The moonlight and his flashlight illuminated trunks that had tripled in size. And the color—the tree bark was terracotta red.

Maybe he had fallen and been knocked out, and this was a dream. He shook his head as though to shake away the nightmare. But the snap of a nearby twig alerted him to very real movement nearby and wrung from his terror a silent cry. Help! His flashlight beam zigzagged between an empty void and a tree trunk. At its base loomed a large dark triangle. As he moved closer, a thick pad of pine needles crunched underfoot, confounding his desire for stealth until the beam illumined a rotted out hole big enough for a body. Hope surged. Shelter.

With the butt of his rifle, he knocked away a tarantula the size of his hand, and then, scrunching and twisting, he squeezed inside. He hugged his knees and stared beyond his cramped fortress, until oblivion, merciful oblivion, shut away the ludicrousness, the displacement of Quartz Mountain.

Though Quartz Mountain beckoned, Eena stood as though rooted in Cedarhenge and asked the crew to walk on ahead of her. Thanks to a mask and firecrackers, they had rescued Caellum. Mission accomplished, they could return home. But she needed a few minutes to linger with Adair and Chas in the nine-sided open-air structure where the impossible happened the day before. Sunlight glinted rainbow hues on the etched glass and reflected on the bronze swirls that formed the symbol holding her captive. Perched on a marble podium, the triskelion seemed so innocuous. She needed to make sense of yesterday's surreal event.

Under Adair's guided meditation, light had streamed from the central symbol to form a shimmering torus, which encompassed the fugitives. Nor could they comprehend the illusion yesterday when the Douglas fir in the stained glass mural expanded to enclose them in its girth. Logic dictated the soldiers swarming through Cedarhenge should see Adair and the crew huddled in the center. At this moment, a day later, the disruptors of Freedom Festival should be jailed in Caellum's stead.

According to Adair they had entered a different dimension as they stood invisible to soldiers scrambling around, searching for them, determined to capture them. After the shouts receded in the distance, the mirage, or whatever it was, shimmered out of view, and Adair, Eena and the crew stood exposed in the real world.

Eena's need to comprehend the experience in that other world persisted. What happened? Why was my experience so different from that of the others? After the glowing strands of the torus receded, a collective sense of wonder lingered for all but Eena. Why was she not portaled to bliss? Why was she transported to the most dreadful place she had ever entered: The Gestation Chamber at Fort Carson? A parade of unsettling images invaded her sojourn in the lighted realm, leaving her shaken.

Babies. Clones floating in glass tubes—petri dish specimens of the planned next generation. According to Dr. Olsen, genetic manipulations throughout childhood would suppress their humanness, rendering them puppets of the regime. Protocols designed to stunt their development; to thwart their independence and creativity would determine their destinies. By now the enslaved future work force of the landlords must include close to fifty children, the oldest, around two and a half years old.

Shuddering from the persistent images, she turned her eyes toward the mural covering three walls of Cedarhenge. The jagged hole in Adair's stained glass work of art, targeted by the soldier's frustration, loomed as a reminder of the troops' search. As though to shatter the very soul of the Douglas fir, the bullet passed through the center of the knothole.

Adair herself was an enigma as she soothed Eena's distress. "The heart of the image is easily repaired, but the soldier's—not so simple... poor guy."

Eena snorted. "Poor guy?"

"Given a gun, he was primed to shoot it."

"He was after *us*."

"We were presented as the enemy."

Eena's retort was vehement. "His kind and the system they serve are the enemy."

"Delusion is the enemy."

With those words that reverberated a familiar chord, Eena turned to Chas. "Who does she sound like?"

He squeezed Eena's shoulder and addressed Adair. "A Lakota elder named Matoskah would likely agree with you."

Adair's chuckle disarmed Eena and prompted an admission. "Even though Matoskah—Grandfather—has taught me a different way, my first reaction is usually to retaliate."

But as she spoke, the question that continued to plague her surfaced. *Without weapons, how can we hope to break the back of the oppressive system of landlords, their social engineering minions and armed forces?*

Though Eena kept to herself the trans-dimensional shake-up, her angst hovered, throttling her breath until the intent of the remote viewing penetrated her consciousness. She realized she would soon be returning to Transtopia and that firecrackers and a mask wouldn't suffice for the next rescue. With a departing glance at the etched glass Triskelion, Eena shook away the still clinging pall. She gazed ahead toward the group crossing the meadow with light-hearted banter as though still buoyed by the otherworldly experience. When Adair said pointedly, "We'll meet again," they hugged goodbye. Eena nodded to Chas, and shouting "Wait up!" hurried to catch up with the crew.

An hour later the group reached the red sandstone formation of massive standing stones known as the Garden of the Gods. The sight of the milling flock of teal-colored birds that dwarfed their human pilots buoyed her spirits and she hurried to single out her bond mate, Cesla.

Tether in hand Leiani looked anxious. "So how did it go?"

"Our mission was a success. Caellum is alive and very likely with his beloved Dora as we speak."

As Leiani cheered, Cesla lowered his head to press his crown against Eena's chest. It was a familiar form of augur greeting, but in this case prolonged, perhaps because she had helped raise him from a chick, and they had been bond mates for three years, and she had been away for two weeks. She chuckled, and after a vigorous scratch below the augur's bony jaw, her fingers moved to the elongated feathers standing erect at his crown and stroked the powerful neck. Full measure, she returned Cesla's gladness to be reunited.

Leiani handed Eena a mango so she could complete their greeting ritual with a hand-feeding. As Cesla grabbed stringy bits of pulp in his beak and raised his head to gulp them down, Eena sighed because the thought of harm coming to this avis gigantus presaged such grief. Since the soldiers occupied Three Mountains Valley, each flight through the portal between Quartz Mountain and Mu endangered Cesla's life.

In response to Gavin's "So are you two lovebirds ready yet?" she shook off the sense of foreboding. Seeing that the others were mounted and ready for flight, she tossed the seed, wiped the sticky juice on her pants leg, and straddled Cesla's tail to scoot to the mounted position. Her fingers ensconced in Cesla's downy breast, the liftoff yielded the heady sensation of escaping the bounds of earth.

The Transtopia skyline receded into the distance, yet a sense of urgency to return loomed. The project at Fort Carson provided the trunk line of the social engineering branches. For humanity, the success or preemption of that project represented destiny's fork in the road. Humankind faced two radically different time lines—one, the achievement of collective and individual sovereignty; the other, workers doomed by the machinations of an oppressive regime.

Eena and the crew approached Quartz Mountain from the north face, hidden from the view of the soldiers in Three Mountains Valley. As they flew over the summit to land in the clearing beside the portal, she scanned for troops crawling the mountain in search of giant birds or them.

Matoskah. The one person Eena didn't expect to see was Grandfather. Why was he standing near the portal, a bandaged wolf nearby? *Valek?*

As the pilots and augurs circled to land, Eena recalled the dream three years ago in which, guided by an eagle, she flew to Blue Lake Mountain. Wearing the man-in-the-maze pendant that matched her own, Matoskah stood beside the lake near the summit as though expecting her. Although she had no memory of ever meeting this Lakota elder, she recognized him. The connection between them transcended time and space.

Today, Matoskah, most often referred to as Grandfather, waited in the clearing beside the portal. He stood as straight as ever, but he looked smaller somehow, the lines in his face more deeply etched, and his smile—his sweet smile—more ethereal, as though of another world. When did Matoskah, her compass for navigating this world, who could outclimb and outthink the best of them, become so frail? When Cesla's claws grabbed the earth, a cloud of dust swirled around Eena and overshadowed her spirit.

Survivors   2

Raymond gazed proudly at the thriving community now named Gaia's Gardens. If only the intrusive nudge of anxiety would allow him these few minutes to revel in all that had been accomplished in three years. If only this little paradise and the portions of I-25 severed by earthquakes could forever keep the control system at bay.

Gaia's Gardens had responded to the capture and recycling of water and soil nutrients by coiling grape vines up wooden arbors and gracing homes with magenta prairie roses. Tall sage bushes, prickly pear and desert willows with yellow flowers lined the lanes of cob houses, comprised of an ancient recipe of clay-rich soil, water and straw. The ten acres of hemp were already producing fiber for both rope and clothing, and offering CBD oil for healing tinctures and soothing creams. Healthy complexions evidenced fresh and abundant produce from the gardens, which surrounded the households and yielded sufficient food for winter storage.

But the memory of the helicopter that circled the town a couple of weeks ago wormed its way into Raymond's gut. Whose helicopter? Why? What were they seeking?

Raymond knew that sooner rather than later, he would have to defend Gaia's Gardens from inevitable invasion by Transtopia to the south and/or Denver to the north. To monitor the recovery of those two cities and surrounding areas became an urgent priority. He began carrying camping gear in a backpack and skirting Gaia's Gardens in ever-widening arcs that encompassed tiny collections of outlying vacated buildings. His third exploratory arc led him five miles north to a small farmhouse. In a fenced-in yard of clucking chickens where an old man harvested tomatoes in tilled rows of vegetables, a dog barked at his approach.

The gardener, balancing a load of ripe tomatoes against his chest, nodded toward Raymond. "Well, hello, there. You a rover?"

"No, sir, just a person looking for fellow survivors. I'm from a little community about a day's hike from here."

Raymond hesitated outside the fence until tail wagging accompanied, and then replaced, the dog's barking.

The old man glanced at his dog. "Scamp's harmless. Come in and close the gate behind you."

The dog and Raymond greeted one another before the host spoke again. "How about a sit with me and a cool glass of water. Name's Cliff." Cliff lowered a bucket into a nearby well, filled a metal pitcher and retrieved two glasses.

After Raymond set down his pack, sleeping bag and tent, and the two were settled at a shaded table, both wanted to know the other's survival stories. Raymond swigged water, then told Cliff about his stay underground during the Earth changes, his family's escape and the subsequent influx of survivors to just north of the Zone of Destruction. Gaia's Gardens.

"I'm living the best time of my life—far from the control structure and close to nature—at least for now. So, Cliff, what's your story?"

The old man looked past Raymond as though transported to a former time and viewing scenes only he could see.

"My wife, Sara, and I live on the top floor of a retirement high-rise located at the edge of downtown Denver. There's been no forecast of a storm when we stand at our glass patio door watching the lightning flashes. I've always been fascinated by lightning. As a child I loved watching the flashes and counting down to the booms.

"But that evening—the night of Solar Flash—remains etched in my memory as the most spectacular event of my life, and since I've just passed my 80th birthday, that's a lot of decades. Mind you, I'm not talking about a single bolt of lightning at a time. Those strikes are continuous—I mean, nonstop. I step out on my balcony. Foolish, I know, but it allows me to see a panoramic view: 270 degrees of currents arcing toward Earth. There are none of the loud booms connected with thunder. Only zaps and snaps of electrical discharges—sometimes a bang when a bolt hits a transformer.

"To the northeast I see a sight I never thought I'd see around here. Across the horizon ripples a sheet of shimmering green waves. It resembles the Aurora Borealis we saw when we toured Iceland. Overhead and from horizon to horizon, the cloudless sky hosts a pulsing bright light as if invisible hands are flicking switches on and off.

"The light show continues for an hour until act two gets even better. But before I tell you about that, I need to backtrack. You with me?"

Intrigued, Raymond nodded. He'd always wondered what happened topside while he and his family were in Cavern City.

"About a month before that night, I'm at the convention center listening to some teen rock star with my 13-year-old granddaughter and a couple of thousand screaming kids. Suddenly, between songs, in the midst of applause, whistling and cheers, two gorgeous, very tall people materialize on stage. The lead singer backs away as the pair step toward his microphone. They tower over the singer. I'd say the male was around seven feet tall, the female about six inches shorter.

"Almost instantly, that auditorium becomes so silent, you could hear a pin drop.

"I wrestle the binoculars from my granddaughter to view the arrivals. They are both astonishing representatives of ideal beauty. Long straight hair parted in the middle—hers golden, his silvery. Oval faces with large, blue-violet eyes. Her brows are perfectly winged, his slightly thicker, slanting down.

"The male begins to speak. He has this real pleasant voice, and a calm settles over the audience.

"'Your sun is about to undergo a momentous change,' he begins. 'It has been very quiet for several years with no sunspots. But you may have noticed its white-hot intensity. Since the turn of the century, it has been packing energy, building an explosive charge. Soon, it will eject a massive solar flare that will wreak havoc on Earth's surface.'

"When cries of alarm erupt among the spectators, the female extends her hands, fingers up, palms facing out, and the cries die down. She speaks. 'There's no cause for alarm. Some of you have aligned with Earth and have chosen to participate in a final showdown with the dark forces that grip your planet. Some of you have been asking to leave. And, indeed, an Earthlike planet awaits your arrival.'

"'We, your genetic sisters and brothers, hearken from the Pleiades Constellation. We have known this time to be coming and have prepared a planet for you: Gaia—2.'

"An astonished uproar rips through the audience and interrupts the speaker. With poised presence, she pauses for the return of silent attention. 'We have ships, each of which can carry thousands. Ships with access to star gates through which you can speedily reach the home that awaits you.'

"Amid disgruntled murmurs, trickles of people move toward the isles and head for the exit. The space woman continues. 'We will take no one against his or her will. You must volunteer to join us. Watch for us. We will appear on your holographic screens, in news broadcasts and at large gatherings. Spread the word. A crisis approaches planet Earth, but so does help.'

"Sara and I don't connect with the aliens. So we decide to stay put. A couple of weeks later the government offices close. Reports fly that the city leaders and a segment of the population have disappeared—to where, no one knows.

"So back to where I started my account—watching the spectacular light show. It's a month after the concert and two weeks after the government shutdown. I'm on my balcony when out of nowhere a huge cigar-shaped craft materializes. Must be a mile long at least. Then another and another until a flotilla of similar crafts cover the Denver sky. I hear shouts and screams at street level. Transfixed by what I'm seeing, I call for Sara.

"Then a beam shoots out from the underbelly of a craft. The cone of light widens as it reaches the pavement. A small group of people steps into the beam and rises straight up as though riding an invisible elevator. There's no sign of alarm, no flailing of arms. They've obviously volunteered.

"One cone of light after another protrudes among the apartment buildings and into neighborhoods. In rapid succession, groups who must have decided to take their chances with the aliens and depart for the new world, rise toward the craft. Amid surrounding flashes and electrical buzzes, the close-up silence is eerie.

"The next morning we're alone in our apartment building. The city's dead. As far as I can tell within a half-mile radius there's not a single living soul. It's creepy. After a week Sara and I, too terrified to step outside, decide to move to the basement. We're hunkered down below street level with candles and food before the electricity goes out and relentless booms shake the building. We hold each other close, sure that our days are numbered.

"Three days later the rains and the wind begin, and we're about out of food, with only a small dry goods storage remaining. Sara and I realize our only hope for survival is to leave the city and come here — to my family homestead, where we have a water source, can live on rice and beans for a while and cultivate a garden. We decide to brave the storms and head out. Fierce gales force us to duck into buildings. We're not sure we can make it.

"Along the way, we pillage grocery stores until taking advantage of breaks in the wind and rain, we finally leave the outskirts of Denver to head into the desert. About two miles from here, our neighbor, Tim Sutters, shelters us until the storms ease. He sends us on our way with a rooster, two hens, garden seeds and a pup, Scamp, here.

"Four months later, on the brink of starvation, still alive thanks to the well water, we celebrate our first harvest.

"Within a year we locate another neighbor about a mile down that dirt road out there and trade corn, bags of seed and an extra plow for a milk cow. She's kinda skinny on account of the scarcity of grass around here.

"Miraculously, the worst of the tornados and horrific winds we've heard about skirt us, so we survive the Earth changes that apparently take a lot of lives."

The tired eyes shifted to Raymond. "How about a sandwich with cheese, lettuce and fresh tomatoes?"

Raymond nodded gratefully.

Cliff stood up. "Sara died last year, so here I am all by my lonesome... and ready to join her."

The screen door creaked as Raymond followed the old man into the kitchen.

"So, you have neighbors?"

"A few. We get together occasionally."

"You took me for a rover."

"Thought you might be one, though we've only seen a couple."

"Were they aggressive?"

"Naw. Just hungry. Passing through. Looking for some town to settle in."

"Any news about Denver?"

"Word is it's a dangerous place ruled by gangs. Best to stay away."

Cliff placed two plates of sandwiches on the table. "The place to watch is the New Denver Airport."

"Why's that?"

"Creepy new world order type place. Robots everywhere."

Raymond had a sense that it was important to know what was going on at New Denver Airport and made a mental note to widen his trek.

The urge to head north to Gaia's Gardens and onward to Denver provoked the restlessness that was growing exponentially in Caellum. Dora had told him of the burgeoning town beyond Rubble Wall. So far, the community had evaded imperial clutches. Denver loomed just beyond. Much larger than Colorado Springs, which was renamed Transtopia by the Scholtzes, very likely Denver was another landlord stronghold. Were Raymond Muñoz's town and the Sovereignty Movement in Transtopia potential allies in the fight for freedom? By the third morning, Caellum fidgeted and paced, and bemoaned his caged status to Cal.

Dora was sympathetic. "I know I said three days and this is the fifth. I've searched the city. Today I'll approach Unit One. Irene and the other residents there have taken a lead role in the Sovereignty Movement."

"I did say 'take as long as you need.'"

Caellum straightened Cal and stuffed an errant strand of straw into his shirt. "I hope Dora hurries up, 'cause I've got to get out of here before boredom turns me into a raving lunatic."

When a knock on the door came, he froze, then moved closer, but dared not open it until a muffled voice came through. "Caellum, open up. It's Shaun."

Shaun. He grabbed the knob and jerked open the door. This was the first time he'd seen him since Cal's hanging. With a flood of gratitude for Shaun's role in saving his life, Caellum hugged his visitor and led him to the kitchen table. "We have powdered lemonade, chicory coffee from the Cavern City storage and sage tea."

"I'll take the lemonade."

When the drinks were poured, Caellum explained that Dora was looking for a room for him. "So how about the Sovereignty group?"

"Number's grown to twenty again. Everyone's pretty creeped out by the SynAnn governor."

"Any successful infiltrations?"

"A couple. The head of the Transtopia Motor Pool Repair Center and the manager of Metro Electrical repairs. I guess middle management is the best we can hope for. The social engineering tier remains impenetrable."

"Nathan still spying?"

"Not so much at the university. I think he's moved onto general surveillance of the working population. The number of runners has increased since Freedom Festival."

Feeling the summer heat, Caellum turned on the fan. "Personally, I think the only way we're going to get rid of this governor is assassination." Caellum's assertion dropped lightly, like a falling feather.

Shaun's glass hit the table hard. "Whoa!"

"I know he's still your grandfather, sort of."

"Besides that, I thought the whole intent of the movement was a peaceful takeover."

The friends quietly swigged their drinks before Shaun spoke again, avoiding the discussion minefield between them. "You know there were two reasons our forty student attendees dropped to a handful prior Freedom Festival."

Caellum nodded for Shaun to continue.

"One was that students were scared of being caught by Nathan's spy ring. The other was that half of them were shipped off to plant and harvest corn at Onmatson Farm."

"I'm ashamed to say, I hadn't given them much thought." Caellum grimaced his embarrassment.

"I pulled royal privilege to visit them. Their lives are miserable. Deplorable living conditions. I would like to help them. Problem is the Sovereignty Gardens' first crop didn't produce enough food for the entire Transtopia population. Without the GMO corn to supplement the food supply, the whole population would be starving by spring."

"What about the cattle herd? Chickens?"

"Not even close to enough meat for a hundred thousand people. And most goes to SEI employees. As you know, the workers get the innards."

Expletives exploded from Caellum's disgust. "I think we're agreed we want to rescue those students. But first it looks like Dora needs to head up an expansion of Sovereignty Gardens so that if the Onmatson Farm folds, the entire population will still have enough to eat. Meanwhile, at meetings let's plan the enslaved students' escape."

"But to where?"

"That's the big question."

"Shaun smiled. "Nudge Dora to hurry up and get you out of here."

"Besides," Caellum added, "We're going to need her and the gardening co-coordinators' full participation for our next moves."

"By the way, according to my mom, that town, Gaia's Gardens, established by Raymond Muñoz already produces enough food to feed its people."

"Sounds like we could learn a thing or two from him."

"Agreed. I gotta run. But I'll be back. Need anything?"

"Freedom. Vipers surround me in this hotel."

"I hear you. Dora's on it, I'm sure."

Shaun's visit nudged Caellum to contact another person residing in the Ritz. Rolf had played a vital role in saving his life. After seeing Shaun out, Caellum's musings turned to the Imperial Governor's son. *Well, neighbor, you're the wild card in this bizarre scenario. I've resented you for being Dora's husband, despised you for being second in line for the imperial governorship, and now I owe my life to you, someone I've never met. Guess this is visiting day.*

As Caellum grabbed Dora's apartment key, he reflected that she and Shaun were in agreement that sovereignty in food production merited a phase two expansion. However, neither accepted the hard reality to be faced—the essential extermination of the SynAnn head of Sector 10. Meanwhile, the issue of increased food production, coupled with the need for an ally, merited a forthcoming visiting day at Raymond's town.

Visitors

3

An extensive search for a safe apartment for Caellum left Dora discouraged. They were filled except for basement storerooms. Anyway, she didn't know the residents. What if snitches lived among them? In desperation she sought the help of Irene, whom she had come to know at gardening meetings. "What do the people of Unit One think of Caellum?"

"They regard him as a hero."

"Everyone?"

"Everyone in this unit."

"Think he'd be safe here? He needs a place to live."

"Sure, but unfortunately, the apartments are filled with families."

"The basement?"

"As far as I know, there too. But let's take a look." Irene grabbed a set of keys from a wall peg labeled *basement*.

Though the basement hallway smelled musty, the floor had been swept and mopped, and the walls were freshly painted. They passed a line of doors with plastic numerals attached.

"These were originally just storage rooms, but we helped childless latecomers turn them into apartments."

Dora recalled the dismal state of Leon and Rita's basement home in the Ritz before their move to the third floor. When she and Irene reached the last room at the end of the hall, the door opened to a small room with a push broom, large mop and bucket beside a double utility sink. The cement floor and cinder block walls were unpainted, and dirty windows near the ceiling allowed limited light through streaked glass. The impression of cramped dinginess withered her last tendrils of hope.

Irene looked apologetic. "I guess this is it. The only available square footage in the building."

"Oh, Irene, Unit One is the one place in the city I wouldn't worry about his safety." Dejection slumped her shoulders she stood in the dismal space. "There's no heat source." Spoken as the death knell to the slim possibility of the room becoming a livable space.

"We all have wood stoves."

"They were provided for you?"

"No, we made them."

A tiny shift lifted Dora's shoulders. "Where can I find one?"

"We've made stoves from empty propane tanks, old metal barrels and such. Tool chests are also options. Soldered metal plates provide cook tops."

"Where'd you get the parts?"

"They're not hard to find. My husband Eric can make you a stove." Irene scanned the room. "We can direct the vent pipe through that window."

"Okay, Irene, I'll take this room." Dora approached cans of paint stacked in one corner. "Paint. I'll need paint. Furniture, I can get from the Ritz."

Irene looked apologetic. "I'd help you spiffy up the room if I didn't have to get back to work.

Dora smiled her thanks and grabbed the broom. "You've helped enough. I've got this."

"I'm fairly certain Eric can build the stove and install it by the end of the week." Irene handed her the key and left.

After a trip to the Ritz to ask Rita for cleaning supplies and paintbrushes, Dora returned to her task without informing Caellum. Struggling to fight down despair at the dismal choice, she couldn't bear to show him his new quarters in this state. Scouring the walls and floor, washing the windows and painting would require several days of secrecy before the room could look remotely inviting.

Slipping the apartment key inside his pocket, Caellum looked up and down the hallway before he hurried to knock on Rolf's door—down the hall and around the corner.

A blond male, a head taller than he with unmistakably German features, opened the door.

"Caellum."

"Rolf... I haven't thanked you for your part in saving my life."

"Please come in. Can I fix you a drink?"

"No, thanks. We hadn't met...."

"Have a seat."

After Caellum sat on the sofa, Rolf dropped into the overstuffed chair across from him and confessed, "I actually had a great time confounding my synthetic old man. But I wouldn't have done it without my... without Dora pushing on me."

"She can be persistent."

"You better watch your step, though. My new dad's a hardcore psychopath."

Caellum remained mute, not sure what to say.

"Does it surprise you that I think of my born-again father this way?"

"It's hard to imagine being in your shoes."

Rolf slouched in the chair, and Caellum looked across the room toward a Matisse print of a yellow cat with a paw in a fishbowl. "My original father never liked me, nor I, him. To be honest, I really don't care much about anything, including your movement. The extent of my involvement with the world includes affection for two people: my friend, my lover, Alexi, and my wife, your lover, Dora."

At first Rolf's droll delivery evoked a blank stare. But when Rolf's pressed lips and hooded eyes failed to suppress the suggestion of a smile, Caellum's laughter broke the tension.

After silent reflection settled between them, Caellum became serious. "It's hard for me to leave Dora, even to live across town from her—especially at this time, while she's expecting. I don't trust Charles the SynAnn."

"Good one. I hadn't thought of that name for my bionic dad."

"I guess I want to ask if you will please look after Dora for me."

Rolf's chin jutted and a haughty expression matched his dismissive tone. "I don't need to be asked to do what is second nature to me."

Caellum drew back as if he'd been slapped. A minute of processing his confusion finally freed his tongue. "Of course, and I'm glad to know it."

With those words the conversation dried up, and Caellum rose from the sofa, glad to have performed his obligatory appreciation visit to the prickly second son of the governor. But Rolf motioned him down with, "There something you should know," so Caellum sat, sensing information important to his and Dora's future was forthcoming.

"My dad has plans for your baby."

"I anticipated this."

"Dear old Dad's present incarnation, which is likely to live indefinitely, at least for another century in his synthetic body, has not a single ounce of affection for Achmed or myself. Progeny of the Scholtz line, we are simply valuable resources for the extension of his empire. He intends his bloodline to become ruling monarchs, to govern Techno City, Denver and beyond as his realm expands. However, since he is now sterile, neither he nor Achmed can sire future rulers. He sees Dora and me as the only supply source of the future offspring earmarked for ruling slots. In short, he intends to groom the child he believes is mine, along with all Dora's future children, to serve his purposes. Don't underestimate the implications of this information. Your children will not be your children. They will be his heirs to be tutored in the art of ruthless expansion of the Scholtz Empire."

Dora needed help with the next phase of her preparations of Caellum's room. She approached Leon who had become far more to her than her driver. In fact, he and his wife Rita, who cleaned her apartment, had become family.

"I have the key to Room 324 which is an empty apartment. Without being conspicuous, we need to transport furniture from the Ritz to Unit One. The only way to proceed and not be noticed by police is to load the limo for several trips."

"Miss Dora, you're not lifting a thing. I'll get help."

After several trips, when furniture filled the room, the concrete floor still looked uninviting, but the addition of small throws and a couple of pillows helped. Although the large utility sink still looked incongruous, they had arranged a twin bed, chest of drawers, easy chair, small kitchen table with chairs, and an ice chest in the limited, but freshly painted space. Rugs beside the bed and under the easy chair, and the shiny black woodstove with a cooktop added a homey touch. Dora declared the room ready for Caellum's eyes.

"So, you're going to leave me here to spend my nights alone?"

"I'll stay with you as much as I dare."

"Twin bed's the best you could manage?"

"I could have chosen a queen bed that would practically fill the room." Irritation thudded the bag containing a hot meal from the Ritz on the table. "We'll just have to make do."

"I see what you mean. The aroma from that bag is making me hungry."

Dora retrieved still-warm plates, and removed the dish towels wrapped around them. "Since, thanks to that narrow bed, you have room for a small table, we can eat our compliments-of-the-Ritz lunch here." The edge in her voice hinted at disappointment in Caellum's lack of appreciation for her efforts.

From behind, Caellum put his arm around her and lifted her hair to kiss her neck. "And then I can express my gratitude as we 'make do' on that small bed over there."

Dora's ire cooled as the hand that had pulled aside her hair, moved to cover the slight bulge in her belly. The ripening in her womb paced the flowering of the summer crops of Sovereignty Gardens. By the time of the planned Fall Festival, when people gathered to feast and celebrate the harvest, she would be six months along.

The present moment, in this tiny homestead, twin bed and all, proffered sweet anticipation of nights when Caellum would press his hand against a small foot, and lay his ear close to listen for the heartbeat. During the weeks her belly swelled, she basked in his growing attentiveness and awaited his return from sovereignty meetings without the slightest inkling of changes to come. Until the early frost turned the corn stalks gold, the cozy warmth belied the night the woodstove would hold only ashes, and the wind would chill a cold and empty bed.

Predators 4

Eena was glad she had decided to remain with Grandfather. When she hugged him, he felt so thin she had to stay. Chas hesitated after the others had passed through the portal, but she nudged him away. "We've got Valek. You need to tend your animals."

Valek raised his head, thumped his tail, and greeted her wolf style by licking her face.

Grandfather reassured her. "Valek will live to lead his pack."

Roughing the wolf's fur, she had murmured, "Our meeting here, remarkable timing," though she knew there was more to the meeting than coincidence.

Grandfather turned toward a strip of leather bound by cords to two sturdy sticks. "I have made a stretcher for Valek." When they had lifted the wolf onto it, Grandfather's eyes, as bright as ever beneath folds of age, glinted his familiar, dry humor. "He was protecting me."

"From what?"

"From a soldier on a reality quest."

She was accustomed to Grandfather responding to questions without answering them. "A what?"

"Matoskah grunted. "We can talk more at my camp."

As the stretcher-bearers followed the network of trails to the elder's teepee, Eena breathed in the pine-scented air of the world she loved to return to. They crossed the field strewn with quartz, the piezoelectric crystals that gave the mountain its unique properties, and maneuvered the stretcher over the stream in the ravine between the mountains. Climbing the steep face of Thunderbird Mountain, they stopped more than once as Grandfather, who in the past had out-climbed those younger than himself, gasped for breath.

When they reached the old man's camp, he sat down heavily on a stump. Eena took charge. *Grandfather, how do I hide my alarm? I thought you'd be viral forever.* "You sit. I'll make the tea."

Grandfather pulled a small bottle and a package from his shirt pocket and motioned toward the wolf. "Mix these to make a poultice."

Valek lay still as Eena tended the wound, and when she completed her ministrations, licked her hand. "Just grazed his shoulder. Looks like he's going to be fine."

"The one that waits behind the trees will be glad." Grandfather gestured with his chin.

Eena detected a slight movement in the surrounding forest. "Of course, his mate."

When the human moved away to start a fire, the female wolf slunk toward Valek to nuzzle and lick a greeting, then lay down on the side farthest from the humans.

With a stab of nostalgia Eena felt the absence of sounds wafting from the valley—the echoing shouts of neighbors and children, the *thwack* of axes and the notes of bows moving across violins as musicians practiced for the next dance. In those bygone days the noises that reached Matoskah's camp comforted the listener with the nearness of community. The soldiers, squatters as far as she was concerned, were much quieter. "Grandfather, you must get lonely sometimes. Do you miss Raiel?"

"The portal connects us."

After they drank the tea and Grandfather rested, they fished together in the pool close to his camp. The gurgle of the waterfall accompanied Eena's account of Caellum's rescue.

Grandfather's face reflected in turn alarm, surprise and mirth. At the end he mused, "Great adventure."

While he removed a fish from the hook and placed it in the bucket, Eena stared at the water, and the swirls at the base of the waterfall stirred the memories repressed for these three years and now resurfacing. She had not talked about the Fort Carson abomination since she first told Grandfather and Chas.

"My daughter, a shadow crosses your face."

A fish pulled on her line. She yanked it out of the water, but it was so small, she freed it and released it back to the pool. "Grandfather, a vision, a specter really, has taken hold of me. I won't rest until I have at least attempted to thwart the plan to turn humankind into an A.I.-controlled, synthetic slave race."

"Ah, you're speaking of the babies at Fort Carson."

When they had eaten fish and potatoes cooked with greens, and the evening shadows lengthened, Eena washed their dishes and grew pensive. "It's hard for me to return to Mu."

The old man's stillness invited her to speak more.

"I had hoped the Sovereignty Movement would have grown more powerful by now. Instead, the new ruler of Sector 10 is formidable, no, frightening — a cyborg with a download from a human brain, synthesized DNA and a skeleton of fused polymers and titanium. A blend of technology and biology, he commands obeisance with an edge like serrated steel.

"After two years the Sovereignty Movement's efforts to seed the townships and infiltrate the power hierarchy have yielded meager results. Those enslaved by the system believe and defend the saviorship propaganda and toss our pamphlets into trash bins. Since Caellum's capture the proliferation of spies and military presence on the streets threaten to squash our movement."

The elder pointed toward the single star twinkling in the indigo sky. "Venus — the first light. To the Lakota, Venus is the star of hope, the one that signifies the return of White Buffalo Woman; when the black, red, yellow and white nations share the pipe of peace. Together we will walk the road of personal empowerment."

Eena sighed wearily. "Amá shared that legend with me. But it's been over three decades since the births of white buffalo calves indicated her return."

Grandfather's expression was stoic as he continued. "Night after night, soon after the evening star appears, Mars, the battle-scarred planet of war, shines its red light."

Eena raised her hands from the soapy water and extended her palms in a "What are you saying?" gesture.

"My daughter, I must tell you something you will not like to hear. In this realm the forces of darkness will never be completely vanquished."

Could these be the words of the mentor who had encouraged her — called her his warrior daughter? "But haven't you always said we are ultimately invincible?"

"Yes, I have. And we are."

"Well, Grandfather, I have to admit I'm stymied."

His eyes twinkled. "Gavin would say I'm making no sense."

As Eena tossed the dish water, the dowse of discouragement left her suddenly feeling weary.

The old man resumed the direction that was clear only to him. "The forces of corruption will always be around, always wielding intimidation and deception. But it's up to you whether or not they rule you."

"So you're not saying it's hopeless?"

"I'm saying the cosmic balance of power supports your efforts."

"Sounds tiresome."

"It's strengthening, like a good day's work. The trick is to stand your ground on your terms, not the opponent's."

"You're referring to Aikido—and to 'the disappearing opponent.'"

"Yes, disappearing in the sense that you prove your sovereignty. The gaze of the opponent can't siphon your strength if you align with the source of all power."

"But they'll always be around?"

"Yes, dark and light coexist in the universe of probabilities."

"Then we should just accept that dark reality?"

"Only as a motivator to spur bringers of the dawn—warriors like the one from Earth's underbelly and like yourself—to take action."

Eena sat up, startled. "Wait a minute. What did you just say?"

"A swirl of red sand blew me a message a few nights back."

"Red sand?" Like in parts of the southwest surrounding Colorado?"

"No. Farther away. Much farther."

"Grandfather, what are you talking about?"

"My impression was of help from an ally."

"Red sand that's far away. An ally. And...."

Grandfather shrugged. "That's all I know."

Eena heaved a deep sigh. Another of Grandfather's undecipherable messages. She shook away her frustration. "So, Grandfather, you said to take action. Which brings me full circle, to the reason I feel so restless in Mu."

"Then fortune shines on you, my warrior daughter. Your next spur to action, the soldier who shot Valek, awaits you there."

Chestnut waves framed Cosima's heart-shaped face as she walked away from her log home in Mu to trek to Blue Lake Mountain and spend a day or two with Grandfather. She wore his gift, the white deerskin dress, because it would please him. With the strap of the bag of offerings from her garden hoisted over her shoulder, the eighteen-year-old headed through the giant Sequoias toward the stream that led to the portal. But just beyond the stream a flash of blue entered a clearing. Cautiously, from behind a tree she watched a man carrying a rifle and wearing a blue windbreaker and a backpack climb a bluff to scan the panoramic view of the savannah.

Wearing a soldier's uniform, his lean frame and profile indicated someone in his twenties. As he peered through binoculars at the sky beyond filled with giant birds, the man whistled his amazement. When he turned around, Cosima recognized Emory, the soldier she had met at Grandfather's camp. He must have been following the stream down the mountain. And now he had discovered that which he had been seeking since the arrival of soldiers in Three Mountains Valley: the home of the augurs. Alarm tumbled unwelcome likelihoods. *He will inform the Union of the Americas Army, and soldiers will invade this peaceful realm. The birds. What will become of them? And the refugees from Three Mountains, now residing in Mu – the military will force them from their homes and herd them at gunpoint through the portal.* Cosi shoved aside the unthinkable and waited beside the stream as the newcomer scrambled down the bluff.

Grandfather, what would you do? Detain him? Familiarize yourself with the one perceived as a threat?

When the soldier spied Cosima, he gasped and stopped in his tracks.

"Hello, Emory. The birds are called augurs."

The confusion in his stare vied with recognition. "Cosima."

"Yes, we met at Matoskah's camp."

"His granddaughter."

"In a manner of speaking."

"What are *you* doing here?"

"I live here." *Grandfather would divert the intruder with food.* "Are you hungry?"

Hesitation. "Starving. Pack's empty. Been trying to find the way back for two days. Where is this place?"

"My home is close by." Ignoring his question, she motioned him to follow as she retraced her steps.

Emory stepped closer. "Big secret, very big secret you people have been guarding."

"Yes, and for important—very important—reasons."

"So what's going on here? These trees. A savannah? Giant birds?"

"We're on an island that doesn't exist in our time."

"Wait. Just wait a minute."

She could tell he had stopped, so she did the same and faced him. "Emory, you stepped through a portal."

His shocked expression demanded she explain their whereabouts.

"The portal you entered brought you back in time to the island remnant of an ancient continent known as The Mother Land, Lemuria or Mu."

A blue morpho butterfly flitted between them, then landed on Emory's shoulder to flex its eight-inch wingspan. Silence reigned as he slipped a finger under its feet, and the bright blue wings opened and closed as for several seconds the creature stood on his extended finger before flitting away.

Speechless, Emory gazed at the fluttering wings until tree limbs hid the blue morpho from view. His look of consternation had softened to one of amazement that took the edge off Cosima's alarm.

"My camp's just ahead."

After several minutes of following the path, the tree canopy yielded to an azure patch of sky, and the front of her log cabin came into view, with something large and black blocking the door. The panther's tail swished slowly as he crouched, green eyes fastened on the pair approaching.

"Whoa!" Emory grabbed Cosima and yanked her behind him as he raised his rifle.

She wrenched her arm from his grasp and commanded, "Do not shoot my cat." Hurrying to position herself between the ready to pounce feline and ready to shoot man, her tone was soothing. "Puma, it's okay." And quietly firm. "Emory, put your gun down."

"Are you kidding?"

"Do as I say and stay where you are."

The bared fangs disappeared and the snarls ceased as Cosima approached to receive the onslaught of affection from the panther that was as large as she. As the powerful jaws nuzzled her face, Cosima rubbed the fur at the scruff of his neck. "Come, Puma. I have something for you. Emory, don't move."

Cosima's commanding sternness managed the man, while her calm reassurances coaxed the cat. Emory stood frozen as the cougar, led by the promise of jerky, paced Cosima. After the cat was closed in one of several bamboo cages, the man visibly relaxed.

As Cosima approached, she explained, "I found Puma when she was half-grown, wounded and near death. Must have been a herd of peccaries. Although she is full size now and can hunt for herself, she visits me almost daily."

"You look only half grown yourself. Too young to manage that wild cat."

Cosima lifted her chin. "I'm eighteen, but look younger because of my size."

The adjoining cages that housed other animals, including an owl, a falcon and three half grown fox pups, drew Emory's attention.

"Motherless young and wounded animals I have found or that people have brought to me," Cosima explained. She felt a twinge of nostalgia for Valek, the motherless wolf she had raised from a pup.

Emory remained silent, only his eyes speaking his confusion. "There are other people here?"

Oh, no. What have I done?" Cosi avoided the question. "Welcome to my home." She hoped her smile relaxed the soldier who had been hit so fast by so many improbabilities. "Let's share some brunch." After dropping dried grass and twigs in the pit of ashes in front of the cabin, she used her fire starter to coax a fire, then placed a grill on the encircling stones and a pot of water beside the grill.

She entered her cabin to return with a tray of food, dishes and utensils. "These potatoes, carrots, beets and onions, grown in my garden, are ingredients for borsch, a Russian soup. My grandmother's recipe. Have a seat on that stump and pull that folding table toward you. Mind slicing the beets?"

While they sliced, peeled and grated, Emory scanned their immediate surroundings. "Aren't you afraid, living here alone?"

She answered "No" and explained that the local spectacled bear and herd of peccaries had allotted this space as hers and the panther's. While she and Emory took turns stirring the soup, the changes wrought by this man's arrival sank in. He represented the most serious threat by far. What would happen with the exposure of both the bird and human inhabitants of Mu, herself included?

The caged panther had begun to pace. "I need to free Puma."

Alarm registered on Emory's face.

"Don't worry. He'll likely head into the forest."

When the cage door opened, Puma paused for a brief rub before sauntering into the shadowed understory to hunt for prey, and Cosima turned toward the more dangerous predator.

Queen Biate 5

The arrival of the helicopter on June 27, 2038 precluded the need for Raymond to extend his exploration arc to Denver Airport. At first he was oblivious of the distant whir because he was intent on repairing the chicken yard fence. Best he could tell, it was a bobcat that got in the night before and took a hen. He stopped hammering when the distant hum caught his attention. The sound grew louder, and squinting skyward he took off his cap to wipe his forehead until the helicopter passed directly overhead.

His eyes didn't leave the craft until it disappeared below the roofline at the edge of town. Probably the same copter that circled Gaia's Gardens a week or so ago. Uneasiness clenched his gut as he placed the hammer on a ledge. Pulling off his sweaty t-shirt, he headed toward the front porch. After tossing the shirt on a chair, he lifted a pitcher of water from a wooden table, drenched his head and torso, and reached for the towel hanging from a nearby hook.

When he had dried off, he hurried inside to grab a fresh shirt and glanced at Elise. "A copter's landed."

Unmoving, his wife, faced him. Her alarmed expression prompted him to pull her close while he collected his thoughts. "You better come too—but not all the way to the helicopter. Just close enough to hear and see what's going on."

While Elise picked up their two-year-old, Raymond buttoned his shirt and ran a comb through his hair. "I don't want to take Ian anywhere near that aircraft."

"Let's drop him off at Amanda and Blake's."

By the time Raymond and Elise handed over Ian, people spilling from gardens and houses filled the dirt lane that led to the helicopter.

Some joined the procession, passing others who were frantically corralling children and spectators who waited behind fences to watch from a safe distance.

The pilot, positioned beneath the still-whirling blades, looked ordinary enough, but his companion triggered a double take. Although he approximated a human, he was a seven-foot muscular assemblage of high tech polymer and aluminum with weaponized arms. Obviously, not designed to blend with the human population but to subdue it, the imposing presence faced the spectators with blank eyes in an expressionless face.

Flanked by his intimating guard, the pilot surveyed the crowd, his head swiveling in an encompassing arc.

The words, "I need to speak to the leader of this town," nudged Raymond to shoulder his way to the forefront of the silent gawkers.

"I am Raymond Muñoz. How may I help you?"

"Queen Biate of New Denver requires your attendance at her court."

Raymond stifled the impulse to laugh at what was obviously a huge joke. "I beg your pardon?" When he crossed his arms over his chest, the robot stepped forward, but an undetected signal detained him.

"Perhaps you are unaware of the regent of this territory—the esteemed heiress to the renowned House of Kellercorfe."

The name of one of the richest families in the world registered without allaying Raymond's confusion. He knew the rich and powerful landlords had royal ancestry, but in the Union of the Americas the presumption of regal titles would have raised both the ire and ridicule of the populace.

The pilot answered his unresponsive stare in a quiet voice. "Sir, the SuperRo beside me can mow down this crowd in mere seconds." Amidst collective gasps, the pilot's tone became forceful. "Queen Biate summons you to her court immediately."

Swallowing the dread that muted his voice, Raymond exchanged a charged look with Elise, who had edged beside him. His gaze held hers for a prolonged moment before he headed for the craft.

Within minutes, when they were passing over Denver, he saw his chance to answer both curiosity and concern about his sprawling metropolis neighbor. Although he thought he saw some movement in the southern portion, most of the city appeared to be a partially demolished city of ghosts.

When the copter reached the expanse of runways that crossed the Denver International Airport, they circled the huge statue of the rearing blue stallion, incongruous progeny of its killed sculptor. The unnatural glow of the red eye that tracked their descent unnerved Raymond until the sight of the stone sculpture of Anubis increased his unease.

The jackal-headed guardian of entombed spirits loomed over their landing as the pilot indicated his next mode of transportation, a decade old Lincoln Continental. When a chauffeur opened the door for him, the continued proximity of the robot quickly squelched his relief to escape its presence. The weaponized machine stood beside the car and as the speedometer accelerated to thirty miles per hour, so did the robot. By the time the limo, paced by the robot, approached the main entrance to the airport, he realized that his escort was more like that of a prisoner than a guest. When the driver opened the car door at the main entrance to the airport, a waiting guard frisked him with robotic precision. He and the SuperRo crossed the expanse of polished stone, their footsteps echoing through stark silence as they passed empty kiosks and counters without attendants.

A woman standing beside an escalator nodded. "It's not working. We'll have to walk it to the next floor."

Sandwiched between his guard and his guide, Raymond continued past shops stripped of merchandise and fast-food counters above empty displays. They headed toward the vacant stare of a gargoyle animatronic, the New World Airport Commission's facedown to rumors about conspiracy. Perched on a pedestal beside the aisle, a winged creature with a humanlike face hunched beneath pointed ears. Hands with claw-like nails supported the chin, and from a mouth sporting sharp canines, a friendly voice formerly welcomed passersby to Illuminati Headquarters. With tongue in cheek allusions to circulating rumors, the creature solicited uneasy laughter. In counter-distinction to its grotesque appearance, the gargoyle beguiled children with its familiarity, evoked spectators' mirth with innocuous comments, and effectively distracted crowds from the swastika pattern of runways and apocalyptic paintings on the floor below.

They climbed another inoperable escalator to approach the double doors of a private lounge that prior to Solar Flash had been a luxurious watering hole where the rich and famous rested between flights. Past high-backed leather chairs clustered around low tables and a bar, Raymond and his guides continued to the far end of the room, where atop an elevated platform, a beautiful woman sat on an ornate throne chair. Against a backdrop of white tufted leather in a gilded frame, a wealth of red gold hair hung to her waist, partially covering the sea foam green of her filmy gown. A bronze clasp gathered the shoulders and a roped belt of shining bronze accentuated the small waist.

Her hands resting on arms that were carved lion heads, her feet between clawed legs, she awaited him with the regal bearing of a queen. On either side of her stood a woman in attendance and flanking them, robots that were identical to his own escort.

Raymond's urge to laugh rivaled an interior sense that forewarned the folly of a false move in the face of formidable power.

While the large green eyes looked down on him and the voluptuous lips smiled, the guide bowed and whispered that Raymond must do the same. But he simply stared.

"Your majesty, I present to you Raymond Muñoz of Gaia's Gardens." And to Raymond, "Her Royal Highness, Queen Biate."

Raymond blanched, but preventing the amused curve of his lips, he offered a brief nod of recognition.

"I am your queen, and collecting the most special of my workers to be in rightful attendance to me."

Silent regard was the best Raymond could muster as disbelief grappled with the absurdity of her claim.

"My scouts tell me you have contributed greatly to my realm with your extensive gardens."

"You are referring to Gaia's Gardens?"

"Gaia's...I like that. Good name for our new beginning. The members of my court face starvation in a very short time. We require monthly installments of vegetables, eggs and meat from Gaia's Gardens sufficient to feed twenty-six people."

Raymond blanched, fighting down revulsion for her pretense to rulership. Such a large allotment of food would seriously deplete their winter reserves.

"It's lucky for you, we have so few people here."

"We produce just enough to feed the families of Gaia's Gardens."

"Unnecessary mouths to feed, I'm sure."

A shaft of anger pierced his gut. "Perhaps I can help you start gardens here."

"There's neither a water source, nor soil, nor personnel for horticulture here. Actually, I'm pleased with the outcome of the Earth changes."

"How so?" He refused to call her 'Your Highness.'

"Because of the lowered population, which was our intention all along. Of course, our arms were weaponized pharmaceuticals, toxic GMOs and such."

Raymond's mind was racing. *We'll have to enlarge the gardens. Can we plant for one more harvest before fall?*

"I intend a majority consisting of robots and cyborgs, with a minority of nanite controlled food-eaters to populate my empire." She paused to peer at Raymond. "This is good news for food producers like yourself."

"It's my understanding electromagnetic pulses fried the central A.I. that controlled the vast majority of robots prior to Solar Flash."

"Yes. As you're aware, the Wi-Fi system, through which the planetary Central A.I. networked exists no more. Only I can access the means to send the signal to either activate or stall my Super Robots—I call them SuperRos—and the nanites that course through the veins of my human staff."

Mulling over her enigmatic smile, Raymond glimpsed the importance of discovering the source of her access to such control.

He persisted, "But isn't there a central A.I. in space, in our solar system, one that controls more worlds than this?"

She fingered the jewels at her throat. "You are well-informed. There was. But Solar Flash destroyed it. "Fortunately, my newly-installed central A.I. can use the still-standing cell tower near the airport to beam its signal within a hundred-mile radius. Were a robot to go rogue, the A.I. could instantly switch it off. After a complete memory wipe, a new circuit would house the body.

"But back to the food. My helicopter will arrive a week from today to load our first shipment sufficient for twenty-six people for a month. I'm sending you back now so you can perform your task. But in time you will tell your wife goodbye and come to be with me."

Raymond fought the scorn that burned his innards. "I will not come willingly."

"You will if the lives of your wife and any children are threatened."

He blanched. The pretentions of the woman who faced him were comical—her threats, cold-blooded. The initial impression of beauty had been replaced by a sense of childish petulance shaking its fists behind a grand façade.

Biate arose to stand poised in front of the ostentatious replica of a 17th century throne, nodded toward the SuperRos on either side of her, and descended the two steps from the raised platform. With a dismissive flick toward the guide that had accompanied Raymond since departure from Gaia's Gardens, she summoned one of the robots.

"SR 5-13, accompany us." Sweeping past Raymond, she crooked her index finger. "Come."

It was the candles, the only light in the darkened room, that first caught his attention. On pedestals, end tables arranged in a large circle on the floor must have numbered fifty or so. Upon closer approach a gold circle inlaid in the black marble floor enclosed the bronze outline of a pentagram.

"My robe."

The robot placed a purple robe on her shoulder and she slipped her arms through the billowy sleeves.

"Hand me my wand."

SR5-13 complied before she stepped into the center of the pentagram and spread her arms so that the sleeves arced upward on either side from her waist to her head appearing to Raymond like a dark angel poised to wreak havoc on her realm.

When she moved the wand he was sure a squiggle of light followed the sweep of the tip.

"Do you believe in the power of spells, Raymond Muñoz?"

He cleared his throat. "Well, I...."

"Well, you should." It was as though a demon grinned at him. "Believe me, my power is great, and endangers whoever deigns to cross me."

She lowered her arms slowly, deliberately, as though to create an indelible impression and turned toward an open book bound in leather beside the candelabra that cast light on her rituals. When a page turned in response to the swipe of the wand, Raymond gasped.

"My treasury of charms and spells. All I need to clear out all impediments and bring a lover to my bed chamber, which is just beyond those double doors."

Raymond's eyes followed the long, slender finger pointing toward the ornate wood carved with reversed swastikas and grotesque faces. Gargoyles, like the ones he had passed in the hall guarded the entrance.

"SR5-13, the doors."

The robot opened the doors and handing him the robe, Biate swept past to throw herself on the enormous four-poster bed, lying seductively on one side to accentuate her hips, small waist and ample breasts. The queen who was also a witch gazed back at Raymond. "Now tell me, is this not an enticing invitation to pleasures on end?"

"I am speechless," he replied. *Nor will I tell you it is an enticing invitation.*

"Then come to me."

Quickly, he scanned for a deterrent and found it in a clawed leg extending from the table to the right between him and Biate. A slight side step and a yank of the tablecloth was sufficient to catch his foot and instigate an ignominious topple as the center centerpiece of marble fruit balanced on a set of bronze scales slid across the table to hit the floor with clashes and clatters.

Stunned silence hovered over Biate's languid stretch as she faced Raymond's spread eagle splay. As he recovered his dignity, Biate jerked upright. "You clumsy ox, you shattered the mood."

He stooped to retrieve a stone pear.

"Leave it. And leave me at once. You will return in one week. SR5-13, accompany this fool to the helicopter."

Prisoners 6

After Puma returned to the forest to hunt down a meal, Cosi returned to her problematic guest.

Emory, eyes closed, lips upturned in pleasure, breathed in the scent-filled steam as he stirred the borsch. After processing in silence for several minutes, he mused aloud, "Russian ancestry, I can believe. But you don't look at all Native American."

"You mean as in related to Matoskah?" Cosima smiled. "Our relationship is of the spirit. Sit."

After she ladled the steaming soup into bowls, Emory reached for his along with a large chunk of bread. Between bread dipping and slurps, he queried Cosima about the portal and their time/shifted presence in Mu until she put down her bowl, refilled Emory's and sought her own answers.

"Why are you so determined to find an auger?"

"Those giant birds? I'm a scientist. An ornithologist." Emory sank the end of a fistful of bread in the borsch. "Well, I've seen what I need to see."

"Not really."

"I beg your pardon."

"You have to look your future captives in the eye."

"Captives?"

"Isn't capturing augurs the reason you soldiers came to Three Mountains?"

"Oh, no. It's a base camp for forays into the mountains."

"So the soldiers seek people?"

"Yes—per the command of Imperial Governor Scholtz to flush out groups hiding from the government. When reinforcements arrive, we will begin extensive searches."

Cosima struggled to contain her alarm as she refilled Emory's empty bowl.

"The birds are a side interest of a couple of guys, myself in particular."

"You have a wing feather, I believe."

Emory nodded.

"If you're a scientist, why are you in the Army?"

"I enlisted before Solar Flash to get a degree and survived with the troops underground in Cavern City. Now I'm stuck. Why do you live alone, here, in this cabin?"

"To remain safe from you soldiers."

Her listener shifted uncomfortably.

"So, Emory, how did you find the portal?"

"I was looking for a nest of giant birds. A wolf was about to attack me. As I shot him, I tripped and fell. You know the rest."

Although the wolf probably wasn't Valek, since he would not likely attack a man, Cosi was concerned. "So the wolf is wounded?"

"Or dead."

The urge to see about the animal struggled against the certainty that she must not lead this man back through the portal.

She looked up to see yet another arrival from Three Mountains.

Eena greeted Cosima, then Emory—his name spoken like an accusation.

"Did someone schedule a convention at my cabin? Hungry?" Interjecting dry humor reminiscent of Grandfather's, Cosima welcomed her friend.

Eena removed her bow and quiver of arrows. "No, thanks. Do you know about Valek?"

Cosima froze.

Eena's tone was soothing. "Don't worry. Fortunately, the bullet just grazed his shoulder."

Cosima's glared accusation at Emory elicited a defensive response. "He was about to attack me."

"Valek was protecting Grandfather." Eena faced Cosima, ignoring Emory.

He drew back. "What? What are you talking about?"

"Grandfather was tracking you."

"But why?"

"Partly for your protection, partly for ours." Eena shot Emory a scathing look. "Nathan Abelt all over again."

"I don't understand."

Cosima responded to his confusion. "The spy that several months ago almost cost us Three Mountains and our freedom."

Eena shook her head. "So what do we do with you?"

"Believe me, I don't want to be here anymore than you want me here. Just show me the way out, and I'm gone."

A sudden realization hit Cosima. *Of course. The wall of stone at the portal prevented his return.*

But apparently Emory's mind wasn't on escape. "Except, first, I really want a day to study those birds."

Cosima wished Grandfather were here. In his quiet way he would manage to befriend the intruder and at the same time quell Eena's zeal, which was likely to culminate in a threat to lock him up. The thought of Grandfather reminded her of how differently her day had turned out than she intended. She touched the carefully worked softness of the leather in the dress, worn to please him while she sought his counsel and their spirits commingled. Her musing yielded an unanticipated suggestion. "Perhaps a hike across the savannah to the nesting grounds is not a bad idea."

Eena shot her a surprised look, paused, and glanced at the rifle leaning against a tree. "All right, Emory. We'll take you to their nesting grounds, but you have to leave your weapon here." This said as she retrieved her bow and arrows. "Cosima, mind if Emory observes augurs with you and Leiani while I attend a meeting?"

Knowing it would be a meeting about how to restrain Emory, Cosima nodded. Disappointed she must forgo a visit to Grandfather today, she ducked inside her cabin to fold and put away the deerskin dress and put on a shirt and pants.

As they followed the stream down the mountain, the water gurgling over its stony bed, the croaks of the frogs and calls of crows distracted Cosima from the tightness in her gut. Even the embedded stones and raised roots that challenged her to focus on each next step in the trek evoked a sense of the continuity that flowed through unexpected, or unwelcome, events—such as the arrival of Emory. So she pulled her thoughts away from the man, while nature, ever her reprieve from life's stressors, pulled her into its harmonies.

At the base of the mountain the trees yielded to shrubs, and those, to the grass-filled plains. As they navigated the path along the stream screened on either side by tall grass, Eena's voice broke the silence, her tone edged with warning. "There's a reason I wear this bow and arrow. My arrow saved Leiani, the person we're about to meet, from being attacked by a giant saber tooth."

"What? You're kidding." Alarm resounded in Emory's voice.

"I'm not. The pre-ice age animals that roam this grassland are huge and deadly. One night the people you're about to meet fought off a herd of peccaries as tall as a man and also a pack of wild dogs."

Emory peered through the wall of yellow and rust-colored stalks.

Cosima suppressed a smile as Eena dramatized her words by unsheathing an arrow to notch in her bow. The newcomer was being played.

Emory, looking more alert now, murmured, "Very low visibility."

"I don't recommend ever crossing this savannah without an armed escort."

"I have a rifle."

"No you don't. Not anymore."

Emory's face registered affront. But as they approached the cypress trees that bordered the river, swirls of augurs landing and taking off in the distance captured his attention.

In the clearing beside the trees Eena dropped behind. "Cosi, I have a couple of things to attend to. Mind if I meet up with you later?"

An exclamation from Emory overrode Cosima's reply as a huge form blocked the sun and extended it wings and legs for a landing. The dry stalks crackled as a rush of air bent the grass, and a puff of dirt escaped the grip of the enormous claws.

As Eena greeted the augur with their customary nuzzling, scratching session, and declared, "This is Cesla," disbelief registered on Emory's face.

"A pet?"

"A bond mate since he was a chick." Eena walked to Cesla's tail feathers and mounted him. "Stand back." She couldn't resist a brief demonstration of piloting an augur.

"You ride those creatures?"

"For two years they have helped save us from the likes of you." With a loud *whoom* and a powerful rush of air, bird and rider lifted off.

After an interval of silently watching the blue-green enormity shrink in the distance before the return arc, Emory shook his head. "I don't think she likes me."

Cosima's response was kind, but direct. "Nothing personal. No one likes threats to their freedom."

Leiani approached, and, following Eena's cold brush-off, her friendly expression was very welcome even to Cosima, who set aside her concern about Emory's *un*welcome presence to anticipate the wonders in store for him. From the impressive nests, to Leiani's chick sitting, to a close-up view of the birds foraging among the exotic fruit-bearing trees, he had landed in a researcher's dream.

He sighed. "If only I had a notebook and colored pens," he said as he scanned the trees. By the time he hoisted himself to a viewing limb, Leiani had left and returned with rare commodities in 2038—a pad of paper and a single ink pen.

"Thanks. Black and white sketches are fine."

Cosima, enjoying Emory's exuberance, pushed aside the fleeting thought that the artwork could never travel through the portal with him.

The rise skyward lifted Eena's spirits, and with arms wrapped around Cesla's neck, she considered how to handle this new challenge. If the rapt expression on the ornithologist's face was any indicator, for the moment, return to the portal was highly unlikely. This was fortunate, because she and Cosima needed to collect Gavin and Leslie and head to the village for an emergency meeting.

After the return and landing, she whispered to Leiani, "Hopefully he's too scared of large predators to attempt to cross the savannah alone."

The man, apparently entranced by an ornithologist's paradise, alternately sketched and trained his binoculars on the mango tree where augurs were ensconced. Nonetheless, Eena urged Leiani to watch him closely before she and Cosima crossed the tangle of kneed cypress roots to approach Gavin and Leslie at their nest. Leslie declined their invitation with apologies that she needed to work in her lab, but Gavin joined them.

They followed the river to the village where within a half hour fifteen people had gathered in Chas and Eena's courtyard. After everyone was briefed on Emory's identity the mood was tense.

Head nodding accompanied Rigel's observation. "We can't allow him to return to Three Mountains."

"I hope I have frightened him sufficiently with tales of giant prehistoric predators. I don't think he'll risk crossing the savannah alone."

"Where will he live?"

"We can construct a nest between Leiani's and Gavin and Leslie's so they can keep an eye on him. It's very important that he never follow anyone to the portal or watch a bird fly through."

"So he's in essence our prisoner?"

"What choice do we have? If Emory escapes, we're likely doomed to removal by Scholtz's military to Transtopia where everyone's a prisoner."

To the students removed by Scholtz's military from Transtopia University to Onmatson Farm last March, they *were* prisoners. The sense of doom increased with every passing month. They had ceased torturous reminisces about their university days. To those dreaming of escape from Onmatson Farm for the past five months, it may as well be a prison and they the inmates assigned to a life of hard labor.

Matt turned the crank on the old machine designed to extract the corn kernels from the cobs and drop them into a bucket while Natalie, close by, ground the kernels to cornmeal with an old fashioned grinder.

The release of the sixtieth cob for that morning yielded a vehement burst from Matt. "I'm sick of this monotonous labor."

Natalie dipped her fingers in the mound of meal. "The state's grinding us to a nub like we're grinding this corn."

That night, after the soldiers retired to their quarters and the guard dogs roamed the compound to secure the prisoners in their barracks, murmurs of malcontent rumbled across the bunks. Some spoke of running into the forest. Others insisted they could survive better in the ZD amid the ruins of Colorado Springs. Someone inserted that whatever they decided should happen as a group.

The next morning something powerful overcame Matt and exploded in an outburst. "I'm climbing on the delivery truck and riding away."

Pouring a bucketful of cornmeal into a burlap bag, Ken shook his head. "Man, you're crazy. You're gonna be shot in the back—if not here then at the destination."

As if on cue all three looked up at the guard tower and the soldier in it with a view to the barracks, the work sheds and the cornfields. Somewhere away from their sight another soldier and police dog were patrolling the compound. They worked silently for another hour, lost in their own thoughts. When the last of the meal was bagged, Matt signaled a soldier to back up the flatbed truck.

When the last of the fifty twenty-pound bags was loaded in the truck bed he glanced at the tower. The soldier was watching the driver and another soldier with the police dog, their backs turned toward the crew as they threw the ball for the dog and laughed at his antics.

Without a backward glance, Matt scrambled atop the mound of bags and frantically burrowed underneath.

His last glimpse was of Ken standing at the foot of the truck bed before he heard, "I'm coming too." Then shouts.

Buried at the rear of the cab, Matt scrunched down, with only a tiny air passage between bags. A slight tremor shook the truck bed as barks and growls escalated. More shouts. "Ken!" Natalie's scream. "Don't shoot!" A shot. Natalie's sobs. "How could you?"

Grief clutched the one who was hidden and whispered chances were good that at the unloading of the bags, his fate would be the same.

The Reception   7

The original Imperial Governor Charles Scholtz, his consciousness housed in his purely biological brain, had often assessed possibilities as he stared out his tenth floor office window. But free of the range of emotions that had once governed his human/anunnaki relationship to the world, sheer, one-pointed logic dictated the outcome of all Charles Scholtz's observations. Gone was the irritation at Astrid's insipid presence; the frustration with Achmed's failure to produce a robot army; and cold fury at Rolf's refusal to fulfill his royal obligations. More importantly, gone as well was the underlying affection for his wife and both sons. Singular purpose activated the intellectual terabytes of a sentiment-free hard drive fused with a biological brain—the drive for ever-expanding power.

Everyone and everything, including the ruler of New Denver just brought to his attention—the one with the ostentatious title, "Queen"—all represented a means to the extension of Scholtz's empire. While the helicopter landing on the roof of the Imperial Ritz surprised Charles the SynAnn, and left him no chance to assemble his forces, it also represented a challenge. When the pilot and formidable robots faced down the guard in the office foyer and announced her arrival, the governor agreed to meet with this self-designated Queen Biate of the House of Kellercorfe. The governor could never resist an opportunity to add to his knowledge bank.

The next hour yielded information but also questions about his visitor. It was curious that she was the sole remaining Kellercorfe—that she was the only family member who escaped Duat Cavern, the entombed subterranean complex under New Denver Airport. Though her reference to herself as 'queen' indicated psychosis, tomorrow night would be interesting. He intended the association to result in a conquest—the expansion of his empire.

Holding a reception and dinner in her honor tonight would satisfy more than his curiosity—to gain full knowledge of her assets was a strategic move. But first he called for a briefing of Dora, his sons and top SEI officials.

In bygone years Charles Scholtz's palatial living room had often hosted landlords and ministers, but never an individual whose ancestral global empire wielded wealth and power far exceeding his own, and certainly no one assuming a royal title. Yet with regal audacity and the hypnotic prowess of one who has convinced herself of the adulation due from others, Queen Biate swept into the room.

Scholtz's aide announced Biate's arrival and, as protocol dictated, the Imperial Governor and his wife Astrid, the governor's son Achmed and his wife Lauren, and Rolf and Dora greeted the queen in a reception line. After polite introductions, she stepped regally from the line into the circle of agog SEI ministers. All eyes closed ranks around her striking beauty crowned by a delicate tiara embedded in an elegantly piled coppery mane.

Minutes later, when Dora was seated on a sofa, the sea-green satin of Queen Biate's gown swept by. The four-year-old perfume that assaulted Dora's nostrils was an affront to her body, which in pregnancy had become hyperreactive to unwholesome intrusions. With a slight motion in front of her nose, she waved away the offending scent and fought down the sudden rush of nausea.

On the sofa facing Dora the younger version of Astrid, the SynAnn recipient of the consciousness of the deceased original, sat beside her bionic husband. Dora shuddered at the sight. She knew a prepared bionic body had awaited the approaching death of Scholtz. *But how was the transfer of Astrid's consciousness possible?*

Turning to Achmed, who slouched in a chair to her right, she spoke in low tones. "Did you have Astrid's cyborg double in stasis for years like you did for your dad?"

Achmed shrugged. "That was no longer needed by the time he married her. Before Solar Flash scientists learned how to replicate adult bodies and insert synthetic organs—brains, hearts—everything ready for activation within a couple of months."

Though Achmed spoke in an off-hand manner, Dora noticed a haggard look about him. Knowing Rolf's mother, Astrid, had no choice but to relinquish her life as a biological human, Dora's next thoughts remained unspoken. *The second murder since the prematurely activated Charles the SynAnn killed the biological original.*

"The project took on an unstoppable momentum." Achmed confided in Dora as though he had heard her silent accusation. Conflict tightened the jaws of the man who often sought the counsel of Adair, his ex-wife of druidic lineage, though he did the bidding of his ruling father and now his father's synthetic replacement. Before he spoke again, morose silence brooded over the interval. "At Adair's urging, I was on my way to save my dad. But I didn't get there in time. In a sense, I'm implicated in the murders of two royals—Charles, mine and Rolf's father, and Astrid, Rolf's mother."

Feeling sucked into a dark morass of cyborg priorities in which human life was deemed expendable, Dora grappled for words of comfort. But, as though to condemn the amoral goo of technological/biological interface, the ghosts of the biological Charles and Astrid, lingered.

Dora shook off the impressions and turned to surreptitiously study the stunning woman, who seated herself in the chair to Scholtz's left, the side opposite Astrid, and commanded his full attention. Delicate strands of auburn hair escaped the pile of tiara bound ropes, and the filmy shawl that matched the frosted glow of the sea glass at her throat accented her cream colored flesh. The sidelong seduction of Biate's long green eyes appeared to capture and hold the unnatural glitter of Charles's gaze.

After ice-breaking pleasantries, the boldness in her tone drew the cocked ears of those standing close by. "While robots requiring minimal maintenance populate my small, but growing empire, you have an excess of bothersome baggage—thousands of biological underlings to house, feed and clothe."

The royal SynAnn's counter clarified his priorities. "You fail to appreciate that our endeavors are a temporary inconvenience in the interest of the future usefulness of a synthetic race."

"A synthetic race?"

"Bionic hybrids that will require less maintenance and accomplish more tasks."

Biate was obdurate in her argument. "We fine-tuned replicators prior to Solar Flash. Why include the biological component? A robotic slave race entails lower maintenance with higher performance."

Charles the SynAnn smiled, his look slightly deprecating. "An army of mechanical soldiers and a staff of servants to perform servile chores, though extremely valuable, offer a limited range of intellectual ingenuity."

His rebuttal rendered Biate speechless, her response only a slight widening of her eyes.

Charles continued. "The global connectivity and swift assessments of supercomputing A.I. needed to run civilization's technological complexities have been wiped out. We currently need the consciousness of the biologicals, including workers, scientists and Anunnaki rulers to transfer to synthetic bodies."

Biate held tight to her corner of the argument. "But in the meantime, why allow the underlings the ability to reproduce?"

"Until we master technological self-replication, strictly controlled biological reproduction remains a valuable commodity."

The SynAnn's forward lean as he adopted a confidential attitude drew Dora's heightened attention. This debate, the weighing of technology versus biology bandied by the royals, had never reached her ears before.

"As we speak, a successful cloning experiment is progressing satisfactorily at Fort Carson. Protocols are in place to apply stringent socialization and indoctrination protocols plus nanite insertions to engineer human clones to be the prototypes of a superior slave race. Eventually, we will transfer their consciousness into bodies with synthesized DNA."

The SynAnn continued to clarify his emphasis on biological/technological fusion. "We need the cloned infants for interim experimentation—to perfect the cloning and reproductive ability of a superior synthetic race.

"You're speaking of both royals and workers?"

"Yes. Our scientists can transfer royal consciousness into disease-free biological/technological blends with extended life spans. My own human consciousness is now enmeshed in a super computing hard drive. Hopefully in the future, SynAnns like myself will have the ability to reproduce royal heirs."

"And the underlings?"

"To remain less well equipped specimens. SynHus will be tireless, docile and disease-free, and provide a durable work force with limited mental capacity and short life spans. Five fail-safes will perpetuate our society: replicators, consciousness transfer, cloning, nanite infusion, and biological reproduction. We are building a society of SynHus to serve as the worker force, SynRos to serve as the armed force, and SynAnn descendants of Royal Anunnaki like me to lead."

"Won't SynAnns like yourself eventually see Anu's biological progeny like myself as a threat?"

"In the future the attainment of the capacity to reproduce by SynAnns will eliminate the need for solely biological royals."

"Such as myself?" Biate drew herself to her full sitting height so as to display her provocative attributes from the well-formed hips to her small waist to breasts lifted like ripened pomegranates to display ample cleavage.

"Yes."

"And?"

"Though we will certainly replicate the seductive attributes that endow you with sexual appeal, your exclusively biological line will eventually be exterminated."

Charles's boldness evoked from eavesdroppers a series of gasps that echoed Biate's shocked response. Nonetheless, her reply flowed with modulated composure. "Well, Charles, it's good to know I'm in no immediate danger of extinction."

"Far from it." The SynAnn straightened in his chair and raised his chin to admire his interlocutor beneath lowered lids, his glittered gaze, more suggestive of an invitation than annihilation.

Biate leaned forward, her high cheekbones slightly flushed, "So tell me, Charles, do you have all the physical equipment and sensations of a man?"

"If you are asking if I'm fully equipped to enjoy sexual encounters, I am, though I cannot reproduce."

Nearby conversations paused with ears directed to the exchange that likely settled private speculations.

Biate's lashes, thickened with mascara, flickered as she leaned toward her SynAnn companion. "No matter, you are practically immortal."

"With the added advantage of powerful heirs in this room and to come."

Biate looked discomfited as though her companion had edged into the conversation the advantages of his familial plurality over her royal singularity.

The governor's glance toward Dora unnerved her, and the shift of Biate's green eyes toward her bulging belly added to her discomfort. Though she crossed her arms as though to shield her protruding abdomen, she was certain that the warmth that rushed to her face exposed her unease.

"So, my dear, you are expecting."

Words failed Dora. Did envy fuel the intensity that Biate lasered her direction? With Dora's affirming nod, one hand drifted upward to rest protectively atop her ripening womb.

The long eyes turned to Rolf, on whom Biate lavished a seductive smile. "Congratulations are in order, I believe."

With his signature aloofness Rolf nodded. "Bothersome business, if you—" Stopped mid-sentence by a discrete jab from Dora.

For a brief moment, childlike wistfulness softened Biate's brazenness as her gaze settled again on Dora's womb. "I long to have a child of my own." Lamented with a child's voice.

Caught by surprise Dora stuttered, "Of, of course. Surely you will... some day."

"Only a royal heir will do."

Dora mentally referred to the afternoon briefing with Charles Scholtz. "A potential father in New Denver perhaps?"

"There are none."

When a quick mental inventory of available royal sires in Transtopia tallied zero, Dora glimpsed Biate's dilemma.

A barely discernible, swiftly contained flicker darkened Biate's irises before the seductress returned her attention to Charles. In a lingering upward sweep, her forefinger flickered over the jewel at her throat, then traced the arc of her neck and brushed her chin to pull provocatively at her lower lip. Charles's transfixed expression remained while she restated the disadvantages of a large population of workers. "Underlings are problematic, especially insurgents."

"To the contrary, our first round of nanite implants to subdue troublesome human traits in our population has eliminated the headaches of rebelliousness and helped set Transtopia's trajectory in motion."

Dora smiled inwardly, recalling Caellum and Dr. Monroe's nanite insertion charade last spring, the thousands of destroyed vials and the currently nanite-free population.

Biate's forefinger compelled Charles's prolonged gaze as she explored the fleshy redness of her lower lip. "Military invulnerability is far more important." Spoken with petulant certainty.

Dora detected a hinted challenge to the SynAnn who had only every human military and civil police at his disposal.

The SynAnn's chin tilted up. "Your guards are strong but bulky." In a shift to a personal trajectory, the SynAnn's chest expanded and stretched the fibers of his dinner jacket. "No match for hard, compacted strength like mine."

Biate leaned in close holding her champagne glass aloft. "My Five Hundred, as I refer to my robot warriors, is an unstoppable military machine." Her displayed cleavage suggested an invitation, while her words discharged a threat.

Spellbound, Dora witnessed a whole new Charles the SynAnn as he grinned, chinked his glass against Biate's and leaned forward, his face inches from hers. "Ours is a perfect alliance."

Whether a proposition to tousle in bed or to meet on the battlefield took precedence, the SynAnn's eavesdropping 'family' had varied responses. Rolf snorted his disgust as he stood and walked to the fireplace to lean against the mantle, his back to the public interplay. Achmed looked down, his lowered lids and shroud of dark, curly hair veiling the embarrassed shake of his head. On the sofa, behind Charles's back, the youthful Astrid the SynAnn stared vacantly.

During the lull in Charles and Biate's layered posturing, Achmed's household robot Jeff appeared at the dining hall entrance to announce that dinner was served. He waited beside the door while a hush stalled the hum of conversations.

The change in Charles echoed the charged vehemence of his predecessor's dislike of the sometimes-bumbling robot. He glared at Achmed, his voice like a clap of thunder "I thought I told you to get rid of that clumsy excuse for a servant."

As Achmed blanched and ordered Jeff to leave the room, Dora recalled the original Charles Scholtz's irate reaction to the dropped china. Unease churned her stomach, annihilating any hunger. Remaining seated during the rustle of guests moving to the dining room, she caught Rolf's attention with an "I need to talk to you" stare.

In response to the motion of her crooked finger, he approached to lean forward, allowing her to speak into his ear.

"I can't eat." Then louder, "Pardon me, Your Excellency, I must forgo the meal." With an apologetic smile, she rubbed her belly. Glad for the SynAnn's indifferent blink and that pregnancy afforded her an excuse to leave, she slipped her hand into Rolf's. He helped her stand, and stood solicitously close as they waited for the crowd to dwindle. When they were alone, Dora urged Rolf toward the opposite end of the room where the robot had retreated. "Get Jeff."

When Rolf returned with the SynRo, she addressed Jeff cheerfully. "I think Achmed will agree it's better for you to serve my household from now on."

Jeff nodded slightly. "Yes, ma'am. That is an agreeable prospect."

Turning to her husband with "You'll tell Achmed?" she kissed his cheek, then chided him. "You must be on your best behavior, Rolf. She's not one to trifle with."

Rolf ran his hand lightly over his every-strand-in-place blond hair and straightened his dinner jacket with a decisive tug, his smug dismissiveness conveying complete lack of concern. "I can handle Biate."

With a shrugged sigh, Dora exited with Jeff to enjoy a peaceful evening with Caellum, while Rolf entered the sure-to-be action-packed stage for the next Charles and Biate performance as they resumed the duel of robots versus humans with synthetic innards.

Red Sand   8

I'll never again step into the cockpit of the Lockheed Martin F-35 Lightning II. The wash of grays from the heavy cloud cover, to the fog, to the concrete landing field matched Jack Merrick's reflections. When he was nine years old the Air Force show at RAF Bentwaters awakened his yearning to escape the bounds of Earth at breathtaking speeds. By the time he was eighteen, determination to fly the fastest jet in existence guided his test pilot career—until Solar Flash crashed those best days of his life. Yet, despite the finality of his fate, he still longed to experience the exhilaration of flying at supersonic speeds, of gaining altitudes high enough to see Earth's curvature below and the blackness of space above.

Since his career plummeted, transporting ministers of this and that in commuter planes consigned him to Earthbound hops between population centers with deteriorating infrastructures. Waiting on the return of the dignitaries in the small café in the mostly vacated airport, he began to feel edgy from drinking too many cups of Turkish coffee until, with a final clink of his cup, he rose to meet the returning passengers.

A couple of hours later, as he sat on the sofa in the shadowed twilight of his living room, an outline appeared beside the fireplace. Before his speechless gaze, the three-dimensional image of a tall, willowy woman shimmered into view.

"Whoa!"

"I'm sorry to startle you."

"How'd you get in here?" He switched on the lamps at either end of the couch.

"Not through your locked entry, if that's what you're asking."
Unable to assemble another question, he stared.
"I'm Anaya."
"Jack. Jack Merrick."
"A new destiny beckons you."
"Another boring choice in this world crumbling into the dark ages?" As Jack mumbled his disillusionment, he noted the exotic slant of Anaya's blue eyes. Silver hair hung over pale skin that reflected the light with a faint lavender hue.
"More than your wish to pilot a jet hangs in the balance."
"I don't understand."
"Solar Flash accomplished a major setback to forces that have oppressed humanity for thousands of years. But an underground complex in the Rocky Mountains has spewed the remnants of that old order. They intend to re-establish their global stranglehold."
"So, in the coming dark age we're to be the serfs and they, the noble owners of Earth's real estate and wealth."
"With a new twist. The landlords, as they are called, further their agendas through control of technology. The lords of science, energy and medicine, bound by lucrative contracts and the threat of the withdrawal of funds, serve the planetary landlords.
"Conspiracy theories...."
"Left unchecked, misappropriated technology will usher in an age of bionic humanity kneeling at the altar of A.I. This is according to an intergenerational design and comprised of incremental steps. Prior to Solar Flash, in phase one, the lords of science linked humanity's devices to a central A.I., also known as CAI.
"So?"
"CAI spied on humanity, collecting information on their preferences down to their food palettes and favorite entertainment venues."
"To what end?"
"Seduction. To influence the population to welcome internalized devices — devices giving CAI an interface for control of human brains."
"So, what about the lords of energy?"
"Humanity's dependence on the petroleum-based transportation and energy grid generated vast revenues. While the lords of energy funneled profits to controlling interests, they closely guarded the secret of available over-unity or free energy devices. By the late 2020s the obsolete energy grid further entrapped humanity with smart meters to

monitor, tax and penalize their energy usage while polluting their homes with harmful radiations."

"And the lords of medicine?"

"Engineered the direction of medicine away from healing and self-responsibility for holistic health by replacing diseased organs and limbs with artificial ones."

"Why?"

"To accustom humanity to an incrementally increasing blend of biology and technology."

"A synthetic race."

"Yes. Within a couple of generations to become human robots directed by CAI."

"So, the arisen landlords in the Rockies want to revive this slide toward total control."

"Yes. Partly because they fear you — humankind, that is."

"That's a shocker."

"At quantum levels both human DNA and the heart link human beings to an inexhaustible source of cosmic potential. The ancient manuscripts possessed by the landlords confirm this."

"I'm not one for New Age dribble."

"This is science. Like a honing signal, your origin and destiny, the Alpha and Omega of your lives, draw you beyond the machinations of the landlords. Your creative, inventive genius expresses the sacred geometries of living systems.

"The controllers hope to sever this quantum connection by replacing biology with technology. With the segue into nanite-bearing inserts, CAI can direct an enslaved race of bionic humans kept ignorant of the unlimited potentials of a biological, spiritual interface."

"Why are you telling me this?"

"Solar Flash disabled the original CAI. However, in the Rocky Mountains the landlords plan to be both the designers and minions of the Earth's new central A.I."

"What does that have to do with me?"

"An opportunity for flight beyond your wildest dreams."

"Beyond Mach 2?"

"Speeds far exceeding the physics of combustible jet propulsion."

"Well, I...."

"Far from an end in itself, this piloting assignment will provide a way to assist this small group of sovereignty seekers to usher in an age of enlightenment. A message will arrive soon. If you choose to take on this assignment, pay close attention to it."

Jack stared at his hands and then toward Anaya. But she was no longer there.

Gazing southward over the tile roofs of Marrakech, Morocco, Jack Merrick patted the cryptic note and map in his breast pocket. In the distance, the sunrise bathed the gray escarpments of Mount Jebel Yagour in a lavender wash and sparkled the white peaks with a hint of turquoise. Enveloped in the stillness of early morning, the spectator on the rooftop scanned the ocean of ochre sand between the city and the foothills of the Atlas Mountains. He estimated if he left soon, a camel could carry him across the twenty-five-mile stretch of Moroccan desert by nightfall.

Days before, a messenger had handed him an old-fashioned envelope stamped *Casa Blanca* with a note inside that referenced *Tahnaout Ring* scrawled in jagged handwriting—nothing else. Puzzled that someone from Morocco would send him a message referencing jewelry, Jack pictured a ring with an exotic stone setting. When he flipped the pages of a well-worn twentieth century encyclopedia, he expected to find that Tahnaout was a type of semi-precious stone. But, if it was, the name wasn't listed.

A week later the same messenger delivered a second envelope, which enclosed no note, only a folded map. As he opened it to stare at a road map of Morocco, his heart skipped a beat. A red line traced a highway that stretched southwest from Casa Blanca to Marrakech and from there, south along P2017 toward an area circled in red, abutting the Atlas Mountains. He peered more closely, until the name Tahnaout grabbed his focus.

Suddenly it hit him. *Ring — Randolph Ring.* Jack knew from their pre-Solar Flash communications that Randolph had established *Blue Kachina Center for Research and Development* at a secret location in Morocco.

But Ring would be over 100 years old by now. Besides, several years before Solar Flash he'd moved to Paradise, California. How likely was it that he'd still be around? A son or daughter maybe?

As though Solar Flash had posed no interruption to a thousand years of ritual, the citywide call to prayers startled Jack out of his early morning reverie. Soon the street market would come to life with noisy bartering as shoppers filed through stalls of vendors hawking shawls, hand-painted vases and Berber carpets. He grabbed his pack, descended the stairs two at a time and hit the floor with both feet. Winding through Guelmim Market he headed toward cud chewing Dromedaries to purchase the services of a guide and camel while his heart drummed anticipation of his trek.

The Wedding   9

With Emory settled in an arboreal home between Leiani's and Gavin and Leslie's nests, and since Cosima kept watch on the mountain, Eena relaxed. To all accounts, Emory was in no hurry to leave his newfound paradise for more reasons than studying the augurs. According to Leiani, when Cosima came around, he could hardly take his eyes off her.

Eena flew Cesla near the base of the mountain, scanned the savannah for predators and reflected on Gavin and Leslie's wedding a week away. A year ago who could have imagined their nuptials occurring forty thousand years in the past in this exotic land known as Mu.

A few hundred yards away, Chas and three others were completing the final sections of the planned 500-foot circumference of the moveable corral. As the grass would soon disappear from over-grazing such a limited area, they were building the eight-foot-tall enclosure in sections they could periodically disassemble and move. In the meantime, the livestock foraged and grazed in the surrounding plains under Eena's, Lori's or Chuck's watchful gaze.

On Eena's watch, the shapes that glided silently through the sequoia forest and down the mountainside evaded her notice until the gray alpha male emerged from the tree line, headed into the plains. Eight wolves followed and at a fast trot self-organized into hunting positions as they fanned out.

Eena notched her bow and screamed, "Wolves!"

While the fence-building crew scrambled for bows lying nearby and notched their arrows, Chas broke into a run in the direction of the disparate herd of rooting pigs; scratching, pecking chickens; and grazing cows and horses.

Hoping to slow the wolves' advance, Eena flew Cesla toward the predators. She didn't want to shoot at them if she could avoid it. Recalling the dead sabretooth with her arrow wedged in its heart, she shuddered. *Are we, the intruders, to pick off one by one the apex predators trapped on this island remnant of Mu?* At that instant she realized that she wanted to forestall the slaughter of the wolves, with the same intensity as to protect the livestock.

With short feints and dives that were new to her and Cesla's flight maneuvers, she managed to momentarily turn one wolf at a time. But driven by an unstoppable momentum and the discipline of a collective instinct, the rest of the pack surged forward. The tight flight shifts to turn them from the targeted grazers strained Cesla unnaturally, and proved to be ineffectual as they rapidly advanced toward the next meal.

Eena turned her attention toward the work crew perched on a section of fencing, a row of notched arrows aimed at the predators. Her cry of "Don't shoot!" came too late as a loosed arrow found its mark under the silver-tinged fur of a massive chest.

A series of whoops and yells drew her attention to Chas who was galloping and swerving atop the mare in a cowboy style roundup. At that instant the vision of Grandfather's faggot setting aflame the tiny pile of grass presented itself, and she knew teamwork was their best means to herd the animals into the courtyard.

In response to the urgency of Eena's psychic command Cesla looped toward Chas and his unlikely herd, and dove toward the surprised alpha leading the pack. Chas was driving the livestock toward the courtyard while a second dive scattered the wolves, which were closing in for the kill.

A glance in the direction of the courtyard enclosure revealed the bamboo door was latched, and Eena yelled to no one in particular, "Unlatch the gate."

From her panoramic perspective she watched Raiel jump from the fence to run toward the courtyard, only to be targeted by a wolf speeding toward her.

With a low swoop Eena and Cesla raced to intercept the rapidly closing distance between the wolf and its target, but with little effect, leaving to shoot as her only choice. As Raiel reached for the wooden latch, Eena's arrow stalled the predator's leap within a couple of feet of his unsuspecting victim.

Seconds after the door opened, the cow led the panicked charge into the corral with Chas and the mare bringing up the rear before Raiel followed them in, and slammed the door shut.

Eena looked toward the wolf with an arrow imbedded in its shoulder. Yet to her amazement, the wounded animal stood up to follow the pack now headed away from the scene of attack. A wolf circled back toward him as though to lend encouragement, but within fifty yards or so, the impaled pack member fell, and after briefly pausing beside him, the wolf in attendance, likely the female alpha, returned to the scattered pack to lead them to the forested slopes.

Feeling the weight of Cesla's exhaustion, Eena signaled the desire to land. Once landed, she dismounted to hug her faithful friend and whisper her gratitude. So the nectar-filled pulp could revive him, she held a mango to his beak as she nuzzled the powerful neck. When the seed of a second fruit was bare of flesh, Cesla opened his wings and flew to the closest cypress grove. He landed on a branch with sufficient girth to support his huge body, and seconds later, beyond the reach of stalking cats and wild dogs, his head drooped, his eyelids blinked shut, and the augur slept.

Relieved to see the exhausted augur rest, Eena hurried toward the wounded wolf. He lay so still she wasn't sure he was still alive until he jumped up, snarling and lunging with bared teeth.

"Don't move." Chas stood beside her. Out of range of the snapping jaws, the pair waited out the wolf's bravado until, with a yelp, he fell to the ground.

"There's a chance he'll pass out from the pain while I remove the arrow. But in case he tries to attack me first, press your bow hard against his neck."

The tightly held bow blocked fanged lunges as snarls turned to whimpers, then distressed cries until, at last, the animal went unconscious. When Chas pulled out the arrow, blood gushed from the shoulder, but he pressed cotton against it to soak up the excess blood. A honey compress to kill bacteria and promote healing, and a tourniquet between the shoulder and opposing rib completed his ministrations.

With grunts and groans Chas and Eena maneuvered the wolf onto a makeshift travois, and Chas slipped harness straps on his arms. As they walked together, Eena was painfully aware that somewhere in the field a wolf lay dead. *We shouldn't be living in this exotic world where we're upsetting the balance of nature, especially since the world forty thousand years in the future, the one we left behind, sorely needs our help.*

Against the back wall of their Mu dwelling place, they constructed a wooden lean-to and placed the wolf inside the pen.

When they closed the door, Eena smiled her love for Chas. "No one but you would accept as a patient the attacker of your livestock."

Leslie. A wreath of vines intertwined with tiny flowers adorned the glossy brown bangs that accented the bride's expressive eyes. The long hair Gavin loved to stroke hung over a white cotton dress gathered below the bodice and above the slight swell of her abdomen.

Awaiting her at the head of the aisle, Gavin watched her take the arm of Chas who would give away the bride-to-be. *I have loved you since I first saw you – when your glasses slid down your nose and I could hardly tear my eyes from your face to pay attention to the machines in your lab. To think I almost lost you after Espirit's death when I pushed you away.*

When Espirit was shot from the sky by the rover, Gavin had plummeted to grief and self-recrimination. Looking back, he was grateful for his acute case of jealousy a couple of months later when Chuck's amorous attentions toward Leslie shook him from his self-absorbed remorse. Undaunted by the eyes that avoided his, he had arranged the meeting that brought her to his side while he fought to save the life of Phoenix – the augur whose beak was still a lethal hazard to his bride, to everyone but himself.

Grandfather. It seemed natural that the elder who had so mercilessly poked his ego, prodded his self-interest and doused his pride, should perform this wedding ceremony. The old man had even honored their nuptials by dressing up his usual attire with two feathers stuck in his headband and a breastplate of fox leg bones sewn together with sinew over his clean but thread bare shirt.

Our child. Gavin recalled over two years ago, when Eena saved him from falling through the missing slat in the bridge. Upon reaching Three Mountains, he had regarded it as a resort from responsibility and fantasized that he would become a world-traveling adventurer. Fortunately, the missions with Eena, piloting augurs to ferret out possible allies hidden in the mountain forests, matured him. But, was he ready so soon for fatherhood? Leslie, with that added glow, stood poised to join him, so for now he hid his trepidation behind a smile.

The flute and guitar music paced Leslie's steps as, flanked by Chas and surrounded by the community of runaway dreamers and renegades, she approached. Marriage and fatherhood beckoned.

More than the happiness of a bride shone in Leslie's countenance, and Eena wanted to celebrate this day and the natural continuity of life her pregnancy augured. But, while the strains of wedding music flowed with the bride's steps, knowledge of the ripening in her womb triggered the memory of the day at Fort Carson Hospital. In the gestation chamber cloned babies grew in glass wombs fed by a system that loved their usefulness but not them.

Leslie glided toward Grandfather and Gavin, her face beaming with an ethereal light—a radiance garnered by the biological perpetuity of a mother and the gestating infant.

A pre-Solar Flash span of two generations seduced humanity gradually so as not to excite resistance. Beguiled device users, eager for each upgrade, slid willingly from a state of accessing technology, to becoming technology. And like soldiers awaiting release from a Trojan horse, nanites, the central A.I.'s obedient warriors, escaped the chip and swarmed the brain—the objective being complete takeover of the slumbering consciousness with the army of invaders claiming the citadel.

Instinct drove Eena's militant desire to fight back, but Grandfather and Chas had influenced her to temper those urges. Momentarily, the sight of her tall Japanese amour with his jet-black hair trimmed to just above the collar held her attention as he stood tall beside Leslie and relinquished her to Gavin.

The example of her parents had fueled her resistance to A.I.'s corporate web, which was seducing GMO-fed humanity to become dependent on pharmaceuticals. Her naturopathic father and mid-wife mother interpreted the body's messages signaling disease, and collaborated with its powerful capacity to self-heal. Amá likened the ecology of the human body to planetary biomes. "The landlords, via corporate tentacles, are trashing both."

After Chas relinquished the bride, he stepped beside the groom and faced Grandfather. His tall good looks and quiet composure still made Eena weak. Tonight, pressed against him with his arms around her, she would push aside her restless frustration.

The bride and groom stared into one another's eyes in this ritual that was as old as humanity itself. What was it about weddings that struck a resonant chord and moved people to tears?

As Eena brushed her cheek, recall of the cold objectivity outlined in red volumes of Social Engineering Protocols at Fort Carson intruded. Plans to grow a mechanized hive from cloned babies, incubating in glass containers and destined for clinical procedures to produce the new generation of SynHus.

With quiet dignity, Chas, the pillar of stillness around which her stormy rebelliousness swirled, handed the groom the ring. In the outdoor cathedral in the ancient land of Mu, the young lovers spoke their vows. Engrossed in interior impressions, Eena felt without hearing the sincerity of their voiced intentions.

Peaceful inroads toward human sovereignty in the townships and Techno City had prevailed for a year and a half. But now, thanks to their forced transfer to Mu, few volunteered to travel to the townships. Without spreaders, as far as she knew, the Sovereignty Movement, if it still existed at all, was dying.

The revered elder blessed the union and together as husband and wife, Leslie and Gavin walked down the aisle, showered with well-wishes, their faces radiant with hope for the future.

Eena wished she could share that optimism. Threatening to overturn the Sovereignty Movement's achievements, the aggressive unrest in the townships was ratcheting up. Ironically, crowds of protestors with activated DNA had stalled the birthing of a positive future—potentials that gestated in both Leslie's ingenuity and her womanhood. Retaliatory martial law and the suffocating grip of the SEI had turned townships in to virtual prison camps and all but snuffed out hope.

The moment the bride and groom passed, an ethereal presence penetrated Eena's gloom.

"Amá! What are you doing here?"

"My daughter, the atmospheric ocean of energy immerses humankind not only in electromagnetic currents, but also even finer energies. Like Leslie's machines, human beings are themselves free energy devices with access to life-

enhancing currents. This all-encompassing flow, when tapped, can deflect attempts to sabotage humanity."

"Amá, what has that to do with me? I'm neither a scientist like Leslie, nor a midwife like you. I am a warrior."

"For your next task, retrieve that ever-available power source. Listen."

"What next task?" Eena asked. But Amá was gone.

As the crowd dispersed, tantalizing smells drew people to heavy-laden tables, and the band tuned their instruments. In the midst of the activity Eena stood still, momentarily bereft, while in the heart of the village and in the midst of those gathered, a spring of sweet water gurgled a message. Eena listened. *Fort Carson, Techno City. The townships. The time for return approaches.*

Indian Summer

Raymond headed with Elise down the lane toward the helicopter waiting to carry him and September's installment of produce to New Denver. "Even after we harvest the second planting of our gardens, we'll be in trouble by spring. Five more shipments over the winter will empty our food storage."

He paused to call out to a gardener sprinkling mulch around the seedlings in his recently extended garden. "Perfect Indian summer day."

Joe waved and shouted, "The additional ten percent's in the ground and will be ready for harvest in six weeks."

Raymond signaled a thumb's up and plucked a branch of spearmint growing beside the front gate. "D'ya mind?"

A friendly hand waved him on. "Help yourself."

"Let's hope the second planting yields a good harvest before the first frost," Raymond called back.

After a deep whiff of the mint, he stuck a leaf in his mouth and caught Elise's mischievous sideways glance. "The mint can't penetrate that onion and garlic smell. You reek."

"How's this for repulsing a romantic advance?" When Raymond pulled a handkerchief out of his pocket, the potency of the smell increased, his eyes reddened and, along with his nose, began to water.

Elise pursed her lip. "No one but me would want you."

"Or this." Raymond faked a nose blow into the cloth.

"Positively obnoxious."

They reached the copter, and as his wife held her nose, Raymond hugged her. "Pray I'm as disgusting as possible." And to the pilot waving away the fumes, "Medical remedy."

The route was familiar now: over the swastika runway formation, past the stallion's red-eyed glare, and descent beside the jackal-headed Anubis. This time, behind the Cadillac waited a flatbed truck, onto which a pair of SuperRos loaded the crates.

Under the watchful eye of SR-whatever, Raymond waved to the Gargoyle. With handkerchief over his nose, he reddened and watered his eyes, and walked into Biate's lair. After pausing to bow, he approached the throne as close as he dared.

"My God. That smell!"

"I apologize, your highness. Remedy for a bad cold."

Biate rose and walked toward the nearby balcony. She passed through the sliding glass door, and crowded to one side under an umbrella. "Over there. And get that thing off of your nose."

Snuffling noisily, Raymond wiped his eyes and nose and moved the cloth to just below his chin so the magic of the onion and garlic crushed by Elise would continue to counter Biate's spells.

Waving her hand in front of her nose, Biate called, "Rebecca."

The servant scuttled from behind the bar and minced a bow.

"Two wine coolers. It's hot out here."

The long green eyes narrowed and glared at Raymond. "Don't ever come in that condition again."

"I came because you insisted I come."

"Then keep yourself well."

After Rebecca reappeared with a tray of drinks and left, Biate leaned on the balcony railing and sipped her wine. "I still need the few humans that I brought to my palace to attend me until the scientists and technicians design their synthetic replacements. Historically, Anu's descendants have referred to common humanity as 'useless eaters,' and that is exactly the way I think of them, especially since our technological advances."

Holding her glass up to signal Rebecca, Biate appeared to be studying Raymond's blotched face. "Oh, but you needn't worry for now. The people in Gaia's Gardens will remain alive as long as they feed me, my technicians and my household—that is, until the activation of their replacements.

Raymond's drink remained on the table. "You honestly think that with a few robots you can control a hundred-mile radius?"

Biate's return gaze—bright to the point of a glitter—appeared to assess the slightest nuances of his response. Yet, the wild stare avoided direct eye contact. "I had two very special reasons for requiring your return today."

"Okay."

"Although a fun little tryst is a no-go with you in that state, I want to provide you with very valuable information to take back to my other partner" — Biate paused to giggle — "Imperial Governor Charles Scholtz, who actually thinks he can beat me in our political chess match. He's scared to come here, you know, my SuperRo Guards and all. And well he should be, and I'm about to show you why."

She turned toward the ever-present SuperRo. "SR-1-15, accompany us."

When they reached an elevator with a light that signified it was working, she commanded the robot to push the button.

"Down."

When the door opened, she said, "You first with the robot. I'm not riding with that smell."

Raymond hesitated. Was he being taken to a subterranean cell into which he would be thrown if he didn't comply with her demands? As he stepped to the elevator floor, he steadied himself to resist an unsettling wave of apprehension.

The ride was smooth past two floors to open at B2. A SuperRo guard stood in attendance on the basement floor, and when the door closed behind Raymond, he waited in suspense until the door opened for Biate and a second SuperRo, its insignia indicating designation SR 5-13.

Upon reaching the double doors at the end of the hall, a smug smile lingered on Biate's face as a guard unlocked the doors and flung them open. Raymond tried not to gape at the vast high-ceilinged, hanger-like room, which held no aircraft. Instead, columns of robots, the entire width and countless rows deep, awaited activation with blank stares.

Biate waved her hand toward the assemblage. "Meet New Denver's Royal Armed Force, more than equipped to conquer our pathetically struggling neighbor to the south.

A whistle followed Raymond's deep intake of air as he forced his body to immobility. "How many are we looking at?"

"Five hundred SuperRos, including the two currently attending me."

The robotic force didn't sport the expected bulging muscles. "They don't appear that muscular."

"In humans such strength requires bulk. In machines such as this, a blow from the fused titanium and carbon-reinforced polymers that are the bone and sinew of this design would be deadly."

Noting the bulges that looked like weaponized forearms, hands and fingers on each robot, Raymond shuddered.

"Though not super smart, they're virtually indestructible war machines. Each is loaded with sufficient firepower to mow down a few hundred human beings in minutes. Able to deflect bullets, they're incredibly strong and fast. A SuperRo can run thirty miles an hour and with a flick of its wrist flip a car or deliver a death blow to a human."

Apparently Biate's gaze had followed his. "They can vaporize a human instantly... and all this power is directly under my control. The SuperRos are numbered SR 1-2 for aisle one, row two and so on. By directing signals via the New Denver Central A.I., I can wake up and shut down the robots. Thanks to a holographic grid that shows me their location, I command them within a hundred-mile radius. If one reaches the border of that radius, a blinking light on the grid indicates its specific designation and location, and the A.I. redirects it movement within the communication perimeter."

At that moment Raymond's single most compelling goal was to find the location of New Denver's central A.I. "So, Biate...."

"You will address me as 'Queen Biate.'"

"Queen Biate, you do have incredible power at your disposal."

Biate eyes brushed his. "Yes, at a thirty-mile-an-hour run, this force would require no more than an hour to reach Gaia's Gardens."

At that instant, in the high-ceilinged hangar, as the weight of Biate's words sank in Raymond's gut, the deafening echo of five hundred simultaneous metallic click/swishes startled him.

Biate doubled over with laughter.

With a second click, five hundred weaponized right arms and hands rose upward aimed straight ahead.

The sweat on Raymond's forehead and in his armpits had nothing to do with onions and garlic. Instinctively, he looked around to seek cover.

The next collective click/swish lowered the robot arms and drew a thousand legs to stand at attention.

Shaken, Raymond wished he could rouse himself from the nightmare that portended a serious threat to Gaia's Gardens, Transtopia, the world.

"I'm sure you agree that this is information you need to take to Transtopia. In fact, I command you to do so."

"You're right. I do see why I must comply and inform others. But there is something I still don't understand."

Fingering the aquamarine pendant at her throat, Biate stood still as though waiting for him to continue.

"Where is the controlling computer, the central A.I. that just activated the force?"

With her chin raised, Biate's eyes explored the space around Raymond. "That, you will never know."

He stared at the expanse of stalled killing machines. But someone in Transtopia does needs to know about this Super Ro threat. Caellum and Dora.

Dora and Caellum need to know about the Fort Carson Cloning and Hybridization Project. A growing sense of urgency nudged Eena to take advantage of the warmth of early September to fly Cesla to Transtopia.

Two weeks into Gavin and Leslie's secluded honeymoon, she drew him away from conjugal bliss to meet under a cypress tree.

"I have an important mission in mind."

He rolled his eyes. "Eena, I can't believe you. I've just returned from a stint as a spreader in Township 26. I'm a newlywed. You can't even allow me just a reasonable reprieve from stress? I'm a father, for Pete's sake."

She paused and looked apologetic, but nonetheless, charged forward. "It's your child's future I'm thinking about."

"Oh, and I'm not?"

The destroyer of Gavin's happy reprieve had the wherewithal to look embarrassed. "Of course you are."

With forceful insistence Gavin resisted Eena's idea. "Look, as I've told you, the days of Three Mountains missions to townships to seed a peaceful insurgence and propagate spreaders to infiltrate the upper management in the townships are over. That DNA thing is happening. People are waking up. But the mood is ugly. Volatile."

The grove hid from view the source of a loud splash in the river before Eena continued. "This is about something different."

Gavin groaned. "Sometimes I wonder if you're fully human."

Her hurt look shook him.

"I'm sorry. That was a mean dig."

Eena peered through the cypress limbs. "Let's head for the river."

Stumbling and lurching, they threaded their way through the tangle of root knees, some a foot above ground. The river, back to its lazy meandering since the monsoon, and flowing well within its banks, hosted a herd of hippos dredging the river bottom with rows of teeth that could snap bones in half. Croaks, grunts and birdcalls serenaded the aquatic habitat as, closer to the river bank, a pair of crocodile eyes perched above the waves that submerged its twelve-foot body. Not far away cranes targeted by the periscope eyes balanced on one leg on a sand bar.

Once Gavin and Eena were seated on root knees, he warily watched the crocodile eyes. Calmer now, he explained his position. "As much as I dislike saying it, I became convinced during this last stint in a township that we're defeated. The leaders of the resistance have nixed our infiltration strategies. As we anticipated, the only change yielded by the citizens' pushback against SEI directives is continuous martial law. The townships have become police states. The jails are overflowing with people awaiting execution. Now life is far worse than before you and I escaped. This time I barely made it out."

Eena nodded. "I agree. Those dramas are out of our hands now. The people will either regroup to resume a peaceful underground resistance, or not. However, I'm thinking of babies."

"What?" He could barely fathom Eena's abrupt changes.

"I don't think I've told you about the babies at Fort Carson."

When Eena turned in unexpected directions, Gavin generally wanted no part of them, and certainly not this one. "Oh no, I already have one baby to be concerned about."

"To the contrary, if you care about your child's future, wiping out a major SEI stronghold hell-bent on generating a sub-human race with a hive mentality and nano technology fused with biology, matters greatly."

"I don't want to hear this." The periscope eyes in the river made Gavin feel like his main purpose was to provide their owner satisfying meal. "Between you and that crocodile, I'd almost rather take my chances with him."

The crocodile lunged for a crane that lifted gracefully just beyond the predator's reach. Undaunted, it resumed its submerged hunting position.

Eena persisted with dogged determination. "I haven't told you what I saw at Fort Carson. Cloned babies, a landlord project to engineer test tube-raised human/robot hybrids directed by a central AI."

"And you want to drag me there to save them."

"Basically, yes."

"In yet another exercise in futility."

"For sure, if we do nothing, the landlord schemes now in operation doom your baby's future."

"Not if we remain beyond their reach."

"Already the military has seized Three Mountains. And now one of them has penetrated this island remnant of Mu."

A gazelle paused at the shore and lowered its head for a drink.

"I've thought of that. Boats. We can build boats and sail away."

Eena's accusatory look unsettled Gavin. He knew he was sounding like his old avoidance-of-responsibility self.

The submerged crocodile eyes and water trail didn't bode well.

"As you know, we have an ally, an infiltration higher than we dreamed was possible. I'm going to enlist Dora's assistance."

Amid tumultuous swirling and splashing, the gazelle, its nose grabbed by crocodile jaws, disappeared beneath the river.

Gavin rubbed his nose. "To do what exactly?"

"Assist us in rescuing babies, toddlers and young children from Fort Carson."

Circles of water expanded until the river's relentless flow obliterated evidence of the kill.

"With Dora's help, maybe we can prevent your child from drowning in a world in which roboticized humans serve a police state without question, without the slightest resistance."

Gavin imagined the gazelle, helpless in the jaws of the beast. *Leslie and I will protect our child from such a fate.*

After a long silence Eena added, "I don't know if we can save those children. But I do know that if we do nothing, Charles the SynAnn and his ilk will devour humanity."

"I was gone for six weeks, and now you're asking me to leave after being reunited with Leslie for less than three. And we've only been married a week."

Tears of compassion reflected the light in Eena's unwavering stare. "I wish we had more time."

"So let me get this straight. Unarmed, we march up to some guard and say, 'Unplug and hand over those babies.' He says 'Sure' and sits on his thumbs while we remove what he's there to secure. Then we somehow transport infants and children to god knows where, to have a nice life with people, who are themselves living severely restricted lives under constant surveillance in a police state."

Long pause. "I admit we don't have a plan. That's why we need to meet with Dora and Caellum, inform them of the cloning/hybridization project at Fort Carson and plan the rescue of those children."

Gavin grunted his disgust. "Eena, I have great respect for you—for your courage, your tenacity. But let's face it. Your idea to seed a sort of contagion of peace and brotherhood in the higher echelons of Sector 10 has failed. Those in charge love their power and know how to keep it. Now, in my opinion, you're concocting another scheme which is also doomed to failure."

When he glanced at Eena, fire had seared the moisture in her eyes. "Okay, so just roll over and play dead." She stood up. "Well, with or without your help, I'm going. We saved Caellum from execution with a hair-brained scheme involving firecrackers... and we can save those children, and as ridiculous as it sounds, eventually, even Sector 10. With or without you, I'm flying Cesla to Garden of the Gods in three days to tell Dora and Caellum about the Fort Carson Hybridization Project and plan a mission to wipe it out of existence next spring."

Eena stood and turned to Gavin with formal stiffness. "Thank you for meeting with me. I know the timing couldn't be worse."

Having decided to put the meeting with Eena behind him as fast as possible, Gavin relayed the details with considerable affront to Leslie. "So there you have it."

Whereupon, Leslie, love shining in her eyes, her tone matter-of-fact, her hand on his cheek, replied, "Gavin, of course, it seems like you just returned from the township. And neither of us wants our honeymoon to end. Neither of us wants to be separated even for a few days. But, of course you must be at that planning meeting with Dora and Caellum. And, thankfully, our child will be born before that mission, which, of course, you must join."

What's Brewing?

When Gavin and Eena were seated in Dora's living room, her "So, tell me what's brewing?" opened a floodgate of revelations. She was mildly surprised to learn of Eena's royal ancestry on her father's side, and how the invitation at Fort Carson to work more closely with the landlords sent her fleeing to Three Mountains. But as she listened to Eena's account of the scheme to engineer a race of SynHus at the disposal of the landlords, shockwaves jolted her.

Eena concluded her narration with, "Persistent memories of what I saw and heard there won't let me rest."

Dora was pensive. "There must be a reason you've made this special trip to give me this information."

"We had to come now before it's too cold for the Augurs to leave Mu. You might call this a pre-brainstorming session. Frankly, Dora, we'll need your help."

"I don't see how."

"First, will you just visit the place?"

Caellum's concern for Dora was obvious. "No doubt there's a strong military presence there."

"The point is, Dora's a royal. She outranks all of them."

Gavin grabbed everyone's attention as he said, "Like you, my wife and I have a child on the way. But our child will not enjoy royal privilege. I can't help but wonder if the landlords or SEI webs of dehumanizing schemes will one day reach our child along with thousands of children."

Eena nodded. "The way I see it, the social engineering project at Fort Carson represents the landlord's scaffolding for the construction of a slave race."

"So, what's the plan?"

"At this point there is none. We only know that we want to save those children and destroy the lab. And we have to wait until spring to take action."

"How many children are there, and what ages?"

"That's what we need you to learn."

"And where would the children go?"

Eena shrugged. "We have a few months to figure that out. The thing is, we need you, Dora, being who you are, to first scope out the place—the layout, how well protected it is, and, equally important, we may eventually need you to pull rank to assist the rescue."

The looming threat to the people of Transtopia haunted Raymond. "I have to return to Transtopia." He braced himself for Elise's reaction.

She grabbed his arm. "Too dangerous."

"When five hundred SuperRos march toward that city, we'll all be endangered." He placed his hand over hers. They both knew he had to go.

Early morning yielded to midafternoon as Raymond followed the road cleared by the military last May for the 'zombie roundup' fiasco. When he reached the gate, he scanned the six-foot-high wall of rubble on the north side of Main Street. Too close to the Imperial Ritz Hotel. However, about 100 yards to the west he tackled a four-foot mound obscured on either side by higher piles of brick and mortar.

He flopped over the top, scrapes, and gashes decorating his shins and forearms, then waited as a retriever vehicle cruised by and a military jeep crawled past in the opposite direction. When both disappeared around corners, he scrambled down the south side of the wall, risking the seconds of exposure required to cross the street from rubble wall to an eight-story building. Seconds after he reached the curb and heaved a sigh of relief, a voice to his right commanded, "Put your hands up and keep them up."

He felt the barrel of the gun press against the middle of his back.

"Now, nice and easy give me your right hand."

After both handcuffs were locked on, the policeman gave him a little shove. "Squad car's just ahead around the corner."

"Aren't you going to read me my rights?"

Raymond's captor opened the door with one hand, pushed his head down with the other and shoved him in.

A cynical chuckle accompanied the start of the engine. "Rights? Where have you been for the past three years? The past decade?"

The officer's glance met Raymond's dejection through the rearview mirror. "I gotta say I'm used to catching people crossing the wall to get out of here, not in."

After they rolled to a stop in front of the station, the policeman got out, opened the back door, and motioned Raymond out with a wave of the gun barrel. At the top of the stairs, Raymond paused to look directly at the man beside him.

"Listen, I need to speak to someone of authority."

"Don't we all. Open the door."

Raymond felt a poke in his back but stood his ground. "It's urgent."

"Always is."

"I'm not talking about saving myself. I have information that someone in Transtopia needs to hear."

"Okay. So tell me."

"Like I said, someone of authority."

His captor shoved him through the door and they proceeded to check in. On the way to a holding cell, Raymond ventured one last try. "Commander Feldner will want to know that Raymond Muñoz is here."

Several hours deepened Raymond's despair until the click of the cell lock echoed down the hall and the guard walked him to Feldner's office. Dora sat across the desk from the commander.

"I thought Ms. Scholtz should hear what you have to say."

With relief he greeted the two people who were allies and who would listen to what he had to say.

After brief pleasantries he dropped his information bomb. "Soon—I don't know when, but soon—five hundred weaponized robots will be on the march from New Denver Airport to Transtopia."

The policeman who patrolled the campus nodded at Dora and Raymond as, flashlights in hand, they headed for the small, unlighted building at the edge of the campus.

Dora answered Raymond's unvoiced question. "He's one of the two sympathizers on the police force besides Feldner."

A flight of stairs led to a room in the basement where a group had gathered around tables. After introductions followed by Raymond's announcement of the coming of the SuperRos, he shocked them with the statement: "I feel partly responsible for the existence of this impending threat. I need to tell you about an event you never heard about — one that is painful for me to recall."

Which confused Caellum. "But aren't you a horticulturalist — permaculture, organic, biodynamic gardening — that sort of thing?"

"Not originally."

"Oh?"

"In two thousand fourteen, I hired on with a top robotics company. We assembled family robots."

"A decade later, I went to work for (ROTE), a robotics technology company with labs and gigantic hangars inside a mountain under contract to the military. It was an Unacknowledged Special Access Project (USAP), a top-secret agency that employed scientists with clearances up to fifteen levels above the president's need-to-know."

Since no comments or questions filled the space of Raymond's pause, he continued. "I should back up. For forty years prior to my arrival, USAPs had reverse engineered the advanced technologies of crashed ET craft recovered by the military. These offered stunning breakthroughs in science and technology and strategic warfare.

"By the time I came on the scene as a twenty-three-old, our work to reverse engineer fantastic off-world technologies had yielded rapid advances in computers, lasers and nanotechnology and space flight far in advance of humanity's need-to-know."

A shift in perspective transported Raymond back to the period of his life spent as a lab technician for Robotics Technology Labs. "In labs such as ROTE a major component of maintaining secrecy is compartmentalization of work. People in the various departments are sworn to secrecy — contractually forbidden to divulge the nature of their work to employees outside their department."

Someone on the far side of the room interrupted. "Why the secrecy?"

"Secrecy ensured no note-comparing so that we could not piece together and leak to the public the alarming capabilities of the assembled robots.

"But back to my career. It never occurred to me that our creations were anything other than benign, labor-saving devices—you know, to take over household chores like vacuuming and dusting, friendly companions and guardians of children—the kind depicted in movies: strong, able to lift and transport items too heavy for humans—furniture, that sort of thing.

"I enjoyed my work because I like designing and inventing. However, I never had a hand in assembling an entire robot. Just parts of them. Nonetheless, through the years I transferred between compartments. In one, I help to improve circuitry to make limbs move more efficiently. And in the last one, my team worked to make the movements of robots increasingly fluid, the facial expressions more humanlike. I had no idea we were developing weaponized robots."

"Weaponized robots?"

"For military purposes. Therefore, top secret."

"Okay, I'm following you."

"But even more concerning was that these are mostly autonomous machines."

"Autonomous?"

"Yes, except for a satellite A.I. interface."

Caellum noted the astonishment on Dora's face. "You'd better explain."

"Okay. Even in this narration, I choose my terms, my designations carefully, having become so aware of the insidious reach of the puppet masters into our lives."

Dora shifted uncomfortably from more than her distended belly.

Momentarily, Raymond's eyes closed, and the past enveloped him as though it were a present reality. "I enjoy coming to work. Often, I work late because I'm so intrigued by new breakthroughs in robotics. I anticipate that our improvements will benefit humanity, even though my knowledge stops at the door to my lab. I imagine a world in which labor-saving technology frees people to enjoy meaningful, creative pursuits.

"Years later, by the time my clearance has moved upward from level fifteen to twenty-five, ROTE transfers me to the department that is the final stop for assembled robots. Our task is to test them before military deployment. Instead of futuristic ray guns, which are to be the next development, this particular line of robots fires metal bullets.

"The thirty-five technicians in this department, the final stop for the fully assembled robots, inspect the new lineup to ascertain a flawless product. I don't understand my sense of unease as I witness the powerful limbs and blank stares of the mechanical replacements for human border patrollers and soldiers. I shake off the tremors up and down my spine. But I reassure myself that it's better to risk the destruction of a machine than the death of a human in defense of nations and their borders.

"After I've been in the final inspection department for about a week, I'm shocked at the intel a colleague shares in defiance of the strict secrecy mandate. Taking care that his actions are undetectable by listening devices and surveillance cameras, he presents each team member a glance at a hand written note. We learn that certain countries have begun to deploy the robots developed in ROTE labs to patrol their borders. Turns out the military has programmed the mechanized border patrol to shoot to kill men, women and children who approach within a few feet of national boundaries. The news syndicates suppressed the fact that a robot has recently massacred a family. Not a word on any of the news programs.

"My enthusiasm for robotics morphs into almost chronic anxiety. At that point, I realize what compartmentalization has hidden from view. Judging by the expressions on team members' faces, others share my concern. Far from docile household energy-savers, the products of our technologies are easily triggered, autonomous killing machines. We are assembling the potential murderers of human beings.

"Nonetheless, we proceed with our assigned tasks. As several technicians with handheld devices surround the robots, others engage with the inspection process through computer monitors. The technician who has the access code to activate the robots awaits a collective green light. After nods from inspectors who have completed their checklists, the head of the department, Dr. Onikawa, addresses Shem, who speaks the codes for the activation of the robots one by one. Within seconds there are metallic clinks as the robots shift slightly. In a weird role change, we, the thirty-five humans, stand unmoving.

"Within seconds the mechanical arms begin to twitch. The eyes fly open. The heads shift incrementally. The eyes scan us one by one.

"When the scan isolates me, my skin crawls." An involuntary shudder interrupted Raymond's account.

"The semi-circle of inspectors stands in a state of suspended animation. Suddenly, they applaud and with handshakes all around congratulate themselves on the success of the project. There's an almost festive feeling in the air.

"A particularly animated technician approaches the closest in the robot lineup. The man reaches up to clasp the polymer shoulder. Suddenly, the robot shifts and raises its weaponized arm. The sound of machine gunfire blasts the room. Horrified, I watch as technicians are thrown back by the force of the bullets, and blood spurts from their bodies. With macabre thuds, they land on the floor—dead.

"But that's only the beginning of the waking nightmare. The next instant, the weaponized arms of all four robots spray bullets in a three hundred-degree sweep of the room. In the blink of an eye twenty-seven people are mowed down.

"To this day the massacre event, which I helped engineer, robs me of sleep." Raymond's voice grew husky.

"So eight of you are still alive. What now?"

"Stealthily, Shem codes their shut down. As if grabbed by the same intent, several who have escaped death move stealthily behind desks and equipment to the rear of the robots collecting electric drills, screwdrivers, even laser pens—pathetic excuses for weapons. The scientists spring as one force from behind the killing machines and begin to tear them limb from limb, pulling heads from necks, whatever they can do to permanently deactivate them. Within moments, surrounded by the twenty-seven humans lying in pools of blood, the four products of extensive research and development lie inert with exposed fiber optic cables, pools of blue 'robot blood' on the floor.

"A momentary stupor grabs the eight of us who are still alive. I shake my head to surmount my shock. As I rise slowly from a squatting position behind my desk, I think the bizarre nightmare's over, but it's not. I hear a noise. I think someone's recovering from the psychological paralysis that has gripped us. But I'm wrong. A robot, the one with a still intact head, sits up. The weaponized arm torn from the shoulder socket dangles beside the exposed innards of the torso. But the head moves side to side in small, rapid jerks. A series of blinks and clicks indicate reactivation.

"When the not-weaponized arm begins to move, a technician springs from behind. Another joins him, and with an electric drill they drill into the neck, pry the head from the body and feverishly hack the fiber optic bundles that comprise the robot's spinal cord. After they have ripped loose every single wire, they toss the tangled mass of wire and metal to the floor.

"'What just happened?' I ask.

"Dr. Onikawa's face is white, disbelief still written on it. His voice cracks. 'These robots were in communication with a satellite A.I. that apparently overrode the shutdown code. The one that revived appears to have been receiving instructions for self-repair. No doubt it was preparing to take on the remaining humans in this room.'

"For the next couple of weeks, we watch the news for word about the lab technician massacre. But every syndicate maintains complete silence on the subject.

"Over the following months I scan the mainstream media for reports on either the lethal potentials or deployment along borders and in war zones of autonomous killing machines. Nothing. Absolutely nothing.

"However, on the alternative media circuit, short-lived whistle blowers leak information that our robots work in tandem with drones to mow down humans with little or no provocation. Not long afterward those who speak out die untimely and mysterious deaths—usually declared suicides.

"The certainty that both my home and my body are bugged with nano technology is in effect a lifelong gag order."

A silence thick with apprehension filled the interval until Caellum cut through it. "Wait a minute. Let's back up to those robots that are to approach Transtopia. Assuming we are able to destroy them, their reactivation is impossible. Solar Flash destroyed satellites, and any A.I. they housed."

"Nonetheless, I watched as an unseen A.I. activated all five hundred SuperRos. Though I don't know how, Biate must have communicated with it. According to her, the A.I. can track and individually control the five hundred designations. And yes, she assured me that like the prototype I helped build, the central A.I. reactivates, and initiates repairs when a robot is damaged."

Fall Festival 12

As Leon opened the car door for Dora, the profusion of tall corn stalks the length of the park affirmed the success of Sovereignty Gardens. Thanks to the guidance of experienced gardeners, the seeds saved from the June harvest provided for the August planting. This October harvest would double the winter storage.

As though to accommodate the Fall Harvest Festival of 2038, corn, beans and squash, the three sisters had reached fruition to fill the baskets of the harvesters by the first of October. Snap beans wound their way up the stalks of corn that formed a green border along the west side of Celebration Park, and a profusion of the broad leaves of butternut squash carpeted the garden floor. Not to be outdone by the three sisters, ripe tomatoes, onions and potatoes awaited harvest.

Dora grabbed a nearby basket and passed the pickers using pruning shears to sever squash from vines, and filling baskets to overflowing with heavy gourds. In response to a heightened awareness of her and the earth's mutual fecundity she felt a quickening in her womb. After a quick scan for Caellum she kneeled among the vines winding up the corn stalks to fill her basket with freshly picked green beans.

Once the green beans were harvested, Dora filled her basket with corn and carried it to the 'shucking' crew that was peeling back the green husks and golden silk to expose the ripe yellow ears

New arrivals continued to stream in as harvesters returned heavy baskets to work stations where food that wasn't put aside to be dried or otherwise preserved was dedicated to the feast. The food preppers snapped the green beans, peeled and cubed the squash and shucked the corn. The cooks receiving the produce roasted the orange-gold butternut flesh over the cooking fires, steamed the green beans before mixing them with caramelized onions, and lightly boiled the corn.

Heading to the potato patch, Dora took a moment to once again look for Caellum. Several yards away where men cleared and raked an area for a bonfire, he was splitting logs. When her eyes briefly met his, she smiled her contentment. After shooting her a grin, Caellum, barely recognizable with black-rimmed glasses, a cap and a beard, balanced the next log, raised an ax, and split it with a *thwack!* that echoed through the park.

As though to bless the day of harvest, the cloudless blue of the sky seemed filled with promise, and the afternoon sun bathed Dora's upturned face with its warm radiance. She reveled in the new and welcome sensations until something dark obscured her view and shattered her serenity. *A helicopter.*

The whirring thumps of the blades grew louder, and as the craft descended, milling people underneath scattered. While the blades still turned, out stepped a robot guard which, with a feeling of dread, Dora recognized as Biate's. He stood by the exit which soon framed Biate herself, wearing a teal blouse and cream pants.

Dora's exalted moment thudded to earth. *Why does her arrival cast such a pall over the lighthearted glow of this day?*

Not wanting to draw Biate's attention to herself, Dora grabbed a basket and trawl, and fell to her knees to dig for potatoes. Glad to reconnect with the soil, she was unconcerned that she had no gardening gloves. At times she even put aside the trawl to dig barehanded, smiling inwardly at her childish love of thrusting her fingers in the cool dirt.

Expecting Biate to head straight to the SynAnn governor, she shook away the pall of the woman's intrusion to recapture the happy camaraderie of the day. But minutes later as she held a just-dug potato, a shadow blocked the sun, and she turned to see the object of her evasion. Chagrin unsettled her as, off balance, she struggled awkwardly to an upright position assisted by the firm clasp of Biate's hand.

Green eyes that were uncomfortably close smiled into hers, and she fought the impulse to flee.

"Dora, how are you?"

"Fine, thank you, and you?" She brushed her palms together freeing a spray of dirt.

Biate scanned her hands and glanced toward her knees caked with red soil. "Dirty."

Dora stifled her amusement when Biate stepped back as though to avoid being contaminated. Dora's equally childish response was to thrust out her hands to flagrantly display the soil stuck to her knuckles and packed under the tips of her nails. A look of startled abhorrence greeted her impudence.

Perplexed by Biate's reaction, Dora bent over as best she could to brush the caked dirt off her knees and pick up the filled basket. Slipping her arm through the basket handle, she headed toward the corn shuckers, but Biate detained her.

"Your hands are dirty."

"Of course. Comes with gardening."

"You must wash them."

The laughter that burst from her couldn't be restrained. "I'll wash them soon enough. Come, Biate."

Biate remained where she stood, stubbornly intent on the immediacy of the need for cleanliness. "You," she turned toward a woman who carried a basket of corn. "Bring a bowl of water."

The woman stopped in obvious confusion.

"Now." A delicate tiara bobbed slightly when Biate issued the command. Amidst surprised onlookers, the woman hurried away to return and place a bowl of water at Biate's feet. Deciding the incident wasn't worth a scene, Dora smiled an apology, placed the potato-filled basket on the ground, and hunkered down to sink her fingertips in the water. As dirt from her immersed hands muddied the water, the corners of Biate's lips turned downward and, like a child, she repeatedly voiced her revulsion. Dora heard the murmurs among the spectators, the whispered observances of those gathered when the epitaph 'the mad queen' was born.

With obvious relief, Biate watched as flesh and nails washed free of dirt, Dora's hands lifted from the water, while Dora contemplated the psychology of whom she was interacting. She couldn't put her finger on it, but something about Biate wasn't right. With Dora's nod and thank you to the woman who then carried the bowl away, Dora retrieved her basket, and Biate fell into step beside her.

She brooded over the just-passed scene, but Biate's focus had moved on. "Your baby, when is it due?"

The expectant mother wondered at the surge of alarm that so shocked her heart, it missed a beat. "I...I believe sometime in January."

"Don't worry. I'll be there to assist you."

From the depths of certainty leaped the words Dora dare not voice, *oh no, you won't*.

After Dora delivered the basket of potatoes to the peelers, Biate hung around for a long few minutes of stalled conversation, before she spied Charles the SynAnn near the row of vendors. In parting, it was not Dora, but the unborn child, she addressed with "Good bye, my little one."

After Biate moved away, the sight of Adair and Sylvia in line at a gaming booth re-grounded Dora in a sane world. Pressing her palms to her belly in response to a volley of kicks, she addressed Adair mentally. *It's you who will assist the birthing*, and as though she had heard Dora speak, Adair turned with a friendly smile and waved an invitation.

But with a return wave she stood apart from the crowd, needing momentary solitude amid shouts and bustling underneath the red-gold glow of the setting sun as the aromas of potatoes, onions and pan-fried fish drew people to the chow line. Relieved to be rid of the creepy queen and yearning to be close to Caellum, she scanned the crowd, but couldn't find him.

Blankets were spread for the workers while the royals sat at three tables joined to form a 'U' shape. Her own plate filled, she headed toward the tables to sit at an obligatory place, perform her expected role, and share a feast she could barely taste. While Biate hypnotized Charles the SynAnn, and Astrid stared, she looked around for Rolf with mounting tension. When he arrived before his cyborg parent noticed his absence, she sighed her relief. At a distance from the banter and Charles and Biate's flirtation, they ate their meal and escaped when leaving the royal table was acceptable.

As they approached the men coaxing the first flames from the fire pit, Rolf turned to her with concern. "You okay? You look pale."

"I'm fine."

Rolf crooked his forefinger and lifted her chin. "I'll stay."

She sighed. "No need. My Biate ordeal has passed since your cyborg dad has grabbed her attention."

"Don't let her get to you."

"You're right, I shouldn't. Now return to Alexi before he resents me."

Not a hugger, Rolf's hesitation was his embrace. "Seems like I'm leaving you alone again."

"You are, and I wish you'd get on with it." Dora pecked his cheek and playfully shoved him away.

The crowd closed behind her tall, gorgeous spouse, and with a tug on her heart, Dora resumed scanning for Caellum until she found him. Sporting his disguised look, with the breeze blowing light brown strands around his face, the father of their child blended inconspicuously with the group of men who were feeding wood to the roaring fire. She wished she could join him and longed for the day they would somehow oust Charles the SynAnn, which would free Rolf and her to shed the marriage and keep their friendship, and allow Caellum and her union to be made public.

But within seconds, her heart lurched as she spied Nathan Abelt and his family approaching from the opposite end of the concession stands. She searched her memory. Had he ever seen Caellum up close? Of course he had. That fateful day after she conceived when Caellum left her at his camp in the forest to attend a meeting of the Sovereignty Network. Nathan was one of the men who had ambushed him. And he was present at the execution.

Caellum, my foolish love, I urged you not to come today.

She fast-walked to intersect the family, approaching the crowd gathered around the bonfire, but they reached it first. As Nathan's wife held the youngest, the two older children's eager dash toward the flames distracted their father who, with apologies, squeezed between people as he bolted after them. When Nathan reached the twins to forcibly halt their pell-mell charge, Caellum, evidently alerted to imminent danger, pulled the bill of his cap over his face and turned into the shadows. Once he had melted to obscurity on the far side of the just-arrived fire gazers, Dora turned to beam a smile at Nathan's wife.

"Mrs. Abelt."

Lydia, looking flustered but pleased, apparently recognized her. "Hello, Ms. Scholtz."

The toddler with downy blonde hair and blue eyes, viewing the world from her mother's arms, captivated Dora with an intensity that was new to her. "How old is your child?"

"Emma's eighteen months, Ms. Scholtz."

"Please, call me Dora."

"Lydia. Pleased to meet you."

As Lydia's glance assessed Dora's state, Dora reached for Emma. "May I hold her?"

Lydia shifted her child for transfer.

Targeted by Nathan's scowl that looked as though he expected her to kidnap his offspring, Dora held Emma sitting upright and alert on her arm and nudged her forefinger inside a little fist. In response, bright blue eyes became animated, the trunk bounced, and the feet kicked.

"When are you due, Ms.... Dora?" Lydia's voice sounded shy, tentative.

"In three months. January." Dora brushed soft wisps from the forehead and admired the delicate ears.

Lydia smiled gently. "I know the feeling. Impatience for the birth of your own."

"I'm new to this."

"I remember how it was before the twins were born."

"I'll need advice from an experienced mother." As Dora looked pointedly at Lydia, the phrase *have you gone mad?* flashed through her head.

Lydia looked flustered, but a pleased smile lit her face. "I'd be happy to help any way I can."

Suddenly, Dora yearned for the companionship of another young mother. Whereas Nathan repelled her, she felt attracted to his wife. "Over a cup of tea?"

"That sounds wonderful. However, Nathan's often away and I do have the twins."

"Of course."

"Next Sunday at my house at 10:00 a.m.?"

"It's a date."

At that moment Nathan returned looking haggard as he gripped the hands on either side of him, tugging against his grasp. "Can we move away from this fire?"

As Dora returned Emma, Lydia smiled a wan-faced apology.

Dora touched her shoulder. "I'm pleased to have met you."

Lydia's former reserve had dissolved and her eyes smiled an invitation to friendship as she moved to follow her husband. "I look forward to our visit."

After the Abelts moved away, the reality that Nathan could have spotted Caellum hit Dora. Shaken, she trembled. Firelight and lanterns had replaced the last vestiges of daylight as she stood alone at the edge of the crowd. Behind clustered couples, a longing for normalcy, for Caellum, sank her into despondency until strong hands gripped her shoulders and drew her farther into the surrounding darkness. Startled, she caught her breath and, though Scholtz's chief spy scanned the crowd only a few yards away, she leaned into Caellum. For brief, unguarded moments she laid her head on his shoulder and breathed the scents of pine and smoke comingling in his Pendleton shirt. His lips brushed her hair, and encircled by his protective embrace, she clung to him.

"I've been watching you," he teased, holding her tight. "Even saw you hobnobbing with the enemy's wife."

"It's worse than that. I'm invited to tea," she confessed, glad she couldn't see his face.

The band started to play, and couples filed onto the deck that had been constructed for dancing while arm in arm they watched, concealed by the milling crowd and darkness. "Oh, Caellum, will we ever enjoy these events as a family like normal people?" She didn't dare voice her actual thoughts: *It was a bad decision to remain in Transtopia. A huge and possibly costly mistake.*

The Monsoon   13

Europe, the Mediterranean Sea, Casa Blanca and three hundred miles of sand behind, Jack relaxed into the dromedary's rhythmic plodding. Shouts and the hum of market traffic receded as, swaying in the saddle, Jack followed his guide through the arched gate of the ancient city of Marrakech. The final phase of his journey began with quiet aplomb on a dirt road bordered by the vast sweep of red dunes speckled with gray scrub. Ahead, the futuristic compound that had so intrigued him a few years back awaited the completion of his trek.

As the November breeze sought entrance inside his leather jacket, he pulled up the zipper, and a smile belied his reflections. In this land of stark contrasts, beyond the ancient walls that yielded this tedious conveyance, a man researched the means to defy the constraints of gravity and traverse interstellar realms.

Three hours into the trek, the creeping soreness in his spread-out thighs and a rumbling belly intruded on his reflections, so he decided to walk for a while. His guide forced the grunting, humphing animal to kneel so Jack could dismount to munch on flat bread and cheese and, lead rope in hand, exercise his legs. Just ahead loomed the first tree he'd seen since the Marrakech orchards that offered figs, dates and olives to the locals. He blinked to bring into clearer focus the blobs of brown and white visible among its sparse greenery. Instead of the familiar fruits, the lone tree appeared to have sprouted goats perched with perfect equanimity on its accommodating limbs as they ingested shriveled fruits and excreted the nut-like pits.

"Argan tree," Jack's guide, Aref, offered. "The women make argan oil from the nuts."

By early afternoon a darkening sky shadowed the dusty road. The gray clouds crowding overhead were a reminder that November was the month of the monsoon though the guide explained that the desert clouds often released only light sprinkles.

To the west, broiling red-brown swirls loomed a warning, and his companion said they needed to pick up the pace to reach the sheltering dunes that bordered the Ourika River before the storm hit. So once again the guide coaxed the protesting camel to kneel, and Jack swayed and tilted precariously upward as the camel rose. Between spurts of trotting, the dromedary plodded on at a maddeningly sedate gait, and Jack's gaze shifted between the still distant goal to the south and the advancing wall of sand to the west.

A half hour later, pursued by the deafening roar of the storm, a small fox disappeared beneath a dune, and a herd of gazelles bounded past. Within minutes, Jack turned up the collar of his jacket in self-defense as the raging torrent of sand engulfed the riders and camels. Crystalline projectiles stung his cheeks and coated his eyelashes as the barely visible guide pulled on the lead rope and induced Jack's mount to lie down. As the camel's knees buckled, a disconcerting *nhhhuuuur* rumbled a protest while Jack leaned back in order not to tumble forward. Then, in awkward haste, he dismounted to huddle behind the humped torso, a meager shield from the relentless barrage of sand.

Eyes closed, locked in near comatose surrender, Jack escaped to interior musings.

Flight. Although Jack's idea of exhilarating flight was piloting a jet at Mach 2, he knew Randolph Ring didn't initiate Blue Kachina Center for Research and Development to experiment with combustible engines. His methods were in alliance with what he termed *Natural Law* — a whole new way of looking at the physics of flight.

Jack recalled Randolph's words: "Commonly, science text books purport the conventional way of doing things. We have a conventional way of doing things and we have a natural way of doing things. And they're totally different."

While Jack grimaced against the pummeling from the storm, he smiled inwardly. His mind's eye presented the incongruous image of a bumblebee — the bee featured in the short documentary titled, *What if Physics Is a Lie Because the Bumblebee Knows Best?* He'd watched the film narrated by Randolph several times, practically memorizing the script.

Randolph narrated. "I was in physics class, and the teacher was saying, 'You know, bumblebees can't fly. It's impossible. Aerodynamically, they can't fly.'

"The classroom was on the second floor, and I looked out the window. There was a big, beautiful bumblebee staring me right in the eye, and he was doing something that this guy said he couldn't do. I've never forgotten that lesson, and so from then on I understood that he was right. They can't fly. They levitate."

As the bee featured in the film hovered over bright orange flowers, Jack started to lose interest. He had no desire to levitate. But at his mentor's behest he continued to view the documentary.

The narration continued. "So why teach that bumblebees *can't* fly and forget to teach that they *can* defy gravity?"

In the film, the bee, attracted to the color and scent of the flower, alighted on the petals to sip the nectar.

"There's a hollow cavity next to the bee's larynx. When the bumblebee starts to flap its wings, the larynx begins to resonate. This resonance is similar to when someone breaks glass with her voice, or uses sound to levitate objects."

Jack had to admit resonance was an intriguing principle. But, to a pilot, it offered an unattractive means of conveyance when compared to the dramatic propulsion of a jet into the atmosphere.

"The resonant energy from the bee eventually reaches the resonance of the surrounding field. It creates a magnetic bubble, and within this field, it can go anywhere it wants."

The gossamer wings began to beat, and the striped body and pollen-laden legs of the insect rose straight up.

"In Natural Law there's only one law. You either apply Natural Law or resist it. And get this: just *want* to understand Natural Law, and soon it will start teaching you."

Jack thought he *ought* to want to learn more about Natural Law. But in truth he would just be appeasing this man who commanded so much respect. Jack resonated with Randolph's way of being—his persistence despite the resistance of moguls of the petroleum corporate empire and the scientists they funded to publicly uphold an outgrown physics model. Though Jack supported Randolph's fight for truth, an unremarkable lift-off to float in resonance with an unknown field held no appeal.

After an hour and an insignificant spray of moisture, the roar retreated as nature's rampage moved past the ochre blanketed mounds that were camels and riders. Jack unglued his tightly closed lids, unscrewed the cap from his canteen and with handfuls of water, freed his eyelashes and face from the moist, clumped sand.

Judging the destination was about ten miles ahead, Jack stood up and shook off layers of sand while the dromedary's irritable *nhhhuuuur* protested the guide's inducement to resume the journey. But they had only progressed a few yards when shining through the retreating swirls of dust, an apparition stalled Jack's mounted impatience. In open-mouthed disbelief, he halted his camel.

The Woodstove 14

After Raymond's account of the robotics lab massacre and his warning about the imminent robot invasion, the October chill in the air added to Dora's angst. She shivered. "This is the coldest morning so far. Shall we start a fire in the woodstove?"

"Good idea." Caellum opened the grate, lit the kindling, blew to coax the sparks to small flames and strategically placed wood retrieved from the bin to encourage the fiery source of warmth.

Dora placed a kettle of water on the top plate. "When does it stop — this parade of awful revelations such as those robot killing machines?

Caellum sympathized. "As one who has spent years sifting through fake news and piecing together genuine whistleblower intel, I understand. The elites, your kind of people with access to technologies hundreds of years in advance of that of common humanity, were sometimes referred to as a "breakaway civilization."

"It's still hard for me to grasp."

When a knock at the door interrupted their conversation, they stared at one another, the unvoiced question: who should answer? Caellum, who was presumed dead, or Dora, who shouldn't be there?

"Caellum, Dora, open up. It's Shaun."

With a relieved sigh, Caellum opened the door, and Shaun burst in. "I need to talk with you."

"Wait," Dora said. "Let's have tea and breakfast before the next blow."

The stove rapidly warmed the small room, and by the time the oatmeal, toast and tea were served Shaun removed his hoody. "First frost expected tonight."

They made small talk until the last bite, at which point Shaun shared the news. "Commander Feldner called me into his office. Turns out a couple of students attempted to escape Onmatson Farm. One was killed, and the other was taken into custody."

"Whoa!"

"Fortunately, the policeman who nabbed him was one of the two officers besides the commander who are sympathetic to our movement."

"So the youth's in jail now?"

"No."

"So?"

"Knowing he would be slated for execution, they called me."

"And?"

"They asked if I knew of any place he could hide. I suggested your old base camp on the far side of rubble wall.

"Okay."

"He's there now."

"You took him?"

"Yes. I think you'll want to talk to him. Seems there's considerable unrest among the students at the farm. They'll be squashed like bugs when my... the governor learns of this."

When Caellum said he had to go, a premonition shook Dora. After dark, after Shaun and Caellum left and the embers in the stove turned to ashes, she put an extra quilt on the bed to ward off the cold and crawled underneath. That night, while unsettling dreams invaded her sleep, the fingers of the first frost crept across the windowpanes.

Shaun and Lieutenant Clark escorted Caellum as far as the gate in rubble wall, where Shaun slipped him a couple of large bags of food, a communication device and a key. "So you can communicate with me or Commander Feldner—Channel 1 is his. Channel 2 is for me. If you can't reach either of us, you can slip back to this side, but knowing the risk, you may want to wait until you reach one of us."

Following the eerily familiar route to his old ZD headquarters, Caellum reached the house with the two crosses in the front yard marking the graves of Raymond's brother and sister-in-law. A faint light glowed through the window.

"Blake, Caellum Nichols here."

After a pause the door opened a crack.

Caellum handed him the bag. "From Shaun."

"I'm glad to meet you, Mr. Nichols."

"I guess you're aware this was my headquarters before my execution." Blake grinned.

"So tell me what's going on at Onmatson Farm."

"We're like slave labor. Now that it's fall, we spend hours—I mean ten hours a day—pushing ears of dried corn through a mechanical kernel extractor, grinding it in to meal, and bagging it. Imagine doing that sun up to sun down. We were college students, headed for careers. Now, along with bad food and bed bugs, we have lice in our hair. Nights are getting colder and there aren't enough blankets to go around. I could go on. It's like a concentration camp."

"So you decided to cut and run?"

"When the soldier on tower watch and the truck drivers were distracted by the antics of a dog, I saw my chance. Climbed on those bags of meal, and dug in. Ken decided to follow me, but hesitated. They spotted him. I couldn't see anything. Just heard two shots and Natalie's scream."

"You were lucky the man who discovered you was Lieutenant Clark. Otherwise, you'd be on death row."

"I know it was crazy. I just saw a chance to escape and took it."

"Did you have a place in mind to escape to?"

"Well, I hoped on this side of the wall I could find a way to survive. I've heard rumors of a town farther north. Or I could hide out in the forest like you did."

"Until winter. The cold drove me to this house. So tell me, Blake, would you say you're feeling more rebellious than most?"

"There are others. I'm sorry to say Larry Owens hanged himself. Misti Russo was shot in the back for trying to escape through the fence that surrounds the buildings."

"What's the mood among those college youths?"

"The mood's ugly. After lights out in the dorm the guys argue about ways to kill the guards and where to escape. It's a toss-up between the destroyed part of Colorado Springs and the mountains. I think something really bad is about to happen."

Caellum's mind went to Dora. *Sorry, my love. I thought I might be returning to you in a day or two. But it looks like we're going to be separated for a while.*

Closing the door on the unlit the woodstove, Dora left Caellum's cold room to return to her apartment. Feeling bereft of his companionship as she gazed out at the Transtopia skyscrapers, she was glad she had agreed to visit Lydia and hoped a Sunday sipping tea and discussing motherhood would lift her spirits. An hour later, Leon drove her to Lydia and Nathan Albeit's two-story four-bedroom home, one of a line of similar houses on that street with restored electricity reserved for top officials in the Social Engineering Initiative.

Lydia's welcoming smile met her at the door. "I just put Emma down for her nap. So we can visit uninterrupted for a while."

Eager to escape her concerns for Caellum and for the future, Dora invited Lydia to speak of hers. "Your children are young. What did you do prior to Solar Flash?"

"As my goal was to help children with psychological problems, a large portion of my master's degree trained me as a diagnostician to deliver batteries of tests to detect symptoms of maladjustment. I continued my education until I earned a PhD in child psychology with an internship in counseling under my belt.

"So, at the local school I face this squirmy eight-year-old-boy, Robbie. He practically explodes with harnessed energy. I'm aware that, to punish him for inattention and interruptions, the irate teacher has taken away his recess. In the next escalation the provoked teacher confines him in a small partitioned area in the back of the room. When neither of those strategies works, she arranges for him to eat lunch in isolation and places him in solitary detention after school. In desperation, she and the principal have sent him to me.

"Aware that tests suggest he has Attention Deficit Disorder and dyslexia, I pull out a nature book for discussion. He starts naming local snakes. Identifies ten off the top of his head. Then he pulls several crystals out of his pocket. Names them too, tells where in the world they're found, and even special properties of each as he lines them up on the table. Obviously, he can sit still and focus on special areas of interest—particularly those found in nature.

"I'm interested in therapeutic measures. My mind flashes images of Robbie running across fields, climbing trees and finding bugs, snakes and interesting rocks. But those elements have been eliminated from school settings with twenty-minute recesses on asphalt. I say to myself, 'Be realistic.'

"I approach the teacher. 'He's a nature-lover, a walking encyclopedia of knowledge of outdoor creatures. Hand him nature books to browse with plenty of pictures and information. Let that inspire his writing.'

"She looks at me like I'm crazy. 'Do you actually imagine we have the luxury of deviating from the curriculum? He needs an effective prescription and/or an insertion. And we need to hit his parents where it hurts.'

"She means a drug or the chip for him and a bank account deduction for the parents. At that juncture in my first year as school counselor, reality strikes. I'm not employed for effective therapeutic measures. My job is to administer diagnostic tests, document endless details of what's wrong with each child, and to render students docile and compliant by whatever means necessary—drugs, the chip, whatever."

Dora rubbed her belly as though to caress the energetic acrobat she carried. *Don't worry. That won't happen to you.*

"Throughout the ten years of my career escalating signs of depression, even psychoses keep pace with punitive measures, emotionally detached teachers and students plugged into technology. Increasingly, AI teaches them and grades their multiple-choice exams. To a growing extent, computer-generated holographic worlds even dominate their playtime. I notice an alarming correlation. Children who prefer computer-generated worlds disengage from reality and avoid eye contact."

My child will have better than this.

"I've come to see regimented schooling as more to constrain intelligence than to expand it—to entrain children to fill corporate slots."

Not my child.

At that moment, two-year-old Emma, rubbing sleep from her eyes and dragging a stuffed animal behind, approached her mother and whining, "I want you," lay her arms across her mom's lap.

Lydia lifted Emma so that the child's head rested on her shoulder as she rubbed and patted her back and sighed heavily. "In just over two years she'll be four."

"Why do you say it like that?"

"That's when the be-still, sit-in-your-chair and attend-to-academics begins. Imagine that. Four years old, when nature designed her to spend her days playing in the dirt, animating bits of fluff and sticks in pretend play."

As my child will.

Seeing that their younger sister had approached mom, the twins did the same. "We're hungry."

Lydia smiled apologetically. "Sorry. I had hoped for more time."

But Dora smiled brightly. "Please don't apologize. I feel like I'm getting the education I never got, and none too soon." As she helped prepare and serve the sliced carrots from Lydia's kitchen garden, Eena's allusion to Fort Carson popped into her head. *The way I see it, the social engineering project at Fort Carson represents the Social Engineering Initiative's scaffolding for the construction of a slave race.*

"Forgive me, Dora, for bending your ear."

"To the contrary, I think you've told me what I needed to hear."

"I do hope you'll visit again. I promise we'll focus on you. I'll teach you about breathing exercises to ease the birthing process."

"Sounds lovely." Dora's smile reflected her intention to return, but hid the intention that surfaced. *In the meantime, I need to further my education in current child-rearing practices someplace else – Fort Carson.*

Apocalypses 15

Raymond's onion, garlic and bad cold ruse would raise suspicions a second time. So, before the Tuesday food drop-off he and Elise concocted a more permanent means to squelch Biate's determination to take him to bed. A lightly dropped suggestion, tinged with embarrassment, that he had contracted a venereal disease would permanently dowse the sexual fires that fueled Biate's advances—thus easing a major portion of his dread of being with her.

So, for the first time in Raymond's association with Biate, he invited her advance, and put his arms around her. She pulled back enough to gaze seductively into his eyes and trace his jaw line with the tip of a manicured nail. Unbuttoning the top of his shirt she leaned forward to kiss the exposed flesh. "Oh, Raymond...."

"Dearest Biate, how many times I have thought of holding you close, your flesh pressed against mine, my fingers entangled in your gorgeous hair."

Biate pulled away from Raymond to pull him through the door to her bedroom.

"But I must share with you one tiny impediment to our long awaited union."

"Later. I couldn't care less about your wife, if that's it."

Raymond yanked her close with crushing strength.

"I must tell you...."

"Tell me later."

She pulled him toward the bed until with hard jerk, the entwined would-be lovers fell across the satin quilt.

"It wouldn't be fair to you." He kissed her neck and pulled aside her strap to bare the shoulder he was kissing.

"I'm not interested in your affairs."

"Nor am I, except for the one in which I contracted a venereal disease."

Relieved the pressure for a sexual encounter was permanently squelched, and to be no longer dogging vases, lamps and candelabras hurled across the room, Raymond buttoned his shirt and breathed deep in preparation for phase two of his visit.

After Vanessa's soothing ministrations calmed her mistress, Biate collected him to join her in a walk down the escalator and linger in the hall with the apocalyptic paintings. Her disappointing encounter with Raymond and the artist's warnings of impending doom seemed to fuel her desire to reveal the apocalyptic currents of her own life.

"I grew up in Chicago. My trillionaire father, Dion Kellercorfe, was one of the two or three most powerful men among the world's elites. He even fancied himself ruler of the world. He insisted that his harshness, his abuse — locking me up, food deprivation, striking me — was meant to provide my personal boot camp for life. To toughen me up, he said, so that when I grew up, I could effectively rule the workers.

"By my teen years my father offered a second type of abuse. I have always been beautiful. And to him any and all alluring females of any age were his consorts. And such dalliances even qualified his attentions toward me.

"Sailing on Lake Michigan offered my only respite from dread of his approach. The yacht crew was at my disposal. At times we sailed on the open sea and at others, the sailors and myself moored at rocky lagoons for swimming and partying. Sometimes I brought boyfriends along. Other times, the sailors fulfilled my need for companionship.

"My father, aware that my promiscuity mirrored his, subjected me to surgery to ensure I could never bear a child.

"When I was eighteen it became known to my mother and myself that one of Dad's liaisons was different from the others. He became so smitten with a worker named Mini, it was as though she were his whole world. It seemed to me this favored mistress had cast a spell on him so that he preferred her above all others. Certainly, my father loved her more than my mother — or me, for that matter. Whispers of Dad attending functions with Mini at his side often reached our ears.

"Mini became pregnant, and a month later so did my mother, and both carried males in their wombs. Mom became very distraught, but not because of my father's affair. As I said, he'd always been a philanderer. Her concern was that Mini's pregnancy was a month in advance of hers, and Dad's illegitimate son would be born first. My mother feared that my father, being so enamored of Mini, would favor her child as his primary successor and heir.

"This situation brought a change to my relationship with my mother—an opportunity, I should say. While she was not abusive toward me, her social circle engrossed her attentions, leaving little room to care for me. My ploys to get her attention through physical wounds, ailments and bouts of depression failed since she simply paid professionals to attend my needs. It was the tension over which child would be my father's male heir that afforded me the means to at last win my mother's approval.

"After concocting a scheme to forge our alliance, I approached her. 'We can trick my father.' As I shared my plan, my mother squeezed my hand and her eyes watered with gratitude. 'That is a splendid idea. Thank you.' My jubilance knew no bounds and during the weeks we conspired together, I imagined I had gained her love. A month prior to Mini's due date, I approached my father. 'Dad, don't you think you should make a public announcement that the next child to be born will be your successor?'

"As I anticipated, Dad's startled expression soon morphed into agreement. My nails dug into my palms until they bled as I hid my outrage at his eagerness to please Mini by elevating her newborn to royal status. Within days he held a press conference to proudly make the announcement. Without naming the mother, he announced his son and heir would be born soon.

"Immediately afterward, my mother, who was nearing eight months along, ordered her doctor to induce labor.

"When my brother Herman was born prematurely, Dad suspected me of conspiring with my mother against him. When he became enraged and turned that fury on me, I turned to my mother for consolation. But positioning myself as my mother's ally didn't merit her indulgence. Mom turned all her attention toward her newborn son and ignored me as she always had. In truth, the conspiracy gained me nothing. My situation actually worsened, since at this point neither parent had any use for me.

"I sought solace in the sea. When I requested a crew take me sailing on Lake Michigan, my father stared past me, his eyes cold, remote. With full knowledge that a storm was brewing, he nodded assent. That afternoon, as the turbulent sea rocked the sailboat, I stood on the starboard side, and each wave that crashed against the hull seemed to shout, 'Leave, leave this world where no one, absolutely no one, loves you.'"

A jagged breath cracked Biate's voice. During the brief interruption to the narrative, she closed her eyes and fingered the jewel at her throat while breathing measured breaths.

Shaken by her vulnerability, by the glimpse through the crack in the imperious façade, Raymond waited for Biate to continue her narrative, which she did as soon as she collected herself.

"Though behind me, the crew struggled to keep the vessel from capsizing, the sea captivated my gaze. Sunlight glinted infinite shades of teal, and the surf drew me into its hypnotic swirls. I climbed atop the gunwale. A slight nudge at my back helped the heaving waves and tossing sloop throw me overboard. My arms flailed and gulps of seawater strangled my screams. Roaring confusion. The angry sea grabbed me and pulled me down. I fought the urge to struggle. I sank. My submerged grave pulled on me. Silence. Stillness. I agreed to die. I forced my eyes to stare into the murky depths. I drowned my lungs. The dark void drowned me."

Silence oppressed the room. Mired in Biate's tragedy, Raymond waited.

"The next thing I remember is rain pelting me while my body convulsed and my nose and mouth ejected water."

Behind Raymond's watery gaze, the image of the drenched waif clutched his heart.

"Strong hands clasped my arm and turned me on my side. Between gulps of air and wracking coughs, my lungs heaved the last of the seawater. The fisherman and his wife revived and fed me. I should have remained with them. But I wanted to return to my father. I wanted him to know that, despite his retaliation, I was alive.

"It's because of that day—the day the sea almost claimed my life— that I always wear this color.

"I will tell you something else that may surprise you. Since then, I have wanted the one thing I can never have: my own infant. You see, although I'm no longer capable of love, as a child I loved my father and mother. And I saw how much my baby brother loved my mother; how he smiled and gurgled at her; how, as a toddler, his first steps were right into her arms. So now I desire an offspring to lavish upon me the devotion I crave. Problem is, thanks to my father's intervention, I cannot bear a child of my own."

The silent interval was prelude to her memoir's finale. "But being queen has its advantages. I can claim any child I choose."

Alarm iced Raymond's gut.

During Biate's sidelong glance, the long green eyes half closed then widened. "Oh, so you have a child. You needn't worry. You're just an underling. My infant must be of royal blood."

While Blake stirred the pot of stew, Caellum placed the provisions he'd brought on the sofa. After he set aside two sleeping bags, a folded tent and a backpack stuffed with food, he opened a duffle bag of clothes and gear and pulled out binoculars, flares, a fire starter kit, carabineers, ropes, four walkie-talkies, four flashlights and a first aid kit. Then he tossed a knife with a six-inch blade and the pistol on the sofa.

Blake whistled. "Man, how'd you ever get your hands on that?"

"To make a long story short, this gun has accompanied me, left me, and returned to me since my escape from Township 26.

"Stew's ready."

The glow from the fireplace provided the only light and the clink of spoons and slurps of stew the only sounds until Blake spoke. "It's hard for me to go back there. If we get caught, it'll be even worse than before."

"That's true. We'll be thrown in jail, then executed, if not shot on sight. I can go alone."

Silence.

"There's nothing you can do. It's too well guarded."

"I still want to check it out."

"How?"

"I need to reach a vantage point high enough to see the layout of Onmatson Farm—buildings, crops, vehicles, MP headquarters. I'm heading toward the mountains at dawn."

Before going to bed. Caellum left the curtains open on the east side of the house, and shifted the sofa so the first rays of morning light would hit his face. But he awoke with Blake shaking his shoulder. "I'm in."

After sharing hot tea and stale cornbread, they headed out the door.

Caellum inquired, "Would you say we're about two miles north of the farm?"

"Yes, and there's a guard posted in a watch tower. We could be seen crossing the valley."

"Okay. We better look for a low point, a gully that stretches from the base of the mountain."

Where abandoned residences thinned out at the edge of former Colorado Springs, Caellum peered south through his binoculars toward the farm, and there it was, the watchtower platform. "Let's head north a couple more miles."

By the time they reached a dry streambed, the tower was out of view and they headed across the sage fields to the foothills of the Rocky Mountains.

"The pine trees are so thick it'll make it hard to see the farm. However, the trees can hide us as we head back south."

"Then what?"

"We'll look for a bluff with a clear view of the complex."

Together they stared at the rock promontory. "Great lookout."

"Except for the large cat on top."

"A flare would scare it away."

"But soldiers would see it."

Caellum retrieved the knife. "We have to wait it out."

Both chose a tree trunk to lean against and sat down, each lost in their own thoughts until Caellum nodded off.

"Caellum."

His eyes flew open.

Cougar. Emitting a low growl, tail swishing, the cat hunkered down, its stare fastened on Blake.

Caellum tightened his hold on the knife and spoke softly. "Over here." The cat's gaze shifted to him as it growled another warning.

Blake spoke barely above a whisper. "Stand up slowly, but don't bend over. Stare into the cat's eyes."

As Caellum fixed his gaze on the green eyes, it seemed the pounding of his heart against his chest must be audible. Struggling to remain erect, he shifted to standing position, back against the tree. As the tail swung side to side, he gripped the knife against his chest, poised to sink into the cat's flesh should it leap.

A growl-whine voiced the cougar's protest as it also stood and Caellum, chest expanded, arms akimbo, stretched to appear as tall and big as possible. When the cat took a step he tightened his hold on the knife, but the cougar broke the clasp of the mutual stare and turned to follow the base of the boulder that had been his sunning place. In an instant, the forest swallowed the animal and it was as though he had never faced the man still alert to kill.

In mute agreement the humans scrambled up the vacated observation point. Only after a careful scan in all directions did either one dare to speak.

Caellum turned toward the youth who was his junior by several years. "Okay, so how'd you know how to handle a cougar?"

"Before Solar Flash I backpacked a lot with my parents. They said looking big cats in the eye establishes dominance. A cardinal rule is to never go down on all fours or turn your back toward a cougar and run."

"It was hard for me to trust your instruction because I know that looking a bear in the eye is a sign of aggression and invites attack." As Caellum spoke, he pulled the binoculars out of his pack and handed them to Blake. "You take a look at the layout of buildings first. Then you can explain to me what I'm looking at. I can already see that though the fields are open, fencing topped by barbed wire surrounds the structures."

Blake clarified specific building use. "Straight ahead are the men and women's dorms. To the left is the equipment shed. Behind that, the grinding/sacking shed. Mess hall left of that. I don't know what's in some of those buildings. The MP headquarters are toward the back beside the road in and out of the complex."

"How many soldiers would you say are around at any given time?"

"No more than four. One in the watchtower, another on patrol. Couple of drivers. There are forty students. Correction: thirty-eight."

Between the viewers on the mountainside and the complex, in a swath as large as a football field, dry yellow stalks, many bent at odd angles rustled in the wind. Silently they passed the binoculars between them.

"The perimeter guard has a dog. Any others?"

"Two dogs in all."

"We'd have to take the perimeter guard down first. Then the one in the watchtower."

"And the dogs?"

"Last thing I want to do is shoot a dog. Hope I don't need to."

"Anyway, gunfire will bring the rest running."

"True. And sure to bring the remaining dog to sniff out escapees hiding in these hills."

"So what do you have in mind?"

"Without exciting the dogs, in a surprise entry, we capture the perimeter and tower guards, and free the students. It'd have to be at night."

"Dream on. Impossible."

As the sun slid behind the mountain, the smug return stare of Onmatson Farm confirmed the impossibility of a rescue.

Fort Carson   16

After a meeting with Commander Feldner to solicit backup from him and the two lieutenants who supported the Sovereignty Movement, Dora turned her attention Rolf. Before Rolf opened his door, she prepared for the coming scene with a long and deep inhalation. "Rolf, I need you to go with me to Fort Carson Hospital."

One eyebrow raised, the sardonic sideways glance signaled Rolf's guard was up. "I'm perfectly fine."

"It's not about you. There is a project involving children that requires checking out."

The guarded expression yielded to a look of horror. "You propose dragging me among a horde of snot-nosed, whining, sticky-fingered brats?"

"Rolf!"

"The acting gigs in Sergeant Starke's office, at Caellum's execution, and in my Dad's office were one thing...."

"On this stage you have to act affronted at the abuse of children."

"Dear wife, at times the unreasonable demands you make on me to aid your schemes are beyond—"

"I knew you'd help. And when we return, you'll be treated to a home-cooked meal."

"Not by you I hope."

"Certainly not. Rita, of course. Shall I ring Leon to meet us out front in an hour?"

Rolf waved her away and closed the door, the resounding click surely a definitive "Yes."

After Commander Feldner introduced the illustrious visitors, he and Lieutenant Armstrong flanked the doorway and Dora and Rolf swept into Doctor Olsen's office. With an admirable rebound from obvious shock, the doctor stood up behind his desk, bowed his head as the Imperial Governor Scholtz required, and arranged his features in an affable expression.

"To what do I owe the honor of your royal presence at this facility?"

Dora had decided to disarm Olsen in order to gain access to the whole truth, hence the extended hand and slight smile. "Doctor, accounts of the admirable progress in the social engineering initiative have reached our ears."

"Well, I... I...."

"And the level of security surrounding this project?"

"Ten MPs are rotated five on duty per shift at these premises on a regular basis, and since our visitors, other than your imminences, include only the top echelon of the Social Engineering Department, our project is quite secure."

Rolf beat Dora to a response. "A tour of this facility could provide us a most edifying morning, if we could please get on with it."

Responding with a gracious, "Of course," the doctor came around his desk. With a gesture, he said, "Please allow me," and led the elite personages out of the room, down the hall and into the Gestation Chamber. Though the dimly lit room was much as Eena had described, the impact of twelve tubes of babies lining the walls like bizarre hydroponics experiments slammed Dora speechless. Instinctively, she placed her palm on the head that protruded on one side of her belly, and massaged it as through to reassure herself and her child of their living connection.

The broad sweep of the doctor's hands accompanied the pride that rang in his voice. "Scientific protocols govern your future subjects, your work force. Throughout their childhoods, we will augment submissive inclinations and engineer desirable behaviors to serve royal imperatives."

Less impacted than Dora, Rolf warmed to the charade and filled the space of her shock. "Having been only recently informed of this experiment, I'm wondering about the inception of this project and how Fort Carson sustains it."

"The lab was installed with our initial subjects and used briefly just prior to Solar Flash."

"And those fetuses?"

"Unfortunately, when the electricity died, so did they. But in anticipation of the grid going down, still frozen embryos had already been safely transported to a temperature controlled vault in Cavern City. After we returned topside, Imperial Governor Scholtz ordered the military to repair the generator and reinstall electrical services to this wing of the hospital.

"So what happens when these fetuses reach full term?"

"We extract them and immediately connect them to a breathing apparatus to establish continuous positive airway pressure, or in other words, ensure breathing kicks in."

Dora's degree in physical therapy had included a broad introduction to medical practices. In preparation for this meeting, she had poured through handwritten lecture notes from her college course on 'Birthing Procedures and Their Impacts.' She launched into her stage one assault on the violations. "But the massaging of the newborn during passage through the birth canal is a vital step in birthing. Research in the twenties indicated that Caesarean section births negatively impacted the DNA pool in the white blood cells of the infants. As children, they were more susceptible to immunological diseases such as diabetes and asthma in later life."

After a surprised glance, Doctor Olsen countered with clinical neutrality. "Millions of C-Section babies have survived just fine, as do our incubated clones." He gestured toward the door. "Follow me to the Newborn to Nine Months Lab."

A viewing window allowed observation of the tiniest babies sleeping in cribs, crawlers moving across the mottled carpet. As the three nurses attended their charges, noticeably missing were eye contact, affectionate touch and smiles to evoke a response. A baby began screaming in the crib. But the check by the attendant was perfunctory, including no sign of comforting engagement in the form of physical or eye contact. They fed and changed their charges with impersonal efficiency. The oldest ones sat in pens as an attendant flashed cards of pictures and words before their eyes.

Doctor Olsen's astute observations voiced his pride. "You will notice our nurses are strictly mandated to maintain an emotional distance from the children."

Dora blurted the counter arguments that inwardly screamed to be heard. "It's my understanding that children, deprived of eye contact, touch and cuddling have lowered IQs and ill health for life—if they survive the neglect, that is."

"No worries. These children's IQs will be augmented with nano technology that will supply the needed comprehension for the performance of designated tasks. As you can see, two nurses attend these ten infants, the latest batch to leave the gestation tubes."

"Shouldn't there be twelve from each birthing?"

The doctor's pronouncement, "Two have died" may have just as well have been a comment about the weather.

Dora's outrage swelled to bursting. "Let me inside the lab."

"I beg your pardon?"

The sound of a baby crying came through a concealed microphone.

"I want to engage directly with the nurses and infants."

"But that is entirely against regulations." Olsen's outburst seemed to surprise even him.

"Surely you have not forgotten who are the regulators." Rolf gestured with imperial authority.

The wails of the infant continued as an unsettling backdrop to the interval of charged moments that preceded Olsen's mollified, "Of course, one moment please. I didn't bring the key cards."

The doctor signaled a nurse to open the door and while Rolf remained at the window, he ushered Dora in. As the project's clucking mother hen, he followed close behind. Dora felt his breath on her neck. Barely able to contain her irritation, which was exacerbated by the still-crying infant, she halted so that he bumped into her, and she commanded over her shoulder "Please wait outside."

She approached the nurse. "The baby's crying. Why don't you pick him up and hold him and soothe him?"

The woman's eyes darted to Doctor Olsen's glare. "He's been fed and burped and his diaper's clean. I'm instructed only to hold a baby when transferring it from one place to another. Protocol forbids coddling or establishing eye contact with any child—ever."

Dora's expression must have triggered the nurse's shift in position so that her back was to her boss, as she whispered, "Believe me. I long— I mean yearn with all my heart—to interact as a surrogate mother, to comfort, smile at and play with these little ones."

When Dora lifted the infant to her shoulder, a primal instinct orchestrated an ensemble of cooing clicking sounds, caressing pats and rubs, walking and bouncing. She recalled Adair's insight that when a mother holds a baby close, the child's heartbeat syncs with hers, and a multi-level communion occurs. The nurse handed her a bottle and Dora imagined, as Adair described, a wash of calm coherence and multi-sensory sustenance flowed into the child.

"What would happen if you did coddle this baby?"

"At the very least I would lose my job. The worst would be blockage from finding another childcare position. I have my three-year-old to feed."

After a soft belch the baby quietened. "I gather your child is in a daycare facility?"

A nodded affirmation.

"So why don't you work there?"

"Regulations forbid working where your own child is enrolled."

Carefully holding the baby's head, Dora returned him to his crib.

"And your name is?"

"Joan."

"Nice to meet you, Joan. I'm Dora d'Arc Scholtz."

Joan started. "I recognize you now from the wedding documentary last winter."

"I need to leave, and I wish I could dictate changes immediately. However, if word reached the SEI and they reported to the imperial governor, my efforts would be thwarted. But don't think that you or this project will be forgotten."

Dora turned toward the two faces staring through the glass — one bored, the other disapproving — and signaled she was ready to leave.

Obviously relieved to restore order to his domain, Doctor Olsen motioned down the hall. "Shall we move on? Two cultures remain to be seen after this one: the ten- to eighteen-month-olds, then the nineteen- to twenty-seven-month-olds: the products of our second and first batch of artificial womb occupants."

They reached the lab of crawlers and walkers, many of whom sat as though in a trance before a large screen of cartoon characters.

"Open the door, please."

Again, a nurse retrieved a key and Dora entered, her expression halting the doctor who was about to follow. She approached an attendant who was placing a crying child on the mat that was already crowded with screen-watching infants.

"How long do they watch those screens?"

"They average four hours a day."

"You are aware that optimal mental and physiological development requires almost perpetual physical movement, sensorial contact and emotive engagement during toddlers' waking hours."

"According SEI mandates, this project has struck the ideal balance between visual stimuli and physical exercise."

"Do you agree with those mandates?'

The woman shrugged. "It's not for me to agree or disagree. I'm hired to perform prescribed tasks and no more."

Across the room another baby began to cry. The second nurse offered the child a bottle without holding it or offering the slightest comfort.

"You didn't engage with that child."

"I adhere strictly to my job description."

"I see. Allow me to introduce myself. I am Dora d'Arc, daughter of Peter d'Arc, governor of Techno City and wife of Rolf Scholtz, son of Imperial Governor Charles Scholtz. And your name, please?"

The nurse chewed her lip and looked anxious. "Beth."

"Beth, you needn't fear me." Dora lifted the baby from the bed, held him to her breast and looked into his eyes as she fed him the bottle.

"So how would you approach a child such as this one if the ban were lifted?"

A look of relief obliterated the fear in the woman's eyes. "You mean if I could cuddle the babies?" She hesitated as though for fear of entrapment.

"I mean if you were impelled do so as though you were the mother tenderly responding to every cue from her child."

The woman said nothing while tears sprang to her eyes and she crossed her hands over her heart.

Holding bottle and baby, Dora circumvented the beds of mostly sleeping babies. Where were the soft and cuddly teddy bears? Where were the soothing colors of a nursery? Where were windows to invite sunlight and birdsong? Two beds away, a baby's whimpering escalated to crying.

She approached the attended she had first met. "Do these children ever go outside?"

The woman shrugged. "Where would they go? There is no playground around here. Besides, their working lives will be spent in cubicles or warehouses, with no need for them to be outdoors, or to play for that matter."

Dora turned toward the collection of children seated motionless before cartoon figures interacting on screen. One figure bopped the head of another, who chased him away. She walked directly to a two-year-old whose brown eyes, slack-jawed, expressionless face gazed at the screen. She spoke to him and tried to make eye contact, but his eyes remained riveted. She waved a hand in front of his face. A tiny hand reached up to remove the obstruction to his viewing. Gently, she pressed on his chin until he was facing her. Eye contact triggered a look of terror. The child flung his head from side to side, arced his back away from her and screamed.

The attendant appeared and quickly resettled the child, turning his head toward the on-screen moving characters involved in a slap-stick food fight. Within seconds after the familiar scenes grabbed the two-year-old's attention, the screaming receded to whimpered gulps. Completely reengaged with the screen, he was oblivious of the fingers that wiped his tears and the snot cascading over his mouth.

The nurse pocketed the cloth while she chided Dora. "They are not accustomed to eye contact."

Turning to the viewing window, Dora signaled the doctor to open the door and they headed to the third room.

The screen held the attention of some, while others moved about the room on tricycles and seated on rolling devices. Collisions resulted in enraged screaming and hitting. Other than a couple of children covering their ears, response was negligible. Similar quarrels accompanied disputes over toys. Sooner or later the frustrations yielded an ignored shove, a cry, and a winner.

When Dora entered, the wary expressions of the attendants and mumbled protocols that governed their jobs answered her queries.

She signaled the doctor and they retraced their steps to his office. When they were resettled, she, asked, "Where do these children go when they leave this facility. And what are the plans for their next stage of development?"

"The implementation of the SEI protocols will extend to the 10,000 preschool age children that are now in day care. I believe there are twenty day-care facilities in Transtopia."

"Won't the prior more normal raising of those children impede your plans?"

"Not my plans. The protocols mandated for this project. To answer your question, much can be accomplished to render four-year-olds compliant by technological insertions and plugging them into external technology. At the very least, the social engineering implementation of B.F. Skinner's deprivation and reward systems will forestall defiant attitudes in the future. When this group reaches four years old we will add the next tier."

For the first time, since entering this subterranean realm, the red binding of the eight volumes behind the doctor flaunted their presence.

Doctor Olsen's eyes followed Dora's. "Our protocol manuals. We adhere closely to the directives, particularly those in the sixth volume: *The Management of Offspring*."

"And the specifications for *your* management?"

"I beg your pardon?"

"Doctor Olsen, are you an Earth human or an Annunaki human?"

The doctor stammered before blurting a coherent sentence. "Well, I'm sure I have *some* Annunaki in my family tree."

"In other words, I presume you understand that like those children, you are managed by rulers of superior blood? I assume that due to your lesser stature, you won't mind eventual loss of *your* individuality to microscopic machines and the directives of a central AI?"

The doctor's only response was a vacant gaze and the silent drumming of his fingers on his desk.

Dora's fingers gripped the cold metallic rim. "I need to familiarize myself with the contents of those manuals. Please find a box or crate for their transference."

"But... but the authorities expressly forbid their removal from these premises."

The casualness of Rolf's slouch in no way hinted at the resounding finale to the scene. "Must I remind you again—we *are* the authorities."

Naiveté   17

Constant stress dogged Nathan Abelt. Runners escaped every day and upon his approach groups of students and people clustered on sidewalks disbanded as though they were guilty of conspiring against the government. The undercurrents of a rebellious population were definitely on the rise. This put him in a difficult spot. With complaints that the nanite chips in the population weren't doing their job, Governor Scholtz was breathing down Nathan's neck. If he told the governor the situation, he and his team of spies would be expected to increase the number of apprehensions. Yet, as loyal as he was to the government, he was loath to arrest innocent people to fill a quota and save his neck.

On the other hand, if the governor stepped up martial law episodes again, and he probably would, Nathan would have Lydia to face, because his wife was sure to connect his activities with this worsened state of affairs. Of the two of them, he didn't know whose ire he dreaded more. During the months of weekly lockdown leading to Caellum Nichol's execution, they had spent half of their single day off each week shut in with the kids. Not fun.

Nathan headed home hoping Lydia was in a good mood today. Lately, since her association with Dora Scholtz, her grumbling had increased. Their commiserations about the poor quality of schools and daycares had provoked Lydia's ire. Women and their gossip. They just didn't know how good they had it. Just when Nathan didn't think his mood could darken any more, he entered his home.

Every fiber in Dora's being shrank from association with Nathan Abelt, who last spring had spied on her and followed her when she met Caellum at the mountain foothills; Nathan Abelt, the spy who was responsible for Caellum's capture and near execution. As Lydia coached and Dora sat on the floor to practice breathing during childbirth, Lydia's husband opened the front door then stood in surprise.

"Nathan, close the door. You're letting in chilly air. I'm helping Dora prepare to give birth."

"Ms. d'Arc."

Like Nathan, Dora could manage no more civility than his name and a slight, unsmiling nod.

Lydia seemed oblivious as she turned toward the kitchen. "Let's have a cup of tea and cupcakes. The kids are next door, dear."

Struggling awkwardly to rise from the floor Dora felt the grasp of Nathan's hand as with equal awkwardness he assisted her until she stood. Only being in Lydia's home restrained her from spewing disgust and jerking her arm free. The prospect of tea with Mr. SEI spy was as attractive as socializing with a worm.

As Nathan retreated several steps, Dora followed Lydia into the kitchen. "I should leave now."

Lydia's protest was swift and smiling. "Oh, no, I made those cupcakes especially for you."

The hastily set table on one side and the spy in the doorway on the other effectively nixed a graceful escape.

"You sit here."

Captive to Lydia's insistence, she sat. *With Caellum in danger, God knows where, I'm to dine on sweet cakes and engage in friendly banter with the enemy. Can't do it.* She didn't expect help to come from Lydia's side of the table.

Lydia faced her husband. "Dear, you've known about my displeasure with the educational and childcare system."

The "oh no, not this again" look on Nathan's face offered a loud and clear message about the effect of former conversations and an introduction to his attitude about the one coming up.

"Dora, do you mind telling Nathan what you learned at Fort Carson?"

After Dora's description of the Gestation Chamber Nathan responded, "Why tell me? My job has nothing to do with that place."

Ignoring him, Dora recalled the visit to the Newborn to Nine Months room with emphasis on the emotional deprivation of the children.

"Yes, that's unfortunate, but...."

"And then came the Toddler to Two Years room." The non-playing children lost in the large screen were the subjects of her next description.

"I don't know why you're telling me all this."

Lydia laid her hand on Nathan's. "The next part will make that clear."

Dora related the SEI intention to step by step dehumanize all children—his children.

After the slightest flicker of his eyes, Nathan retreated to his customized mantra: "The government does everything for our own good. It's irresponsible to suggest that the social engineering objective is to dumb down rather than augment the intelligence of future generations."

"As promoted by the SEI newsreels?"

"Just so."

"And the controlling AI? Will it be so kindly?"

"There is no, never has been, nor ever will be a controlling AI. That's sci-fi malarkey."

As mothers do, Lydia returned the conversation to their children. "Nathan, teachers who are cold to our children's needs and a system that deprives them of play time will stunt their growth."

"That's your department. My job is to keep food on the table and a roof over our heads."

His bland avoidance invited Dora's barbed assertion. "And to hunt down and execute those risking their lives to save your children."

"I remove from society the scumbags engaged in criminal activity."

Dora's voice softened, "Scumbags like Caellum Nichols."

Fear flickered across Nathan's face as though he just recalled whom he was talking to.

As Lydia's nonplussed expression navigated the space between her guest and her husband, Dora managed the fury flaring with an intensity that would have gladly nailed the spy to his chair. "Yes, the Caellum Nichols I led you to."

The stupidity of pursuing this discussion with a dehumanized SEI official hit Dora, and she stood to go. When she thanked Lydia for the snack and breathing exercise lessons and promised to practice them, she noticed Lydia's peculiar and very pointed glare at her husband.

When the door closed behind her, and Leon ushered her into the car, acute discomfort tinged her flashbacks of the conversation with Nathan. An impression, vague, yet intrusive, resisted Dora's denial that in the recent past she and the spy had shared an identical liability: blind trust in those who govern. Peter d'Arc loomed in the foreground. *My dad convinced me of the noble obligation of Annunaki descendants to manage the human herd. Similarly, the lie that the spirit of the founding fathers of the former United States of America governs current political policy colors Nathan's perceptions. Dear God, in this, our naïveté, our natures are the same.*

Dora stewed over this elephant in her headroom for a month, until the first snow flurries swirled over the sidewalk, and she tried in vain to cover her belly with her coat. The twenty eighth of November was an eventful date: the day she went into early labor, and the day Nathan Abelt spied a helicopter landing on the roof of the Imperial Ritz Hotel.

Nathan hurried to inform the Imperial Governor who stood and faced the door while directing Nathan. "Sit over there, in that corner. Any detail, however small, concerning this woman may be important."

The dark teal of the wool suit in perfect contrast to the aquamarine silk blouse and the leather bag strapped over Biate's shoulder signaled she was on a strictly business mission. The governor walked around his desk to seat her, but she waved him away and seated herself.

After perfunctory greetings she leaned back, clasped her hands in her lap and cocked her head as she dove into the reason for her visit. "When we were last together we discussed an alliance."

"We did."

"Have you given it any further consideration?"

"Only that we both have valuable assets."

"No doubt word has reached you of my army of five hundred SuperRos. What can you possibly have that approaches the value of such an asset?"

"Your SuperRos are no match for Transtopia's might. In addition to my military and police force of two hundred each, plus a population of two hundred thousand that can be armed as necessary, I control a military base and arsenal at Fort Carson." Scholtz paused for effect. "How about an armed fighter jet to mow down your tin men."

Biate drew back as though considering her opponent's unanticipated moves on the chessboard. "My titanium men carry sufficient explosive power in one arm to crash your puny plane."

As Nathan mentally tallied the negotiation volleys between the supreme leaders of Sector 10, he was aware that Scholtz had lied. No mechanics capable of overhauling jet engines existed. The queen's sense of being in the more powerful position, thanks to her SuperRos, was based on fact. But each time Biate spoke, Lydia's accusing expression inserted itself in front of the long green eyes and provoked the spy's mental protest. *Lydia, one or the other of this pair will rule us. It's tweedledum or tweedledee. Take your pick. In order to keep you at an arm's length from harm, I serve as the right arm of the governor now, but perhaps the queen later.*

Scholtz, leaning forward with glittering eyes, resumed his litany of self-acclaim. "But of more interest to me to ensure our continued dominance is our long-term SynHu project at Fort Carson. There, Transtopia's future workforce, as smart and responsive to our commands as we desire, is incubating."

"I desire only one of your incubating assets... As you know I cannot bear a child. Yet I very much want one to call my own. But only a child that is of royal blood. I am willing to extend to you the protection of my five hundred SuperRos in exchange for the baby that Dora Scholtz carries—your grandchild."

"You can forget that idea."

Nathan blanched. Thankfully, Emma, with her cupid face and golden curls, had only dribbles of royal blood. The spy shook himself back to attentiveness.

Biate looked peevish. "If you have some silly attachment to your predecessor's bloodline, then let us form an alliance. You will enjoy the protection of my SuperRos in exchange for Dora's child."

"We can marry, and you can be my grandchild's grandmother."

"You have a wife."

"She's expendable."

"As I would be. An alliance best serves the balance of power between us."

"My heir remains just that... *my* heir."

"Then we have no alliance."

Cave of Crystals   18

Puma lay panting in the shade as, once again, Cosima, dressed in the white deerskin dress, stepped through the door, headed for Grandfather's. "So, you have arrived in time to guard our animal refuge while I am gone."

Puma stood up to rub against her.

"Oh dear, not today." Cosima leaned over so as to grab Puma's head and scratch behind her ears with the white leather skirt at a distance from an increase in the freshly delivered swath of black fur. As she turned to follow the path, Puma returned to her shady refuge at the intersection between the path and the homestead clearing.

After witnessing Emory's enthrallment with the augurs, Cosima started up the mountain trail unconcerned he would follow her. Days before when she left him in Mu, the tall grass and augurs milling around a guava tree on the far side of the savannah hid him from view. So much for concern about predators.

She *was* concerned about soldiers after crossing the portal, but the familiar forest screened her passage as she headed through the field of crystals and up Thunderbird Mountain. Before Matoskah's camp came into sight, the pungent smell of his tanning solution wafted to her nostrils, and though not compelling in itself, hours spent with Grandfather made it so.

She had missed the Lakota Elder more than she realized, and relished warming her hands beside the crackling fire as they sipped tea in his camp. When they had finished eating, Valek lay down next to Cosima. She stroked his fur recalling the tiny, orphaned pup that had accompanied her, riding in her backpack and pursuing squirrels and butterflies as they followed the stream to Three Mountains. White-gold light splayed her memory of the day they reached the valley, and Grandfather told her he had been expecting her.

The cadence of the old man's voice captured her rapt attention as he held up a large crystal from Quartz Mountain. "This stone, our grandfather, speaks of a world before the time of the two-leggeds."

Matoskah's eyes smiled his appreciation for the sacred crystal. "Grandfather holds ancient memories. His records reach before the time of our earliest ancestors, beyond the time of the giants, and the rise and fall of unknown civilizations, to the time before land, when the waters covered the face of our mother."

The elder addressed his student. "Are you ready to take a journey with me?"

Eagerness danced in Cosima's eyes as she glanced toward the cautious approach of Valek's mate. Side by side, the two wolves lay on their bellies, heads and ears erect, as though they also attended Grandfather's story.

"Sister and brother wolf will guard our bodies when we leave them." After a pause, Grandfather continued. "You already know your connectedness to nature. For now, connect with me also. We will journey together."

While together they breathed slow deep breaths, it was easy to unite with Grandfather, even as her spirit entwined itself with the trees and all within the timeless embrace of the Presence. Moments later, standing before his student, Grandfather beckoned with the words "We are going to the Cave of Memories," and in a flash disappeared.

When shafts of light once again penetrated Cosima's eyes, it took several seconds to make sense of the surroundings. Similar to when sight has been restored to a blind man and the bandages removed, a confusing array of colors, outlines and forms presented a blurred abstract. Shards of aquamarine blue to turquoise to green light stabbed her eyes in random slivers. She blinked and a single straight edge came into focus. Steadying her gaze she followed the shard several feet before it angled sixty degrees to end at a point. Reversing direction, her eyes followed the shaft to the undulating wall of a cave.

She blinked, and a scene of unspeakable beauty rewarded her clarified sight. Dozens of enormous hexagonal crystals protruded at varying angles from the walls and floor of an enormous cave. In semi-transparent splendor, blue to green hues comingled their radiance.

Over a symphonic cadence of aquamarine waves, light danced in a staccato of brilliant flashes that blinked out to reappear elsewhere.

A glance away from the cave revealed the crystals reflected the undulating ripples of a vast sea. Expecting to see a sunlit sky, her lifted gaze traced the ceiling of a huge cavern filled with diffused light, its horizon meeting the sea in the far distance.

At that moment she recalled her patient companion. "There is no sun. Where does the light originate?"

"The stones in this cavern are chemiluminescent. Similarly, the algae-like plants that cover the ceiling produce light for this world. Even the sea life is bioluminescent."

Cosima's attention returned to the cave of embedded crystals that was enclosed in the cavern's vastness. A feeling of awe prevailed as she breathed in the spectacular glow of the crystal array. "So, Grandfather, you called this the "'Cave of Memories.'"

"These quartz crystals hold many thousands of years of Earth Mother's memories."

Cosima stared at her mentor in amazement. "How?"

"Resonance. Events recorded in sound. Scientists have used quartz crystal resonators in technology for several decades now."

Grandfather stopped abruptly, to stare toward the sea. Cosima followed his gaze to see someone rowing across the water. When the boat abutted the floor of the cave, Grandfather moved forward to secure the attached rope under a stone. Then he lent a hand to a tall willowy woman as she stepped ashore. Hues from violet to cobalt blue to blue-green undulated around this translucent being from whose heart a golden glow pulsed.

The radiant arrival smiled her thanks at Grandfather and assured Cosima, "You and I need no introduction."

Cosima knew she had never met anyone even remotely like this otherworldly being.

"We shared the experience of the Presence in the desert, and also in the forest."

With a peeved expression Cosima asked, "Who are you? I don't recall such familiarity."

"I am you, and not you. I am Earth, but more than the planet."

These were confusing riddles.

"It's hard to pin down my identity. Some refer to my planetary aspect as Gaia. Suffice it to say, you and I share the resonances of the planet and its resident creatures."

She gestured toward the crystalline array. "These crystals, Earth's treasure trove, are continuously growing life forms." Gaia approached a single crystal, the longest one in the cave cluster.

"Ten thousand years ago, this crystal was only this long." Gaia indicated a measurably shorter end point. "Though crystal growth is too slow for humans to measure."

The diminutive Gaia paused as though to let this information sink in. "These hexagonal clusters of silicone record our collective song. Listen."

The woman's elegant body swayed, her hands twirled gracefully and her arms moved in a captivating dance as a symphony of sound evoked both wrenching pathos and exquisite elation.

When the tones receded into stillness, Gaia continued. "The atoms in these crystals resonate in response to finer energies than current technology can measure. Such frequencies resonate every event on Earth and in the human family."

"Those frequencies often assist me," mused Cosima. "After a helicopter crash, I felt the call of the pilot Nathan lying in pain, his arm broken."

Gaia nodded. "Quantum level frequencies travel through the skin and bones of Mother Earth to record eons of history in these living libraries."

Cosima's imagination wrangled an image of volumes of recorded history becoming a library of invisible quanta.

"Whereas people operate in time spans of years, the crystal quanta oscillate a tonal/photonic history of eons of evolving life."

"Mother Gaia, they look solid, unmoving, as if frozen in time."

"Let's compress space and time to go inside." Gaia touched Cosima's forehead and suddenly she was inside a realm of pulsing light. Unlike the traveling waves of an ocean, these were standing waves that rose and fell as a rhythmic sequence of light and tone. During the brief moments of Cosima's observation, the crystalline quanta pulsed millennial scenes of a primeval world.

A touch on her forehead transitioned the girl's perspective from the world of standing waves to the cave of jutting crystals. Cosima drank in the mystical beauty of the Cave of Memories. "Mother Gaia, I have the feeling that you and Grandfather brought me here for more than a science lesson about crystals."

"As you observed, according to our space and time, these crystals are frozen sound. Just as a stethoscope amplifies the beat of the heart, with sensitive equipment, we can hear these oscillating waves as musical tones."

"So what am I to learn here?"

"Look toward the sea. See the pulse of waves as the mental, emotional and physical flow of human experience."

"I still don't understand why we are here."

"Deep down, you know why."

"To add our experiences to the crystalline library?"

"Yes, and to hone your unique abilities. Like these giant crystals, you and Grandfather tune into frequencies unheard by most. Come into me to listen to your inner self. You, all humanity, are poised at the crest of a wave of destiny, which like the waves that cross the ocean for thousands of miles, has traversed eons and is poised to crash upon the shore of your future."

Suddenly, Cosima felt herself staring outward from Gaia's body. In that state of ecstatic connection she stood on a raft flanked by ships adrift at sea. A giant swell loomed ahead and transfixed Cosima's gaze. Its crest so far overhead it extended beyond view, the enormous wave approached until the raft began to rock and bob dangerously.

As Cosima fought to steady herself, a ship of iron loomed to the left, bearing a crew of men with eyes half open who labored beneath a banner bearing the words 'Ship of Fools.' And on the deck, wizards in pointed hats and alchemist robes stirred pots, which discharged lightning bolts and dispensed gadgets, electronic devices, including mechanical men. And from the chaotic swirl emerged an artificial intelligence with a brain, but no heart. And by means of electrical cords, the AI wielded godlike powers over biological/mechanical blends of men—synthetic men adrift at sea on the Ship of Fools.

And straight ahead, ominous in its walled assault, the wave towered overhead.

And to Cosima's right, above the stormy sea, bobbed another ship where alchemists stirred their pots and electrical discharges freed gadgets and devices and vehicles. But aboard this 'Ship of Those who have Learned,' the heart collaborated in inventions that supported living forms—plants and creatures and humans. Connected by a single cord to their Source with eyes wide open, humankind freely traversed the lighted realms.

When the wave crashed onto the raft, annihilating the vision, Cosima exited Gaia's perspective, and stood somewhere between terrified and transfixed. She looked to Gaia for clarification of the vision, but no explanation was forthcoming. "The meaning is for you to decipher, the timeline is humanity's to choose. Help them."

"Timeline?"

"Humanity stands at the crest of two timelines. One to relinquish freedom to technological enslavement for untold generations, the other to embrace freedom through the heart's connections."

"But how do I help?"

"A task will present itself. Yours to accept or refuse."

Lovingly, Mother Gaia stroked the girl's cheek. "We'll be in communication—and communion." She smiled as she turned toward the boat. Grandfather helped her in, handed her the rope, and pushed the helm toward the sea. "Together we'll record a new chapter in the Crystal Library," she called back as she rowed away.

The quartz crystal that had first clarified its faceted beauty was the last in Cosima's line of vision before a haze of color obscured the Cave of Memories and she and Grandfather sat together on the mountain.

How real was that experience? Cosima followed the trail to her camp, still half-ensconced in its dreamy essence. But the menacing growl, the leap of the black blur and the man's cry as he fell, shattered her reverie.

"Puma!"

The enraged animal ignored her. She grabbed a stick and threw it hard at Puma's jaws. With a loud and heart-stopping scream, claws still sunk into her victim's shoulders, fangs bared, Puma's head whipped around to face Cosima. Snarling as though at an unknown enemy that dared to encroach on her kill, the cat glared. Cosima's "Puma, no!" commanded the cat's attention for several seconds as not only Emory's but her own fate hung on the cat's next move.

Her voice coaxing, Cosima slowly approached the panther. "I know you were protecting our home."

Visibly, the rage ebbed from the animal until, willing to release the man, but not in the mood for a conciliatory gesture, Puma slinked into the forest.

Cosima turned to Emory, noted the bloody marks on each shoulder, and delayed alarm surged. "Puma is a wild and very dangerous animal."

Emory sat up looking sheepish. "That was stupid of me."

As he rose shakily to his feet, she trembled with the thought that he could have been killed. "Why didn't you stop to think about Puma?"

Emory's eyes sought hers. "My only thought was of you."

The Disk

A silver disk parked in the middle of the road audaciously blocked the way, gleaming an invitation to approach and investigate.

Glancing at the guide's face, which was frozen in a shocked expression, Jack declared, "I need to dismount."

With unintelligible grumbling, Jack's gawking companion induced the cantankerous beast to reverse the just-completed mounting sequence and lower his unwieldy torso to the ground.

Hyper-focused on the object ahead, Jack hardly heard the shouted warnings of the man departing with camels that could move at a fast clip after all. He approached with caution and tentatively extended his fingers to brush the metallic surface. Since there was no shock or sensation to repel his touch, he continued around the disk, exploring the shape with his eyes and fingertips. The ten-foot diameter object was shaped like two saucers, the top one inverted, the edges molded together to form a seamless circumference.

As Jack traced the smooth exterior, he found no break to indicate an entrance point, and detecting no notches or knobs, his fingers inched forward. The continuous edge with no apparent gaps offered no hint of a way inside until, without warning, a portion of the wall began to pull away. With a gasp, Jack jumped back and the section arced outward until, within seconds, the end rested on the ground.

As though invited by an unseen host, Jack moved to the edge of the ramp to stare into a gaping hole and hesitantly leaned forward to peer inside where an array of lighted colors splayed across the interior from a central point. He stepped toward the entrance until his transfixed gaze settled on the center of the floor where a multifaceted crystal emitted a breathtaking spectrum of over twenty distinct hues. Behind the crystal was a chair, which must be the pilot's, and beside that an oddly-out-of-place sheet of paper lay on the floor.

A tremor of apprehension shook Jack as he looked over his shoulder to spy his means of transportation and guide galloping toward Marrakech. Nonetheless, after an instant's hesitation, he climbed the ramp and stepped inside the craft. But when the ramp soundlessly lifted and then closed with a metallic click, a solid wall blocked retreat through the opening, alarm shot through him.

Soft light enveloped the closed space, and the rainbow array so intrigued the newcomer that the instinctive sense of panic soon yielded to tingling anticipation. He approached the chair. But oddly out of place in this futuristic domain, the sheet of paper inscribed with familiar, scribbled writing, beckoned first. After he walked around the chair to retrieve the scrawled note, an undecipherable riddle jumped out at him.

"Hand on helm, resonate with indigo blue. Wherever you want to go, intend it. — RR." Puzzled, Jack turned the paper over, hoping it held more than this cryptic, new age-sounding tripe. But the reverse side was blank. In exasperation, he shouted aloud, "Randolph, here I am enclosed in this UFO, and all you have to offer is bloody dribble."

Disgusted, Jack turned toward the pilot's chair and eased into it. In the center of the armrest to his right a slightly raised mound and three indents invited his palm and fingertips. The surface was otherwise smooth and blank except for a row of symbols along the front edge.

He moved his finger over the first glyph. A microsecond before contact was made, a holographic array appeared, pulsing a steady stream of lighted strands. A central, tightly wound double helix of glowing cords streamed between the top and bottom. The spiraling bands arced outward at the apex and base, expanded to form a torus, and re-entered the helical core at opposite ends.

With a tinge of excitement, Jack mused aloud. "Must be the anti-gravity propulsion system."

He extended his finger toward the next glyph, and a lighted hexagon known as Metatron's Cube appeared. The lighted complexity drew his gaze to its center where a single white light pulsed and the next zoom inward revealed a white sun and its solar system. No sooner did the third sphere from the sun, the blue and white image of Earth, beckon, than a closer view revealed goats perched on an argan tree in a sea of red sand. As Jack stared and the view extended down the stretch of dirt road, he chuckled to see the guide and dromedaries, already miles beyond the silver object, racing toward Marrakech.

Excitement mounting, his finger hovered over the third glyph on the panel. Instantly, the 3D image of Randolph Ring flashed into view. "Good to see you, Jack."

A shocked, "Randolph!" was all Jack could muster.

"So get over here!" The expression beneath bushy brows was deadpan.

"Okay, so tell me how. I thought this was a navigation control panel. But the first is to monitor the power source, and the second, location. And from the third I get a holograph, or ghost, or whatever."

"I did tell you. See you when you get here." The screen went blank.

Exasperated, Jack shook his head and dropped his hands to the arms of the pilot's chair. "Bloody hell, you can't just leave me hanging like this." Shouted expletives bounced impotently around the compartment.

The screens having vanished, he faced a meaningless play of lights and behind those, a blank curved wall with no clue as to how to navigate the craft. He was stuck with no way out of an immovable UFO parked in the middle of a desolate wasteland. As though enjoying a childish prank, Randolph had offered only the strange gibberish resting in Jack's lap. The would-be pilot groaned and read the note again.

"Hand on helm, resonate with indigo blue. Wherever you want to go, intend it."

Helm. He transferred the paper to his left hand and again placed his right on the palm-sized hemisphere in the center of the panel, three fingertips in the indents. *Hand on helm.* Crinkling the edge of the paper in his fist, he stared at the indigo band of light until the color seemed to draw him in. *Intend.* An instinctual deep intake of breath accompanied the mental utterance, *Take me to Blue Kachina Center for Research and Development.*

For several moments silent stillness mocked his psychic command, provoking an exasperated shout. "So take me there, you useless piece of junk with no navigation controls!"

Angry with Randolph, feeling profoundly let down, Jack sat in the pilot's chair as nothing—absolutely nothing—happened.

Michael 20

Dr. Monroe lay the preemie newborn between Dora's breasts. "Well, he's tiny, but his heart and lungs are well developed."

In an exquisite haze of exhausted achievement and a wash of oxytocin, known as the love hormone, Dora's hands covered Michael d'Arc Nichols for the first time.

Adair laid a receiving blanket on Michael. "So, no complications even though he's a month early?"

"No. Though hardly more than a handful, he's strong and healthy."

After Michael weighed in at five pounds, ten ounces and Dora's blood pressure tested normal, the doctor nodded toward Adair. "Mother and child are doing well, and I have surgery at ten. Can you take over from here?"

With Adair's reassurances and Dora's thanks, Monroe left. That night, Adair remained with mother and child, insisting she would stay as long as Dora needed her. The next morning Dora was up and about, and the following day, grateful for the guidance in syncing with her newborn, she shooed Adair out the door. "I imagine Sylvia misses you and needs a dose of your care."

Enclosed in a cocoon of bliss, her baby satiated with colostrum since her milk had not come down, Dora buttoned her blouse and rocked Michael. A soft sigh escaped her lips as she admired the fingers and toes of the baby nestled against her breast. "If only your father could see you. He's away from us now. But he adores you already." Her fingertip brushed a wisp of hair. "Did you hear him speak to you before you were born?" She wrapped her hand around a tiny fist. "Did you feel his hand caress your foot as it pushed against the wall of my womb?"

Although Michael's eyelids were shut in sleep, the tiny mouth puckered and the fist enclosed in her hand moved. "Michael d'Arc Nichols, I do believe you just replied 'yes' to my question."

She changed his diaper, then swaddled him before placing him in the cradle. "You know, your father made this cradle, which, though he is miles away, helps to bring him close to us."

Hardly able to tear her gaze from the miracle that she and Caellum had produced, she placed Michael on the pillow that was his mattress and lingered to kiss his forehead and push the teddy bear close to him. *I didn't know. How could I? Nothing could have prepared me for this sense of wonder – this deep connection with you.*

Jeff, now her robot instead of Achmed's, stood unmoving in the corner of the room. "You and I are on a steep learning curve," she confided to the mechanical man. "But for now let's accomplish some chores while Michael sleeps. Please put a load in the washing machine while I tidy up."

Reluctant to leave the newborn, making a mental note to locate a used baby sling, she followed Jeff out of the room. But overcome by a wave of tiredness, she detoured from her intention and collapsed in the recliner, promising herself the respite was only for a moment. But the closed eyelids triggered a deep sink into dreamless sleep in a timeless realm – until a loud noise intruded. What was that banging? She shook her head in a futile attempt to drive away the insistent pound. Where was it coming from? Exerting exhaustive effort, as though to pull herself from a deep well, she forced her eyes open.

The knocking persisted. Jeff, positioned behind her chair, inquired whether he should answer, but she motioned him to wait.

With difficulty she climbed from the well of oblivion to summon a weak voice. "I'm coming." She lifted her body from repose, though it felt heavy, reluctant to move, and still shrouded in a sleepy mist, crossed the room. With the intention to send Rolf away, she opened the door.

Biate's glare was accusatory. "You didn't inform me that birth was imminent."

Dora gasped. The dreamy fog cleared; her brain suddenly charged to full wakefulness. Danger.

"I...I... Hello, Biate."

"Well, aren't you going to invite me in?"

Dora blanched as the intruder all but pushed her way into the room. Alarm surged adrenaline to her extremities and clutched her heart when two SuperRos proceeded behind Biate.

"Boy or girl? What's its name?"

"His name is Michael."

"I need to see him."

"Michael's sleeping. If you come back in a couple of hours he'll be awake." Dora's over-amped heartbeat banged against her chest and constricted her breath.

"But I'm here to see him now."

The pathetic attempt at a stall tactic had proved futile, of course. *I'm dealing with a crazy person. I must remain calm.* She fought down terror as she imagined Biate grabbing her baby and dashing out the door with him.

Biate's full lips curled in a poor imitation of a demure smile. "Just a peek."

Words failed Dora. In the face of the invasion of the determined woman flanked by ominous looking machines, she stood frozen. As Biate breezed past her and proceeded to the partially open door, Dora snapped into motion to hurry behind her, but an iron grip stalled her.

"Let me go." She jerked her arm in a futile attempt to wrench it free. "Biate, tell your robot to free me."

Biate ignored her, shoved Jeff out of the way, pushed on the door and disappeared from view.

She's here to kidnap my child. Then as though her worst imaginings were a script for what was to come, Biate reappeared holding Michael. With slightly extended arms, she held his head in one hand, the rest of his body in the other. The support was awkward, devoid of maternal tenderness.

Unrestrained tears streamed down Dora's cheeks. "He's due to nurse soon."

But Biate, oblivious of the mother's distress, cooed and swayed, smiling at the infant.

Unable to tear her gaze from Michael for more than a split second, Dora glanced at her captor. "You're hurting my arm."

The robot's only response was a tightened grip.

"Biate, he's only three days old. Please put him down. He needs to sleep."

Finally, Biate looked up at her. "You act as though I'm kidnapping this baby."

"Biate, I know you want to hold him. But he needs to rest in his crib for now."

"You are very ungracious. Selfish woman, you don't deserve such a child."

"Biate, what do you want that is so urgent?"

The corners of Biate's lips turned down as she frowned at Michael. "This is not the heir of that ridiculous SynAnn."

Fearing to make matters worse, Dora didn't trust herself to reply. Her eyes were glued to her baby as the self-proclaimed queen shifted the tiny form from the extended reach of her arms to a possessive clutch, his nose squashed against aquamarine fabric.

"Do you want this Annunaki child to be the heir of a SynAnn?" Biate glared at Dora. "You and I are pure Annunaki. It's to our bloodline he belongs."

Michael, his face scrunched in discomfort, shifted his head. Dora's brain raced as she croaked, "I see what you mean." The tiny body squirmed.

Unresponsive to Michael's signals, Biate clasped him as though he were a coveted possession. "We—you and I—will care for this baby. You will live in a suite of rooms in my palace."

A gasp escaped before Dora could stifle it. Michael's whimper and the rag doll contortion of his body further amped her alarm.

Biate spoke over the baby's cries, still oblivious of his distress. "This is my heir. You will be his wet nurse, his nanny.

I have to get to him. "Biate, your robot is hurting my arms."

The Annunaki queen continued. "He will love *me* as his mother." Michael's blanket opened, and his legs dangled as in one hand Biate clasped his head and torso while with the other she tossed the mane of red hair over her shoulder.

In no way subdued by Biate's shouted, "Quiet!" Michael's distress escalated to loud cries.

Mustering every ounce of self-restraint, Dora assumed a quiet but direct tone. "Biate, you need to hold Michael like this." Though the guard held her forearm, she managed to enact enfolding a baby in both arms against her breast.

Ignoring Dora's instructions, Biate extended the arm that held the screaming child, commanded the SuperRo to release its hold, then addressed Dora. "We're leaving. Gather its things."

The distressed wails of the newborn grew more insistent as the mother rushed to him.

Biate shook her head, her features contorted. "What's wrong with him?" She thrust the child toward his mother.

As Dora slipped her hands under the still-screaming baby and drew him close, Biate covered her ears. "Stop him. Make him stop that noise now." The volume of her scream matched Michael's.

"Mind telling me what's going on here?" Rolf, looking elegantly detached, leaned against the doorjamb, his strong male voice slicing through the mayhem.

Biate, wild-eyed and distraught, turned toward the husband and supposed father as Dora, her wet cheek pressed against the baby's head resting on her shoulder, comforted Michael.

As the cries subsided to muffled sobs, Rolf affected an uncharacteristic, albeit exceedingly charming, smile. "Why, Queen Biate, how delightful to see you."

Emphasizing every word as though pleased beyond measure to meet up with an old friend, Rolf swept toward Biate. With Biate's slack-jaw attention riveted toward the new arrival, Dora, protectively hunched over Michael, backed up toward a chair, grabbed a receiving blanket, and covered the still crying infant as her breast offered the ultimate comfort. From her background retreat, she observed Rolf's staged friendliness as he approached the self-proclaimed queen.

At her command, the robot guards halted their advance toward him. Biate's eyes glittered an abrupt attitude change as Rolf took her hand in both of his and clasped it warmly. "We are indeed honored that you have come to give your blessing to our child." He raised her hand to his lips to plant a gallant kiss.

A pleased return smile lit Biate's flushed features before, with a brief nod, she retracted her hand. "I...He...That baby is very noisy."

"Drives me crazy," Rolf confided—the first hint of being himself. "Be glad you don't have to live anywhere near such a screamer. You do look upset." He turned toward Jeff, who stood behind Dora. "Bring her majesty a glass of water."

With solicitous ease, Rolf took Biate's elbow and steered her toward a chair. "Please, dear, do have a seat."

With kitten-like submission, Biate all but purred as Rolf eased her into the chair. She sipped the water offered by Jeff, set the glass on the end table, and smiled tentatively at her rescuer. "Your father... Does he like Michael?"

After the slightest pause as though to process the query, Rolf eyed her with an 'are you kidding?' look. "This being Michael's first week, Dad hasn't met him. But no, he can't stand crying babies."

Biate turned toward Dora, who had curved her back into the chair to pull Michael into the protective cave of her body. The hysteria of the would-be kidnapper had dissolved into reflective wistfulness. "Babies love their mothers. My brother loved my mother like that."

At that instant, while Rolf's expression grew more perplexed, Dora's terror receded. Behind the bizarre scene of super robots poised to attack at the command of a crazed woman intent on kidnapping her newborn, she glimpsed the underlying need that drove Biate's insanity. Accessing her intuition, she mused aloud, "So Biate, that's what you want? Love like your brother had for your mother?"

Biate nodded with childlike openness. "You want that child's love, but I need it more."

Dora shuddered and grimaced a smile. "One day you'll have your own child to love you." The empty reassurance fell flat.

Biate eyes blazed. "No, I won't." She turned imperiously to Rolf. "That baby's heir to the Annunaki, not a robot."

Rolf eyes shifted as though he were unable to decipher Biate's meaning.

Dora tossed Rolf a clue while addressing Biate. "You mean robots as in SynAnns... as in Charles, the imperial governor."

Biate stood up, her air imperious. "Absolutely. He's hardly more than a machine." Her look scoured the mother and baby embrace. "You will care for that young royal until he knows me to be his queen and true mother."

Rolf, leaning against the wall with feline ease, looked startled, then raised his chin, accenting his finely sculptured features. The affable façade was wearing thin. A barely perceptible twitch of his jaw accompanied his emphatic response. "Make no mistake, Michael *will* know his true heritage."

Biate proffered a queenly nod. "It's fortunate for all concerned that we are in agreement about Michael's future role. And you make no mistake that, if necessary, my force of five hundred SuperRos will prevent that SynAnn's abduction of this child."

"Abduction?" Spoken with a sardonic edge.

Ignoring Rolf, Biate gestured toward her guards and faced Dora. "Take good care of my heir."

As Dora choked and Rolf's brow shot up, Biate flounced out of the room followed by her mechanical entourage. Rolf followed them to the doorway blocking it until the clank of the elevator door removed the intruders from view.

Dora approached from behind and, when Rolf turned, leaned forward to rest her forehead on his chest with Michael sleeping between them. As she felt the perfunctory pat of the husband who loved her in his own way, a jagged sob escaped, and the full impact of the just concluded drama hit. "You saved Michael and me from being kidnapped."

Clasping Dora's forearms, Rolf spoke with measured sternness. "I believe I'm the only one other than Shaun who comes to your apartment unannounced. I'll get him to agree that we call on the in-house phone before coming. Otherwise, do not open that door. Ever. Do you understand?"

Dora nodded meekly. Thanks to Rolf, her would-be actor husband, sanity had shoved away the nightmare where insanity had prevailed. She wanted to hug him and gush her gratitude, but knew nothing would repel him more. The affection between them must always be nuanced, seldom expressed, and then only with the slightest brush of implied caring—and that had just happened.

She turned to Jeff who stood in attendance. "Jeff, I appoint you Michael's guardian.

"Yes, Ms. Dora."

"You must protect him from Biate."

"I will do my best, Ms. Dora."

"Never open the door to the apartment without my approval."

"I will follow your instructions, Ms. Dora."

As the horror of Biate issuing threats and swinging Michael around receded, she turned toward Rolf, a mischievous glint in her eyes, and lifted Michael toward him, "Do you want to hold your stepson?"

With a look of abhorrence, Rolf shrank from the offer. "I do *not* like children, and as a matter of principle, *never, ever* hold babies."

Smoke 21

The students at Onmatson Farm slept under the watch of the guard who stood atop the tower that loomed just outside the military compound and at the edge of the cornfield. Inside the chain-link fence a pair of freely roaming dogs provided additional security against a nocturnal dorm breakout.

One night in mid-December at around three in the morning, Natalie had to pee. She padded through a chorus of shifts and sighs and snores to enter the restroom/shower room through a door on the right at the far end of the barrack. At the opposite end of the room frigid night air intruded through a one-inch space at the bottom of an outside access door, and she braced herself for the chill. As Natalie eased her backside onto the cold toilet rim, a German shepherd scratched and whined at the door, and after returning to her bunk, she lay awake until morning and thought about that dog.

One night in late December a snarling ruckus—a standoff between coyotes and dogs on opposite sides of the fence—awoke several sleepers. But the guard radioed the officers' barrack assuring them that the all too frequent canine challenge was underway. And when the pack of coyotes, bored with teasing their imprisoned cousins, veered away to resume the hunt, the soldiers returned to sleep while the tower guard continued his watch.

That same night a couple of hours passed before the smell of flesh and blood just behind the women's restroom door compelled the dogs' interest. After whines and yips, the alpha dog managed to pull a chicken leg through the opening under the door and snarled at his salivating companion his right to eat first. His appetite barely whetted, the dog pressed his canines under the door to grab more flesh. But the bulk of the meat remained out of reach in the middle of the floor, that is, until the door opened slightly, enabling the dogs to force their way through before the jerk on a rope slammed it shut. After the rapid close of a second door, the alpha dog devoured the plate of sliced chicken parts and the beta grabbed the bits of bone and flesh that scattered on the floor.

The subsequent scratching and whining of the trapped dogs failed to awaken the soldiers sleeping in barracks a hundred yards away. The muffled barks even failed to rouse the tower guard from predawn slumber. But when the acrid smell of smoke reached his nostrils, he jumped up and leaned over the rail to see flames licking one leg of the tower. Jolted to wide-awake alarm as a tongue of flame curled around the bottom rung of the ladder, he switched on the radio. His frantically yelled, "Fire!" accomplished what the canine calls could not, and in the barracks bright lights blinked on.

The guard scrambled awkwardly partway down the side of the tower that wasn't burning and jumped the remaining distance to the ground. Still yelling, he unlocked and threw open the perimeter gate and ran toward the officers' quarters. While a shower of sparks torched the nearest cornstalks, tiny flames devoured corners of the officers' and soldiers' barracks.

In response to the cacophony of shouted curses, loud enough to be heard throughout the compound, across the cornfields and on the hillside that overlooked the complex, a pair of eyes aided by a quickly grabbed pair of binoculars, peered through the dark and saw the blazing tower.

Blake scrambled up the rock to stand beside Caellum. "What do you see?"

"The watch tower is in flames. Lights are on in the officers' and soldiers' barracks."

"I see it and it looks like the cornfield's caught fire. What else?"

"Flashlights zigzagging, scattering all over the place. Wait... I can't believe it."

"What?"

"The military barracks are burning."

"What about the students' barracks."

"Dark. Can't see anything. Wait... flickering light inside both the men and women's dorms."

"Inside?"

"Yep, interior fires."

"Anything else?"

"Figures. Running between the compound fence and burning corn."

As they traded the binoculars back and forth, darkness obscured briefly glimpsed shadows, but the sickening rounds of gunfire were unmistakable.

"Oh, God."

Imaginations took over as the *pop-pop* followed the figures crossing the cornfields beyond the scope of the fire.

Caellum handed Blake the binoculars, dashed inside the tent and emerged wielding the gun. "I'm going down."

Keeping his flashlight pointed toward the ground he stumbled and lurched down the mountain, his pace maddeningly slow as more gunshots followed shouts of 'Halt!' and he wondered how many students, if any, were still alive.

As he neared the foot of the escarpment, dawn broke, and he shot a soldier headed for the forest. Still hiding behind a tree he spied a second soldier about fifty yards away, firing into the trees. He took aim, and the man fell. Farther away, another hundred yards or so, the rounds came from the mountainside, the shooter hidden by the forest.

The faint light of dawn was both Caellum's friend and his foe. With increasing danger that he'd be seen first, he pursued the sporadic gunfire. That the sound of shots went silent was a blessing because he could imagine students climbing to safety, but also a curse because he could no longer locate the soldier. In a nerve-wracking creep from trunk to trunk, he intuitively calculated the soldier's speed and trajectory up the slope and moved to intersect him.

To his right and farther up the hillside, bright orange flashed across his peripheral vision. As he turned, the youth paused to stare at him. He pointed in the direction of Blake and the camp, and after a quick nod, the orange shirt moved on and Caellum resumed his pursuit.

In the forest, in the silence that was devoid of birdsong, the slightest snap of a twig announced each footstep necessitating extra caution until Caellum saw the soldier and took aim a split second before the man spotted him. After the volley of shots, a burning pain sliced through his side and he slumped behind the tree beneath a frantic flapping of wings before silence returned to the forest.

That smell. Adair pushed back the covers. The fire in the woodstove had died, which increased her anxiousness about the smell of smoke. *Is our cabin on fire?* In the early dawn light she lit the oil lamp and held it up as she peered from corner to corner. *Nothing.* She flung open the front door, then slammed it shut. The air outside was thick with smoke. Barely breathable. But she had to know.

"Mom?" Sylvia peeked over the loft.

"Quickly, come down." She lifted the child away from the ladder, threw a jacket over her shoulders and clasped her hand. Choking, she flung open the door. "Cover your nose." To preserve the better air quality that was inside in case they'd be back, she shut the door behind them. When they reached the bottom porch step, she grabbed Sylvia by the shoulders and backed her several feet from the cabin. "Stand here."

"Burns my eyes."

"Close them."

Sylvia's coughing and gasping heightened Adair's state of near panic as she circled the cabin in search of a blaze. None. She peered all around in the forest. No fire.

"Let's go inside."

As they gasped deep breaths, she knew it was dangerous to stay there. They could be trapped if a forest fire was approaching. "So sorry, sweetheart, we have to go back into the smoke. We need to know where it's coming from. Let's pass Cedarhenge and head up the mountain to see where the fire is. If necessary, I know a place we can go."

"The place in Cedarhenge that's out of this world? The other dimension?"

"Yes, that one. Hurry."

They ran, coughing and hacking, through the forest and into the meadow surrounding Cedarhenge, and scrambled up the hillside until they reached a ledge. The early light revealed the dense flow of a river of smoke following the valley. Adair peered into the distance to discover the source of the acrid drift. *Must be the farm, the buildings and the corn. Looks like the entire complex is ablaze.*

Relief over her and Sylvia's intact cabin and concern for the students heaved her sigh. "It's a couple of miles away."

"Let's go home," Sylvia whined.

With Adair's eyes watering so much she could barely see, she led Sylvia through the smoke into the breathable air of the cabin where she bathed both their eyes in distilled water. She was preparing breakfast when a knock at the door surged a fresh charge of adrenaline. Adair's "Wait, Sylvia" was too late. The child opened the door to a young woman, who appeared to be in her late teens. With a coughing blink and nod toward the child who couldn't see her brief greeting, she looked toward the mother.

"Quickly, come inside and close the door."

Adair retrieved a bowl of distilled water, eyedropper and a cloth as the young woman stumbled inside. "Three of my friends and a man who helped us are wounded. They need medical assistance, fast." The girl looked stricken.

Caellum. "Sit here. This is distilled water for your eyes. Use this eyedropper. Any dead?"

As Natalie squeezed the water into her eyes, she sobbed "yes" then hid her face in her hands. Adair embraced the shaking shoulders for several minutes before asking, "How many fatalities?"

"I know of a couple." The girl's voice broke. "But I'm afraid there are several closer to the burned corn. We were running for our lives. In all, there are about twenty-five not accounted for."

"How'd it start?"

"We set fire to the barracks and the watch tower. The corn field caught fire." The girl breathed a deep, jagged breath. "I'm Natalie, by the way. We're at a camp on the mountainside."

"Adair. My daughter, Sylvia." Adair's mind was racing. *Dr. Monroe.* "Can you show me where the camp is?

"Not with all the smoke. But there's a large boulder sticking out from the hillside. It's above the farm compound."

"I know where that is. My son will be here in an hour. Tell him to get Dr. Monroe. Sylvia, go with your brother and tell him to take you to Dora's. Natalie, you can lead the doctor to the camp. Hopefully, they haven't been found yet."

"If the dogs are okay, they'll find the camp fast. May have already."

Can this get any worse? Adair started a fire under a kettle of water and placed two quart thermoses on the table. "We'll boil enough water to fill these. She pulled a folded sheet from a drawer and grabbed a pair of scissors from the desk. "Here. Cut this sheet into strips. So, Natalie, you said *if* the dogs are okay."

"Well, it wasn't my intention for them to be burned alive."

Sylvia gasped, and Adair took her hand as they awaited an explanation.

"I trapped them in the barrack restroom about half an hour before we started the fires and escaped. There's a chance the soldiers found them still alive. I imagine the closed door to the dorm spared them smoke inhalation—at least for a few minutes."

"Blake and a man...."

"Caellum."

"Yes, they have a tent on the hillside. We laid Caellum beside it, then brought the other wounded. I think we got everyone. We left the soldier Caellum shot lying on the ground."

"How'd you find my place?"

"Caellum gave me directions. From that location we could see your building, Cedarhenge."

"So, they could be sitting ducks for a dog-led search."

"I guess, but now they have the wounded soldier's gun plus Caellum's."

"Wounded, not dead?"

"He was moaning."

Adair placed a jar of calendula ointment, a bottle of lavender oil and the last of her pre-Solar Flash supply of cotton balls in a bag along with the sheet strips.

"Let's make sandwiches. How many people?"

"Fourteen, including the wounded."

Within minutes Adair stuffed thirty sandwiches and a flask of brandy into bags before hoisting one on each shoulder. She tied together the two bottles of water to hang from her neck and placed a wet sheet strip over her nose and mouth.

"Help yourself to whatever you need. Food's in the larder through that door. Sylvia, you help Natalie. I have to move fast."

She wrote a quick note to Shaun. "Give this to my son."

With a quick hug and assurances to Sylvia that it'd be okay, she took a long, deep breath of breathable air and hurried out the door.

The rope with the water bottles attached at each end cut into her neck while the load she carried became heavier and the burning in her lungs intensified. With gasping stops and start-overs she followed the gradual upward slope of grass and sage until she reached the foot of the escarpment where the stone outcropping loomed overhead. Overcome with dizziness and exhaustion, she dropped to the ground and with her hands cupped over the cloth that covered her nose and mouth, she gasped for air. Unable to stand, she sat resting her forehead on her knees, until voices penetrated her semiconscious haze.

Strain etched the lines in Monroe's face as he greeted Shaun. Though Sylvia's sightless gaze was devoid of expression, her cheeks pressed against her brother and arms wrapped around one of his signaled her terror.

"Don't worry, Sylvia. We'll take care of the wounded." Then to Shaun, "I'm the only doctor here today and have two surgeries scheduled."

"Mom's already there with ointments and other supplies."

The doctor looked dubious. "Does your mother know what she's doing?"

"She's a natural healer."

"Hope she knows to sterilize the open wounds."

Shaun bristled. "Dr. Monroe, with all due respect, you're a heart surgeon. How much about natural healing did your courses cover?"

The doctor shot Shaun a half grin. "Matter of fact, in a single course we learned about the herbs from which pharmaceuticals are derived and that was the end of it."

"So, Doctor Monroe, for sterilization will it be sufficient for us to boil bandages so we can reuse them?"

"Yes. Rinse and boil. I can leave here by 6:30 p.m., which is good because the early darkness of winter will hide me as I head beyond the patrolled outskirts of the city. Will I find you at the cabin?"

"Yes, after I leave Sylvia with Dora. One of the escapees, Natalie, is waiting at Mom's to lead you to the camp."

Since the tightly closed windows of the tenth floor conference room of the Imperial Ritz isolated its occupants from the smell of smoke, no one questioned the haze that darkened the December sky. Dora hadn't wanted to bring one-month-old Michael to the meeting, and anxiousness about leaving him for the first time precluded attention to the weather. So she left Jeff the number to the meeting room, a full bottle of milk, and strict instructions to not open the door to anyone but Shaun or Rolf. Wishing to be any place but near the SynAnn governor, she forced herself to tune into his words as the morning sky darkened.

"It's matter of force. We have to destroy New Denver's robots with a superior might." The SynAnn governor's chin jutted imperiously as he spoke in a staccatoed monotone.

Rolf's voice jerked Dora back to the present reality as he risked the ire he had weathered so many times in the past when he addressed his father. "Our military and police force combined are no match for five hundred weaponized robots."

Dora braced herself for the predictable outburst, but the governor replied with an even tone. "You are correct."

Charles the SynAnn turned toward the older brother. "Achmed, we need your assessment of the capability of our labs."

Achmed swallowed and pushed back his hair, which immediately re-curtained his left eye with dark waves. "We are seriously handicapped by a shortage of necessary equipment."

An eerie stillness like the calm before a storm held the listeners in suspense. Cold logic governed the reply. "I assume that currently, we have neither super robots nor the capability to produce them?"

After Achmed's hesitant "Correct," it seemed as though the five people in the room almost ducked in anticipation of a fist pound and spewed profanity. But neither were forthcoming.

The SynAnn governor doesn't bang the table or turn red in the face like his predecessor would have. As his steel-edged logic sliced through the room, Dora speculated on the cause. Since he's an augmented clone, a human heart still beats in his chest. Adair had explained that communication wasn't just one way, from the brain to the human body, but was a two-way information exchange between every system, organ and cell—and that included input about feelings from the heart and solar plexus. So, the only thing that could account for the SynAnn's lack of reactivity was the heavily augmented brain that overrode emotion with serrated logic. Dora smiled inwardly. *Admittedly, this is a marked improvement on past 'family' meetings.*

"I know of only two ways to halt that invasion. First, we locate the controlling AI at the Denver Airport, and force the pass code from Biate."

A slight rustle in the room greeted that unlikelihood before the governor voiced the second option. "Or fighter jets. A squadron sufficient to mow down the robots."

The only response was Rolf's droll, "And where might we find those?"

"The place to look would be Fort Carson airfield. Our technicians have already refurbished two commuter planes. I threatened Biate with an overhauled fighter jet."

"We've discussed this already. The overhaul of a fighter jet requires considerably more expertise than the repair of a small plane We don't have a mechanic with such training in Sector 10."

As Rolf's replicated dad opened his mouth to reply, his wife, who was gazing vacantly toward the window, interrupted with, "Is that smoke?"

First in the darkening room to respond was Dora, who jumped to her feet and ran out. Shaun and Sylvia were waiting for her when she reached her door, crying, "Michael."

Wounds   22

Glad to see no soldiers or dogs, Adair hurried to the wounded, including three students and Caellum, who had been placed side by side on blankets. Kneeling by the youth who was moaning, she reached into her bag and lifted his head. "This brandy will help numb the pain." After he downed a couple of swigs, she washed the entry and exit wounds on his shoulder and applied lavender oil around the openings for soothing sterilization under cloth bandages. Repeating that procedure on a young woman's grazed thigh and the split earlobe of another, she assured them, "The doctor will be here soon."

While Adair ministered to the wounded, the remaining seven students gulped swigs of water, devoured sandwiches and discussed their fate.

"We're sitting ducks."

"Yeah, any minute now they'll be crawling these hills."

Adair asked the unexpected question. "The wounded soldier?"

Someone muttered, "Who cares about him?" and several looked at her as though she were crazy.

"I need help locating him."

The silence was thick with resistance. Adair turned to Blake who stood on the stone outlook staring through the binoculars. "We have about three hours until dark. Blake, what do you see?"

He lowered the binoculars. "Air's clearing a little. Charred rubble from buildings. Still smoking. Students tied up. Twelve sitting on the ground surrounded by soldiers. Bodies scattered around the burned field. Oh God, the bodies of our friends."

Adair grabbed the bag of medical supplies. "He could be dying."

"Let him die." A murmured chorus.

"With all due respect...." A tall strong-looking youth stepped forward.

"If I have to, I'll do this alone."

"Ma'am, while you head into danger to save the enemy, why don't we stay out of their way and save ourselves?"

From the stone vantage point, Blake voiced support for Adair. "I'm in."

A young man strapped on a water bottle. "I better join you. I heard where the last shots came from. I'm Jeremy."

"Thanks, Jeremy. I know it's not easy."

Caellum groaned. "They're likely on their way now. We need to get away as soon as possible."

"Won't help. The dogs will track us."

"If they're still alive. Natalie locked them in the shower room."

"For now, we need to act as if they're on our heels."

Caellum persisted. "Exactly. That's why we need to walk a distance in the stream before we cross to the other side."

"It's December. The water's freezing."

"Yep."

"We'll all die of pneumonia."

A sardonically voiced, "Sure, Caellum, you and the other wounded just lead the way."

Caellum half-grinned. "I get your point."

Blake kept the binoculars trained on the compound. "A jeep's headed into Transtopia. Must be going for reinforcements."

"In about an hour they're going to be crawling all over these hills."

"Let's break camp and get out of here." Caellum winced as he sat up. "With help I can make it. Alexis, can you walk on that thigh?"

A look of pain shot across her face as she struggled to stand. "If I had a cane."

"Someone find Alexis a walking stick."

"Navigating that water will be tough."

"She'll need two people to support her."

"Gemma, sorry about your ear. You okay to walk?"

"Yes."

"Can four of you carry Phil on a blanket stretcher?"

After nods of agreement, Caellum turned to Adair. "Please, don't go."

She shot a question back at him. "So where do you plan to head?"

"To the Zone of Destruction."

"Why to the ZD?"

"My old headquarters is there."

"Wait a minute." Adair hesitated. The last thing she wanted was to lead the enemy to her home. To Sylvia. "Dr. Monroe's going to my cabin before coming here. After a trek, you're going to need his help even more. But I'm worried in case Sylvia's still there. Should troops arrive, hide her."

Caellum nodded his understanding.

Jeremy pleaded with her. "Adair, come with us. The troops will find that wounded soldier."

"Yes, but immediate first aid may be the difference between life and death for that man. I shouldn't be more than a couple of hours behind you."

That face. I've seen it before. But where? "Drink this. It'll dull the pain." The soldier groaned as Adair held the flask of brandy to his lips. *Chest wound. Not good.* The front of his shirt was a sticky mass. By far the worst wound she had seen that day.

As she opened his blood-caked shirt, he clutched her arm. "Am I going to die?"

"Just stay with me." She poured water onto the cloth strip and began cleaning the bloody opening."

He moaned.

"Here, drink some more. What's your name?"

"Titus."

"Adair."

When the torn flesh was clean, she tended the wound and studied the face that had etched itself in her memory. "Now, I recall where I saw you." Blood stained the freshly applied cotton strips. "I watched you shoot my stained glass."

Straining to speak he rasped, "Are you crazy? What are you talking about?"

"The day of Caellum Nichols's execution. You soldiers were searching for the group that escaped Celebration Park. The group that launched the firecrackers. We were in the building with the stained glass mural."

"No way you could have seen me." He grimaced and uttered a low groan. "No one was there or even close by except the search team."

Holding his head, Adair offered him another swig. "Actually, you glimpsed us for a moment."

His eyes, dulled by the pain, closed for a moment. "How'd you do that—just disappear?"

She dipped a damp cloth in lavender and wiped his neck and forehead. "When you're on the mend, I'll explain."

"Didn't make sense. Still doesn't."

"I know. You were quite angry and shot a hole in the stained glass tree."

"You mad at me about that?"

"Not if you agree to help me repair it."

"I won't be alive."

"I'm counting on your help next spring."

Blake's voice broke in. "Ms. Adair, we better go. Reinforcements are crossing the burned field."

When she moved, Titus grabbed her hand. "I'm afraid to die."

"Help is on the way. They'll take you to the hospital."

"I don't want to die alone."

Adair stared at the hand that clasped hers. "Blake, Jeremy, there's not a moment to lose. Go. You know what you need to do."

Jeremy stood behind her. "Ms. Adair, please come with us."

"Don't leave me."

"I'm staying."

Blake remained unmoving. "We should stay with you."

"They won't hurt me. But they'll take you prisoner. Move... quickly."

As Blake and Jeremy disappeared among the trees, Titus's clasp of Adair's hand loosened." "I'm cold."

"Here." She pulled off her sweater and covered him. "How old are you?"

"Nineteen."

Same age as Shaun. Youth turned against youth. Madness. "Now you hang on, Titus. You're going to live."

"Will you stay with me?"

"I'll be right beside you."

His eyes closed, and before he lost consciousness, a six-year-old voice whispered, "Mom." She placed two fingers on his neck. A slight pulse, dangerously faint. Close by, a soldier spoke into his walkie-talkie. "Over here! Who are you?"

"Adair."

"What are you doing here?"

"Came up the mountain to investigate the source of the smoke."

The man's expression was dubious as he lowered his gun. "No one's allowed to live outside the Transtopia border."

"No one except the mother of the grandson of the Imperial Governor Charles Scholtz." *Mid-twenties. All so young to be caught in this mire.*

Adair's interlocutor stood as through processing his surprise.

As two others arrived at the scene, the soldier raised his voice as he lifted the sweater. "I guess this is yours."

"Leave it on him. He's cold."

Two others shifted the wounded man to a stretcher.

More troops arrived and milled around them.

"Ma'am, you must have seen some people running for their lives."

"Why would they be doing that?"

"Maybe because they're arsonists. Set fire to four barracks."

"And why would they have done that?"

"Because they're sniveling insurgents against the Union of Americas."

"Strange. Sounds more like a prison break."

The lieutenant ignored her. "You guys spread out. They're somewhere in these hills."

"Thanks for your help, ma'am. We'll leave you now."

"I promised Titus I'd stay with him." She gestured toward the unconscious youth. "He needs to get to the hospital fast." Jolted to action, the men beside the stretcher began the trek down the mountain.

Under the darkening sky, as they descended into the smoke-filled valley, smog burned Adair's throat. But the worst was to come. She fought down the nausea that assaulted her as they passed the blood-soaked corpses of slain youths, vibrantly alive hours ago, now strewn across the field, blanketed by nightfall's indifference.

"Could any of them be alive?"

"All dead. We checked."

"We can't just leave them."

Shrugs and silence.

"Are you as dead as those corpses?"

Angry counterblows gloved with profanity pummeled Adair. The lieutenant put up his hand to quiet the riot of protests. "Show respect."

Adair's survey of the soldiers was without rancor, her tone calm. "I'm not the threat."

"We had our orders."

"From a regime that threatens our humanity."

"Ma'am, step aside."

"Those bodies need to be picked up. Now."

She leveled her gaze at the commanding officer. "A truck, lieutenant, and three men. That's all it will take."

After a moment of straight-backed hesitation, the officer barked three names and pointed to one. "Aidan, drive the cargo truck. Move out!"

As the three ran ahead, Adair and the soldiers crossed the scene of smoldering rubble past a charred dog carcass lying amid piled and blackened beams, metal frames minus the cots and cracked glass in frames of mostly disintegrated photos. She stifled her sobs so that those who glanced her way saw the streaming tears, but could not hear the internal screams of outrage that wracked her soul. *An inferno of insanity.* It was as if humanity had descended into the darkness of Hades where she and all seekers of sovereignty were condemned like Sisyphus to forever roll a boulder uphill.

Caellum waited for the chorus of exclamations and curses, including, "this water's ice-cold" and "damn," and "we'll all die of pneumonia" to sputter out before he declared, "We have to wade downstream for a hundred yards at least."

"Easy for you to say."

"We can't do this—carry you guys and walk on these slippery stones."

"Put me down." Exasperation sharpened Caellum's tone.

The group holding his stretcher tried to stop him.

"Help me walk."

Scott glared at the complainers as he supported Caellum. "Now look what you've done."

"Move!" As Caellum struggled between the two who supported him, the re-opened entrance and exit wounds screamed at the violation and oozed fresh flood.

Gemma carefully navigated the stream behind Caellum. "Think we should head across that field while there's still light?"

"No. Too exposed. We should head through the forest about a mile, then hunker down until dark and pray the dogs don't find us."

"Hurry."

They had only progressed a short distance before a stretcher-bearer slipped, nearly toppling the patient, which triggered a new round of complaints.

Crazed with pain, Caellum growled, "Quit acting like babies," before the world turned black. So he didn't know when Jeremy and Blake entered the creek several yards back or about the next two slippages before the group left the stream, nor did he hear the chorused, "I can't stop shaking" or the approach of the sound of barking.

Shaun opened the door for Doctor Monroe and after introductions and a brief conversation, just long enough to boil water for tea, he handed Natalie and Doctor Monroe a thermos. "I'll stay here and wait for my mother."

Flashlights in hand Dr. Monroe and Natalie headed past Cedarhenge in the direction of the camp. Fortunately, although the smell of smoke was still pronounced, the air was more breathable.

"I hope I can find it in the dark."

"Is there a marker of any kind?"

"A stone outcropping partway up the mountain overlooks the farm. It's about two miles south."

They trudged silently through the sage and yellowed grass until they neared the base of the mountain. Natalie's flashlight beam shined on the stone prominence. In the distance a dog barked.

"Doesn't sound like the noise is coming from the direction of the camp."

"But it's a search party for sure."

Monroe shined his flashlight on the stone overlook. "So that's it?"

"Yes, but should we go there?"

"The barking was some distance away. Let's continue upward with caution."

They climbed without speaking, beams from the flashlights moving in erratic zigzags across the forest floor until they saw the tent.

"No one's here."

"Oh, but you're mistaken. Put your hands up." The pair whirled to face the soldier as he pointed his gun at them and held up his walkie-talkie. "Caught a doctor and a *pyro* at the tent. Over."

"Hold them there. We're still searching. Out."

The soldier motioned with his gun. "Drop that bag and sit over there, hands behind your back... both of you.... If those arms so much as twitch, I'll shoot you dead."

As he faced the seated pair, they blinked and turned their heads to avoid the bright beam directed toward their eyes. "You two sleaze bags are in very, very big trouble. Doctor, you're gonna face trial for aiding the enemy. And as for you, Ms. Pyromaniac, endangering the troops, destroying federal property, running away—all giant no-no's. At the next Freedom Festival, we're gonna watch you hang."

Seasons   23

Cosi dipped her bucket in the spring, flowing slower now than it would from the summit's snowmelt next spring. "So why did you become an ornithologist?"

Emory was on his knees beside her. "When I was nine years old, I asked for binoculars for Christmas because I loved watching the quick hops of robins searching for worms, and blue jays carrying sticks, twigs and string to build their nests in the crotch of trees. I laughed at the squabbles of crows, endured scoldings from mockingbirds and exulted in the piercing cries of hawks as I focused my lens skyward."

As Cosi righted the half full bucket to ladle more water inside, he took the handle. "But that's not the whole story. I loved exploring and setting up little camps in nature."

"But the augurs...."

"Listen, even if I had found a nest in what you guys call 'Three Mountains,' I probably wouldn't have told my fellow soldiers.

Emory carried the full bucket, and as they followed the path toward Cosi's cabin, her interior resistance, refusing Emory entrance, wavered. The essence he exuded, the clean aura of time spent in the sunlit outdoors, unsettled the space between them, and though she knew every protruding rock and root on the trail, she stumbled. Water sloshed over the side of the bucket as Emory grabbed her, pulled her closer than necessary and further dismantled her defenses.

Confused by the prolonged moment of charged contact and the urge to lean into his strength, she pulled away and recovered her voice. "So you weren't searching for them as a soldier?"

"Lord, no, and now that I have seen those magnificent creatures and their bonds with humans, how could I inform the military about this secret?"

For several more steps, she dared not acknowledge the shift that made her yearn for another excuse for their bodies to collide until Emory set the bucket on the ground. His eyes confessed his attraction as he crooked his finger under her chin. "And now that I've found you, how could I ever leave you?"

They stared into the fire for hours under the stars, and as an entwined being entered Cosi's cabin to alternately share stories and physical pleasures until well after sunrise, when a nudge, quiet but persistent, intruded on Cosi's bliss. "Grandfather is calling me."

"Where?" Emory looked around.

"He's not in Mu. I hear him with my heart."

"You mean at his camp."

As she nodded, her forehead rubbed against Emory's chest, and his embrace tightened. "Cosi, I just found you...."

She drew back to gaze into his eyes. "Though it's hard to leave you, I must go." As she sat up, her back to him, his fingers traced her spine and she shivered. "The fox is ready to be set free, but while I'm gone the wounded hawk will need help."

"I'll care for it." Emory sat up to kiss the nape of her neck and pulled her close again.

"I don't trust Puma with you when I'm not around."

"Nor do I."

"There will be a room for you in the village. I have a cage for transporting raptors. Will you take the hawk with you?"

"Sounds good."

"The children bring strips of meat to Raiel's school for the raptors."

"I'll check in with them." Emory hands clasped her shoulders.

"I should be back in a couple of days." She couldn't resist the backward pull toward her pillow and Emory.

"Okay." He explored her with his lips. "As long as you'll return to me. As long as you'll always return to me."

"Shhh...." She pulled him close. *How could I not?*

Cosima put the hawk in the portable cage. "Eena would warn me not to trust you."

"She thinks I'm a snake. So, what about you?"

Glad for a reason for her back to face Emory, she filled the bowls of Puma and the hawk with fresh water. "I would classify you as the garden variety."

"So that means you trust me?"

While handing Emory the cage, Cosima's eyes avoided his persistence. *I feel trust, but also unease.* His query remained unanswered as he pulled her close and kissed her.

"Cosima, since yesterday... We made love for the first time, and it's hard to let you go."

Words failed her as she leaned against the strength of a body toned by outdoors, a nature grown reflective by bird watching.

He lifted her chin to look into her eyes as he spoke his feelings. "Cosi, I love the endless depths of your blue gray eyes and how small you look standing beside that mountain lion. I love that you live in the forest surrounded by wild beasts. I love that you care for motherless and wounded creatures. I want to be one of those creatures." A glint of humor flashed in his brown eyes. "Though not wounded, of course."

Glad for the relief brought on by shared laughter, she pulled away with a backward glance toward the cages. "You called me Cosi."

"Is that okay?"

"Of course. That was my father's name for me."

She unlatched the door to the fox's pen and opened it wide. Though the world beyond the door beckoned, for several moments red fur hugged the mesh of the rear wall, while bright eyes peered at the opening until, in response to an irresistible call, the fox darted to freedom. As the black tip of his tail disappeared, the last vestige of the gate guarding her heart's separate peace dissolved.

The old Lakota's smile radiated like no other. "The Mother destined that doe skin dress for you."

Though Matoskah sat on a stump, Cosima chose not to sit on the one beside him. Instead, she folded her legs on the ground at his feet. "The Mother?"

"The Earth Mother who also dresses in clothing that's pleasing to the eye and protects her skin when the season brings a big change."

Cosima's breath barely moved as she smoothed the soft, white leather that covered her lap.

"My daughter, are you preparing yourself?"

A shaft of alarm shot through her. "For what, Grandfather?"

"For what is to come."

She waited for the old man to continue, but nothing was forthcoming. For a while, attentive silence sat between them until she looked into the eyes that peered underneath wrinkled lids, and asked, "Am I to know what is to come, Grandfather?"

"No. Only to prepare yourself for the unexpected."

"Soon?"

"Always."

"How do I prepare myself?"

"Attune to the language of feeling. The Mother will speak to you through the heart. Attentive to the heart's nudges is a helpful way to navigate life."

Alerted to the presence of the one who had mothered him as a pup, Valek emerged from the forest. Cosima scrunched her face in defense against the wolf's barrage of quick, wet licks and ruffled cascades of light and dark gray as his mate hung back.

After the wolves lay close by, Grandfather stood. "Herbs hang drying in the shed. Too many for me to finish."

"Then I'll help you."

Cosima followed him to the small log building. As he opened the door, she breathed deeply of the blend of fragrances.

"My grandmother always harvested herbs in the morning, just after the dew evaporated. She told me that is when essential oils are at the most potent concentrations."

Grandfather motioned her inside the room where dried plants, their flowers still intact hung from slats near the ceiling. "These herbs will store up to a year, but they are ready to be crushed and packaged now. On that table squirrel skin pouches await filling."

"Good. We can work together."

"Listen closely." He pointed to a cluster with purple flowers. "Echinacea encourages the immune system and reduce symptoms of colds and flu."

Two types of pink flowers merited Matoskah's next explanation. "Both the pink bee balm, here, and magenta bergamot beside it treat infections and digestive issues, such as gas and bloating. Wild bergamot is antimicrobial, anti-inflammatory and diaphoretic. It brings on a sweat to break a fever." Cosi's teacher looked at her pointedly. "Submit this information to memory."

Cosi glanced toward the wolves just beyond the doorway. *I have always welcomed this beloved shaman's instructions. Why do I want to cover my ears and run from the room?*

"Calendula oil has antifungal, anti-inflammatory and antibacterial properties that make it useful in healing wounds, soothing eczema and relieving diaper rash.

"Motherwort calms stress and headaches and is woman's friend during her menstrual cycle."

The protest, "You're going too fast. How will I remember all of this?" burst from Cosima, confusing her with its vehemence.

Grandfather's response was even-toned, kind, as though he understood her angst. "The book on that table has labeled drawings and reiterates what I am saying."

Cosi clasped the thick reference book as he turned to the basket of pouches. "The drawings and labels on those pouches indicate the seed varieties. Knowledge of the conditions for their planting is vital."

Matoskah glanced at Cosima's face and declared, "Enough for now."

The volume of information presented in the room Cosima had entered with a light heart now weighed on her. Since the age of fifteen she had welcomed Grandfather's teachings. Yet, today, she was glad to escape the enclosure and his instructions. But outside of the hut, sitting on the ground as she leaned against a tree with her eyes closed, their wordless camaraderie brought relief, and the peaceful interlude calmed the electrical surges that made her uncomfortable in her skin. The speckled sunlight that warmed her upturned cheeks had almost restored equanimity, when she opened her eyes to see a large dark blob followed by two more intrude on the periphery of her vision.

Grandfather's greeting floated past her alarm. "Mato, and first and second son, welcome."

Though the mother bear hung back to sniff the air, her offspring, having tumbled and romped as cubs near the old Lakota's tanning frame, approached for a greeting. As each nose presented itself inches from Grandfather's face, he scratched the fur underneath the chin.

Cosima, who considered herself the surrogate mother of a wolf and a panther, hugged her knees close to her chest and wished herself anywhere but near Mato and her nearly grown cubs. In her interior ear echoed the mother bear's enraged roar two years before as she loomed seven feet tall and waved lethal claws at the young girl clutching the wolf cub.

Now larger than their parent, the black bears padded around the camp, stuck their noses in Grandfather's house, rose on their hind legs to sniff the drying shed and circled the ashes of the fire until only one object remained to be investigated. When not one, but two, noses neared Cosima's face, she knew the bears would smell her fear, so she breathed deeply to quiet the pounding of her heart. Left with no choice but to follow Grandfather's example, she scratched beneath the thick fur of the jaws until first one then the other tired of the greeting and plodded into the forest with Mato following.

"The spirits of the bears came together for a brief farewell."

An unwelcome prescience shadows Grandfather's explanation. Cosima's expression queried her mentor.

"In December, the bears slumber. We entered their dreamscape."

"They seemed as real and present as in any spirit traveling we have shared."

As the sun disappeared behind the trees that circled Grandfather's meadow, he drew a circle in the dirt; then filled it with nearby stones. As he laid the last stone, he said, "It is complete."

Trepidation yielded to the softly uttered "Meaning, I can walk these trails alone without fear?"

Grandfather beamed as though glad his apprentice comprehended the bears' message.

"Tomorrow, morning let's hike to the summit of Blue Lake Mountain."

That night Cosima snuggled under the wool blankets with Grandfather on the far side of the teepee, and throughout sleep-deprived hours, awaited each soft snore.

Below the summit of Blue Lake Mountain, the lake where grandfather had met Eena sparkled in the sunlight, and hid in its depths the plane piloted by Nathan Abelt. The panoramic view from the mountaintop was so vast, it seemed to encompass the entire world. Mountains undulated in every direction, welcoming the sun's rise to the east and reflecting its descent to the west.

Momentarily, a labyrinth superimposed itself over the seemingly random pattern of mountain summits. From the heart's perspective, Cosima's gaze zoomed in on the scene of people, known and unknown, following the path that spiraled to the center and back. In an even closer enlargement of the lens, Cosima recognized Leiani, to whom the Augurs entrusted their chicks, and Eena, the first from Three Mountains to bond with and pilot an augur. There was Gavin, who barely escaped death on the rickety bridge to Quartz Mountain. The account of Gavin's rescue by Eena as he dangled had become a favorite around campfires, embellished until listeners waved their hands and laughed at the exaggerated "hanging by one finger."

A few steps back was Leslie carrying her machine that still, after three years, pulled energy from the ethers. And Rigel, who risked his neck to protect Cosima from the rover Jimmy who wanted to make her his sixteen-year-old bride.

And there was Caellum, who had gone to Techno City and landed in jail. And Dora, known as 'the Landlords' daughter,' who came to Three Mountains to plead for help. And Chas, who drove the ambulance that carried the crew and boxes of firecrackers to save Caellum from execution.

The teacher Meyer accompanied Raiel, with children coming up the rear. Cosima herself walked accompanied by a wolf and a panther. And in her arms, was a small bundle. But the being it enclosed remained hidden.

And approaching the center of the labyrinth was Grandfather.

Evidently, Grandfather saw the vision too. "Event strings carry each one to fulfill chosen destinies."

"But by following the labyrinth to the center, don't the people share a common destination?"

"Yes. The paths wind together like a strong rope.
"To where?"

"Symbolically, the Return of Buffalo Woman—a shared event that looms large in humanity's future."

The image of Anaya, the enigmatic healer able to teleport between the city deep in Earth's honeycombed crust and Three Mountains, sprang to mind. "I didn't see Anaya on the labyrinth."

"Anaya's people, the Erathans, took a similar journey many thousands of years ago. This is our adventure."

"I do miss her wisdom."

"And she defers to the growth of ours."

"So, Grandfather, why has this vision presented itself?"

"For you to grasp the strength of the collective rope during what is to come."

"Do you foresee the outcome, Grandfather?"

"With my old eyes?"

"So we're to follow a confusing maze to an unseen goal?"

"The labyrinth spirals as though around a mountain. Near the summit broadened views are possible."

Their climb down Blue Lake Mountain was quiet; their time at Grandfather's fishing hole filled with laughter as he poked fun at Emory. But, trout in hand, he hastened to assure her the bird-watcher was a good catch.

That night, after they crushed the dried herbs and transferred them to squirrel skin pouches, Cosima was so tired she knew she would sleep. But before she dozed off, Grandfather's last words to her were, "My daughter, when you leave, the herb and seed packets must travel with you."

Brainshifts 24

Coming to Morocco was a bad idea. Disgusted at his gullibility, Jack Merrick sat unmoving in the unresponsive craft in the middle of the Moroccan desert. During the intervening seconds, he mocked himself for coming to Morocco, for the camel trek, for entering this useless saucer. When the opening reappeared as suddenly as it had closed and Randolph Ring's face beamed at him, Jack started in surprise. "Randolph! How did you get here?"

"I live and work here." Randolph's expression was matter-of-fact. "This is my lab."

Jack stared in bewilderment. "In the middle of the desert?"

"You better come have a second look at where we are."

When Jack reached the top of the ramp, the surrounding terrain elicited a gasp. A foreground of green foothills that skirted the steep escarpments of Mount Jebel Yagour had replaced the reds and grays of the desert. As he descended the ramp, his gaze returned to the man standing on the ground in front of him. "But, Randolph, you must be over a hundred years old."

"Now, Jack, do I look that old?"

He didn't. "What's going on here?" In a robotic daze, Jack descended the ramp to a gravel surface.

A mischievous sparkle lit Randolph's eyes. "Seems like a pilot would know."

"Surely, you're not implying that this vehicle flew here."

"How else would you have reached Blue Kachina Center for Research and Development?"

After a stunned silence, Jack protested. "But the saucer didn't move."

Randolph's eyebrows raised in response to Jack's bemusement. "Then you better fetch your camel."

A reflexive scan of the immediate surroundings confirmed there was no camel and everything was wrong. They stood in a large cleared area bordered by stately cypress trees reigning over a green substrate. To one side rested an impressive aircraft hangar. Several yards away from that structure, level ground yielded to a mound with an apex about four feet above ground level.

Randolph's voice interrupted Jack's attempt to orient himself. "Ten miles is an instantaneous shift for a craft like this."

"None of this makes any sense." Bewilderment edged Jack's voice.

"Not to your brain, which is locked in 3D. The memory is in there. It just hasn't surfaced yet." Randolph turned toward the mound and signaled for Jack to follow.

In confused docility, Jack unlocked his legs to approach a raised archway on the far side. The pair entered an open door to descend stairs spiraling to a floor about six feet below ground level where a recliner and table lamp clustered around a sofa gave the room a cozy feel. A fresh-from-the oven smell wafted a homey invitation.

A woman welcomed him with a warm smile. "Nice to see you, Jack."

He responded with pleased surprise, recognizing Marsha from video interviews prior to Solar Flash. Randolph relied on Marsha to keep his answers from drifting among an ocean of memories. By helping him retrieve dropped strands of thought, she astutely steered him back on course.

After introductions, Marsha glanced at her husband. "Let's head into the kitchen."

A plate of muffins sprinkled with yellow-gold saffron triggered Jack's hunger as, seated around the table, he and Randolph waited for Marsha to pour hot tea into their cups.

Jack addressed Randolph. "Since hearing your interviews, your work has fascinated me. I recall bits and pieces of the story of your discovery of natural law, but I'd love to hear from you how it all fits together—the bumblebee, Tesla, Otis Carr and Blue Kachina Research and Development."

Smiling, Marsha lifted the plate, and Jack grabbed a still-warm muffin.

Randolph leaned back in his chair. "It's a long story. Thankfully, my partner here will help me stay on track." His expression conveyed deep love for his companion. "You could say my life trajectory originated with the great inventor and humanitarian Nikola Tesla. A man out of time, he offered humanity an endless source of free energy by erecting Wycliff Tower. But his plan to transmit electrical power through the Earth and the ionosphere without any wires or telephone poles fanned the ire of his primary funder, J.P. Morgan."

Jack bit into the cardamom-flavored sweetness. "The wealthy tycoon was in the business of making money."

"Yes, and Tesla's invention offered zero returns on his investment. So Morgan withdrew funding, had the tower demolished and basically shut Tesla down. He made sure Tesla never found another investor willing to fund his visionary projects."

"Humanity plugged into the grid promised vast wealth to the few." Jack chugged his tea.

"Yes, while access to free energy devices to power people's homes and vehicles would free them from dependence on electrical generators and countless miles of power lines."

When Marsha replenished his tea, Jack nodded appreciatively. "Seems odd. Halting scientific progress to enable powerful financial and industrial interests."

Randolph nodded understanding of Jack's confusion. "The power structure of the elites requires the continuous funneling of funds from the many at the bottom to the few at the top. It's that simple."

Jack shrugged. "We could all prosper from paradigm-changing breakthroughs."

"Those who control the world hoard such knowledge in secret programs. But you're right. People could express the creative power they were born with—which has been suppressed because they've had to plod as children through rote learning and as adults in mundane jobs. Many could be tremendous artists and engineers, beyond our dreams.

"Now back to Tesla. While he was an impoverished resident in the New Yorker Hotel, a college student by the name of Otis Carr supplemented his income by working as a clerk at the hotel. A sponge for science, he became the great inventor's protégé for several years. Tesla taught Carr about natural science in which propulsion and energy generation is simple—in compliance with natural law. It was Tesla who first put into Carr's head the idea of a craft that could levitate by generating its own magnetic field."

"Like the bumblebee."

"Exactly. The famous inventor once told him, 'In my time, humanity's not interested. I want you to take everything I teach you and see if they'll listen to you in your time. And if not, you're going to have to pass it on, because otherwise we're on a self-destructive course.'"

Marsha shoved a muffin on Randolph's plate and signaled him to pause to take a few bites and drink his tea. After Randolph wolfed down the muffin, complimented the cook and sipped his tea, he resumed his narration.

"So Carr established his own lab for building a special type of free energy devices—small ships that levitate and traverse space and time according natural law. In the 1960s I joined his team."

"So what led you to connect with him?"

"Looking back, the path to OTC Labs began in my boyhood, as I followed a forest trail between home and school. Hours spent observing life in the surrounding wilderness revealed the fascinating habits and abilities of the forest creatures. The bumblebee, which taught me the rudiments of natural law, was to have a profound effect on my life, especially after I discovered I had a technical bent and a knack for invention. Persuaded of the value of a college degree, I entered the university, only to have a bee teach me that the physics taught by the professor was a lie."

Jack nodded. "I know that story practically by heart."

Randolph leaned back in his chair. "Clearly, nature could teach me more about physics than academia. So I left. Through a group of scientists I was affiliated with, I learned of Otis T. Carr Labs, and soon joined Carr at his lab in Apple Valley—a decision that changed my life."

An interlude of silence prevailed as Randolph stared past his guest.

"Carr's often-repeated words were, 'We live in an energetic sea of moving vortices and frequencies. We ourselves are energy packets that are local, yet interconnected with everything everywhere.'"

Randolph downed a cake in two bites. "According to natural law, an abundant energy source surrounds us—and it's free." Randolph's emptied mug clunked on the table.

"You mean the field in which bees and craft, like the one I rode in, levitate. But I still don't understand how."

"Remember the bee's resonating chamber? Similarly, the OTC-Z1's propulsion system resonates with Earth's electromagnetic field. Drawing from that source, it generates its own magnetic energy bubble, allowing it move freely in the atmosphere."

The implications of Randolph's words sank in. "Then we don't need rockets to blast into space."

"No. Haven't for many years. But corporate interests are determined to control energy resources, not to mention the most advanced technologies."

Quietly, Jack voiced his musings. "So, the government has known of this energy source since the fifties."

"Not necessarily elected officials. Behind the scenes, through extortion and bribery, corporate powers wield political clout in academia and on Capitol Hill."

"Yet, Tesla died a pauper, his files confiscated by a secret agency."

Marsha had cleared the table before the inventor spoke again. "Prepare yourself. The next phase of Carr's instructions requires a real switch in perception—the relationship between physics and our minds."

Espionage   **25**

Nathan's straight-backed attentiveness belied the wetness in his armpits. The scorn in the governor's gaze sliced to his core. "Abelt, unfortunately, your sorry ass is all I've got for this next assignment." Nathan dared not flick an eyelash or move a finger for fear of igniting imperial wrath.

"Those students can't be running around the mountains in this weather. They'd die from exposure. They have to seek shelter. I'm sending MPs to search the ZD, while your spies and the police search Transtopia. There are around ten on the loose, and we're going to capture every one of them."

Nathan kept silent about his initial hunch they were hiding at Adair's. Assuming an air of determined certainty, he met the governor's dismissal with assurances.

Nonetheless, the governor's mouth remained turned down in disgust with his parting shot. "Abelt, don't blow this one."

At the entrance to the Ritz, the limo waited and with a long sigh of relief Nathan sank into the seat, directing the driver to his house. The moment he entered, the homey smell of pot roast drew him to the kitchen, but he greeted the twins first, relieved that they had outgrown the rambunctious assaults of past years. In the kitchen, Emma was in the highchair, playing with the peas, carrots and potatoes that filled the tray. Lydia was preparing a salad at the counter.

Lydia, his refuge. He took her in his arms, glad that her embrace was as responsive as when they first married, her kiss both tender and sensual. With her full lips and breasts, her solicitous care of the children and himself, she was all woman, the one he would fall in love with all over again. How was it that she worked long hours as he did, but never complained about coming home and preparing dinner for her family?

Lydia was also a woman with fire in her veins, which was great for marital relations, if only that passion didn't carry over into other aspects of life. He couldn't fathom her opinionated notions about politics and education, and inwardly ducked and ran for cover when topics arose concerning the school's indoctrination of their children and their inundation with mind-dulling minutia. When Lydia ranted about martial law—the government's frequently declared way to flex their muscles—Nathan took offense at her ungratefulness and usually ended up on the sofa for the night.

Nathan also dreaded exciting Lydia's ire over his line of work. To ameliorate that unpleasantness in his home, his refuge, he had developed a strategy of silence when it came to the aspects being a spy that triggered Lydia's disgust. The less said about the unsavory aspects of his job, the better.

Lydia's friendship with Dora Scholtz made matters worse. The recently fanned flames of Lydia's smoldering objections to systemic policies exacerbated his resentment of Dora and the wish he could prevent her coming to his home. Instinct warned him that Lydia must never know that the year before he had tracked Dora to apprehend Caellum Nichols.

Lydia reached up to brush the swath of hair from his forehead. "You look as though today was a particularly trying day, dear."

"I'm just glad to come home to you. Let me help you."

"Thanks. Would you please scoop the peas, carrots and potatoes back on Emma's plate?"

Nathan made silly faces as he loaded a spoon and coaxed Emma to take a bite. But she clamped her lips together and batted away his hand, sending peas rolling across the floor. While Nathan returned carrots one by one from the tray to the plate that Emma gleefully re-emptied, his mind turned to his latest challenge.

When that pharmacologist died, leaving an open work slot, Lydia urged him to request a transfer out of the Social Engineering Initiative. But he just couldn't bear the thought of days spent behind a counter dispensing prescriptions and pills. Not to mention reduced status and income which would nix the long dreamed-of two-story house with Lydia wearing the necklace with the ruby pendant as she directed her staff. Besides, workers like pharmacologists didn't get paid vacations, which though spent in the confines of Transtopia, still offered two weeks of relief from stress.

As Nathan removed the plate Emma had perched atop her curls, he made a mental note to approach the SEI work-assignment official to promote a speedy replacement for the position in the pharmacy so he wouldn't have to dodge Lydia's persistence.

Lydia handed him a damp cloth. "I think Emma's finished eating, dear. Let her go play. The twins have already eaten, so it's just us."

The opening of the oven door immersed him in the aroma of pot roast smothered in onions as Lydia asked, "Did you by any chance inquire about the pharmacologist position?

Stall tactic time. "My work kept me too busy today." After Nathan washed the chubby hands and face, Emma hugged his neck as he lifted her from her seat.

Lydia placed the salad on the table. "That smoky haze has lasted all day. What's that about?"

Thankfully the job transfer topic has been avoided. But the fire can also be a minefield. "Fire at the Onmatson Farm."

"Judging from all that smoke, it must have been a large one."

"Uh-huh."

"I have a feeling it was more than an accident. Have you learned any particulars?"

"M-m-m-m, that roast smells delicious."

"Nathan, are you avoiding my question?"

"You know the strictures on a spy's communication."

Undaunted, Lydia pressed on as she placed a slice of meat on his plate and shoved the roasted vegetables beside it. "There's a rumor that the students started it."

The tender meat yielded easily to Nathan's knife and he hurriedly loaded a large forkful in his mouth for a long, deliberate chew. After cooking and seasoning the meal to perfection, Lydia would allow him the prolonged and exquisite stimulation of every taste bud.

She served herself as she prattled on. "A student rebellion's no surprise. It was cruel to tear them from college and conscript them to live like prisoners in a labor camp. Who could blame them if they did start that fire? So was it them?"

Of course you would champion those youths. Your tender heart is my delight, and yet, it's the bane of a spy's existence.

"Well, if you won't tell me, Dora will."

The well-chewed clump clogged Nathan's throat. As he struggled to breathe, his wife ran around, hit his back and lifted the glass of water to his lips. After he swallowed and ceased gasping for breath, she sat down, and he croaked, "Dora?"

"Of course. She's on our side, you know."

Our side? "What do you mean?"

"Although she's a royal—"

Nathan guzzled his water and as his glass arced to the table, interrupted Lydia. "Dora has betrayed the government, her own kind, Sector 10."

"Nathan, where do you get such ideas? She's our best hope for a better life, for freedom."

Nathan's fork and knife stood erect on either side of his plate as though guarding his stance. "We are alive, free and enjoy a nice lifestyle, thanks to Charles Scholtz and our status in the SEI.

"Calm down, dear, and eat your supper. I do love you, even though you are so deluded."

Dora's image loomed as his fork jabbed the roast and his knife sliced with a vengeance. The worst thing that could happen to a spy was for the object of suspicion to make his line of work suspect to the object of his devotion. To the final forkfuls, he devoured the roast as though to clear his plate of the hateful image until the oven timer rang.

Lydia, adept at more than lovemaking, fetched the potholder to remove peach cobbler from the oven. Before her next declaration, the tantalizing aroma and Lydia's well-timed small talk wafted across the table. "Oh, by the way, I took the liberty of speaking with the SEI job placement official today and told him you may be interested in that pharmaceutical position." Said with an air of childlike innocence as she ladled a mound of dessert browned to perfection with golden peaches encased in still-bubbling syrup. "Tell me when, dear."

The doctor and Natalie had left two hours ago and Shaun awaited his mother's return. His concern growing with every passing minute, he paced for what seemed like ages until he heard steps on the front porch. When the door opened, the first face he saw was Caellum's with a youth supporting him. Eight more coughing, shivering people pushed through. Several collapsed on the floor to remove their shoes and socks.

"Your feet. They're soaked."

"Iced is more like it."

"Move closer to the fire."

The flood of coughing, sneezing youths, including some soaked to the bone, snapped Shaun to a whirlwind of activity: bringing towels and changes of clothes for those soaked through, placing the kettle of water on the stove for tea.

"My mother. Have you seen her?"

"Hours ago. She went to help a wounded soldier."

"Soldier? Wait a minute. She went to help you."

"She did. Then she left."

"Where is she now?"

"I'm surprised she's not back here with you."

"And what about Dr. Monroe and Natalie?"

"Never saw them."

Concern silenced the murmurs of people warming bare feet near the fire.

"We did see a new round of troops from Onmatson head up the mountain in the direction of the wounded soldier."

"I have to find my mom and figure out what happened to the doctor and Natalie." Shaun grabbed his parka and a wool scarf from the coat hook.

Caellum clasped Shaun's arm. "Tell Dora... tell her I...."

Shaun nodded as he grabbed his coat. "I'll fill her in on everything and let her know you're okay. "Caellum, you know about the larder. Help yourselves to food. Stew's simmering on the stove."

So great was Dora's fright at the smoke darkened sky, Michael had not left her arms, and she held him as she opened the door to Shaun for the second time that day.

"I'm looking for Mom, Doctor Monroe and one of the students."

Before inviting Shaun inside, Dora stared uncomprehending.

"I need to be on my way. But I'll give you a brief synopsis."

In the rocking chair Dora held Michael close and listened.

"The students burned down their barracks and escaped early this morning. Several were killed."

Gripped by the horror of the deaths, her burning question concerned Caellum.

"He's been wounded, but he's okay. Mom left the students to help a wounded soldier. The doctor never arrived."

Anxiety nagged her about Adair and the doctor. But she had to get to Caellum.

"I'm headed to the jail. May I leave Sylvia with you?"

"The jail's closed by now."

"Ah, I forgot how late it is.

"Let's check the hospital."

"The hospital?"

"At least for your mom. It's possible she accompanied that wounded soldier to the hospital."

Dora reached for Sylvia's hand and squeezed it. "We'll all go together. Call Leon while I make sandwiches and a thermos of hot tea."

Shaun called Leon on the in-house phone. "Leon, I know it's late. I'll drive myself."

After Shaun hugged his mother, Dora reached into the bag, handed Adair a sandwich and poured steaming liquid from the thermos. "When you're ready, I want to hear about everything."

"You wouldn't believe how welcome this is. I'm famished." After a grateful sigh and a few bites, Adair shared her story of the fire and wounded students and why she accompanied Titus to the hospital.

Dora turned to Shaun. "Did Dr. Monroe meet up with the students at the cabin?"

"No," Shaun replied. "Natalie was leading the doctor to the camp. But they never made contact with the students. We don't know what's happened to them."

"Oh, dear. That can't be good."

Dora shifted Michael so that his face rested against her shoulder. "I'm so worried about Caellum."

Adair squeezed her free hand. "No need to worry. It's just a flesh wound."

"So the farm? The students?"

Glancing at Sylvia, Adair spoke in a monotone while Dora's eyes reflected the understated horror. "We better brace ourselves. Serious ramifications are likely."

Dora noted the exhaustion on Adair's face. "You need rest. Why don't you come to my apartment?"

"I'm staying until Titus wakes up. If he wakes up. I promised to be at his side."

At that moment a nurse approached. "Ma'am, you've been on that bench all night. The doctor on duty said to break hospital policy and give you a room."

"A bed and a shower. That'll be heaven. Thanks." And to Dora, "Hopefully Dr. Monroe's home in bed as we speak."

"I'll check with you in the morning. Adair, I'm desperate to see Caellum."

"I'll go with you in the morning after Titus, is out of surgery and awake. I just need to reassure him."

"Adair." Doctor Simms touched her arm. "Titus Graham could wake up any time now. He's in room 307."

"So he made it through surgery."

"It was touch and go, but yes."

Adair shifted her legs over the side of the bed. "I'm concerned about Dr. Monroe."

"His shift began two hours ago, but he hasn't showed up."

Titus was still asleep when Adair pulled a chair beside his bed. She drifted in and out of sleep herself until he blinked and looked around the room. His eyes settled on her, and after a brief stare, he uttered, "You're here."

He moaned and she took his hand. After the nurse came with water and a painkiller he fell back asleep, his fingers wrapped in Adair's hand.

"Any word on Dr. Monroe?"

"None that I know of, ma'am."

Adair remained at Titus's side until he awakened again mid-morning and she told him she had to leave, but she'd return soon.

Dora played with Michael, and adored his angelic smiles until he nursed and fell asleep. As she paced between the living room and kitchen, and back again, awaiting the arrival of Adair and Shaun, her concerns oscillated between Caellum and Michael. She thought of taking Michael along, but he was just too tiny. Calculating she could be back in less than two hours, she grabbed the in-house phone.

"Rita, Caellum's seriously wounded. Can you keep Michael for a couple of hours?"

After Rita's enthusiastic "yes" and Adair and Shaun's knock on the door, she collected Sylvia, a full diaper bag and Michael and burst through the door.

With the look of adoration and exclamations that accompany women's introductions to babies, Rita took the bag and Michael. "I know you're anxious about Caellum, dear. Hurry on."

Dora hugged her gratefully and Leon escorted her to the waiting limo. Once she was seated, Shaun drove as fast as he dared. They hurried the final yards through the trees and up the stairs. But an uneasy feeling caused Dora to pause, look back and scan the forest.

At Adair's 26

Nathan Abelt agreed with the Imperial Governor that, although the military was combing the forested escarpments to the west, the band of arsons would seek shelter from the cold and a meal source. After instructing the driver to hide the car, he hurried through the pines to situate himself in the forest facing Adair's front door. The curtains were drawn, and since it was daylight, there were no shadows from inside light to expose the student's presence. Nonetheless, he fully expected to see escapee vandals from Onmatson Farm emerge sooner or later, if for no other reason than to visit the outhouse.

Nathan had been watching the house for an hour when something, call it a spy's sixth sense, alerted him that someone was approaching. Lowering his binoculars, he hunkered down behind a tree.

Dora, and three others. It was his job to anticipate the moves of suspects and accomplices. But he couldn't have been more surprised. He knew from Lydia about the premature birth. He also recalled that his wife was in constant attendance at home during her babies' first month. What was so important that Dora left her newborn and braved the cold to come to Adair's cabin?

Resentment flooded the spy as Dora disappeared through the cabin door. Although he was certain of Lydia's love, her look of happy camaraderie was reserved for times with Dora. Sure, they were women and shared women's concerns. But he wished that same glow emanated from Lydia when they shared his goal to provide a better life for her and the kids. Problem was Lydia didn't appreciate the importance of his role as a spy, nor his dream of elevating her to elegantly dressed, spectacularly housed status in the SEI.

Dora played with Michael, and adored his angelic smiles, until he nursed and fell asleep. Though accustomed to sleeping herself for at least part of his daily afternoon nap, she paced between the living room and kitchen, and back again awaiting the arrival of Adair and Shaun. Her concerns oscillated between Caellum and Michael. She thought of taking Michael along, but to get from the end of the road to Adair's door entailed a five-minute walk in the cold through the forest. Besides he was just too tiny to take among all those people. Calculating she could be back in less than two hours, she considered Jeff, but decided she'd be too far away to entrust her baby to a mechanical man. *Lydia? Two of her children have colds. I'll call Rita.*

"I need to get to Caellum. He's seriously wounded. Would you be free to keep Michael for a couple of hours? I'll leave a bottle of milk."

After Rita's enthusiastic yes, Dora told Sylvia to get dressed to go and waited for Adair and Shaun's knock on the door. Grabbing her coat and muffler, a full diaper bag and Michael, she burst through the door to ride the elevator to Rita and Leon's apartment.

With the look of adoration and exclamations that accompany women's introductions to babies, Rita took the bag and Michael. "I know you're anxious about Caellum, dear. Hurry on."

Dora hugged her gratefully and Leon escorted her to the waiting limo. Once she was seated Shaun drove as fast as he dared. They hurried the final yards through the trees and up the stairs where an uneasy feeling caused her to scan the surrounding forest.

Caellum was sitting up, but as she hurried to him, she noted his wan expression. "Thank God, you're okay."

"Of course. Didn't I promise you I would be?"

"But are you in pain?"

"Only a little. Adair took good care of us yesterday, and I see that she's back at it now."

Steam from a pot of water with camphor oil humidified the air for the benefit of sore throats and dry lungs. Moving quietly among the patients, Adair cleaned and re-bandaged wounds, and gave the one with the leg wound, which she was concerned could fester, especially attentive care. Next, she made her way through those who had contracted colds, which was the majority, while giving extra care to the one that was feverish and in all likelihood had pneumonia.

Though reluctant to leave Caellum, Dora asked, "Adair, how can I help?"

"You need to keep your distance from sick people. Just attend to Caellum."

As Dora nodded, Caellum clasped her arms and pushed her away. "Dora...."

"As I'm sure Adair told you, Michael d'Arc Nichols, was born November 22, 2038."

"Our son."

The softly uttered congratulations of a youth close by reminded them that they were in a room crowded with people.

Caellum spoke over the ongoing conversations. "I have an important announcement. Our son Michael d'Arc Nichols is one month old today."

After the claps and cheers, he squeezed Dora's hand. "Let's grab a little time alone."

Neither noticed the frigid wind as they stepped on the porch. A blizzard would have barely distracted the pair from their mutual absorption.

"Our challenge is feeding these guys. Adair's winter food supply is rapidly diminishing. I'm hoping there is sufficient food for them at Gaia's Gardens."

"Caellum, come to my apartment and let me take care of you for a week or so. We can bring some food from the Ritz."

"You know I would love to be with you and Michael, but in a few hours, soldiers will likely arrive at Adair's door. I have to lead these teens to Gaia's Gardens. Since the wounded are all reasonably healed, we're leaving early tomorrow morning. All except the one with pneumonia and the one with the leg wound. It's a matter of days before the MPs discover Adair's cabin and realize it's a likely hide out. Do you think you can get Shaun to drive the ones that are too ill to travel to the hospital?"

Dora nodded as with an uneasy feeling, she scanned the trees beyond.

Caellum's extended hand collected tiny crystals on his mittens. "Hopefully, we can trust Dr. Simms. I should be back in a couple of weeks. But for now... "Tell me about our son's first month as we walk toward Cedarhenge."

Nathan waited and brooded as late afternoon cast shadows over the cabin until a man emerged through the front door followed by Dora. But it was more than hard to believe his eyes. It was impossible. Caellum had been hanged in Celebration Park during Freedom Festival. He had witnessed the execution himself. He had memorized that face. Though it made no sense, the man was either Caellum or his double. Dora's arm hooked around his confirmed it was not his double.

In the brief opening of the door Nathan's suspicions were validated as he peered into the brightly lit room, enabling him to see others milling inside. Not just Shaun, Adair and her child. Several people. His hunch had led him to an even greater bonanza than he had anticipated. The students plus a resurrected Caellum Nichols.

This intel would be a real shocker to the governor. Even better, the whole business implicated Dora d'Arc Scholtz. A mine field to be sure. But, if handled with care, one that could bring Nathan public acclaim along with a raise in status and pay. Of course it would be a monumental task to convince Lydia of Dora's guilt. And truth be known, facing her could be as hazardous as sitting in the governor's office. But it had to be done, and as always, he would face his task with courage.

The wind had picked up, confounding his immediate task, so he sneaked as close as he dared to follow within earshot of the pair. But gusts carried away their voices and the bits and pieces he picked up were as sparse as the first flakes of snow.

Caellum's, "You know I would love to be with you and our son," confirmed the explosive truth. *I suspected as much. Their time together at The Garden of the Gods Monument. That's when she conceived. That baby is Caellum Nichols'. Therefore he isn't Imperial Governor Scholtz's grandchild.*

It would be tricky conveying that insight to the governor who at first would call him an imbecile and ridicule him for jumping to such a conclusion. He'd never told the governor three days passed between Dora's departure across the valley and Caellum's approach. But he'd dribble the unbelievable in small palatable sips, beginning with the info that Caellum was alive. The baby's true lineage would be the final gulp. That revelation would come after the governor was forced to credit

Nathan with the most spectacular spy work since the capture and removal of the student insurgents to Onmatson Farm.

The wind blew parts of phrases his way and extracted others. "ZD... no food... too exposed."

So no depositing the targets in the Zone of Destruction. Where then?

"... Gaia's Gardens."

Gaia's Gardens? What or where is that?

"Raymond Muñoz"

Who? Never heard that name.

Dora's muffled words.

Caellum's reply "Can't hang around another week" alerted Nathan to the need to act fast. He followed them past the dirt spirals of Adair's garden to the entrance of Cedarhenge. The last words he heard were "tomorrow morning." The snow was falling fast, and the chimes of Cedarhenge conspired with the wind to cover the suspects' remaining conversation, which had become sparse, as they kissed and held tight to one another until a heavy curtain of snow hid them from view. But Nathan had seen and heard enough.

He cut through the forest and rode home beside himself with glee. He'd found not only the escaped vandals, but also a very alive and well Caellum Nichols. And he knew where the suspects were headed. He could hardly wait to see the astonishment on Scholtz's face. This event could yield accolades beyond his wildest dreams.

Second thoughts crowded in. But not if he reported to the governor this very night and the military police arrested them in the morning. Sure, he'd be credited with the discovery. But to Scholtz he'd be doing his job, nothing extraordinary. Recognition of himself as the one who found an alive and well Caellum Nichols would fade into the background. The military was sure to get the credit, and his chance of fame and glory would implode—again.

Nathan had forfeited the opportunity of a lifetime over a year ago, when he flew over Three Mountains. As he circled with Charles Scholtz in the passenger seat, he knew his supreme moment approached. He knew the holographic forest engineered to hide the valley was in operation. He knew discovering the location of that valley and its occupants was Scholtz's foremost goal.

But above the valley, at the summit of Blue Lake Mountain, stood Matoskah, the only one of the whole group that called him 'friend'—Matoskah, who had saved his life. The old man's wave diverted him from his mission. If only he, Nathan Abelt the spy, had said to Scholtz, "See that forest? It's a holograph, and we're about to fly right through it." Thanks to him, the governor could have captured the runner most despised by both of them—Eena. And he would have received full credit for the bust. If only he had ignored Matoskah and revealed the truth then, he would have earned the governor's admiration and be treated with respect now.

Well, I'm not throwing this opportunity away. This explosive intel, the location of the arsons and Caellum alive and well, could offer me the fame I deserve. Instead of allowing Scholtz to send the MPs first, what if I track the fugitives to this place, Gaia's Gardens? What if I inform the governor of its location? What if I catch Raymond Muñoz harboring enemies of the state? Then Scholtz will add to my list of credits, the apprehension of the head of Gaia's Gardens. Second chances are hard to come by. And this is mine.

Visitations   27

When Nathan reached home that evening, he removed his coat, but not the pressures of work. Though he usually welcomed the role switch from spy to family man, he hardly responded to the kids and even Lydia.

"Sorry, the smell of your baked fish is wonderful, but I just can't eat."

"Are you alright, dear?"

He had to carefully downplay his current state of agitation. Anything negative or stressful about his work had become Lydia's segue to protest yet another aspect of his work. "I may eat later, honey. Just need to finish some paperwork." After delivering a peck on her cheek he quickly detoured to his office and closed the door. Steering this event to his advantage required strategic planning.

Two hours later, Lydia entered. "You need to eat and come to bed, dear. You're not the slave of the SEI."

"Be right there." He had to think this through with clarity.

He finally crawled in beside Lydia, but being in bed didn't equate sleep. An hour before dawn, after hours of tossing and imagining scenarios, he filled a backpack including a rain slicker and radioed the driver.

The car reached the forest enclosing Adair's cabin at sunrise and just in time for Nathan to see the last of the group exit the cabin. Following them through open snow-covered fields would be tricky because he was highly visible, which necessitated he hang back sufficiently not to be seen and yet keep them in view.

Flanked by mountains to the west and the Zone of Destruction to the east, they had covered about 10 miles, when the thunderstorm rolled in. As heavy raindrops spattered the snow, they ducked into a farmhouse on the outskirts of the ZD. Nathan blew on his gloved hands and longingly watched the interior glow from the fireplace. The nearby barn offered the only other shelter from the rain, but scant relief from the bitter cold. Careful to remain out of sight, he gathered wet grass and sage branches outside, and inside found a loose wooden rail that was six feet long. He ripped it away, but it was too strong to break and he had no means to chop it in half, so for three nerve-wracking hours he watched the entire plank burn. He climbed the loft in hopes of finding hay to sleep in, but it had mostly turned to dust, which he formed in small piles around himself for meager warmth. The cold intensified through the night until his shaking body made sleep impossible. So he descended to the ground and with shaking hands swept together bits of charred wood and dragged more planks to the pile to start another fire.

Shivering he stared into the flames until a voice startled him. "Nathan, that's a hazardous line of work you've chosen."

Instantly he recognized the voice and the man beside him. "M-M-Matoskah, how'd you ever f-f-find me?"

"You called me."

"B-b-but that's absurd. I didn't call you. Even if I did, you c-c-couldn't p-p-possibly hear me."

"You asked for my blanket. Here, wear this."

When the old man wrapped his blanket around Nathan's shoulders, the weight of it was proof that he wasn't dreaming. Blissful warmth spread around and through him until it cocooned him from his neck to his folded knees, and his trembling ceased. Nathan gripped the edges that overlapped at his chest, forming a wool tent that enclosed the fire at its core—himself. He glanced toward the stoic profile of the benefactor wearing neither coat nor blanket. "Aren't *you* cold?"

"No. I'm beyond that now."

"None of this makes sense. If you're really here, then why?"

"In response to a call from a friend."

"You said that to me once before."

"When I found you on that foolish trek with the rascal that betrayed you."

Certain he was delirious from the cold, Nathan pulled the blanket up to his head. As the image of his delirium poked the fire, he muttered. "I could have died out there."

"Uh-huh. Took us two weeks to hike to Transtopia."

"You disappeared that day, kind-a like you appeared today."

"We each had to attend to our own business."

"You know, I had to report my findings about Three Mountains to Imperial Governor Scholtz."

"Uh-huh. You also protected Three Mountains."

"You mean from discovery by Scholtz when I flew over in the plane?"

"Uh-huh. Part of our friendship pact."

"I took a beating from the imperial governor over that fiasco."

"But he must be a good friend otherwise."

Nathan looked at Matoskah like he was crazy. "Why would you say that?"

"Because you continue to share his camp."

"There you go again speaking in riddles. Grandfather, why are you here really?"

"You and I move together through this dance of life." The native elder pulled out a braid of sweet grass and touched it to the fire until the ends glowed, and it began to smoke. "You and Scholtz and I are like this braid.

"It's caught fire."

"Exactly. Gesturing with his hand Grandfather brushed the fragrant smoke over himself and Nathan. "We're bound up together until we catch fire and free our spirits...Now lie down and sleep warm for a few hours. I'll tend the fire."

"I must be dreaming anyway." Obediently, Nathan lay down while something more than Grandfather's blanket covered him, made him feel safe. He blinked a few times observing the play of fire light on his strait-backed companion before, sheltered from the reach of the frigid night air, he slept."

When Nathan awakened at dawn, fingers of cold penetrated his coat, and he swept together pieces of unburnt wood to start another fire. *The dream.* While thawing the biscuit that was breakfast, he ruminated on hours spent in the company of that superstitious old Indian—times he felt safe to be himself. Nostalgia for the one person that called him 'friend' warmed him until the sounds of the suspects' departure for Gaia's Gardens dowsed his reverie. He kicked dirt over the embers, snuffed out last night's memories, and stepped out of the barn and into his role.

To the west the gray December clouds flashed with lightning as the copter flew Raymond and the boxes of produce past Gaia's Gardens headed for New Denver. Minutes later they sank toward the cracked asphalt beneath the inscrutable stare of Anubis, guardian of Biate's stronghold and the underworld, about which rumors flew prior to Solar Flash, and from which, of the royal family, she alone had emerged.

As Raymond followed his host, the grins of stone gargoyles mocked his passage until he reached the double doors that opened to the room with the throne that, minus its queen, flaunted gold leaf trim bordering plush white leather. His guide led him through another set of double doors to the dining room, the windowless center of the palatial complex. Biate entered from a second door and, after polite greetings and a perfunctory nod of her visitor's head, approached the dining table, which was long enough to seat two-dozen, but set with place settings for two. As the waiter seated her at the head of the table, she gestured toward the chair to her right.

While a servant poured Raymond's wine, another lifted the silver lid that covered the serving tray on the teakwood butler, and the aromas of the commandeered produce from Gaia's Gardens escaped—a reminder of the winter storage, which the airlifts to New Denver would deplete before spring.

The all too familiar sense of dread accompanied this command appearance and even though the venereal disease ruse spared Raymond from sharing Biate's bed, he had learned to steel himself for the unexpected. But insight into the schemes brewing in the not-quite-right mind of this woman with the pretentious title and five hundred SuperRos was vital to his town's survival. Additionally, knowledge of the location of and access to the central A.I. that controlled the SuperRos, was his best hope to forestall an invasion, against which his town would be helpless.

As the waiter filled Raymond's plate, the fragrant freshness of the roast chicken, with green peas, and rosemary potatoes grown in nutrient rich soil at Gaia's Gardens, teased his nostrils. He waited until their forks had effortlessly speared the tender flesh and they had savored their first bites, to broach a question that had been brewing for the past weeks. "So, Biate, there must have been many more people underground with you."

"Oh yes, over two hundred thousand citizens received tickets to our underground city."

"Yet, only a handful has survived here with you."

Biate emptied her wine glass and signaled the waiter to fill a second. "Organizing the transfer of two hundred thousand people plus vehicles, food storage, electronics and other equipment is a huge undertaking. Since we were below the Denver Airport, my father, receiving reports that gangs of thugs survived in Denver, determined to make this building his headquarters. He sent crews to renovate this wing of the airport, and turn it into this palace with plans in due time to mobilize the SuperRo force to invade and capture Denver, followed by Colorado Springs to the south, Fort Collins to the north and every town in between. His main concern being the advantage of invasive forces on the surface, he counted on the activated SuperRos to be the unstoppable division of his military might.

"In phase one he commissioned soldiers and workers to restore running water and electricity to this section of the airport and began sending ahead portions of the food storage. In phase two he ordered installation of the science lab topside for the maintenance and continued design and manufacture of SuperRos."

"So, your Majesty," Raymond's throat constricted as it did each time he forced his lips to pronounce that title, "how is it that you are the only royal topside? Are the others still to come?" A queasy feeling in his stomach anticipated her response.

With slow deliberation Biate chewed a forkful of potatoes as though savoring her next revelations. "When the desired construction of this," she gestured indicating her palatial residence, "neared completion, scouts informed my father that we could safely return to the surface. It was agreed that the majority of the submerged population would continue to live in Hades until Denver had been secured and prepared for occupation."

In the silence that followed until their plates were cleared, Raymond barely tasted the last of his food. And Biate's suggestion to retire to the veranda while they enjoyed the bowls of baked apple cinnamon prolonged his suspense.

As they approached the patio where they had stood at opposite corners the month before, pelting rain blown by a fierce wind forestalled opening the glass doors. Surprise halted Raymond's steps, not because of the storm, but because unlike his home in which the sound of rain pelting the roof of corrugated aluminum interrupted conversations, and windows framed dramatic displays of Earth and sky, the walled-in dining room in the center of the palace had completely isolated the pair from Earth's change of mood and her dramatic displays.

Lightning flashed in the distance seconds before Biate's voice overspoke the subsequent rattles of the glass. "After a year of living underground like moles, I longed to return to the surface. But surprisingly, when that time came, depression haunted me. There was really nothing to look forward to. I would simply continue my persona non-grata existence, avoiding both my father's wrath and his advances, while my mother lavished attention on Herman, by then a toddler.

"I began to scheme how to get away from my parents. But to where? Was I willing to forfeit my royal stature to live among the workers? In an ironic twist of fate, my father, who had withheld his love, handed me the knowledge I needed to once and for all escape him and his abuse. My dad, lubricated by a few drinks, revealed not only the secret location but also the means of coded access to the central AI."

Poised at the edge of attaining vital Intel that at some future date could afford Gaia's Gardens a powerful advantage, Raymond waited, his stillness charged with anticipation. His spoon, balanced between his thumb and forefinger, hung motionless over his bowl as he watched Biate empty her third glass of wine

Biate paused, her cheeks flushed, lips wet from the last swig. An impish smile accompanying her sidelong gaze indicated her delight in her listener's suspense. "But that location and access code you will never know."

Miles from the verdant landscape Raymond had wrested from drought ridden land; from the desert willows that shaded his walks, and the mesquite-scented breezes that quieted his soul, he felt dwarfed in the high ceilinged room; emasculated by the seven foot mechanical man that loomed behind Biate's evasion. But his sinking sense of despair was jolted to high alert with her next words.

"I intended to be absolutely in control topside. So, as a crew remodeled this area of the airport for occupation by my family and our servants, secretaries and aides, I proceeded with plans of my own. I knew of two points of access to topside: one of which was a mile away, and the other, the elevator shaft hidden in this airport. After my father deemed the above ground infrastructure sufficiently in place, including this palatial home I now live in, I schemed to accomplish my coup d'état in a single night. I didn't trust the military, which he had alerted of an imminent move—I was doubtful of retaining their loyalty and feared a topside revolt. So I decided to leave them to their fate along with the others.

"While my father slept a sleep from which he would not awaken, I secured the central A.I. Most of the underground city slept in a section removed from the hub of storage depots and military and robotic activity. I activated three SuperRos, and with them approached the soldiers that guarded access to the explosives. In surprise attacks, the Robots murdered them, plus the remaining troops on night duty, and collected the explosives. I singled out twenty people to serve my immediate household escorted by two SuperRos up the elevator. Two more explosives-toting robots followed them up the elevator. I retained seventy-five additional robots to leave by way of the elevators with carts loaded with the food supply that lasted us until now. Finally, I activated another pair of SuperRos to retrieve additional explosives and as part of the remaining four hundred and twenty-five SuperRos to march five abreast through the corridor leading to the rear exit which is a mile northwest of the main airport. As soon as we were topside, I ordered the simultaneous demolition of the elevator shafts from the main airport and the exit point one a mile away. Both are now buried beneath several tons of earth and concrete.

"Leaving two-hundred thousand citizens plus the military personnel behind?" The incongruous urge to wash his hands accompanied Raymond's grasp of the horror of Biate's memoir,

"Yes, basically entombing them with my family." She signaled with her glass for a refill.

"Do you think they are still alive down there?"

"Oh no, they are cut off from air and by now would have run out of food."

"I'm curious as to why you have not invaded Gaia's Gardens, Denver and Transtopia Metro yet."

Against the backdrop of lead gray clouds Biate lifted her glass and as she swirled the wine, light from the chandelier turned the elixir blood red. "Oh, but in my way I have. Denver is most certainly my territory, though I have no intention of residing in that lawless frontier. Likewise,

I claim rulership of Gaia's Gardens and have taxed you in the form of produce. As for Transtopia, in time that city's military will help subdue Denver, and a population of relocated workers will occupy it. But first I must pay a visit to that synthetic buffoon, Scholtz. If he does not agree to form an alliance rendering Transtopia a satellite of New Denver, then, thanks to a SuperRo invasion, the people of Transtopia will soon pay homage to Biate, Queen of Sector Ten.

Arrivals   28

Glad to be back home, the command visit with Biate concluded, Raymond knew that his next visit would be a challenge at best, because New Denver's next food delivery would be a fraction of today's. He kept meticulous track of the town's food storage, a growing proportion of which was potatoes. The numbers didn't lie. The town was running out of winter storage. Feeding the town and Biate's group until the next harvest, which was six months away, would soon become impossible. With the rapid depletion caused by shipments to New Denver, he estimated that by April hunger pangs would plague the residents.

Two weeks ago he had called an emergency town meeting about growing food in the middle of winter to feed the people until mid-June. The following day he and several others headed out with landscaping wagons to find wood and translucent covers for green houses in and around the ZD. A week-long search had yielded the remains of several small greenhouses at neighboring farmsteads, most dismantled, the bits of plexi-glass and corrugated plastic flung about by high winds. After several trips to gather, dismantle, and load materials on the wagons they possessed sufficient materials to begin building the first of the three greenhouses. While foraging for every nail, screw and bolt continued, another crew had already begun construction. The final excursions were to seek and find wood stoves and/or **chimeas** to heat the greenhouses once they were completed. To have begun potting seeds a month ago would have been none too soon.

The rain had stopped when a knock at the door diverted Raymond pouring over his ledger. *It's early in the morning for someone to be knocking at my door.* Feeling a little irritated he put down his pencil and opened the door to a man who looked vaguely familiar.

"Raymond, I hope you remember me. Caellum Nichols."

Processing his surprise he stared for a moment before extending his hand. "Of course. Good to see you, Caellum." He noted the youths crowded on his porch behind Caellum and nodded.

Caellum introduced the others. "I'm sorry to bother you. We have a situation of some urgency."

Raymond welcomed them inside while his gut protested the entrance of a life-threatening dilemma just turned nightmare.

Nathan lowered his binoculars. *A spy's dream.* This bonanza was well-worth the hardship he had endured. Caellum and Raymond—one, a fugitive presumed dead, the other giving aid to the Onmatson Farm arsons. With no time to lose, Nathan circled the town until south of it located the single cleared road in the ZD, which led south to the Imperial Governor's office.

By mid-morning his anticipation was almost as unbearable as last night's bitter cold as he waited until the receptionist opened the door and he seated himself facing the imposing desk, the imperial governor and the crossed swords on the wall that extended like silver horns over Scholtz's head.

Nathan leaned forward, his gaze intense, fingers clasped atop the shining surface as though to convey the solemn weight of his intel. "There is a settlement called Gaia's Gardens at the far end of the ZD."

Scholtz eyed Nathan coldly. "You imbecile. I have full knowledge of that settlement and consider it to be already annexed into Transtopia. Do you not remember the Military Police and Zombie fiasco?"

With an emotional thud Nathan's first announcement plummeted. That explained the cleared road. "I know the prisoners were returned to the ZD. But I'm here to tell you that the students have escaped to that same location."

"Where?"

"Gaia's Gardens. Small settlement of around three hundred people."

"Do you know this for certain?"

"I followed them there."

Scholtz leaned forward. "But the students couldn't have known about that location."

"Caellum Nichols did and does."

Scholtz simply stared. "You mean *knew*."

"I mean *knows*."

"I watched him hang."

"So did I. Whoever or whatever hanged in his stead, he's alive and well."

Scholtz called for his secretary. "Get Captain Starkey right away."

Once Caellum and the students were seated around the living room, Caellum's announcement, "These people need asylum," confirmed the sense of dread in Raymond's gut.

Raymond slowly scanned the newcomers. While he couldn't turn these people away, a dozen additional mouths to feed had just been added to his worries. "From who? And why?"

"From Transtopia Metro military police. For arson. For burning down the barracks at Onmatson Farm."

Raymond, who seldom cussed, inwardly cursed the situation that endangered his family and town.

After the group brainstormed through the lunch hour, unwashed dishes remained on the table and they pulled the chairs around the sofa and chairs in the living area. Silent expectancy followed the scrapes and shifts as Raymond shook his head. *As though a dozen additional mouths to feed weren't bad enough, we're being asked to harbor fugitives from the law.* "I just don't know a place to hide all of you in this town. I do know of a couple of farms about 5 miles from here. I stayed with an older couple and their dog a few months back. They can help you scatter among neighboring farms."

"To be stuck there indefinitely?"

Caellum nodded. "Safe havens while we figure out the next phase of the Sovereignty movement."

No one made a move to leave as they chewed on that possibility a while longer.

"Listen. We're short on food as it is. And we're all likely to be hauled in when soldiers arrive. I ask you to at least try to find some local farms. Why don't you stay tonight and head out in the morning."

Caellum nodded. "I agree with Raymond. That's our best plan."

The rubble mound a hundred yards south of the far edge of Gaia's Gardens, the one which, close to a year ago the child had climbed to catch sight of the MPs herding townspeople to Transtopia, had become a favorite play area of the kids. A place to play King of the Mountain, races to the top over sharp edges from bricks and mortar often resulted in scrapes and bruises.

It also remained the best lookout near the cleared road between Transtopia and the town. Jeffrey, the most recent winner of the King of the Mountain title, was vigorously defending his turf from interlopers when the approach of soldiers caught his attention. Cora's shove almost toppled him, but met little resistance. Ignoring her look of surprise and her loudly proclaimed victory, he scrambled down Rubble Mountain and ran toward the town.

The boy arrived gasping for breath at Raymond's door. "Soldiers are coming."

The scrape of chairs accompanied the impressions colliding in Raymond's brain as he faced the panicked expressions on the faces of the now standing group. Elise flew into motion, scraped bits food left on their plates into a slop bucket and rushed outdoors to feed the pig.

"Any place we can hide?"

"They'll search every closet, every corner until they find you."

"Then we better head out now."

"Too open. Just scrub out there. You'd be easily spotted with binoculars."

"We have to do something fast."

"For starters, fold up your sleeping bags, and take your gear to the back door."

Plates clattered as Elise and Raymond hurriedly washed, dried and put them away while the students and Caellum hoisted their gear.

Raymond faced them, his brain racing. "The only way I can think of is to hide you in plain sight."

"If the soldiers are from Onmatson, we might be recognized."

"Keep busy. Keep your heads down and pray these troops were stationed in the city—not the farm."

Raymond ran to his closet and collected several hats from the shelf. "Just for good measure, Put these on." To a couple more, he gave pairs of reading glasses, and to those remaining, "keep your hoods up."

He looked at Renae, her face framed by long hair. She began pulling a section over her eyes. "Got scissors?"

"Yes." When he returned with the scissors, she finger combed the forward section and sliced bangs hanging to her eyes.

As Elise swept up the clump of hair on the floor, Raymond headed for the back door. "Follow me to the root cellar."

At Raymond's shoulder Caellum spoke quietly. "I'm sure to be recognized."

"Even though you're supposed to be dead?"

"Too great a risk. My presence will endanger the whole group."

Possible places to hide Caellum circled in Raymond's brain as he opened the cellar door and signaled students to pass him the gear, which he shuffled under the piled burlap bags of potatoes covering the floor. After a final glance to ascertain that the packs were well hidden, he closed the door behind him, and addressed the youths, "Wait here." Then to Caellum, "Follow me."

He hurried toward a bale of hay in the chicken yard and grabbed an armful. "Climb into the coop."

Caellum looked at the small structure on posts that elevated it above the ground. "Is it big enough?"

"Barely."

"Will it hold my weight?"

"Yes. Get in."

After Raymond had stuffed hay in front of Caellum until only a yellow mound was visible at the rear of the coop he grabbed a couple of hammers, ran back to the students and motioned for them to follow him. "The townspeople are gathered just ahead to build green houses. Scatter among them."

After the anticipated gasps and protests, he continued. "Pull your hat bills down, get to work, and look as inconspicuous as possible."

"Doing what?"

"Push wheelbarrows. Haul lumber. Hammer. Dig postholes, whatever."

As they reached the construction site, Elise carrying Gabe hurried toward them. "They're close." The students looked frozen with fear. Raymond extended the two hammers. "You and you, take these. You, grab that wheelbarrow. You two, grab some wood from that pile of lumber. You, take the shovel leaning against that corner post. Keep your eyes covered with those bangs." And to the group, "Don't run. But scatter and get lost among the people. Look busy."

"Elise, let's spread the word to give them work."

As Elise hurried away, Raymond likewise melted into the construction crew, garnering seconds to concoct a story. From the corner of his eye he saw an officer approach the closest woman. "I'm looking for Raymond Muñoz."

Raymond stood up, sucked in a deep breath, and approached him. "I'm Raymond Muñoz."

"I'm Lieutenant Yanniv Lebedev. My troops and I are trailing a group of fugitives from justice. You may have seen them?"

"Yes."

"They're in serious trouble for destruction of government property. If you will tell me where they are, we won't have to search the houses."

"A few hours ago, I sent them on their way.

"Headed in which direction?"

"North."

"I'm sure you understand, Mr. Muñoz, we have to search every inch of this town before we head out."

"See these greenhouses we're building? We don't have enough food to feed our current population through the winter, let alone a group of runaways."

"Are you quite sure you can't direct us to their destination?"

"Like I said, they were heading north. Could be anywhere by now."

"It's a shame you can't be more specific. Now, before we search every nook and cranny in this town, I should warn you. It will go very badly for you and all of Gaia's Gardens if we discover you are aiding and abetting a group of arsons."

As Raymond returned the lieutenant's stare, he made his expression inscrutable. He was glad only he could hear the pounding of his heart.

"As we search in and around Gaia's Gardens, the town will serve as our base. Of necessity the residents will house our men while we search for the suspects. You won't mind if your house is my headquarters will you?"

"As a matter of fact, I do. Surely, you have brought along tents to house your men and yourself."

"As matter of fact we have not, as we intend to conclude our mission quickly."

"Our food storage is seriously depleted."

"We brought a week's supply. Let's hope for a speedy capture of the criminals."

"I repeat. We will very much resent your invasion of our homes."

"And I do apologize for the inconvenience, Mr. Muñoz. Perhaps if you rethink the situation, you will give us better assistance. The sooner we find those responsible for the destruction of government property, the sooner we will be gone. Raymond, I think you know where they are. I think we could be gone today, if you make the wise choice to help the government of Sector 10." He looked pointedly at Raymond. "Which would be far better for you than landing in prison and facing execution with them."

Raymond felt Elise beside him with Gabe in her arms. "Is there a problem?"

"My wife, Elise."

"Lieutenant Lebedev. Glad to meet you, ma'am. Apparently, you are already aware of the runaways. I was about to inform your husband of a factor which adds to the urgency of our search. It seems a convicted felon is leading the fugitives."

Lieutenant Lebedev paused as though expecting a response. As Gabe prattled and wriggled in his mother's arms, both parents faced the officer with blank expressions.

The officer scrutinized their faces as he continued. "The hanged criminal Caellum Nichols is reportedly resurrected and helping the fugitives."

"That doesn't make sense."

"I admit it's a mystery. But it's true, none the less, and we *will* find him."

Gave wriggled out of his mother's arms, slid toward the ground and started pulling on her hand. "Mamma, come."

Elise, her hair an unruly torrent and her face smudged with dirt, stood a head shorter than the officer and faced him with a defiant glint in her eye. "Search our town, if you must. But the best outcome would be for the military to capture the *real* criminals in this fiasco. The ones responsible for college students, Transtopia's future, becoming prison camp laborers and hunted fugitives."

"I beg your pardon, ma'am?"

"You heard me."

The eyes that were scanning Elise, shifted without blinking to her husband. "Muñoz, I like you and your pretty wife and little boy here. It's for that reason I choose to ignore the treasonous implications of your wife's statement. One last time, I remind you that your cooperation is vital for all concerned. I'm giving you one more chance to tell me if you are hiding the suspects. I would hate for anything to happen to you and your family."

Preparations **29**

Suddenly, Jack felt overwhelmed. Randolph's information download had become overload, and he felt restless.

Randolph seemed to sense Jack's need for a break. "Before it gets dark, let's take a stroll outside to stretch our legs."

As they circled the leveled area with a few out buildings, it was the hangar that drew Jack's attention. "I'm curious about what's in the hangar."

"Soon. I haven't finished preparing you for what you'll see. For now, join me on my favorite path."

As they strolled a narrow path winding through the foothills of Mt Jebel Yagour, Randolph resumed his narration. ""I was overjoyed when Carr asked me and two other crewmembers to test pilot a 45 ft. craft named the OTC-Z1. We got on board, and positioned ourselves around a large crystal ball in the center of the craft. A laser shined a white light through the crystal, which splayed a rainbow across the interior.

"As we waited, eager to pilot the OTC-Z1, Carr instructed us. 'I'm telling you ahead of time, your brain won't comprehend what's happening. So go to your higher mind. Reach into your heart and focus on aquamarine—the color key to your destination.

"Carr exited the craft before giving us final instructions. 'When you're ten miles down range, get out of the ship. Pick up rocks, sticks and grass, and put in them in your pocket, because you're not going to remember.'

"The door closed. We waited for the thing to move. Nothing happened. The door opened. We filed out, disappointed that the experiment didn't work."

Jack recalled his own experience. "Like me."

Randolph nodded. "Carr just looked at us and said, 'Reach into your pockets.' We pulled out all this debris, proof we had been somewhere. But we had no memory of leaving the craft, let alone picking up sticks and stones. Only months later did fragmentary recall begin.

The invigorating coolness of the morning air nudged a brisk walk as Jack processed yesterday's information download. He probed for more information. "So you had actually piloted the craft?"

"Yes, we were surprised to learn we could target a landing spot by mental resonance..." Randolph paused as though to let that sink in.

Jack stopped in his tracks. *Just intend it.*

Drawn further into the scented realm of cypress and saffron, the pair paused to listen as birds alerted others of their tree real estate.

"Also Carr taught us the resonance varies between locations on the planet. Accompanying him to areas within a few miles of the lab, we used a spectrometer to ascertain local resonances. On the color spectrum one locale might register orange-red, another, yellow-green and so on.

"Carr taught us to meditate so as to quiet our brains, in order to access our minds.

"Aren't they the same thing?"

"The mind is the non-physical intelligence that communicates with the brain. The brain is an interface that transmits information between the body and mind. Carr helped us understand that to pilot the craft we had to align the mind/body/brain with the pervasive flow of energy—the spiraling conveyance of galaxies, planets and craft alike through space. We learned to mentally tap the potentials of natural law."

From its mountain willow perch a cream-colored lark with a black striped wing swooped down to a grab its morning repast. When the trees glowed the last of the evening light, Jack contemplated his place in the strangeness of this world apart, yet entangled with his own. "So Carr distinguished the mind from the brain."

"In Carr's words, 'the brain is just there to operate your body. Unless the brain is in touch with the higher mind, it doesn't comprehend what's going on.'"

"But what was the function of the large crystal?"

"To exude frequencies in resonance with our destination."

As the walkers' circular path returned them to the complex, the sun exited the sky with fanfare, casting in its wake a profusion of red and gold. When they stepped into the clearing, Jack recalled the crystal in the small ship that had transported him here "So, the ship flies to a destination response to the pilot's intention."

"Yes." Randolph's eyes moved sideways as he accessed more memories. "As avidly as the crew listened to Carr, the gate-keepers of the status quo thwarted public access to his invention. The Patent Office refused to give Carr a patent for a levitating flight vehicle, acknowledging his invention only as a carnival ride.

"So, the elite group you've often referred to even controls the patent office?"

"Remember the key to the elite stranglehold is information-blocking tentacles.

In the fading light the enigmatic hangar teased Jack's longing to see inside.

But once again Randolph said the dreaded word, "Soon."

"Jack, let's grab our coffee and a biscuit and head out."

Once again Jack's anticipation mounted as he followed Randolph up the stairs.

But again they skirted the padlocked hangar to cross a meadow of grass and dried up wildflowers headed toward a cliff in the mountain complex.

Among several burning questions Jack voiced the one that had plagued his since the headed across Morocco to meet with Randolph Ring. "Randolph, please explain how you can be here with me today."

"What do you mean, Jack."

"I mean, though you don't appear to be over a hundred years old, you must be."

"Oh, that."

"Randolph, just answer the question."

"I flew here."

Jack stopped, and grabbed Randolph's arm. " We're not discussing distance. We're discussing time."

"Remember, I told you the OTC Z1 traverses fourth dimension?"

"Yes."

"You might say time is stretched in third dimension. Stretched time allows us to experience our adventures in 3D."

"Okay. But you still haven't answered my question."

"An instant's flight in 4D in the OTC Z1 brought Marsha and me ahead in 3D time. To this time."

"But why?"

"Honestly, I'm not sure I entirely understand. However, I'm told this meeting is part of an event string connecting Tesla, Otis Carr, Marsha and myself, and you." Randolph paused as Jack silently processed.

"I'm told we're connected to a momentous event in the history of humanity."

"What kind of event?"

"Sorry, I don't know the specifics. I just know if this achievement on behalf of the human race is to happen in this century, our participation is crucial."

"So you time traveled. That's why you don't look incredibly old."

Randolph resumed walking and Jack followed him to the foot of a cliff. Chins raised, they stared at the top.

"About a thousand feet high I'd say," Randolph mused, "like the one I'm about to tell you about."

Jack stifled his groaned disinterest in a geology lesson.

"As an engineer I've learned about interesting phenomena connected to acoustics."

Summoning enthusiasm for any lesson was impossible when all Jack wanted was to see what was in that hanger.

"Now Jack, I want you to imagine a large rock between us that's about waist high. Then, with our backs to the cliff, imagine a semi-circle of drummers and horn players facing us.

"A concert?"

"Instruments played to accomplish the acoustical feat I'm about to tell you about. Let's sit."

"The primary source for what I'm about to tell you is an article named "Lost Techniques" written over seventy years ago by the Swedish civil engineer Henry Kjelson. The author recorded the accounts of a colleague. Dr. Jarl and his flight manager who witnessed a group of Tibetan monks' demonstrate the science of acoustics. By using chants and musical instruments, they combined various vibrations to create a resonant field, which nullified the power of gravity.

"When Dr Jarl, was touring Egypt for the English Scientific Society, a messenger approached him with a request to come to Tibet to greet an old friend, a Tibetan lama. Dr Jarl traveled by plane and Yak caravans to arrive at the monastery where the old Lama and his friend, who was now holding a high position, were living. During Dr. Jarl's stay, among many wonders he witnessed was Tibetan acoustic stone levitation.

One day his friend took him to a sloping meadow, which was bordered on the northwest side by a high cliff. In the rock wall, at a height of about 800 ft. was a large opening to a cave. Monks were lowering themselves by rope to a platform jutting from the cave. On the platform was a partially complete rock wall.

"Centered in the meadow, about 250 meters from the cliff, was a polished slab of rock with a bowl-like cavity in the center. The bowl had a diameter of one meter and a depth of 15 centimeters. Monks used oxen to maneuver a block of stone, one meter wide and one and a half meters long, into the center of the cavity. Imagine that cavity holding the stone block is here, between us, and 800 feet above where we stand is the platform that opens to the cave."

Randolph extended his arm to trace an arc in front of them. "Facing the stone wall, nineteen monks with instruments form a 90° arc with a carefully measured radius of 63 meters. Evenly interspersed between thirteen drummers are six monks holding long trumpet-like instruments called ragdons. Behind them, like spokes in a wheel, two hundred priests, assigned to sing chants, fan outward in straight lines of 8 or 10.

"Are you with me, Jack?"

Jack nodded his engagement with the tale.

"When the stone is in position the monk behind the single small drum gives a signal to begin. The singing and chanting, trumpeting, drumming monks slowly increase the tempo creating a terrible din, above which the very sharp sound of a small drum can be heard.

During the first four minutes nothing happens. But, as the speed of the awful raucous increases, the stone block starts to rock and sway. Suddenly, following a parabolic arc, it takes off into the air with accelerating speed. After three minutes of ascent it lands on the platform at the base of the cave and eight hundred feet above the meadow."

Jack couldn't stop himself. "Wait a minute, that's impossible. It must have been a trick. Something hollow. Papier-mâché to imitate rock."

"Okay let's say it was a trick. So how would you explain levitating lightweight papier-mâché painted to look like a rock to a height of eight hundred feet?"

"Why haven't I heard of this?"

"How often have has British Broadcasting reported the activities of Tibetan monks?"

"Well, never, I guess. But with all due respect, they are spiritual seekers, not scientists."

To Jack's relief, Randolph motioned for them to retrace their steps to his complex.

"By the second decade of this century scientists discovered the physics of sound and light that govern cosmic form and motion from galaxies to quantum particles. They confirmed the ancient science of 'sacred' geometry, which governs the opening of a rose, the beauty of a face, Beethoven's 'Ode to Joy, a galaxy—beauty that inspires a spiritual experience: reverence for life."

Jack shook his head as though to shake away the confusion that overwhelmed him. The information download from Randolph had become overload, and he gazed longingly at the padlock on the hangar door. "Why am I learning about Tibetan monks when all I want is to see what's inside that hangar?"

"Because, in order to operate what's inside that hangar, you have to open your mind to the seemingly impossible, to laws that transcend 3D assumed limitations."

Concluding with the words "Prepare yourself. The next phase of Carr's instructions requires a real stretch in understanding the relationship between physics and our minds."

But Jack didn't hear him because they were headed toward the hangar and the object of Jack's desire.

Snow   30

The next morning, though heat still radiated from the coals in the center of the teepee, Cosima was reluctant to leave the warm covers and enter the frosty December air. To help the transition out of bed she had slept in the two layers she wore beneath the leather dress and coat, which lay under the covers on either side of her. A glance at Grandfather's empty bed promised a pot of hot water for tea was boiling in the kettle over the outside fire, a welcome incentive to dress and head outside.

Passing the circle of stones, she saw that it enclosed a newly drawn symbol, a half sun over a horizon line and three marks below. She would ask Grandfather for an explanation today. When she reached the campfire, the kettle sat near the edge of the grill, not boiling, but steaming hot. But Grandfather was not around. *Must be fishing*. She sprinkled sage in her cup; then poured the water. *Thank you, Grandfather.*

As she stirred her tea in the silence pervading grandfather's camp, a snowflake drifted toward the toe of her shoe and she raised her face to catch more flakes. The cloud cover released a gentle barrage of crystals, yet neither wind nor crow nor birdsong announced the soundless accumulation of winter white that soon covered the ground and veiled her solitude. The flames sputtered and almost died before she threw on a fresh log to keep the fire going to warm Grandfather's return.

After a few sips of tea, she carried her cup to the drying shed, took down an Echinacea stem and using the mortar and pestle crushed the remaining dried flowers. Between glances beyond the door, the number of filled herb pouches grew to completion until finally, pestle in hand she walked to the entrance and glimpsed movement between the trees on the path to the fishing hole. She paused, looking for the familiar bowed legs and red bandanna until the passage of a deer, jolted her vague unease to insistent alarm. She returned the pestle to the bowl and hurried into the tent, glad she had brought along thick socks and hiking boots.

When she reached the fishing pond, the diminutive waterfall that fed it gurgled the familiar greeting to no one but her. The fishing pole leaning against the tree and the empty bucket beside it added a mute reiteration that this morning grandfather had not come to fish. Her call to him sounded loud in the forest of quietly falling snow while her gut screamed that something was wrong.

In ever widening circles Cosima made her way up the mountainside to the ledge where two years ago the grizzly had sent the rover to his death. Who could say whether the entwined events, the entrance of the grizzly and the rover's pursuit, had culminated in doom or relief to a tortured soul? She recalled her psychic image of the soul that evaded the body's impact fifty feet below, and the motherly face that smiled and embraced the child that had been brutally ripped from her arms. That day Cosima's second sight clarified the outcome, but today fear muddled her second sight while hastening her search.

She fell on the ledge, made slippery by ice particles melting on the sun-warmed granite, but the thought of grandfather's broken body far below compelled her to crawl to the edge. But layered pine boughs hid any evidence of a fall, so she circumvented the stone promontory to descend to its base. Grabbing hold of branches and tree trunks, she braced herself for the worst as she slid and stumbled downward. And when the ground below the protruding granite yielded no body, she sat, oblivious of the wetness of the snow while a mixture of relief and dismay drove her tears.

When the sobs became less insistent, she resumed calling and listening for replies that never came as she wound her way down the slope along the stream that led to the bridge between Adair's old cabin and Grandfather's teepee. At the bridge she recalled her terror the time Valek, a half-grown wolf pup, ran away and enraged the momma bear by barking and darting back and forth in front of her, until she rose up to seven foot majesty.

Grandfather had appeared out of nowhere, and Mato went down on all fours to focus her outrage on him. But that old man who knew bear-talk, faced down the bear without looking into to her eyes. And after head swings, stiffened leg stomps and indignant *humphs*, Mato must have decided she had made her point. She backed away from the unyielding human who somehow managed to look bigger than a four hundred pound bear.

Grandfather had taught Cosima much about the steadfast stance of one's larger self, and she called on that instruction now as her larger, braver self carried her to where she least wanted to go — into the military settlement.

As the soldiers led her to the captain, the last person she expected to see was Emory. Her brain struggling to grasp what her eyes revealed, she dragged her gaze from him to the speaker.

"Ma'am, where have you come from? We've been all over these mountains, and that old Indian is the only one that lives here."

Uncertain how to answer, she remained silent. *Of course, I have to account for my presence here. Why didn't I think of that?*

"Did you come through the same portal as this soldier?"

Startled, she glanced past the officer. Standing in the background among three others in uniform, Emory had nothing to say while his eyes pleaded with hers. But an interior warning nudged her to veil both confusion and recognition. The urgency to find Grandfather, who might be dying in the snow somewhere left no time to contemplate the extent of Emory's betrayal or suffer the loss of him.

"I'm from a far distance."

The Captain sized her up. "Others must have accompanied you."

"I came alone to see Grandfather. He's missing. It's freezing and snowing. Please, help me find him."

"You must mean Matoskah. We know the old Indian very well." He turned toward the soldiers and barked a command. "Gather enough for four search parties of three men each. Carry medical supplies and stretchers. Fan out from the base of Roosevelt Mountain and spread to Lincoln and Kennedy. We only have about three hours of daylight left. Move out."

The captain called her into his tent and offered a rare treat, steaming hot chocolate.

"Now, ma'am, I know that you are worried about that old man. We're fond of him too, and we're doing our best to find him. But in return I need assistance from you. Once again, where did you come from?"

"As I said from a place far beyond these mountains."

"From what direction."

She grappled with how to tell the truth while evading his question. "I came to Three Mountains from Township 21."

His expression was incredulous. "Without retrievers catching you?"

"I was almost captured. But a wolf saved me."

"Your pet?"

"No."

Over the captain's head his forefinger traced a loop in the air "So you call these Three Mountains?"

"Yes, Blue Lake, Quartz and Thunderbird." She pointed to each.

"You're not a Native American. What is that old man to you?"

"He's my teacher. I assist him while he teaches me."

"On that mountain, I believe the one you call Blue Lake Mountain, we just found one of our soldiers. Been missing for month. Found him less than an hour ago. Says he came through a portal."

"A portal?" A fresh wave of heartache assailed Cosima. Under the officer's scrutiny, heat burned her cheeks.

"We're going to search until we find it."

"Sir, if you don't mind I'm very tired and worried about Grandfather."

"Why do you call him Grandfather?"

"All the people from Three Mountains called him that. We have deep affection for him."

"Where are all those people now?"

"You mean the ones that are living as free individuals someplace beyond your reach?"

"Cosima, we have a job to do. You're too young to understand."

"I learned plenty in the township about the lock down on human rights and dangers of trying to escape those who control."

"The government is concerned about the people who may not know about the protection of the post Solar Flash government."

"Many wish freedom from such protection."

"You're not making sense."

"I'm quite sure you didn't earn your commission with the intent to chase people from their homes.

"We didn't chase the people from Three Mountains from their homes."

'That's true. They spared you that awfulness by leaving first."

"And where did they go?"

"If a friend was hiding from a rabid dog, would you lead the dog to him?'

"Cosima, it's a shame you don't appreciate the military's interest in your security."

In the silence that signaled a dead ended conversation, the Captain turned toward Emory and the remaining soldiers and Cosima went outside to stand on the porch.

Cosima stood on the pavilion porch listening to voices that shouldn't be there.

The surrounding snow covered the areas where at gatherings the musicians had played and the dancers had danced. And over there, the stump that by tacit agreement was Grandfather's seat of honor. And to her right the place where Martha had stabbed Jimmy, the rover determined to marry Cosima. Though kept away from the inebriated rover, she recalled the accounts of Eena's blood-drenched blouse after the rover shot her, and Anaya holding her as the two of them disappeared. When Eena returned from Anaya's mysterious home world, she showed them the scar. It was the size of a freckle.

Then there was the day, when the townspeople heard the airplane circle and thought it was the end of Three Mountains until the pilots landed the augurs and announced that the hologram was working at last and had hid them. Soon after the sound of the engines died away, grandfather came down from Blue Lake Mountain. Though Grandfather never took credit, she knew they had been saved by his friendly wave. Those were good times, those years before the soldiers arrived. She turned her attention to the dialogue on the opposite side of the room. *This heartache is punishment for allowing myself to be seduced.*

"Emory, take us to that portal."

"I'll do my best, sir."

"What do you mean do your best?"

"It was night both when I fell through and when I returned. I had left the main trail.

"And what were you doing up there at night anyway?"

"Looking for a nest of those big birds. I figured nighttime was the time to find the birds nesting."

"And did you find one?"

"No."

"And how was it that you fell through the portal."

"A wolf was about to attack me. I backed up, stumbled and fell into a strange world. Solid stone blocked my return. Yesterday, when I stumbled back to this side, I wasn't looking at the portal. I was hurrying down the mountain. You can imagine how I felt after being exiled for a month."

"Wait a minute. How is it possible that you returned looking as strong and healthy as when you disappeared a month ago."

"There were people in the other world."

She addressed the officer. "I'm going to take a walk in the fresh air." *Away from the stale air of Emory's betrayal*

In the shadow of a lone pine, beside the wall that separated her from Emory, Cosima's spirit pulled away from this man who had insinuated himself into her heart, and from the depths of her isolation she called Grandfather. But the only response was the image of the circle and the gnarled fingers placing the final stone—the stone that signaled a completion: Grandfather's life on Thunderbird Mountain. A sudden awareness burst upon her musings. *The soldiers will never find Grandfather nor his body No one will. He didn't want anyone to weep over his death at his camp or at a funeral. I should have known. That's just his way.*

On the heels of that realization a familiar voice spoke loud and clear. "This is your chance. If you stay you may never escape the army's clutches. Leave. Leave now."

Without a backward glance, she walked off the porch to approach the bridge over Destiny River. In need of support, she clasped the railing as she gazed at Thunderbird Mountain and the fast falling snow blanketed her grief with treasured images: Grandfather—sending the flock of crows to confound the wolf pack's claim on Valek. Grandfather—who welcomed her to Three Mountains and restored her full name because it meant 'harmony.' Grandfather—whose spirit traveled with hers to the Cave of Crystals where Lady Gaia, taught her of Earth's stored memories.

At Grandfather's camp the philosophy of the disappearing opponent disarmed the unarmed insurgents. When his friendly wave turned Nathan Abelt's plane from Three Mountains' holographic forest and their location remained a secret from his passenger, Imperial Governor Charles Scholtz, the opponent did indeed disappear.

At the conclusion of her heart's eulogy, Grandfather's eagle, as though winging a final salute, soared overhead and circled the Lakota Elder's camp, and Cosima knew that she would remain the last person to see her mentor alive. Her heartfelt message, *Our undying gratitude goes with you, Grandfather,* ascended with the eagle to the mountaintop.

Today reminded her of another day when she lost two people close to her; when her mother died and she knew she must leave the township; the day she and Johnny Holcomb clung to one another in heartbreak. Today she lost two people that had become equally dear to her and loneliness penetrating deeper than the cold of this snowbound world froze her heart. Reminiscent of the day she left Township 21, a nudge propelled her to leave.

With the pavilion completely hidden by a wall of white, she hurried up the trail to grandfather's camp in case anyone followed her. Once there she melted into the trees. After waiting several minutes she skirted the path down the mountain, crossed the ravine and reached the bed of quartz crystals where she hid in the trees once more. When she was certain no one was following, she continued up the mountain to the portal.

But she didn't go through right away. First she dragged logs and branches in front of it and left them askew, so that the arched doorway to Mu was less conspicuous. When she had brushed the scraped marks in the ground and backed up covering her tracks with snow, she paused to watch the snowfall continue her work before she climbed over her handiwork, ripping her deerskin skirt in her haste.

Eena was relieved to see Cosima heading toward them.
"We never found Grandfather's body."
"Maybe he's alive."
"He hinted that he would be dying soon. Besides, he has confirmed his presence in the spirit world since then."
Cosima waited until after the memorial to tell the group gathered in the center of town beside the well the second alarming news.

"The soldiers know about the portal."

Stunned silence greeted her disclosure.

Eena was first to speak. "So Emory squealed. Leiani informed us early this morning that he had gone missing. We wondered whether it was to seek you or to snitch."

Cosima felt some responsibility for his leaving. "If I hadn't gone to see Grandfather... it's just that I felt his call."

"It's not your fault, Cosima."

"It's only a matter of time before they show up here, to upset the Augurs and to round up us."

"What can we do?"

"In the middle of December with several feet of snow covering the mountains on the other side of the portal?"

Eena who formulated strategies had none. "All we can do is sit and wait for the soldiers. We are snowbound. All we can do is hunker down for the winter. Let's pray that the volcano doesn't blow while we wait.

"Have you noticed that our sky if often purple due to the increased smoke and activity?"

"It seems we are doomed on all sides."

In Plain Sight

As Raymond put his arm around Elise's shoulder, he could feel her trembling. "Despite your threats, Lieutenant, we stand on our truth. While you invade our homes, we'll construct our greenhouses. Now, if you'll excuse me."

"If you don't mind, I will join you in your labors."

But I do mind. Get out of my sight, out of my town. Raymond released Elise and turned dismissively as the Lieutenant moved to Elise's opposite side. When the threesome reached the work crew, Raymond had no choice but to announce the unwelcome hanger-on. "Hey, everyone, with me is Lieutenant Yanniv Lebedev who has offered to help. Please give him due respect and consideration as his soldiers search your homes for fugitives from Onmatson Farms.

After several charged seconds, all eyes on the new arrival, the pound of a hammer returned everyone's attention to the work at hand.

While bantering and small talk covered people's unease and the students worked in plain sight among people sawing, hauling and hammering, the soldiers, instructed to be respectful of people's belongings, searched every nook and cranny of every house and garden shed. As the frames of the greenhouses took shape, Lieutenant Lebedev introduced himself and his aide to individuals and ingratiated himself by handing them tools and wood and acting as though they should naturally invite his friendly presence. With the lieutenant's arrival a subtle transformation shifted the mood of the construction arena from lighthearted collaboration to uneasy subterfuge. Tense performances by nervous actors covered the battle being waged for human lives, while the newcomer relaxed into playing his most congenial self.

By nightfall as Lieutenant Lebedev irritated Raymond by entertaining Gabe on the living room floor, the soldiers were sharing meals with their host families, well-coached children and a newly adopted oldest son or daughter. The following dawn as parents awakened their children with whispered reminders of the secret they must keep, Raymond stood beside the Lieutenant gazing out the window that overlooked the chicken yard.

The lieutenant broke through the wall of silence. "Last night at dinner your wife spoke eloquently about your dreams for Gaia's Gardens."

"Beyond the sullied reach of the landlords."

"Landlords?"

"The controllers. The ones who invade our sovereign domains with the likes of you."

"You are a bitter man, Raymond."

"Toward Puppet Masters with pretentious titles who send armed puppets. Yes"

"Puppet Masters?"

"Imperial Governor Scholtz, or Queen Biate."

Lebedev chuckled. "A queen on this continent? "

"She resides at New Denver Airport in her refurbished palace. Prepare yourself for a show down with her five hundred robot warriors. Maybe you'll all destroy one another and each other's leaders and the rest of us can create a New Earth"

"Ouch! Isn't keeping an orderly society at the heart of your endeavors?"

"An orderly society of free people."

"Some would say preserving order is what frees the people. That is my job."

Raymond had nothing more to say and an uncomfortable silence hung between the men as they watched the chickens peck the ground.

"Looking at your hens, I'm thinking we have more in common than maintaining an orderly society. I like chickens. As a child I had a pet hen named Vasi."

The lieutenant turned to Raymond. "Mind if I visit your chickens?"

Raymond gazed at the coop, psychically shouting to Caellum *don't move* as he gestured. "Be my guest." Hardly breathing, he followed the officer into the yard.

"May I toss some feed?"

Raymond reached into the bin and scooped out enough to fill the officer's hand. As he scattered the feed at his feet, the chickens collected around him.

"Will one of the hens allow me to hold it?"

"Speckles, the black and white one is docile.'

Amid clucked protests and flapping wings the lieutenant picked up Speckles and adjusted her so that she sat comfortably in the crook of his arm against his chest as he stroked her. "A little more feed please." Raymond scooped some into Yanniv's hand, which he cupped under Speckles' beak. She pecked hungrily while he scratched her neck. "Notice how her protests have turned into pleasure since I am feeding her. Time spent in the chicken yard has taught me that chickens and people are quite similar."

Raymond listened feeling slightly sick and wishing he could work off his queasiness by an early start in the greenhouse. At that moment Gabe appeared and dove into a pile of hay. On impulse, Raymond picked up a handful and began forming the stalks into a little man. From a nearby shelf he retrieved hemp twine to twist and tie at the neck and joints so that the straw man would retrain his shape. Gabe's eyes were bright with anticipation as he watched his father until clutching the completed doll, he ran off to show his mother.

Abruptly, the Lieutenant lowered Speckles to the ground. "I think I would like to collect some eggs for this morning's breakfast." He walked over to the coop. "You have elevated the hen house."

"Yes when we remove the ladder and close them inside for the night, the height helps to protect them from predators."

"But you have a tall fence around the yard."

"Occasionally, wild cats, coyotes and badgers manage to break in nonetheless." Raymond peered directly into the lieutenant's eyes. "At times unwelcome predators plague the peaceful lives of both people and their animals."

Avoiding the hook, the Lieutenant maintained a blank expression. "I see that you open this little hatch to the side here to reach the eggs."

Although the temperature couldn't be above the mid-thirties Raymond was sweating. Through the open hatch it would be easy to glimpse the toe of a shoe.

The Lieutenant unlatched the narrow door and which hung down giving access to the eggs. As the opening was at elbow level, he bent down to peer inside. Remarking "It takes lots of hay to keep a chicken house clean," he gave the pile of hay at the rear of the coop several pokes with his gun barrel and swept long strands right and left, before he paused, walked around to the front of the coop and reached in.

Resignation collapsed Raymond's facade as he watched the officer and waited for Caellum to emerge at gunpoint. But instead Lebedev pulled out a bit of torn fabric. "Unless your chickens have taken to wearing clothes, it appears you have had a coat-wearing visitor inside your coop."

Raymond's heart slowed its erratic race as he watched, flooded with surprised relief that Caellum had escaped, but also recognition that he stood exposed.

The lieutenant unzipped his coat and reached inside to pocket the remnant, while Raymond accepted his fate. *Elise, we are undone. I so deeply regret my stupidity. What will become of us?*

"Got a hammer?"

Shocked by the incongruity of the request, Raymond moved in a daze to fetch the only hammer that wasn't at the construction site.

The Lieutenant took it from him. "That nail head sticking out could hurt one of the chickens." When it was hammered in to his satisfaction, he returned the tool. "It seems there are no eggs to collect today. Most unusual to not find a single brood hen sitting on her nest."

Raymond's dread of reprisal, of an accusation of harboring a criminal followed by the threat of jail at any moment, continued throughout the breakfast of hemp pancakes and bacon. Covering for his silence, her cheeks slightly flushed, Elise was at her most charming as she fielded Lieutenant Lebedev's questions regarding the art of firing the clay plates they ate on.

"Please, call me Lebedev." The Lieutenant's eyes hardly left her face and as he spoke, and when he praised the meal, his tone was almost tender, his attention to her spiced with friendly intimacy.

As he helped Elise and Raymond clear the table, his next declaration surprised as much as it alarmed them. "With your permission, I will help to build the greenhouses each day."

Carrying the hammer he had used at the coop, the officer walked with his shoulder touching Elise's and inclined his head so that his face brushed her hair as they conferred about the turquoise jewelry she made and wore. Glancing at her radiance and the arm that Lebedev held briefly as he examined the stones on her bracelet, Raymond fumed. *If he doesn't move away from my wife, I'll give him more than one reason to take me to jail.* But, once they entered the hub of builders, Elise smiled at the officer and moved away.

At the construction site, after the Lieutenant positioned himself beside one of the objects of his search, Raymond had the satisfaction of witnessing his ignorant camaraderie. But concern that the officer was subtly probing the student and that the youth might unwittingly reveal his identity wormed his gut. Needing hard work to expend nervous energy, he grabbed a shovel to dig a corner hole and dragged a three by three post to it while wondering about Caellum. When had he left? Where had he gone? How could he survive?

That evening while Elise, curled on the sofa near the fire, and the lieutenant entertained her with tales of Ivan the Terrible at the Kremlin, Raymond slipped out the back door, and flashlight in hand, headed to the root cellar. No Caellum. He hurried down the stairs. A quick scan revealed the burlap bags that covered the packs had been disturbed.

"Expecting to find someone?"

The lieutenant's query, aimed at his back, shook him so that he dropped the flashlight. He covered his alarm with indignation. "Damn! Must you sneak up on a person like that?"

"I do apologize. But yes, I must, when I am searching for a convicted felon."

Raymond retrieved his flashlight and rifled through the lowest shelf, just above the disturbed burlap. "Ah, there they are." He grabbed a jar of pickles. "My wife, who you seem to like so well, made these. An excellent bedtime snack." As he spoke, he was aware of the erratic path of the lieutenant's flash light beam around the cellar and across the burlap-covered mounds.

Raymond filled the suspicion-thickened atmosphere with talk. "This top shelf holds apricot, pear, and apple preserves, compliments of our orchards. Next shelf down holds herbs: rosemary, basil, Italian oregano and cilantro to season the produce from our gardens, along with canned peas, green beans, pickled beets, corn and..." seeing that the lieutenant's light persisted in traversing the bumps and wrinkles of the burlap, he covered the panicked glitch in his oration with a dramatic flair, opening the bag closest to the officer. "And on the floor, potatoes. Lots and lots of potatoes." After exposing the contents of the bag, he made a show of tucking the burlap around the potatoes. "Anything I can get for you from our storage, Lieutenant? Butter and jam for toast? Dried figs?"

But he spoke to the air. The lieutenant had walked away. Clasping the jar of pickles, Raymond slowly climbed the cellar stairs, and when he had closed the door, leaned against it to wait for his legs to stop shaking while he probed the stars as though their light would steady him.

Nor did the ceiling above his bed an hour later quell his worries as he lay on his back, and Elise turned out the light. She scooted close to him and slid one arm over his chest. The closed door afforded the trying day's first opportunity to be alone and talk.

"That creep has a thing for you."

"His friendliness is a sham, as is ours."

"He's too familiar with you."

"Don't tell me you're jealous."

Silence.

"He will do what it takes to upset our stability.

"Well, you don't have to let him hang all over you."

She pulled away and the distance between them thickened the silence.

"Yes, damn it. I am jealous, insanely so. I'm your husband."

"Exactly the reaction he wants."

"Next time he touches you it'll be a lot worse. I'm gonna punch the bastard in the jaw."

Again silence filled the space of their long awaited time alone.

"I want him to fall in love...."

"So you kid yourself that by ensnaring him, you'll turn him from his sworn duty? Or perhaps you are the one falling in love."

"You interrupted me."

"So speak — tell me the whole truth."

"Then let me finish. Though we live in a small house made of mud and straw; though we are in the midst of a food crisis; though ruthless overlords threaten us to the north and south; I wish him to know the satisfaction of living in this house we ourselves built; of the fulfillment of the harvest and biting into strawberries we have nurtured; I tell him how we have greened the desert by the intelligent management of every drop of water. I confess, I am seducing him — not to fall in love with me, but with our way of life."

"He's beyond that. Besides, what good will discussing our lives do?"

"Don't you see?"

The midnight chill in the room crept into the space between the sheets and their argument. While Elise pulled on the covers for warmth, Raymond lay frozen on his back his arms folded over his chest. "I guess I see only that I could lose you."

"Foolish man." Elise slid forward on the cold sheet and pressed the length of her body against Raymond's. "I promise to keep my distance from Lebedev, while I attempt to draw him into our world."

As his possessive anger loosened its grip, the day's accumulated tension, moments when the precariousness of their dilemma moved from bad to worse, sought release. "It's just that he has informed me that he can't return empty handed to Scholtz. And with just one slip up, those kids could reveal their identity, and we would be implicated, and that'd be the end for us."

Raymond pushed his arm under Elise's back and pulled her close. "I thought he was going to come down the root cellar stairs and uncover those packs."

"God help us."

"Caellum escaped last night, leaving behind a piece of cloth torn from his jacket. When the Lieutenant pocketed it, I expected him to arrest me."

"Is that why you were in the cellar?'

"Yes, to see if Caellum was there or if his pack was gone, which it was."

Elise found his hand and clasped it tight. "If he had been there..."

"I don't want to even imagine that scenario."

"I've never seen you eat a pickle before bedtime."

"The jars were just above and closest to the area where my flashlight beam located Caellum's missing pack. The lieutenant had sneaked up behind me. Awful bedtime snack, pickles. Gave me heartburn."

To stifle her giggles, Elise pulled the blankets over her head and pressed her face against Raymond's shoulder. He turned toward her and wrapped her in his arms. "I wish I weren't insanely jealous when he fawns over you. I wish a single slip up couldn't threaten our way of life—our lives."

"I wish, for now, you would just hold me and make love to me."

His lips brushed her forehead as he pulled her close, tight enough to crush to oblivion the space of separation. "Among all the probabilities swirling in my head, that's the no-brainer."

The sun was at about ten o'clock when Caellum approached the barking dog behind the picket fence. The dog's behavior wasn't threatening. Urgent was more like it. He let it smell the back of his hand, opened the gate, and walked into the yard. The animal ran in frantic loops between him and the house, jumping each time he approached the well. After knocking, Caellum opened the door and walked into the kitchen where the dog's empty food and water bowls sat. He had put a bowl under the tap to fill it, when he noticed the man in bed. No water came from the tap so he put down the bowl and approached the elderly man, who, before the flicker of his eyelids, looked dead.

The man touched his throat. "Water."

"Be right back."

Grabbing the bucket by the door Caellum dashed to the well, sloshing water as he hurried back to the kitchen to fill the dog's bowl and a glass for the man. He lifted the craggy old head and placed the edge of the glass between the parched lips.

For the first time he realized the cabin was freezing cold. After the man pushed away the empty glass, he offered to start a fire. Underneath bushy brows and wrinkled lids, renewed life shone through the eyes that surveyed Caellum while he started a fire in the wood stove.

"You reached us just in time. A couple of days ago a light stroke got me. Couldn't get up again after I fell into this bed. Still can't move my left arm. You saved my dog's life. The wizened hand ruffed the fur on the head that nuzzled his arm. Sorry."

"So where'd you come from?"

"A place called Gaia's Gardens."

The old man beamed. "I bet you know Raymond Muñoz. Showed up here several months ago."

Caellum grinned. "I just spent part of a night in his chicken coop."

"Doesn't sound like the best accommodations. So what's your story?"

The Lieutenant 32

"Thank you, Elise, you are a superb cook."

"And who is the cook in your household, Lieutenant Lebedev?"

"Please, call me Yanniv. Mostly, my wife."

"Surely, the recipient of such compliments." She turned to Raymond. "Honey, will you pass the stevia syrup please?"

Raymond lifted the jar, his gaze fixed on the officer. "So, Lebedev, how long are we to have the honor of sharing our very small home with you?"

Lebedev, swallowed his last forkful. "I afraid we're forced to stay as long as it takes."

Irritation peeled away Raymond's polite veneer. "And what is that supposed to mean?"

"It means the Governor has commanded us to return with Caellum Nichols and the students. Our orders are to remain until we find them."

Raymond gripped the table. *Not in our home, you won't.*

The lieutenant stood and looking down upon the wife and husband, the suggestion of a smile upturned the corners of his lips. "You see this is an ideal headquarters not only for ourselves, but also for starving renegades. I'm quite certain that sooner or later they will turn up here. Until then, I'm afraid I am your guest."

Elise, until now all smiles and prettiness, shot an incisive look that cut through the polite pretense. "You have just clarified that far from hosts, we are your hostages."

"As I am hostage to my superior's orders." A slight click of his heels punctuated Lebedev's rebuttal followed by a polite nod. "Thank you, for breakfast. Now I will leave you two to enjoy some time alone while I walk about the grounds. If we are lucky, today, I will capture some criminals, you can reclaim the privacy of your home, and I can return to mine."

Later the morning, when Elise faced Lebedev at the construction site, she insisted henceforth he keep a respectful distance. Which he did. And Raymond resolved to remove jealousy from his vigilance, until through the plexi-glass he was framing in, he witnessed the lieutenant's puppy dog response to Elise's smile.

When the officer was not working beside Elise he was ingratiating himself to either a resident or a student. But as the days passed, Raymond noted that Lieutenant Lebedev increasingly positioned himself beside the youths, until he worked exclusively near either his wife or a student. *He knows. When he's not salivating over Elise, he's probing for a slip-up, for proof from the suspects themselves.*

As Raymond worked among the people, he inquired about their reactions to the officer. No one doubted that while Lebedev helped with the construction, he was alert to clues about the vanished arsons. Even when the shelters were complete and the stoves hauled inside, the intruder further insinuated himself into their lives as he helped pot over nine hundred cabbage, pea, and carrot seeds as well as garlic and onions.

The lieutenant attended the town meeting to discuss their next big challenge, which was to feed the fires in the greenhouses to ward off the freezing nighttime temperatures. After much debate, the townspeople agreed to post two people to sleep in each greenhouse and awaken twice in the middle of the night to replenish the wood in the stoves.

As though he weren't there to spy on the town, to apprehend the guests in their homes, Lebedev asked in the manner of a friend if those around him would like to hear a tale told to him by his Russian grandfather. After affirmative nods he recounted how past generations saved the crops and orchards from freezing. Raymond seethed as the audience murmured an invitation, and the officer walked to the front of the room.

"In my great grandparents' day, the farmers devised an effective alarm system to alert them to the arrival of freezing temperatures. In late fall and early spring, when any night might bring frost and kill the plants or ruin the young fruits, they placed kindling and wood for fires all along the rows. Then matchboxes in hand, they slept under the stars among the crops and in the orchards. But even that was risky. In the warmth of their blankets they might sleep on, oblivious of the temperature drop. They decided that at least a part of their bodies must feel the chill, and so it was they agreed to sleep with their big toes exposed to the elements. Thanks to this personal warning system, the discomfort of freezing toes, they would awaken to light the fires and thus save the crops."

While the people applauded, Raymond's hands closed in tight fists. To all appearances Lebedev was increasingly one of them. The following week, he even took a shift to tend the fires and joined parties that crossed Cyborg Highway, the former Interstate 25, to the base of the mountains to fell trees, chop wood and haul it to Gaia's Gardens. As the days dragged on, Raymond's hostility grew until he simply ceased speaking to the intruder.

Although Raymond shunned their uninvited guest, he was often within hearing distance when Elise fielded questions about their hopes and dreams. Clearly, the cadence of her words intended the dream of a New Earth to ride straight into the heart of the listener. The lilted tones layered charm within descriptions of the rewards of joining Earth's natural cycles. The musicality of her voice as she spoke of governance of co-creative peace captured Lebedev's undivided attention. Listening at a distance momentarily quelled Raymond's irritation at the intruder's infatuation with his wife, as she also mesmerized him.

During community meetings discussions of greenhouse shifts, firewood retrieval treks and food rationing flew around the lieutenant and his troops. At times moods grew irritable, tempers flared over disagreements, and meetings were adjourned to re-convene with clear heads. Through it all, the participants persisted until they achieved mutually acceptable resolutions to their differences, because the spirit of their joint endeavors in Gaia's Gardens necessitated dedication peaceful relationships.

Nonetheless, the lieutenant's presence sentenced the townspeople to ongoing entrapment, and Raymond's hostility festered as January yielded to February, then March. Whenever possible Raymond positioned himself close enough to listen to the banter, when the officer probed people for their history. He noticed the troops similarly buddying up to the youths as they cut firewood, repaired roofs or helped till kitchen gardens. *They are closing ranks for an ambush.*

Raymond's resentment threatened to erupt at least once daily, when Lebedev sought the company of Elise. He showered her with seductive charm as he hauled the basket of wet clothes to the line, arranged jewelry lessons with her and after March blew in, helped till her kitchen garden. Outrage consumed Raymond as Lebedev's gaze followed her every move with lust that undressed her.

When the officer presented his wife with the bird pendant he had made in the jewelry class, Raymond could take no more and he presented a fist in the lieutenant's face. "I can't stop you from spying on us. But I can and will stop you however necessary from attempting to seduce my wife."

Lebedev eyed him with the supercilious ease that he reserved for Raymond. "If you wish to fight me, let's do it." He began to peel off his officer's jacket."

Elise walked up at that moment and positioning herself between them, postponed the inevitable confrontation. "Come on, you two. There's work to be done."

When the first green sprigs of grass forced their way through thawing soil, a young child ended months of tension by handing Lebedev the clue he had been seeking. Having harvested the last of the winter produce from the greenhouses, he and Gaia's citizenry were potting the seeds for the spring crops. Though the people were gaunter than last December, they appeared for the most part healthy, indicating the reduced food portions remained high in nutrition. Reflecting the next harvest would come none too soon, Raymond worked two tables away from Lebedev as the planters used trowels to shovel dirt into small pots.

As Raymond poked a seed in the soil and covered it, a child approached Lebedev and in all innocence asked, "Have you seen Will?"

"Your brother is at the community wood pile."

"Will's not my brother." The child had to shout over the wind that was gathering momentum. "He just lives with us now."

Lebedev responded as though he hadn't just heard the incriminating evidence he'd been seeking for four months. "Sorry, I haven't seen him today."

The brief encounter sent shockwaves through Raymond. Mechanically, he filled his trowel with dirt. *Will, the youth that looks nothing like his would-be parents, who appear too young to have a son his age.*

Several minutes passed before the lieutenant sauntered away, followed at a discrete distance by Raymond. Hidden from the view and removed from the hearing of any townspeople Lebedev radioed the troops.

In response to a shout that someone had stepped on a nail Raymond hurried back to the greenhouse while he grappled for a way to save the students, the town. Short of begging the man who he had treated so coldly, he had no inkling of a way out.

Prepared to plead for mercy toward his people, Raymond entered the late afternoon gloom of his front porch. The wind tore the screen door from his grasp, and once inside the howling and rattling of the window panes was so loud, it was difficult to hear anything more than a foot away. Not seeing Elise or Lebedev in the living room he headed toward the kitchen before recalling that he was supposed to retrieve Gabe from two doors down. He was about to turn back when he heard Lebedev's voice. Something in the man's tone halted Raymond's steps behind the wall beside the kitchen door. Apparently, neither Elise, nor the officer had heard him enter.

"Elise, a child has revealed the presence of a recently moved-in boarder in his home."

An intermittent banging on the roof punctuated the ensuing silence in the kitchen. The wind had loosened the edge of a strip of aluminum Raymond had intended to nail down today.

"So, what does this mean?"

"It means I must perform the duty that brought me to this town."

"Yanniv, you have lived among us for months; you have shared our meals; you have worked beside us to plant and harvest the winter produce. Today you potted seed for the spring harvest." Desperation wrenched Elise's plea.

"And, I have grown to love you."

Raymond's fists clenched and unclenched as he restrained himself from striding into the room.

"Then surely you wish no harm to come to this town, to me, to my husband."

"I wish to relieve your town of the presence of criminals."

"Desperate youths, what future they had torn from them. Victims of the horrible dictatorship that consigned them to prison-like labor."

"Elise, the corn from Onmatson Farm saved the lives of the citizens of Transtopia. I'm quite certain you would not have wished the entire city to starve to death."

"They collectively grew their own corn."

"But by no means sufficient to survive the winter."

"Lebedev, those young people will be murdered. They will either hang or face a firing squad."

"A lesson to the people to put the needs of the collective ahead of self-interest."

"Like that pompous buffoon with the self-assigned supercilious title 'Imperial Governor?'"

"Those are treasonous words, Elise."

"Lebedev, I'm begging you, don't take those students to their doom."

"I assure you, it is a most unpleasant task."

"And, and Raymond, and me? What about our child?"

Her voice was so low Raymond could barely hear her above roar and bangs that were growing louder, more insistent."

"Elise, where you are concerned, I find myself derelict in my duty. How can I arrest you who have been my companion and confidante for four months? You, with a smile that lifts me from the dullness of my life; you, who hold a feather or a stone or a glazed pot so that it becomes a thing of beauty; you, so feminine wearing a baseball cap and overalls — for my own survival I must know that you are alive in this world."

"And... and Raymond?" Her tone was tentative, childlike in its pleading.

"I must apprehend him."

All semblance of restraint dissolved in Elise's torrent of desperation. "No, please, do with me as you will, but leave my husband here. I know you want to have sex with me. Take me. Whatever you want from me, I will give, if you will only spare Raymond."

After a prolonged screech, the banging on the roof ceased. The moment the wind finally ripped the strip from the roof, Raymond had heard all he could stand. Within seconds of Elise's last words he entered the doorway to see the length of her pressed against Lebedev, her arms flung around his neck. Standing on her toes she kissed him with passion that should be for Raymond only. He strode toward them, jerked Elise away and punched Lebedev in the jaw so hard the man reeled, stumbled backward and fell. With a leap forward Raymond flung himself astride the officer pinning one arm under the grip of his thigh. He delivered a second blow as Lebedev's free hand reached toward his waist. *A handgun.* The men struggled to retrieve the weapon, the tip of the handle now visible under the belt.

A loud *rattle, crack!* and the sound of shattered glass interrupted Elise's screams for them to stop.

Raymond hit Lebedev's arm away with his fist and held it away with his left hand. In an attempt unseat Raymond, Lebedev's body writhed, and he struggled to wrench his arm from his assailant's hold. Raymond grasped the gun handle and pulled it from under Lebedev's belt. As Raymond straightened his arm to raise the handgun toward the ceiling, the officer wrenched his arm from Raymond's restraining hand and reached for the weapon, able only to grab his wrist. The struggle loosened Raymond's hold, and the gun clattered to the floor. As both men looked at the weapon, Lebedev pulled his pinned arm free, twisted his body sideways and moved toward the gun. But Raymond hit him and hit him again and again until Lebedev rolled backward and his arms went limp. Ignoring Elise's screams, Raymond pummeled the pinned man's blood smeared face until a gunshot startled him from his blood lust.

Elise! In a single motion he spun around and jumped to his feet to see her facing him. The fallen tree limb that had broken through the kitchen window extended over the sink inches from her head. The wind blowing through the opening swirled around his wife, twisting ropes of hair from her scalp and tossing them into a hapless halo, except for the strands that blew across her cheeks and caused the flickering of her glare. The gun hanging limply from her hand, she faced her husband without moving until she laid the gun on the counter. When Elise hunched her shoulders and wrapped her arms around herself, her violent shivering brought Raymond a step closer. But she held out her hand, palm forward and looked behind him at the unmoving figure on the floor. "Please, cover that gaping hole, while I tend to Yanniv's bloody gashes—hopefully, he's still alive."

A knock at the front door punctured the pall of violence and destruction, reminding them they had a child. Raymond, his blood-smeared knuckles behind his back, opened the door to their neighbor who held Gabe on her arm. Attempting to fake normalcy he greeted Cindy and his son. "Do you mind letting Gabe play at your house a little longer?"

Cindy's eyes searched his.

"Glass from a broken window is scattered over our kitchen floor, " was his lame excuse.

"Everything okay?"

"I can explain more tomorrow. I'll get Gabe in about an hour."

Cindy nodded and turned. "Hey, Gabe, you and Julia get to play together some more."

After pulling the severed tree limb away, Raymond boarded up the shattered window, while Elise nursed the unconscious man with the shattered face.

Sulfur   33

    A ride with her bondmate was Eena's relief from stressors. After greeting Leiani, Gavin and Leslie, she stood between the grove that lined the river and the savannah that stretched toward the mountain. The winter though mild on the Island of Mu, had triggered the fruit trees that dotted the savannah to drop their leaves and browned the grass stalks for a brief rest. But the return of spring winds coaxed green sprouts to push through the straw residual of last year's grass. The fruit trees had leaved out and magenta and white blooms heralded the fruit to follow. At the inception of spring before mangoes, starfruit, and papayas ripened, the birds still scratched the river mud for crayfish and foraged on pine nuts and evergreen foliage beneath the giant redwoods.

    Eena psychically called Cesla and looked toward the mountain, her heart responding with the familiar tremor. But when the splash of aqua marine appeared, an image intruding on her peripheral vision unsettled her joy. Though she tried to focus on the augur, she couldn't ignore the smoke rising several thousand feet above the mountain peaks. Last year's wispy white curls had reminded the inhabitants of the presence of the sleeping giant, but this year's dark and heavy spew warned of his awakening. The shaking underfoot nudged the emigrants' from Three Mountains to flee. But where? For now Eena stood her ground and focused on Cesla's approach.

    Close now, the wing shoulder arched the twelve-foot wingspan for descent before the claws gripped the ground releasing a cloud of dirt. As the wings folded against Cesla's body, Eena ran forward to throw her arms around his neck. When her fingers pushed through the layered feathers, she felt the hard muscular strength, more like that of a horse than a bird. But preferring a good scratch to a hug, Cesla pulled away. So Eena reached into a pouch and extended her palm—the mound of dried tomatillos, a meager offering. "Sorry, Cesla, it's that time of year."

Forgotten were Eena's plans to soar beyond the reach of persistent concerns. "How about a ride to check out that Volcano?"

They flew beyond the ridge that walled the geothermal activity sandwiched between the ocean and mountain range—the miles where subterranean unrest stirred the volcano's gastric juices, and earth belched bubbling caldrons. The sulfurous broth released noxious fumes and Eena wrinkled her nose at the smell of rotten eggs.

Cesla's gurgle-wheeze signaled flying so close to the volcano, while unpleasant for her, was exacting a price from the augur. Abruptly she and Cesla reversed direction. As they escaped the hellish landscape, the prediction of Leiani's father surfaced. Any day now the giant would explode an inferno and sink the island beneath the waves.

The realization that it would also entomb Cesla, all the augurs, wrung her heart. Their time lay forty thousand years in the past, unknown to the future world where men of science and religion, in order to keep jobs and funding flowing from Annunaki funded grants protected simplistic stories and denied remote human dramas on planet Earth.

They landed, and she stroked Cesla's neck and murmured her gratitude to the wheezing bird that had been so vital to their survival in Three Mountains, from the hoisted food to the transported parts of the holographic structure that hid them from the plane that carried Imperial Governor Charles Scholtz. She recalled the day she rode Cesla to the mountaintop that overlooked Lemon Reservoir, the day the soldiers that were sure to return, spied the falling feather that caught the wind as they held it in the jeep headed for Durango.

An hour passed before Cesla's breathing returned to normal. With a heavy heart, she returned to the little settlement that would soon rest on the ocean floor.

Chas rode the mare and led the yearling, pigs, cow and her calf to the abundant spring grass in the recently moved corral, then herded the scattering chickens in with them. Eena followed Chas and his brood and climbed the fence to sit beside him.

He put his arm around her and drew her close. "Eena, I wish I could spare you this angst. I have never seen you so low."

"Don't you see, despite all our efforts, we are doomed. For generations to come humanity will continue to provide the Landlords' work force. Despite efforts prior to Solar Flash, despite our efforts since, we are defeated.

"Any day now forces from the Union of Americas will march in."

"I'm not so sure. The entire continent has surely met the same fate as Sector 10. You know, Chas, my deepest regret is Ft Carson: those babies which technology has engineered; children who will serve technology rather than the other way around. They will never know they are being contorted into the likeness of machines rather than expressing their full biological magnificence.

"There are stories of children raised with wild animals are their only companions who became like them, howled like them, walked on all four like them. This is like that. But the future orphans will be integrated with robots.

"Throughout the winter I have dreamt of returning To Fort Carson and whisking them away.

"How did you imagine that?

"I'm sure an undisturbed arsenal sits on that base."

"But Eena, you tossed away your gun, to seek peaceful means to oppose the system."

"Well, has it worked?"

"On the surface no."

"No, Chas, not at all. Peter d'Arc and Charles Scholtz grow more entrenched with every passing day."

"Remember, Eena, without a sword, and eighty years of age, Mordechai defeated an armed warrior...."

"Nice story. Nice philosophy. *Disappearing opponent*, not true. To me, your Aikido philosophy offers only a compelling fairytale."

The grief on Chas's face alarmed her, and she clasped his hand. "I'm sorry, Chas, look what I've done. I've brought down you, the man I love, for me the single mainstay of strength that endures through the vicissitudes of life.

"No, Eena, you are mistaken. "You have not brought me to doubt the philosophy. I weep for you, you who have the courage of a Thousand Warriors, but have lost your grip on your sword."

"My sword?"

"Of Truth; of your connection to power that overcomes all odds."

Gavin and Leslie, carrying April asleep in her sling, had arrived with their belongings to choose a house in the village. Gavin announced, "Sulfur fumes are saturating the air a mile from here."

A week later he walked to the auger nesting site and returned to stand wan faced in in Eena's doorway. "It's the augurs."

She hurried out the door and as they passed the corral, waved to Chas. By the time they crossed the stream that bordered the realm of the Augurs, Eena reeled from the rotten egg smell. The noxious gas had spread across the savannah, increasingly affecting the browsing birds. The absence of their *rumble coo*, collectively referred to as the savannah lullaby, intensified Eena's sense of gloom. She glanced toward the fruit-bearing trees gracing this portion of the savannah. Only trampled grass hinted at the former teal sea of foraging augurs beneath fruit-laden limbs. As though to escape the volcanic smog known as vog, the brown edges of the leaves remaining on the trees curled inward.

Many of the birds were no longer standing. Because their sky domain had become toxic, they hugged the ground, heads hanging to rest their beaks against the earth. Small groups still stood and huddled together. Phoenix and Cesla stood apart, but as their bondmates approached, their lids protected their eyes without the slightest flicker of recognition.

Phoenix, still the most spirited of all the augurs, seemed to have reverted to his former wildness, snorting and shaking his head as though to toss away the smoke that burned his eyes and nostrils. Desiring to soothe the bird, Gavin reached toward Phoenix's neck and received a bloodied shoulder for his efforts.

"The smoke is unbearable here. We have to get the ones we can away."

"Yes, let's lead Cesla and Phoenix and that still-standing group to the village."

"I can attach a lead rope to Cesla, but how can we get Phoenix to move?"

"I have an idea." Leiani came up behind them with a blanket on her arm. "If we throw this over his head, I think the relief from the burning smoke will calm him."

Gavin tried and failed. "He's eight feet tall."

"Talk to him. Soothe him. Tell him to kneel."

His eyes burning, Gavin coughed, and Leiani and Eena's coughs formed a chorus of gasping and throat clearing.

Psychically he sent the sensation of relief to Phoenix. "Lower your head and allow me to cover it."

But Phoenix tossed his head violently and lunged again. But ready for him Gavin had jumped back.

"Here," Leiani handed him mango past its prime. "This might help."

Still wordlessly reassuring the bird with the sensation of relief and comfort, knowing he was putting himself in harm's way, Gavin sat on the ground and crossed his legs in front of Phoenix. "When your wing was healing, I fed you like this. You came to trust me and closed your eyes and slept."

The head swung side to side then lowered toward him and he braced himself for the dagger-like slice that would sear his flesh. But within seconds Phoenix tucked his beak under his neck and pressed the crown of his head against his bondmate as he lowered his body to the ground.

"That's right. Tears washed the smoke and cinders from Gavin's eyes. "This fruit's over ripe, but its juice is sweet."

Gavin put the fruit on the ground so he could slip the halter over Phoenix's head. And as the bird devoured one of the last edible fruits on the island, Leiani lowered the blanket over his head.

Gavin felt his bondmate grow still under the false night, and as he gazed toward the sun obscured by dark clouds, he recalled two years ago; the thrill of Phoenix's first approach, at first a distant speck, sunrays glinting on the fourteen foot span of turquoise splendor that landed in response to his call. *Can this be the end of you, of your kind? Can it be that humanity will never know of the* sky travelers *soaring the skies of ancient Mu? Of your assistance in mankind's quest for sovereignty thousands of years after your world's demise?*

"We better go." Through the break in her coughing, Eena's voice was gentle, softened by her own grief.

Trust me. Gavin tugged on the lead as his psychic urging struggled to overcome the resistance of the resting augur.

After attaching a lead rope to Cesla and the other birds to him, with sinking hearts, the pair led them into the corral, not to prevent flight, but to protect them from the migrating predators that also endangered the town.

The Hangar 34

When the lock was unbolted and the tall metal door pushed open, the pair entered the high-ceilinged building. But it wasn't the long anticipated equivalent of a *Lockheed Martin F-35 Lightning II* jet that met Jack's gaze. A circular craft, that dwarfed the one that had transported him to Blue Kachina Research and Development, filled the hangar with its immensity. At the crown the letters OTC-Z1 blazed its identity.

Randolph beamed his pride. "The 45 footer. The largest saucer produced at OTC Labs."

"But, I thought the U.S. government confiscated the lab, the prototypes, everything."

"They did."

Jack was incredulous. "I'm quite sure they didn't fly it to you."

Randolph's poker face met Jack's bemusement. "They couldn't fly it at all."

"You're kidding. My understanding is the government has back-engineered craft like this."

"Similar, but different."

"How?"

"There are many varieties of gravity defying propulsion and piloting systems. The government has back-engineered UFOs and designed replicas of the ones they could fly."

"You're saying they couldn't pilot this one."

"You got it. The concept of attuning to natural law is outside the physics and goals of scientific materialism."

"Okay so how did it get here?"

"In a sense I called it to this location."

"Damn! Stop speaking in bloody riddles."

"I simply synced with it. The magnetic attraction between the saucer and me resonated outside 3D time and space."

Jack processed this information before speaking. "Impossible. This thing was guarded deep inside a mountain. In addition to the distance, solid rock separated you and the OTC-Z1."

Randolph seemed to appreciate the stretch in comprehension. " Maybe this will help. I recall the time a technician at a place I worked called Advanced Kinetics asked me to put my thumb under an electron microscope."

"My buddy said, 'Let me show you something. Put your finger here and look through the scope.'

"I did as he directed.

"'Now what do you think you're looking at?' He asked.

"'Well, it's my finger,' I said.

"And..."

"It disappeared. There's only space." That day I learned that even atoms are widely separated, invisible packets of energy. My life changed because I found out I'm invisible. There's so much space between the particles, it's as if I don't exist."

"So..."

"So, Jack, I'm explaining how this vehicle flew through the atomic spaces, the energetic space in what appears to be solid rock."

Jack groaned. "My world is disappearing."

Ralph's expression sympathetic, he nodded. "I've thrown a lot at you over a few days."

As though circling the disk would bring clarity, Jack walked the circumference. He had anticipated defying the constraints of gravity, light and sound as he flew an exotic jet at terrific speeds. Instead, Ralph was turning his whole reality wrong side out. As he completed the circular stroll he heard, or rather felt, a soft hum, a vibration.

Ralph's voice broke through the pleasurable experience that was like an energetic massage. Apparently the inventor hadn't finished shaking up his world. "Our reality is like malleable plastic. Watch this."

Ralph put his hand on the resonating metal surface. Then he pointed his finger. Was it simply a magicians' sleight of hand that soon obscured the end of it? First the finger, then the whole fist penetrated the shell as though pressing on a giant glob of putty.

"What the...?"

Jack's fist emerged from the vibrating shell. "My hand simply entered the energetic flow that's producing the hum."

Jack grappled with an internal skirmish between enthrallment and disbelief. "You're dismantling my reality."

Ralph turned toward him. "It's dismantling itself. Welcome to 4D."

As deepening shadows in the hangar indicated the sun had completed its descent below the mountain ridges to the west, Jack groaned. "My world is disappearing."

Randolph's expression was sympathetic as he nodded. "In just a couple of hours I've thrown a lot at you about the astounding possibilities available through natural law—without the use of force. But it's only the beginning of the preparation for your mission."

Mission? Did he just say mission? "Randolph, wait a minute. What are you talking about? I came here to fulfill dreams of flight, not set off some blimey mission."

"The flight's part of it, Jack. But we're both here for a purpose beyond personal thrills. Let's head toward the house."

After Jack locked the hangar and they headed toward the mound Randolph's voice was matter of-fact as though forecasting the weather, as he dropped the next information bomb. "Our home is well stocked with food to last you a week."

"What? You're leaving me?" Jack stopped and placed a restraining hand on Randolph's arm.

"You'll be fine, Jack. Here's the key to the hangar. See you a week from today."

In that instant, where Randolph's arm had been, a puff of air brushed Jack's hand, leaving him alone with the contemplation of a world that wasn't there.

Departures 35

Gabe slept in his bed while on the sofa in the living room indigo and purple had begun to ring the swollen lids that covered the eyes in the torn and bruised face of the barely breathing man. In the aftermath of the storms that had raged both inside and outside Raymond and Elise's home, in the stillness of the house and the solitude of their bedroom, they faced one another.

The indelible image of Elise embracing another man cut deep. Raymond's look was accusatory. "You threw yourself at him. You were kissing him."

"You would rather I hang onto my virtue and lose you?"

"I've seen the way your face lights up when you speak to him."

"Your jealousy has blinded you."

"I've seen clearly."

"Have you not seen the intent behind my actions?"

"But you..."

"Stop. It's my turn to point a finger. "You could have killed him."

"Whether he's dead or alive, I face execution."

Elise's shoulders sagged. "After four months of hanging onto our lives by a thread."

"At least that bastard won't let you die."

"I've never seen you so angry, so violent."

"For months I've watched him lust after you. Today, thanks to a child, the slip occurred that I have dreaded day after day. This day is our undoing."

As Raymond's gaze turned inward, neither said a word until a psychic boil erupted accumulated bitterness. "I'm up to here," Raymond gestured under his chin, "with sharing meals, not to mention my wife, with that sorry excuse for a man. Such fastidious manners, while he invades our home and threatens our lives. Day after day he joins the greenhouse construction, all politeness and helpfulness and sickening friendliness. Through four tense, miserable months our town is his lair as he waits for the slip that comes from a child. He intends the murder of those to whom we have given sanctuary— I admit. Today, in those minutes of insanity, I wanted him dead."

Elise's fingers pressed his cheeks and cooled the heat that consumed him. He grabbed her hands and kissed her palms.

Tears filled her eyes. "Leave, Raymond. Go now before morning."

He clutched her to him and began unbuttoning her blouse as he kissed her neck, her face, her eyes, her lips. "All I need now is you, all of you, as much of you as possible through this, our last night together."

An hour before dawn Elise pushed away from Raymond. "Leave before Lebedev awakens."

"I can't run."

"Why on Earth not?"

"Don't you see? I'll be an escaped criminal like Caellum and those youths. My absence will just mean extended months of military occupation in our town as they search for me—Lebedev in my home with my wife."

Lebedev's eyes were so swollen when they first opened, only a slit of his iris was visible; his bruised and battered face barely recognizable. But as the rest of his body had escaped Raymond's battering, he sat up to reach for the glass of water Elise handed him. Careful to avoid the split in his lip, he inserted the straw on the opposite side of his mouth.

"Are you hungry?"

"I cannot eat... I would like you to know that because of your desperation; because you offered yourself to me, I was tempted to spare your husband. Do not cry. I cannot bear to see you weep...Elise, please understand. I must face my troops who will see that I have been beaten within an inch of my life. I have no choice but to arrest Raymond. I am sorry to see your distress. I wish I could spare you this grief. But things turned out the way they must."

Raymond collected himself in the bedroom, hardly trusting himself not to finish off the man that was disassembling their lives, until Elise's sobs drew him to her side.

Lebedev arose from the sofa to his full height to address the couple. Authority rang in the voice that emerged from the disfigured face. "My men will be here shortly. They will have rounded up all the youths in your town. The arsons will have no choice but to reveal their identities. Now, Raymond, as leader of the town you have a choice. My troops can escort you and one adult from each household guilty of treason to Transtopia. Or we can offer you alone to the Imperial Governor as the scapegoat for this fiasco. The choice is yours."

"You know my answer."

"In that case, there is something I must tell you. Although admittedly I have fallen in love with your wife, I would not have taken advantage of her offer. Yet, her plea did tempt me to betray my military oath. You see, in a manner of speaking it was not my seduction but hers that saved the town. Calm down. I'm not referring to sex. She handed me a sprig of rosemary, and the scent filled my nostrils; she described a stark landscape of sage and sparse grass and I could see the transformation into lanes of flowering shrubs and trees; She scooped a handful of clay rich soil and recounted the construction of these thick walls of mud and straw that kept us warm and snug last winter. Thanks to Elise's persuasions, I desired the friendship of families enjoying a fresh start, living in harmony with Earth."

The present reality intruded with a knock at the door

"Wait, I'm not finished. We scooped snow into a barrel and I came to understand how conscientiously you cycle every drop of water. I glimpsed Elise's pride in you, the acknowledged leader, who has invited equal voice in the governance of this town. I held hemp fabric dyed yellow with turmeric and touched the edges of your dreams of sovereignty. Because Elise spoke with such love, passion even, for this way of life, I wanted to remain forever — to become part of this... this... whatever it is."

The second knock banged louder, more insistent.

Raymond stared at the face disfigured by his rage. "I'm not the only one with a choice."

"But you see, my yearning can never be fulfilled. Like you, for the sake of the town I must return to Transtopia. Otherwise the governor will deploy more troops here. And if they are led by my commanding officer, Lieutenant Starkey, your little Camelot is doomed. That is why you and I must go."

The third knock ended the interlude.

Raymond opened the door to a young soldier. "I need to speak with my commanding officer."

Raymond scanned the crowd collecting behind the soldier. To one side soldiers surrounded over twenty youths. Families filled the yard and lane, and angry shouts erupted.

"They have taken our sons and daughters."

"Return our children."

"Raymond, do something."

"I will handle this." Behind Raymond's shoulder, Yanniv spoke, his tone commanding. Raymond hesitated before yielding the doorway to the officer. A collective gasp greeted his appearance.

"Sir!" The eyes of the soldier who had knocked, widened.

Lieutenant Lebedev raised a hand, and his half open eyes faced the crowd. "Please be quiet." He waited for the shouts and shocked exclamations to subside. "Pardon my appearance. I stumbled in the dark last night, and my clumsiness left me with this face. Now, about your sons and daughters. We will sort this out. It is very simple."

Lebedev turned toward the troops and youths they surrounded. "Every person who participated in the arson at Onmotsan Farm and is a fugitive from justice step to the porch."

After a moment of hesitation, Blake stepped forward, then one by one the remaining eleven followed. When Blake said, "This is all of us," the lieutenant nodded to the soldiers, who stepped aside as sons and daughters hurried to their parents. Those who had gathered watched, calmer now, but in as much a state of shock as relief.

Lebedev raised his hand to silence the hum of voices. "For the past four months several among you have aided and abetted criminals, arsons responsible for the destruction of buildings at a military outpost. According to the laws of Sector Ten of the Union of the Americas this is treason against the government and punishable by death."

Gasps and shouts shattered the quiet, and with a signal from Lieutenant Lebedev, the troops closed ranks around the families of Gaia's Gardens.

Again the senior officer called for silence. "However, because the leader of your town has agreed to take full responsibility for harboring the criminals, those of you who have opened your homes to them have been spared arrest—your lives are saved."

Lebedev raised his hand to quiet the cries of relief as parents and their offspring clung to one another. And to his troops. "You two, guard the prisoners. The rest gather your gear and report back here immediately to take these soldiers' place while they retrieve their belongings."

Longtime friends and collaborators approached Raymond to shake his hand, to express their regrets and embrace him until the only sound was the shuffling of feet as the families dispersed to return home. His arm around Elise, Raymond whispered to her that he would like a few minutes alone with Lebedev. Gabe pulled on his mother's hand insisting that he was hungry.

"I'll be in the kitchen."

Raymond remained on the porch and conferred beyond his wife's hearing with the man he had attacked hours before. Beginning with an apology, he told him about Biate and New Denver. Then he grabbed both Lebedev's eyes and his arm as he conveyed his sense of urgency to the man who loved his wife. "I fear for my family; this town. Biate is ruthless. No telling what she'll do when she sees the inadequate shipment of food. As I can no longer do so, I urge you to employ whatever authority you possess to protect Elise and Gabe; Gaia's Gardens "

The Lieutenant insisted on leaning against the porch railing as he ate his meal, while Raymond, Elise, and Gabe shared their first breakfast alone as a family in many weeks, and very likely, their last. After Gabe devoured his plateful, and the parents picked at theirs, the family retreated to Raymond and Elise's bedroom to discuss the harvest to come and with trepidation, Biate. Although meal portions more meager than ever, the town had set aside a portion that was half the size agreed upon to send to New Denver. This would enrage Biate. Raymond moved to the writing desk where a sharpened stick and a sheet of hemp paper lay beside a bottle of homemade ink made from charcoal. "I'd better send Biate an explanation."

While Elise distracted Gabe, Raymond scribbled a note. "Attach this to the shipment. I'm worried that this will not go well for the town. I can just see her face contorted in anger. In this letter I've apologized to her, explained about the food shortage and assured her that after the

June harvest we can send full shipments again. I've also written that it will be the largest harvest ever, so that there will be sufficient storage to last through next winter for both Gaia's Gardens and New Denver. Surely she is capable of understanding we weren't prepared to send large portions of our storage her way this past winter, let alone feed the troops. What worries me is that she is a vindictive woman, not right in the head. She is capable of anything.

"I hesitated to inform her of my arrest, but otherwise she would send her mechanical goons to search for me... Elise, I should be here to protect you and Gabe, the town."

In the few minutes remaining Gabe's eyes filled with tears as he asked his parents why they were crying, and they explained that Raymond had to go away. The final moments hastened Raymond's departure as the troops waited in formation beyond the porch, and the family clung to one another. When the Lieutenant appeared at the door, Gabe ran to his room, and when he returned, clutched the tattered leg of the little homemade man of straw, and pressed it into his father's hand.

Reflections 36

Caellum's account kicked off the story exchange that dragged on from late December to April. By January Cliff rallied and daily Caellum helped him to a chair by a window. By mid-February, the preserved garden vegetables ran out and they lived mainly on potatoes, eggs and chicken — one leg or thigh or breast at a time.

In March the old man no longer left the bed to sit by the window and slept through the final days of his fragile hold on life. In April the old man's waning strength bound Caellum to his side, while the warm breezes of spring teased his restlessness. Daily walks were his only escape from the too-warm space that confined his urge to move on. Circling the farmstead, he followed a maze to nowhere through narrow spaces between sage bushes with the dog meandering nearby. The hours he paced beyond the weathered fence enclosing the weed-filled garden more closely resembled exercise in a prison yard than release from captivity — even his thoughts traveled in repeating loops. When his musings circled Gaia's Gardens, he wondered about the fate of the students. In the other path to nowhere, images of Dora and Michael tugged at his heart. Both directions reinforced the frustration that he was neither a freedom fighter nor available as a protective husband and father. Bound by the old man's helplessness, he longed to be on the move. Yet what could he accomplish in a world in which he did not, could not exist.

By April the milk cow was too old and skinny to provide Caellum and Cliff milk and butter. The rooster had been killed by a bobcat and they were down to two hens. Desperate to resume activity, any activity, in support of the sovereignty movement, Caellum fashioned a cushion-padded, wooden travois to pull the old man behind as he headed out. Somehow without being discovered by the MP's, he had to leave the old man at Gaia's Gardens and a sneak a visit to Dora and Michael before heading to his forest camp. Warmed by the noisy gusts of a southerly wind, he walked and planned until a thumping sound in the distance pulled his gaze to the northwest. He ducked behind a bush to watch the helicopter head south toward Gaia's Gardens. *Must be the one from New Denver Airport going retrieve a food shipment for the crazy redhead with the five hundred SuperRos. If she ever launches them, how will we cripple such forces?*

When the helicopter and it's intermittent whir receded into the distance, he called to Scamp and headed into the house to prepare the old man some eggs and hash browns with the last tablespoon of butter.

The old man was usually awake by now, but as he walked into the bedroom, plate in hand, the eyes were still closed. He called Cliff's name and gave his arm a little shake, but it felt heavy. He put his hand beneath the man's nostrils. No breath. He felt for a pulse. There was none.

It took another day to dig a grave and bury Cliff before he freed the cow to share the fate of aged wild ungulates. A half dozen eggs and a roasted chicken in his pack, he circumvented the town to head toward the mountains, but couldn't resist swinging by Gaia's Gardens. He had to know if the students and/or the military were still there.

Hunkering down to peer through his binoculars, he looked at Scamp. "You can't bark." Two hours revealed the passing back and forth of the town's people without a single uniform in view. He decided to risk a closer look. Holding tight to Scamp's collar he crept from bush to bush until Elise appeared, walking toward the greenhouse.

"Elise!"

She stopped and peered into the sage brush.

Caellum raised up so she could see him. "Is it safe?"

Her expression solemn, but welcoming, she motioned him to approach.

Over tea her story spilled out. The news of Raymond's incarceration fell like a weight on his shoulders. "If we hadn't come..."

Elise shook her head. "We're all just trying to survive. What can we do but help one another? We have no means to fight them."

"Our plans to fight the system by means of peaceful infiltration won Dora to our side, and the reluctant aid of her husband. But that was the end of it.

"What about Commander Feldner?"

"Well, yes. Also three other officers. Nonetheless, our plans have gone nowhere. The future looks even worse than it did a year ago. With this Biate and the Five Hundred we are the puppets of not one but two despots, and an unbeatable army of robots."

Elise's gaze was reflective. "You know, I suspect that many police and military personnel who rely on jobs that support this regime, would choose a different ordering of society."

"What makes you say that?"

"Well, actually, the officer that was here. Lieutenant Lebedev, the one that took away my husband." A sob escaped, and Caellum, held her wrist and waited for her to compose herself.

"He wanted to know all about this town, its vision, the practical aspects of managing water, the construction of our homes, our organic gardening, the uses of hemp.

"You sure he wasn't gathering information to turn against you?"

"I don't see how. He seemed genuinely interested. Wistful. Worked right alongside us."

"So how long were the MPs here?"

Elise poured second cups of tea and shared the tensions of the four-month saga. "I often sensed Raymond was about to explode." She reflected quietly for a moment before she related the child's disclosure and the fight between Lieutenant Lebedev and her husband the night before the soldiers left.

"Raymond beat him up badly. Nonetheless, the Lieutenant spared everyone in the town but Raymond, and seemed to regret the need to take him. In command of the mission, he couldn't return to Transtopia empty-handed."

"Lieutenant Lebedev's invasion of the town and especially your home must have worn on you and Raymond."

Elise's nod and evasive glance flashed the impression of more to the story. But clearly it was not for his ears.

The hand holding the thick paper fell to Biate's side, as she glared at her maid Vanessa. "How dare they? How dare the town send us a half shipment of food? We'll starve to death by the time of the harvest. And Raymond...." Her intensity raised her tone to piercing. "I won't give him over to that pompous half man."

She turned toward the pilot who stood awkwardly near the door. "We're flying to Transtopia. Be ready for the flight in half an hour.

"Vanessa, pack an overnight bag for me, then dress me in something alluring."

With a brisk walk to her bedroom she chose a dress from the closet and tossed it on the bed. The mirror beckoned and she gazed at her reflected beauty as she piled her hair on her head, and then allowed the red strands to tumble over her shoulders. "Down today."

A cascade of shining waves yielded to Vanessa's brush strokes while ire dulled Biate's expression. "I've been counting the days until Raymond's return. I had chicken cordon bleu prepared especially for him. At this moment we should be seated on the veranda in the nice spring air with Rebecca pouring our wine."

With the vehement shake of Biate's head, the brush flew from Vanessa's hand and clattered across the floor. "No, that's not right. Put it up. I look more regal when it's up."

Retrieved brush in hand, Vanessa held up a fistful of hair and brushed hanging strands into it.

The green eyes reflected in the mirror filled with tears. "It's worse than Raymond missing this visit for some stupid reason. I'm sure he's locked up in a Transtopia prison cell. That could mean no more visits—ever."

Through the window, sunlight glinted on the ropes of burnished copper Vanessa had wound at Biate's crown. "Mistress Biate, your tears are smearing your mascara."

"I can't, I won't let Charles have Raymond." Biate gazed through the mirror at her dresser. I don't even know why it matters if I never see him again. I get good sex from the men of my palace, yet Raymond is rarely here and can't even give me that. Why do I long for him so?"

Vanessa hung a pendant that sported a large diamond at Biate's throat and pushed the posts of diamond earrings through her lobes.

"I rely on monthly doses of his quiet listening. Raymond's strong. When I get angry he never cowers like other men. He started that town, you know."

Biate stood as Vanessa retrieved the dress and slipped it over her head, carefully avoiding the artfully piled hair.

"A more honest man than Raymond I have never met. I know the reason he restrains himself from seducing, even kissing me is his condition, that awful venereal disease. If not for that he would be my first choice in bed."

The belt around her waist accentuated the small waist between voluptuous breasts and hips. "The teal suit I wore during my previous visit to Scholtz was to give me a professional look, to complement my power as I presented the threat of the Five Hundred." She admired the sea foam colored gown that exposed creamy flesh reflected in the glass. "But today's gown is the garb of seduction.

"I'll demand food from Transtopia as they're more likely to have it than that little town. And I will demand the release of Raymond to my custody."

"My Lady, wear this shawl. It's lightweight in case there's a chill in the spring breeze. A nice complement to your dress."

Biate allowed her maid to slip the shawl over her shoulders and loop it over her arms. "Scholtz fears the power of my forces. Yet, actually, from my perspective a SuperRo attack is the least attractive option. I'd much rather assume control of the city boasting strong robotic and police and military forces combined. You see, Vanessa, I'm sure we won't always be alone here in Sector 10. It's only a matter of time before external forces invade."

George the butler announced the pilot was awaiting Biate.

As she climbed into the helicopter, the early spring breeze caressed her bare arms and she lowered the shawl. *The baby.* Biate waited for the initial roar and lift off of the copter before resuming her monologue with the pilot, her new audience. "You know, Paul, there's a baby being raised in Transtopia that is actually mine, my child by adoption. Destiny has given me the right to claim a child of royal parents. I'm waiting for him to outgrow that awful noisemaking. Such a nuisance, his screaming. Besides his helplessness right after birth was alarming. And babies need milk, which meant the mother coming along. I really don't want the birth mother around to confuse him. He's to know me as his true mother.

"The most challenging obstacle to transferring my baby to my palace has been the milk supply. But since Vanessa has recently given birth, having her as the wet nurse solves the problem. That baby, whatever his name, is going to return with me soon, I'll rename him, and he's going to know me and love me like my brother loved my mother."

"My best course is to ensnare his grandfather. Next step, assume joint custody and after that, whisk the child, my child, to New Denver."

After a night on the sofa, carrying homemade bread and dried fruit in his pack, Caellum was crossing the sage field toward the mountains when he heard faint thumps to the north and looked skyward. Biate's copter. He dove for a clump of sagebrush. Making himself, his pack and the dog as small as possible, he scrunched close to the ground covered by a meager mid day shadow. Holding Scamp close, he hardly breathed as the sound grew louder until the copter bypassed Gaia's Gardens and receded into the distance apparently headed toward Transtopia.

Dora and Michael. I've been away from my family too long. These past months I should have been there to protect them. And something tells me I may not reach them soon enough.

The helicopter landed on the roof of the Imperial Ritz. The driver gave Biate his hand as she stepped out. A guard opened the stairwell door and sandwiched between her SuperRo guards, one ahead of her, one behind, she descended the stairs. When she arrived at Scholtz's waiting room, the startled receptionist headed for his door rather than using the in house phone to announce the arrival of the illustrious visitor.

Negotiations   37

Sholtz's face held the glare he reserved especially for Nathan Abelt until Nathan excused himself and walked out. Alerted to the next visitor, the governor' features brightened to properly greet another royal, to beam at the person that best loomed as a competitor, at worst, a serious threat.

"Biate, to what do I owe the pleasure of your company?"

"Why, Charles, a friendly visit to further our alliance is long overdue, don't you agree?"

Scholtz held the chair for her under the watchful eyes of her robot guard.

"The Five Hundred have remained at attention below my palace throughout that long, cold winter. How can you not want to visit me for a change and view the unbeatable force you could gain in an alliance?"

Scholtz's chair squeaked as he sat down. "Biate, dear, I would love nothing more. But my responsibilities here are relentless."

"Charles, you men simply don't give due respect to a woman's intuition."

"I beg your pardon."

"It's just a matter of time before we are invaded from the outside. You know as well as I do, in Sector 10 alone, thousands of acres remain unscathed by the post Solar Flash storms. There are bound to be other survivors, powerful metroplexes recovering on this continent."

"I'm fully aware that's a likelihood."

"Then you must admit the advantage of an alliance backed by the might of my five hundred SuperRos and your four hundred police and soldiers combined."

"An outside force will likely approach from the air first."

"All the more reason to be prepared."

"An alliance, yes."

"More than that. Marriage."

"Biate, you know as well as I do that we are both very strong and demand the right to dominate the herd, all others."

"Yes."

"Well, whose word will prevail in a disagreement—yours or mine."

"We'll work together."

"Certainly, but when we strongly disagree who decrees the outcome?"

"Whoever brings the strongest force to the marriage."

"Meaning you?"

"Of course."

"Biate, for obvious reasons, no deal."

Feminine petulance lowered Biate's jaw. "Matter of fact you've already invaded my territory."

"What are you talking about?"

"A place called Gaia's Gardens."

"First of all that town is a satellite of Transtopia."

"As a matter of fact Gaia's Gardens is the essential food producing corner of my Queendom."

"Queendom?"

"New Denver and its outposts. Which brings me to the second reason for this meeting. Your military have captured Raymond Muñoz, the leader of Gaia's Gardens."

"The man was harboring criminals responsible for arson in Transtopia's satellite town."

"He is my Chief Advisor in charge of our food supply."

"They can still send you food."

"Their storage is depleted until the next harvest."

"So you are prepared to attack Transtopia over a food shipment?"

"That and the return of Raymond Muñoz."

"The first we can offer. We will send aide from our food storage to your tiny, struggling realm. But, the second demand we cannot, will not honor. My citizens must see justice done for the crime of hiding fugitives from the law."

Biate leaned forward to offer the governor a glimpse of her deep, cleavage. "Charles, perhaps you need an opportunity to reconsider the terms of our agreement. Let's put aside our differences for now." As she stood to arouse him with a view of her shapely proportions, the guards stepped forward, but she waved them away and walked around the desk to perch on its surface close to the governor's surprised expression. Then she leaned forward again, tantalizing her host with her nearness. "I hope you remember our first encounter as longingly as I."

With an involuntary lick of his lips, Charles nodded and glanced at the robots. "Must it again be in front of your mechanical goons?"

"Always."

Baring his complete indifference to the woman still lying in his bed, Scholtz sat on the edge of the bed naked and spent, his back toward Biate.

"Charles, I will return to resume our negotiations. But for now I have one tiny request."

"Which is?" He faced the wall as he spoke.

In response to the impatient edge in his voice, a caught breath, a twitch of the body still tucked beneath the sheets filled the interval of Biate's slight hesitation. "I would like a suite available to me whenever I visit you."

"That's easy. I'll have an apartment prepared for you immediately."

"And the shipment?"

"We'll load your helicopter tomorrow."

Biate sat up, her hair tumbling over the sheet she pulled across her breasts. "Because we are stronger as an allied force, that is married force, I offer you two weeks, until mid-April to reconsider my proposals.

"Which are?"

"To plan an unforgettable wedding and to turn over Raymond Muñoz to my custody. In the meantime I will choose the location of my Transtopia abode. Please direct me to the office of your building manager."

Charles Scholtz, the seventy-two year old man housed in the muscular body of a man in his twenties, shrugged before he stood up. "Suit yourself."

An hour later Biate had what she most needed, which was neither sex with her despised rival, nor a suite of her own, and which she prized much more than both together.

At four months old Michael was on the move. Though he couldn't crawl, he could roll and propel him across a baby blanket by means of belly scoots. Gone were the days of leaving him bumpered by pillows on the sofa or her bed. The floor, kept scrupulously clean by Jeff, was Michael's domain of exploration. Dora watched him scoot to the edge of the blanket. "Jeff, please watch Michael while I dress."

She shuddered as she slid the dress over her head for the command visit to Scholtz to present Michael to the man who believed he was the child's grandfather.

Rolf dutifully arrived to escort his wife and stepson for their next charade as they faced the father that looked like his younger brother.

Rolf sized her up. "Dear wife, it's nice to see you in something other than jeans and a T-shirt. The lavender of that silk blouse complements your dark hair and blue eyes. You are beautiful, you know."

"Thank you, dear husband. At times you can be almost nice..." Her eyes searched his. "I'm not sure what to expect from dear ole dad."

"Remember he doesn't care about us as family. He values us as commodities. We're the royal *ass*ets of an ass."

"Here take this."

Rolf grimaced. "I'm to carry a diaper bag?"

"It's that or Michael."

Rolf sighed, bent his sleek torso and coifed blond head to retrieve the bag and hoisted it over one shoulder.

"You should hold Michael on your knees part of the time. And don't give me that horrified look. Just think of it as part of your performance. When he get's squirmy I'll take him."

Dora lifted Michael from the floor, traded the hair clip in his fist for a rattle and the family took the elevator to granddad's apartment. When the butler opened the door the first person in sight was Astrid, Rolf's youthful replacement for mom, her vacuous gaze fixed on them as if trying to recall their identity. As full thespian mode kicked in, Rolf strode over across the room to offer the mother that looked more like a younger sister a peck on the cheek, then turned to his synthetic parent with a nod of recognition.

Scholtz eyed the baby for the first time. "So this is Michael."

As Michael's eyes took in his surroundings he sat still, but knowing he wouldn't remain that way for long, Dora gave Rolf a "now's the time" look and thrust Michael toward him. "I need to get a rattle from the bag."

Perched at the edge of Rolf's knee, the baby returned the governor's gaze as he surveyed his grandchild.

"He doesn't look much like our side of the family. I see more of Peter d'Arc than myself."

Rolf assumed an offended look. "He got those blond highlights in his hair from me."

"There are no Sholtz's with brown eyes."

They're Caellum's eyes. Dora assumed an offhand look. "The d'Arcs have French blood. Plenty of hazel and brown eyes in our family."

Since Michael began to squirm, Dora took him as promised and turned to Charles. "Would you like to hold your grandson?"

Charles Scholtz's response to the offer was similar to his son's, but Astrid extended her arms. "I'd like to."

It was the first expression of connection to another human being Dora had seen in Astrid since the consciousness transfer. As she supported Michael sitting on her lap he waved his arms and gurgled, eliciting smiles from his admirers until he forcefully flipped himself sideways, to belly flop on the sofa. With his head close to Charles, he reached a tiny hand toward the hand resting on the seat, grabbed the closest finger and held on tight.

While no emotion other than surprise registered in the governor's gaze, and the hand resting on the sofa arm withheld the slightest gesture of affection, the finger clasped by the tiny fist, remained its unmoving captive. The governor's comments catapulted his present audience into the future. "This is the one who will expand my empire. He is the one that I will send to subdue the far reaches of the continent."

"Dear Father, this expansion is a good twenty plus years away. What about in the meantime? My impression is that Biate has the capability to be a world conqueror."

"I intend to wrest the Five Hundred SuperRos from the control of that insane excuse for a queen."

When the toothless gums clamped on the end of the finger, the hand jerked itself free to wipe off the saliva. The sour lemon down turn of the Governor's lips signaled Dora to hastily remove Michael.

Rolf persisted as though he cared which despot won the struggle for supremacy. "How do you expect to wrest control of the SuperRos from that nutcase?"

As Dora's gaze darted between the blond look-alikes she noted a gratified look flit across the countenance of the elder. *He's pleased Rolf's engaged.*

"I have a plan. We have a certain Raymond Muñoz in custody as our bargaining chip. Biate wants him. I think she's sweet on him."

Michael began twisting his body and pushing against Dora. When bouncing no longer sufficed, she spread a blanket on the floor and placed him on it.

Rolf crossed his legs and spread his arms along the back of the sofa. "So, Dad, you're planning to trade Muñoz for access to the codes to direct the robots."

"Precisely."

Amused at the extent Rolf was warming to his role as Charles's son and right arm man, Dora followed Michael's rolling, scooting progress across the blanket. When she felt Scholtz's eyes lock on her, a bone cold chill shook her. "You will raise him to be a leader so he will one day gather the world under my banner."

Having established the global destiny of the designated conqueror scooting across his floor, the governor ignored him. "But our first and more immediate task is to separate Biate from her guards."

"How? They're with her everywhere she goes."

"Well, make your sorry ass worth something. Figure it out."

Neither Rolf's statuesque posture, nor his fixed stare hid the slight twitch of an eyelid in response to the psychic slap. Dora covered his speechless state with the question, "Then what."

"We'll eliminate her of course."

At Rolf's door with Michael asleep on her shoulder, Dora reached up to kiss Rolf on the cheek still drained of color. "Don't let his verbal cuts demoralize you. Your courage has saved Caellum and Michael and me. You have my love, my gratitude, my admiration."

A caught breath betrayed Rolf's near loss of composure and his sardonic facade crumbled for an exposed moment. He grabbed Dora's arm. "You and Alexi. You're all I have." His pained look glanced off Dora's gaze, before he released his hold, unlocked his door, and wordlessly disappeared behind it.

Anticipating he would drown his suffering in several glasses of wine, she continued toward her apartment. After opening the door, a double take revealed two look-a-likes seated on the sofa.

As she gasped, Caellum turned to face her, and still holding Michael, she ran into his arms. That evening, he and Scamp played with Michael until his bedtime before Caellum and Dora lay in bed to share stories and satiate months of longing until dawn.

As Caellum stroked Dora's hair, she listened to his heartbeat and a single tear rolled across her cheek. "I so long for us to be together. I wish we could have shared Michael's first smile, the first snow of winter, evenings beside the blazing woodstove in your apartment. Yet, I'm afraid for you to be anywhere around Transtopia. The MP's are looking for you in and around the city."

"I agree. But I had to see you and Michael before I return to my old base camp for a couple of weeks. From there I can see if anyone's coming after me. And now I have Scamp to alert me. But I suspect they'll be returning north through the ZD and head toward Raymond's town and surrounding farms.

"In the meantime, I have a request. I want you to arrange a meeting with Lieutenant Yanniv Lebedev of the Military Police. According to Elise, he felt an affinity for Gaia's Gardens. Will you probe him to ascertain the extent of his leaning in our favor? The Sovereignty Movement could use his help."

Emma 38

"Lydia, the people of Unit One have asked me to attend a meeting. I know this is last minute, but it popped into my head to invite you."

Lydia's expression was her answer. "I need a moment to take the kids to my neighbor. We help each other this way."

"Sure. We have time before we need to leave." Dora waited quietly as Lydia rushed to her neighbor's and back, and left again with three children in shorts and T-shirts.

Dora wanted to tell Lydia about her visit to Ft. Carson, but hesitated. On the one hand, she didn't want to upset her. Yet, Lydia deserved to know the truth. So with Leon at the wheel, she dove in. "Lydia, at Ft. Carson, I witnessed the awful future we are heading into. Unless we can intervene, the childcare and education system is going to become worse much worse. If the social engineering project succeeds, our children may be the last generation to be raised by biological parents ...

"What can we do?"

"Nothing I know of right now. Eena and Gavin are due back in spring, and I'm hoping we can put our heads together for a solution. But I'm not planning to bring it up at tonight's meeting since we don't have a plan yet. However, would like you to join me in a meeting tomorrow to discuss childcare with the Governor?"

"He's an intimidating man."

"He is. No obligation."

"But I wouldn't miss the opportunity for close up interaction with his psychology."

The only available space in Unit One was the foyer, which was larger than the main rooms in the apartments, but till too small to hold a hundred plus people. Crowded into corners, those standing covered every inch of wall space, while the majority sat on the floor hugging their legs, with two abreast seated on the stairs. Some spilled into the apartments on either side with the doors open. Black out curtains covered the windows flanking the locked front door.

Winter's toll of coughing, sniffling and blowing noses had yielded to the ruddy health of spring days spent in the sun, working the soil of the Sovereignty Gardens. The downcast eyes that had avoided Dora's gaze over a year ago, now bespoke the people's air of self-sufficiency plus something more that was in the air today. After she introduced Lydia, the meeting began.

Tom, the one who had walked out on the first gardening meeting spoke up. "Ms. Dora, we have a proposal."

"I'm all ears."

"We want you to become the Imperial Governor."

Dora gasped. This was not one of the scenarios she had imagined in her speculations about the topic of the meeting."

"Well, I'm honored by the spirit of your request. But even if it were possible, I would never be an imperial anything."

"Well president, whatever."

"The reality is that whoever would presume to suggest that anyone but Charles Scholtz be governor would face a sure and swift execution on suspicion of fomenting a rebellion."

"Actually, we have discussed his assassination. The voicing of such drastic measures settled into a prolonged silence. "Then voting you in as his replacement."

"First of all we have no guns."

"But the police do. The ones that helped rescue Caellum."

"I see what you are thinking. Such action is out of my league. You will have to take it up with Lieutenant Feldner."

"We have."

"And...?"

"He's considering the idea."

"I see. So your reason for meeting with me is to see if I would serve as your president. Certainly, I would act a as an interim figurehead, while you nominate candidates and hold an election. But to tell you the truth, though I want as badly as you do to restore human rights to this Sector, I'm feeling uncomfortable. I had hoped for another kind of takeover than a bloody coup.

"You won't have anyone's blood on your hands, Ms. Dora. We only want your leadership when there is a vacancy."

Nathan blanched. "You did what?"

"Dora and I went to see the Governor."

Dora again.

"He would hear nothing of our argument about a more intelligent population learning through enlightened child guidance principles.. Horrible man. Compliant army of specialized workers is all he wants. Has an SEI think tank. But he doesn't need your fellow advisors to think. Just to do his bidding."

"Stay away from her."

"Who?"

"Dora. She puts ideas in your head. Do you want to ruin our lives?"

"I want to save our lives."

"You are treading on dangerous ground consorting with the lover of a convicted criminal."

It was Lydia's turn to be nonplussed.

"Caellum Nichols. He's the father of that baby."

"You said *is*. He's dead."

"To the contrary, he's alive and well. I saw them together. There's big trouble afoot about more than the fact that his execution was faked."

"And? You can't just leave this announcement hanging in the air."

"He led the students to a place called Gaia's Gardens on the north side of the ZD. The governor sent in the military police. Thanks to my efforts, they've probably been apprehended."

"I know nothing of Caellum's exploits, of course, but Dora has told me about that town."

"A town of sitting ducks."

"A settlement of self-governing people."

"Lydia, you have all the rights and privileges of a SEI spouse. I provide for your heart's desire."

"*Your* desire, not mine. I'm concerned about our children's right to be children."

"Groundless. The SEI insures the best of care and education."

Lydia's eyes glistened deep sadness though she spoke with firm resolve. "I've made a decision."

Nathan stared and waited.

"I'm leaving you."

It was Nathan's turn to be taken aback. Her words knocked him to the moment in the barn when he woke from the dream of warmth covered by grandfather's blanket; the moment the frigid air clutched him. "Leaving me? Why?"

"While our children are still children, I want them to run wild in open spaces. I want our family to participate in natural cycles between Earth and our bodies and our spirits. I want to drink in sunlight and live simply and collaborate with others in a free and open society."

"Where will you do that?"

"Gaia's Gardens."

"In time that town will be brought under the jurisdiction of the governor and SEI. Then as now I'm your best protection; my position, your source of security."

"Not for me. For yourself. Our children are like Hansel and Gretel. Caged and fattened for future consumption by their captor."

"Captor?"

"Imperial Governor Charles Scholtz."

"He heads up a scientifically ordered society."

"A soulless regime managed by people like you, who have lost touch with their humanity."

Nathan's body jerked as though struck. Shocked by Lydia's vehemence, he walked out of the room. That April night, so unlike the December night spent in solitary misery on powdered hay in the frigid barn, he crawled into a snug and cozy bed in his home — alone. Under the cool sheet, an even frostier cold seized him than the night he thought he might freeze to death.

"Dora, I know about Caellum Nichols." Lydia's tone was gentle, a non-alarming segue into alarming news.

"What do you know?"

"That he's alive."

"Who told you?"

"My husband. Also that you are lovers."

"We are. I was forced to marry Rolf."

"How sad. Tragic."

"Caellum is Michael's father."

"Nathan told me that too. Brace yourself, for I must also tell you Caellum's in grave danger." Lydia relayed what she learned from her husband about the drama at Gaia's Gardens, the apprehension of the students and Caellum's escape..

Dora slumped in a chair. "Thank you Lydia, but I'm well aware of Caellum's predicament. If I didn't have Michael I'd go to him. Sometimes I wonder how I will survive the next days, weeks, months, not knowing where he is or if he's even is alive. I've been through this once."

Lydia put her arm around Dora's shoulder. "I know it's a cliché, but 'one day at a time.'"

"Oh, Lydia, despite the rallying of the people, it appears the sovereignty movement is not only at a standstill—we are losing ground. Caellum and I were ecstatic, to say the least, after he, the only one slated for execution at Freedom Festival, survived. Now it appears June will host an entire line-up of executions."

Feeling keenly, the loss of Lydia in the inviting expanse of their bed, Nathan abandoned it. After a month of going to sleep and waking up alone on the sofa, he didn't expect to see her standing over him when he opened his eyes. He sat up to make room for her on the disheveled covers, but she remained standing. "I have an idea."

"Yes?"

"We visit a pre/school, operated according to strict SEI protocols. According to your standards, the ideal place for Emma."

Nathan groaned. Checking out a daycare facility—what could be more boring. "You take her. I have a full day ahead."

"I want to be clear. The proposal I am presenting may be the only way to save our marriage. Because Emma shrieks with joy when you give her pony rides and toss her in the air; because you hold the twins hands so protectively when we cross the street or navigate a crowd; because the children love to snuggle with you when you read them bedtime stories, I offer this slim chance for a wakeup call, an opportunity for us to stay together-- your attendance with me at this facility."

Nathan sighed and nodded. *Truth is I'd go to the ends of the earth to keep my family together, to remain your husband.* "Okay, I'll go."

"Oh, and one last thing. Our visit will require you to employ your status as a high-ranking SEI official to demand the viewing I desire."

"Dr. Olsen, I'm Special Agent Nathan Abelt in charge of Espionage for the Social Engineering Initiative. This is my wife, Lydia, and our daughter, Emma. We're here to take a look at this facility."

An odd expression crossed Olsen's face. "Sir, for a family to tour this top security operation is unprecedented. Regulations mandate...."

"Doctor, surely you recognize that I out-rank you?"

"Well, I... Yes, sir."

"Then let us proceed."

"Er... Of course, Agent Abelt, Ma'am." The doctor pulled on his white coat as he stood up. "Pardon me. I'll just scoot by you to lead out the door. First we'll observe the Gestation Chamber, where according to strict protocols, the engineering of the citizens of the future begins."

"Thank you. But we just want to see...."

Lydia touched Nathan's arm. "Dear, remember, before the birth of our next child, we want full knowledge of the entire sequence."

There's no mistaking that tone. Next Child? "Doctor, take us to the Gestation Chamber."

A few steps later the doctor's gesture at a doorway welcomed his guests to the room's dim interior. "Mr. and Mrs. Abelt, over here."

The visitors followed him to a glass tube in front of which the Doctor spoke to the attendant, who moved away. "By means of the audible monitor you can hear the strong heartbeat. This eight-months along fetus receives precisely metered nutrients for optimal growth.

Lydia's next words overlay the rhythmic whoosh until the doctor switched off the sound. "In uterus the baby responds to the mother's speech, her loving touches on the womb, even the surrounding environment."

"Precisely. In a human womb the mother's mood swings, less than perfect diet, unpleasant exchanges with people, and other irregularities of life subject the fetus to negative impacts. The Social Engineering Initiative dedicates all endeavors to eradicating the environmental flaws that inhibit human development. Pure, unadulterated science is currently steering the evolutionary trajectory of the human species."

Nathan wished that Lydia didn't have that look on her face as he asked the Doctor, "So, so how long does the baby remain in this manmade womb?"

"For precisely nine months. That part, evolutionary forces got right."

"These fetuses all look alike and the same age."

"Yes, every nine months we extract twelve clones and prepare the environment for the next batch. We are on our fifth production line since solar flash."

"I assume they came from frozen fertilized ovum."

"Exactly."

A fake cheerfulness rode on Lydia's tone as she asked, "And emotion? Among these carefully enumerated objectives, where on the list is love?"

The doctor avoided her gaze. "Love—generally an expression composed of syrupy words to maintain attached dependency. He turned three hundred and sixty degrees and with the sweep of his arm, included the dozen fetuses on the wall. "If this dedication to precise monitoring is not love, what is?"

Irritated at Lydia's lightly snorted disgust, Nathan nodded agreement with the doctor. Yet, an unexpected memory inserted itself: the recollection of their shared joy when he placed his ear on his wife's belly to hear Emma's heartbeat. *Where did that come from?*

"Shall we proceed to the nursery for the most recent extractions and one and a half year olds?"

"Extractions?"

"From the tubes."

Nathan was beginning to be glad he had come. The scientific inception of life was the power source of the driving force of his career.

This was where it all began. He wished he could ignore the disapproval radiating from his wife while he absorbed the scientific rationale driving these procedures.

He looked through the nursery glass. Four attendants for twenty-four babies. "One to six is a good ratio. What about those crying ones?"

"Be assured they have been fed, changed and walked on schedule. Crying in between is simply aberrant behavior. SEI protocols strictly mandate ignoring such pathetic bids for attention. They finally disappear if denied the slightest bit of coddling."

Nathan glanced at Lydia. "Doctor do you have any tissues?" Emma leaned from his arm toward Lydia. In her mother's arms, she hugged her mother and patted her cheek. "Momma, don't cry."

Lydia waved her hand at both men. "Nathan, ignore me. Focus on the other side of the glass. Please proceed, Doctor."

Doctor Olsen, appearing relieved to not chase after something to dry tears, resumed his cheerful tone. "We owe a debt of gratitude to the Stocktavi Institute."

"A Nazi enterprise to disorient victims and engender dependency on the regime." Lydia's mild tone invited more information.

"Yes. During WWII their scientific experiments yielded methods of breaking down the ego to render individuals completely unsure of their position in the Reich. Actors, impersonating officers and doctors, threatened the subjects, making them fearful of painful reprisal if they failed assignments. On the other hand the actors dangled possible rewards — benefits that never actually came. These specimens...."

As infant cries interrupted the drone of the doctor's voice, an uncomfortable feeling crept over Nathan. *I'm surprised Lydia wanted to check out this place. It's nothing like her descriptions of a suitable nursery for Emma.*

Emma reached for him so he situated her on his arm and patted her back.

"Shall we move along to the two and three year olds?"

At the next window, Nathan quickly tallied numbers. "There are twenty-two in this room. Shouldn't there be twenty-four?"

"Unfortunately, we lost two."

"Lost? How?" As Nathan spoke, Emma squeezed his cheeks in an attempt to force him to look at her.

The doctor shrugged. "Died. Inexplicable crib deaths."

As Emma swayed restlessly back and forth, Lydia, for the first time in months, looked into Nathan's eyes. "Nathan, Emma needs to run around. She's such an outgoing, fearless child. I think she'd like to play that room."

"But this is highly irregular." The doctor shook his head.

Lydia gave Nathan an, 'I'm counting on you, this is pivotal to our marriage,' look. He had let Lydia drag him to this place in a desperate attempt to win her back, not alienate her.

"Doctor, your compliance will contribute to a favorable report to Imperial Governor Scholtz."

The moment the doctor ushered Nathan into the room, Emma squirmed out of her father's arms to run among the children. Most of them ignored her as they viewed cartoon figures on a large screen where a monster was chasing a terrified child. One observer who looked around three years old had just broken from the fixated audience to enact the scene by pursuing a screaming two year old around the room. In his dogged pursuit of the victim, the growling monster knocked Lydia down. After a moment of shock, she burst out crying. Nathan started to go to her, but Lydia, of all people, restrained him. Nathan looked from one to the other of the attendants, who were ignoring Emma. Their faces were unsmiling, their eyes hooded, as they interacted with other children.

Emma sat on the floor screaming in a room of eight adults, including her parents, who ignored her cries until Nathan could take no more. *Lydia, what's come over you?* Breaking from her hold on his arm, he picked up his daughter. "I've seen enough. We're leaving."

The Erathans 39

Feeling like an interloper in the kitchen where he had felt so welcome, Jack raided Randolph and Marsha's well-stocked refrigerator and wolfed down eggs and toast before heading toward the hanger. Each time he stepped through the door, the vehicle, behaving as though it were alive, initiated the hum. After circling it, he replicated Jack's disappearing hand magic. He had yet to enter the vehicle, but today he intended to do so. While wondering how to gain access inside, a slight movement to his right initiated the ramp's descent to the ground.

As though in response to an invitation, he slowly mounted the ramp to an opaque enclosure that barely suggested separation from the clearly visible hanger. Hesitantly, half expecting his foot to go through the floor, Jack felt one sole meet a solid surface, and stepped inside. The densification of the surrounding wall transitioned an uneasy sense of no boundary, to the safety of a womb-like interior. When he looked toward the ramp, it was gone as expected, but he wasn't prepared when an instant later a starry expanse replaced the comforting wall of the ship. As he continued to stare around himself, an instant of non-descript darkness preceded the appearance of a wall of rock, which dissolved into inky space, which yielded to streams of light.

Then the familiar wispy clouds of Earth brought relief. But something was wrong. In the distance in every direction a solid rock wall curved overhead. And the stone ceiling peeked through the moving clouds as though he were inside a vast cavern. Jack's confusion increased as his gaze followed the upward arc of the stone to a single point. Within the vast, but walled, realm, bright rays extended from a central sun-like object overhead.

But fascination yielded to alarm when he realized that three craft similar to his own floated in the surrounding skyscape. Feeling exposed he wished the walls to protectively curtain him from whoever or whatever might be peering at him. As though in response, the walls darkened, and only a huge screen disclosed the proximity of the silver disks. As the need to sit overcame him, a seat looking like a captain's chair appeared, and the screen revealed he and his companions had landed on a grassy knoll.

Desperate to ascertain his safety, he desired to know if the craft were of alien or Earthly origin. He had heard of various races, including the grays, the Nordics, the Tall Whites and the Reptilians as well as rumors of both alliances and aggression among off world races. And he was well-aware of back- engineered craft from Earth. *Which is it that surrounds me? Am I about to be shot at?*

Bracing himself for the unknown, Jack took comfort in the solidness of the chair that melded to his body as he gripped the arms and closed his eyes. Feeling more than a little irritation toward Randolph for abandoning him, he berated himself for walking, rather flying, into this fix."

"You probably want to open your eyes for this conversation,"

Jack was shocked to hear a woman's voice as clearly as though she stood beside him. But when he opened his eyes he saw her step forward from two men standing on the ground among the landed craft.

"Greetings, Jack." She waved, but her mouth didn't move.

After a moment of confusion Jack realized he heard her voice in his head. Feeling uncomfortable, he mused, *we're communicating telepathically.*

"That's correct. Why don't you join us now, and we'll use our audible voices since you're more familiar with that form of interchange."

The ramp descended and he walked into a world that though nestled in a huge cavern offered its own land and cityscape. Nearby, a river flowed beneath a bridge leading to a gleaming skyline of polished stone skyscrapers. The river meandered past the grassy hill where he stood and then separated into two arteries, one flowing through what appeared to be cultivated fields, and the other disappearing in a forested realm.

Jack approached the group of men and women who averaged a head taller than his own 6 foot height.

The speaker introduced herself as Anaya. "Let's sit here." Anaya gestured toward a wrought iron table and chairs on the grassy knoll."

As Anaya introduced her brother Ealar and a friend Jonpur, Jack felt the non-threatening presence of the trio, and his fears evaporated.

"So where are we? Has my ship flown me to an alien planet?"

"Oh no. You haven't left Earth. You're in a cavern several miles below the surface as large as Britain's main island."

"And the lighting for this subterranean world?"

"We ignited the self-perpetuating plasma ball that serves as our sun. Even without it, the chemiluminescent plants that crowd the cavern walls lend a soft, glowing twilight to the atmosphere here."

Jack surveyed each of his hosts in turn. "It was rather nerve wracking to see your vehicles positioned around me. I didn't know whether I was to be greeted or shot at."

"Your apprehension is understandable. But believe it or not, in the past century, attacks have come from *your* craft, not ours. Surface Earthlings are known for their aggressive tendencies."

Her statement rankled. "Well, I doubt we're all that bad."

An impish smiled softened her assessment. "On various occasions prior to Solar Flash, you were on the brink of an atomic war."

"True."

"Make no mistake. If it weren't for our interventions at your silos where missiles were poised for attack, a holocaust, far worse than Solar Flash, would have devastated this planet."

"I assume topside bombings would affect you as well."

"Yes. We share a common interest in preserving Earth."

"So who are you? For that matter who are we?" How did you come to live inside the earth's crust while we walk the surface?"

"Our ancient history has many layers and complexities. The simple answer is hundreds of thousands of years ago we removed ourselves from extra planetary explorers extracting gold from earth. Through genetic manipulations they developed a slave race from surface populations to mine the earth for gold."

"So you abandoned us?"

"At the deepest levels, your ancestors chose the very challenging learning curve offered to surface dwellers. After countless centuries of struggle, current generations are preparing for graduation."

"From?"

"The university of third dimension oppression. Many of your courses have involved becoming like the oppressors, others being on the receiving end of usurious agendas. However, currently, growing numbers are mastering sovereignty and brotherhood and have issued calls for help."

"Help? From whom?"

"From ourselves, for instance. Our connection with our surface relatives remains. However, our task is not to save you, but to help you help yourselves."

"How do you do that?"

"This meeting with you is one way."

"Me? What do you expect me to do?"

"We have no right to expectations. We can only inform you of a dilemma challenging a group of sovereignty seekers. We leave you to decide if you want to assist or not."

"With all guns confiscated, rebellion seems foolish."

"Set aside the myth that counter violence will defeat powerful dark forces."

"Then it's futile."

"No. To the contrary, we are permitted to lend a hand to powerful alliances with a clear vision of respect for individual rights, for all life and the ecosystems of this planet."

"Okay. So what's the secret?"

"Remember Star Wars? The force?" The *force* refers to the dynamic field that spirals around and through every star system, every planet, every human. Your field and *The* Field interact. You draw strength from this field like an over-unity device. The Cosmic energy force is ever available. Especially now.

"I don't get what you're talking about. Give me examples."

"On every continent on Earth we have observed members of the human race save trapped, starving, or ill-treated animals, including dogs, whales, elephants—you name it. We have seen the selfless desire to help humanity and save the planet spur inventions such as water-fueled and electric cars, recycling and organically grown produce. We have seen the urge to heal promote the proliferation of natural healing modalities such as color, light, argon, sound, and homeopathy.

"On the other hand we have observed the defamation, sometimes murder, of truth tellers, inventors, and healers that have sought to empower humanity.

"But why didn't their connection to the "Force" save them?"

"Various reasons, one being that they were willing at a deep level to sacrifice themselves to a greater cause. Outrage at their fates triggered the awakening of many to the need for action. Prior to Solar Flash the numbers who saw through the ruthless tactics employed to suppress the truth of your sovereign powers grew exponentially. A super charged plasma field that intersected this solar system penetrated your DNA, your collective heart and consciousness. Since then Cosmic forces support the flexing of humanity's amazing potentials for ingenuity and valor."

"I took off in this ship having no idea where I was headed, with the intention to carry out an unknown mission. Why has that led me to you?"

"We can answer surface humanity's calls for assistance in the form of encouragement, warnings, and information. But no benevolent race, no matter how powerful, will deny you the completion of your season of harvest through your own efforts. Your graduation to self-empowerment must be *your* achievement if you are to gather the fruitage of thousands of years."

"Our meeting is to inform you of the following: sovereignty seekers from Sector 10 have put out a call for assistance. As a surface earthling you can actively intervene in ensuing events."

"What happens if I don't?"

"I'm not sure of the outcome. But I do know, minus your assistance in this current show down, the surface humans' quest for unified strength will be considerably more difficult and likely stretch into several generations."

"How can I assist when I don't even know what I'm supposed to do?"

"Sync your heart and mind with the need of the group and the supporting field."

"That's it?"

"That will guide your ship to the most helpful location in the time/space continuum."

"Your replies seem evasive."

"We've given you the key. You have to open the door. In the words of Yoda, "Become one with the Force."

"Look. I'm a practical sort of guy. My sole passion is to become airborne at terrific speeds. But I count on being able to pilot my craft to the correct landing field. For this I need coordinates. Now, Randolph, you are evading the simple answer I need. "Where the bloody hell am I to land this craft?"

The Institute   40

After the subdued drive home, Nathan followed Lydia into their bedroom. "Why did you want to go there? Even if we wanted to, that's not a center where we could place Emma. "

"But the day care facilities and schools available to our children, the ones you have refused to visit, follow those exact protocols. They just don't include artificial wombs—at least not yet. Remember the doctor's reference to the Stocktavi Institute? Recently I unboxed an old textbook that referenced their procedures.

Nathan responded with pride in his voice. "I know about the Stocktavi Institute. The avant-garde organization in the field of mental health. That institute spawned the Social Engineering Initiative. So how do you know about them?"

"In college I studied their methods thinking they only applied in war to the psychological dismantling of captured enemies.

"That's war."

"But, Nathan, the application of their psychiatry ranges far beyond wartime interrogations. By the twenty-first century the high-sounding phrases and scientific jargon of The Stocktavi Institute referenced the behavior modification techniques that proliferated with we have just witnessed on common people—like ourselves.

"We're not common. We are of the Annunaki bloodline."

"We're hybrids. Fifty percenters. Although we enjoy certain perks, we're like the workers, under the thumbs of the pureblood landlords. The Stocktavi Institute, a Landlord right arm, used wartime experiments to declare war on humanity."

"That's absurd. In what way?"

"Dora showed me the protocol manuals, which credit their originators."

Dora. That hated name again.

"Nathan, don't look so disgusted. Who would understand better than Dora the real agendas behind our political structure? Her disclosures jive with my intuitions."

Woman's intuition, nothing could be faultier regarding the tactics needed to run this world. "Back to Emma. Surely, we can find a better choice for her."

"Even if we can spare Emma, can we ignore the plight of nine-tenths of the people of Sector 10? Nathan, this is my last attempt to reach you. Social Engineering is anti-humanity. Remember, I was a counselor in public and private schools. I now realize they unknowingly followed Stocktavi mandates. Of course, it was hidden behind layered jargon to appeal to people's concern for their children to be the brightest, the most secure, the most successful. Its totalitarian thrust turned schools into factories that inhibit individual creativity and independent thought while demanding unquestioning obedience.

"Lydia, that's absurd."

She grabbed a heavy psychology text, a rarity in book form by 2030. "This textbook, copyrighted 1956 includes a chapter on John Rawlings Rees, a pre-imminent figure in the Stocktavi Institute and wartime psychiatry during and after the war. "Listen to this direct quote:

Especially since the last world war we have done much to infiltrate the various social organizations throughout the country, and in their work and in their point of view one can see clearly how the principles for which this society and others stood in the past have become accepted as part of the ordinary working plan of these various bodies...Similarly we have made a useful attack upon a number of professions. The two easiest of them naturally are the teaching profession and the church: the two most difficult are law and medicine..."

"Did you hear that? 'Attack upon the teaching profession.'"

"Well I..."

"And you and your cohorts, Nathan, who obey the imperial governor's dictates and know full well the extent of his threats, would you say the system you support is more democratic or totalitarian? Listen to this: 'If we are to infiltrate the professional and social activities of other people, I think we must imitate the Totalitarians....'"

"Where are these purported quotes from?"

John Rawlings Rees M.D.'s address to the Annual Meeting of the National Council for Mental Hygiene June 18th, 1940.

"I know of that council."

"The term *Mental Hygiene* sounds benign, doesn't it? Totalitarians are not stupid. But they do count on *our* ignorance—our susceptibility to their high-sounding terms for means of entrapment. Like magicians they use appealing slogans for slight-of-hand subjugation. Audience looks the other way; rights disappear."

Nathan was sure Lydia misunderstood Rees. *He meant an attack on what was wrong with psychiatry. That's why he wanted to infiltrate psychiatry and the teaching profession—to rout out archaic practices that were not therapeutic. Surely, by 'mental hygiene' he meant mental health.* "Lydia, why don't you understand?"

The next day he returned from work to a house in which once again the fragrance of Lydia's cooking didn't meet him at the door. And the twins didn't hug him and tell him about their day. And Emma wasn't playing with her food in the high chair. He wandered alone in a mute and lifeless house where not even his easy chair welcomed him. The only communication came from sheet of paper attached by a magnet to the refrigerator. "Nathan, we've gone to stay at Jean's house until I figure out how to obtain an escort to Gaia's Gardens."

Nor did he welcome the ghost of Matoskah sitting beside him as he sat in his pajamas. "Thank you for sharing your ghost blanket that night in the barn. I don't know how, but it did keep me warm. But I'm warm tonight."

Suddenly, Nathan realized Matoskah and he were no longer on the sofa. "Hey, how'd we end up in your camp?"

"I didn't want to interrupt this challenge."

"What are you doing with those rocks?"

"Making a perfectly balanced construction."

"What a waste of time."

"For you maybe."

"Please, go away. You are depriving me of badly needed sleep."

"That's one way to escape."

Nathan watched the stack of rocks grow to five. "Escape? What are you talking about?"

"All kinds of living creatures do it. Ground hogs, moles, rats. They burrow underground to escape storms."

"You're implying I'm escaping?"

"Uh-huh, Lydia's anger. The whirlwind departure of your family." Eight perfectly balanced rocks.

"Go away. I think you're here to torment me."

"Okay. Better your boss than me." The image flickered.

"Wait. My boss?"

"The imperial governor."

"I can't rid my life of him."

The column grew to nine stones.

"Alright, I'll leave. Good luck with your life."

"Hold on a minute. That sounds like a final good-bye."

"Your choice."

"It's not like you to declare an ultimatum. Why are you holding that rock over the stack you just made? You've always supported me, even when I've made stupid choices."

"Uh-huh."

"So you're implying I'm making the wrong choice now?"

"Not if it's the one you want."

"That's a large rock you're holding over that stone pyramid."

"For now I'll just suspend it above."

"Grandfather, what am I supposed to do?"

"Don't ask me. I don't run your life."

"Are you implying Scholtz does?"

"Isn't that obvious?"

"Hey, are you going to drop that rock or not?"

"You say when."

"Now, for God sake!"

"Okay." The rock fell and smashed the meticulously balanced stack. As stones flew in every direction, Nathan looked toward Grandfather, who was gone.

Oh, no. This can't be the end.

A sound ahead of him riveted Nathan's attention. *That bear.* "Grandfather!"

No response. The bear padded forward, its eyes fixed on him as the great head swung side to side.

Urine trickled onto Nathan's underwear, as he muttered aloud, "This *is* the end."

When the beast stood on its hind legs and roared, Nathan covered his eyes. *Let the end come swiftly.* Then the image spoke to him. *Bears don't talk and that's not grandfather's voice.* Nathan spread two fingers to see the speaker whose voice he recognized. *Scholtz?*

The dream shook him awake and he stayed that way until morning, battling the intrusive vision. The next day, when the knock at the door brought the summons from Scholtz, the dream still enshrouded Nathan in its pall.

"Well, Nathan? I repeat, I'd just as soon throw the whole lot of them in jail."

"Sir?" The feeling of déjà vu derailed Nathan as he faced the governor's bearish swing of his head.

When I face you, why must I tremble? Why can't you be like Matoskah?

"What's the matter with you? Listen up, you imbecile. "It's time for the hammer to fall."

The impact of the rock, shattering the balance, cracking the supportive stones.

"Take the names of any and every person in Transtopia who speaks against my empire. After the Attitudinal Cleansing here for a month, you'll proceed to Gaia's Gardens to complete the cleanse there. The ones you catch are likely to be those who were complicit in hiding the arsons. Captain Starke's men will march them to jail. Along with the recapture of Nichols, that round up will be the final sweep up of insurgents. Don't leave a single stone unturned to cause us future headaches. Are you clear about this assignment?"

"I am, sir."

During the ride to his house, Nathan struggled to clear his brain. *How did I move in one day from grieving the loss of Lydia and the kids, to that dream of conversing with Matoskah's ghost and facing a bear attack, to Scholtz' assignment to smash the dissent here and in that town that's dazzled Lydia? At least, for whatever good it will do me, I'm eventually headed in the same direction as my family – Gaia's Gardens.*

The Attraction   41

Dora insisted the prison guard allow her inside the cell with Raymond. As there was no chair, she faced him seated at the opposite end of his bunk. "I want to hear all about Gaia's Gardens."

When Raymond began describing the principles behind their practices, she touched his arm.

"I'm a great admirer of what you are doing. But since we have limited time, I want you do tell me about the past four months. Maybe, some insight will help me to get you out of here."

He shot her a wan smile. "Thanks, Dora, but I don't see how what I have to relate could possibly help."

"Tell me anyway."

"Well, it began with the arrival of students followed by the occupation of our town by the military police."

"Please include key names."

She watched the emotion crescendo on Raymond's face as he described the final scenes involving Lieutenant Lebedev culminating in their fight.

"Raymond, I need to ask you something that may make you uncomfortable."

"Go ahead."

"In your estimation, which attracted Lieutenant Lebedev more — the town or your wife?"

Raymond got up to circle the cell and stand at the bars with his back to Dora. The pain in his voice was unmistakable when he replied. "In the beginning, my wife. But by the time he left, he seemed equally attracted to our way of life."

Dora opened the door to Lieutenant Yanniv Lebedev.

"I appreciate your willingness to come to my apartment, Lieutenant. I realize this is unorthodox."

"It's a pleasure to meet the royal princess. I'm familiar with your face from news reels."

"Have a seat. Jeff, tea and sandwiches please."

"So you have a robot to serve you."

Ignoring her guest's statement of the obvious, Dora plunged forward. "You were recently in Gaia's Gardens."

A closed look descended over his features.

"Please, don't assume I'm going to rake you over the coals for not returning with as many people as possible to throw into jail."

Jeff returned with the tray and set it on the coffee table. "Thank you, Jeff. That will be all. Please watch over Michael." She, the royal princess, served the officer tea and cucumber sandwiches, fully aware of his surprised expression.

"Yanniv, may I call you that? Raymond Munoz is a good friend of mine."

Yanniv's cup clattered against the saucer.

"Yanniv, if I drop my royal façade, you can discard the deference for my status. I request information as your equal."

"I apologize, Miss...."

"Dora. Only Dora."

"Alright, I'll do my best to meet your terms of engagement."

"Although I have crossed paths more than once with Raymond, I haven't had the pleasure of meeting his wife."

Yanniv looked down, the hand that held the sandwich resting beside the plate.

"According to Raymond, she is quite passionate about their project, the earth friendly town they are growing."

When his eyes met hers she knew they had segued past the danger zone into open conversation.

He nodded agreement. "She spoke so eloquently of their dreams, it was hard not to become lost in her descriptions."

And Elise herself, if I understand correctly. "According to Raymond...."

"You've seen him since our return?"

"We had an in depth, revealing meeting." The telltale sideways shift of Yanniv's jaw confirmed her suspicions.

"Yanniv, there is something personal I want to ask you. As an equal, you retain the right to refuse to reply." *Poor man. She was jerking him from one emotional minefield to another.* The veiled look returned to his eyes. "Which did you admire more, Elise or the way of life she described?"

A long pause prefaced his reply. "Truthfully that is hard to answer. Dora, I have a wife."

"I'm aware of that and don't consider your marriage any of my business." *He looks relieved, more relaxed.* "Now I will confess to you as an equal." *That got his attention.* "Let me put it this way. Elise's explanations, time spent at Gaia's gardens would inspire me also."

He's taken aback. Confused.

She persisted in her single-mind pursuit of higher ground that was also common ground with Yanniv. "I want to insert that way of life into Transtopia."

"Is that possible?"

"Probably not entirely, not now anyway."

"Why?"

"You know as well as I, Charles Scholtz would block such efforts. He has no interest in such a life for common people. They are his chattel."

A guarded expression distanced the Lieutenant from Dora's explanation. "Dora, I think you are leading me into dangerous territory. I'm not willing to go there."

"Of course. But I simply must express my concern for the escaped prisoners you captured."

"I captured arsons, criminals, who were not prisoners."

"To the contrary you returned with young people who were students by choice, who escaped from a forced labor camp, and whom Scholtz deposited on death row."

That's the look I want – shaken and confused. "I see we disagree on that issue. So let's switch to another topic. Currently, I'm concerned about the treatment of the cloned children at Fort Carson. Are you aware of that project?

"Only that we rotate MPs for guard duty at Fort Carson."

"Do you have any children, Yanniv?"

"Not yet."

"I think having Michael really woke me up. Also my association with Lydia Abelt."

"Abelt, I am familiar with that surname."

"Special Agent Nathan Abelt. He informed Scholtz of Caellum Nichols leading the students to Gaia's Gardens. His wife has a Ph.D. in child psychology. To get to the point, she's concerned about the effect of current education and childcare practices on an entire generation of children — with dire implications for our future."

Yanniv crossed his leg, glanced at Dora, and stared straight ahead.

His state of disconnect with this topic is obvious. "SEI protocols at Fort Carson and schools and daycares throughout the city forbid the insertion of adult to child understanding and compassion, what the head of the project, Doctor Olsen, describes as 'coddling'. The government fears, and correctly so, that benevolent practices would trigger self-assertiveness, the desire for individual expression in human offspring. This is not the goal of the system. The engineering of a submissive race, workers on autopilot, is."

"Dora, I'm struggling to comprehend why you are telling me this. Mine is a black and white world in which good guys capture bad guys."

" Yanniv, for countless generations, warriors like yourself have protected societies from criminals and foreign invasions. Women like Lydia and myself, wish to attend the nurturing of the hearts and souls of our children, of the people in general. But to do so requires an alliance with our male counterparts — men like yourself."

I've lost him. "Yanniv, am I correct in assuming you connected at a deep level with Elise's descriptions, the way of life at Gaia's Gardens?"

"I suppose there is truth in what you say."

"Thank you. Please forgive my invasion of your private space. My sense of urgency drives me to reach out to you. Elise taught you of the importance of respecting planetary ecology: sustainable relationships with earth's land and air and water. I wish to persuade of you of the equal importance of nurturing the interior terrain of human beings: psycho-ecology is a term coined for this: sustainable relationships with the human heart, mind and soul."

"Dora, the essence of Elise's persuasions, moved me deeply. Today, the spirit of what you are saying shakes the foundations of my world. But wondering why you are telling me these things distracts me. My job description defines me as both a police and a military man. What does my role have to do with ecology, terrestrial or human?"

"Everything."

"Why me?"

"Because you listen; because you feel. Because you are more than your job description. I have a request of you. Simply a request, not the flexing of my royal muscles."

The embodiment of polite restraint, the soldier waited.

"What I'm about to tell you puts me in grave danger of your betrayal. Should Scholtz learn of my vigorous support of the Sovereignty Movement, he would throw me in prison along with Raymond and the students."

"Ma'am, I would rather not be privy to your secrets."

"Truly, I am risking everything to trust you with this information. In an even more self-incriminating, but calculated move, I ask for your support of our movement while you carry on as Lieutenant Yanniv Lebedev of the Military Police."

As she exposed her traitorous leanings, surprise lifted the lieutenant's brows, but only for an instant.

Dora stood up. "Lieutenant, I leave you to further reflections on this conversation in private."

With impeccable dignity and a polite nod, Lieutenant Lebedev rose to his feet, clicked his heels and faced the royal daughter-in-law of the imperial governor.

As she showed Yanniv to the door, she looked deep into his eyes. "Raymond and the students need to be freed before the tragic taking of their lives."

As the two faced one another on either side of the door, a final query was irresistible. "So, your impressions, Lieutenant?"

"Since you have invited me to speak freely, I will do so. Here are my impressions. "Elise was leading me in a tantalizing direction. You are forcing me into territory where I dare not tread."

Dora nodded and sighed. *I've blown this. Thanks to my bungling, a vital link for the Sovereignty Movement has slipped through our fingers. Too much too fast.* "I apologize, Yanniv. It just that lives are at stake and the future of humanity hangs in the balance. But don't worry. I won't bother you again."

Wordlessly, his expression blank, the soldier saluted Dora, turned on his heels and walked away.

The last person Raymond expected to see on the other side of the bars was Lieutenant Yanniv Lebedev. Only a red line over his left brow remained as evidence of the disfigured face smeared with blood. *You have cost me everything. My town. My family, and soon my life. How can you look so composed as you face the man whose life you ruined?*

"Raymond."

"Lieutenant."

"I've been ordered to return to your town to once again and use it as headquarters."

"And get my wife into bed, no doubt. But you may as well. I won't be around much longer, and I did ask you to protect her. But why rub it in my face by telling me? Go, take the spoils of the victor and leave me alone."

"Though I admit to feelings for Elise, she is married and I am married. Raymond, I have no intention to betray my wife or you. I assumed sooner or later you would find out I was stationed at Gaia's Gardens. Naturally, you would imagine me to be in your house. But I've come to set your mind at rest. I will not stay in your home, and I will maintain a respectful distance from your wife."

"Then why are you returning?"

"The governor has ordered me to seek and find Caellum Nichols. We will be searching the Zone of Destruction, surrounding farms, wherever he might be hiding."

"Yanniv, are you aware that Caellum's only crime was seeking human rights for the Onmatson Farm forced laborers?"

"My troops and I helped save those same workers, hiding in caves, stranded on farms, many of them close to death from starvation in the aftermath of Solar Flash."

"So is that the best a man can ask of those who govern? To feed their stomachs, yet just as easily kill them for seeking human rights?"

"I understand your point. My grandparents escaped a harsh regime. But I think Transtopia's recovery since the decimation by Solar Flash and high winds has been remarkable. Electricity is restored where needed. People have running water and safe places to live.

"Yanniv, you're an intelligent man. You know I am speaking of more than comfortable lodging. I'll tell you something that may surprise you. I think you're at heart a man of honor, although you support the dishonor of the rogues in power.

"You're the second person today to talk to me like that."

"Oh, yeh, who was the other?"

"Dora d'Arc."

Raymond smiled. "Of course, I know Dora very well. Did she mention that she and Caellum are lovers? That they have a child together?"

"Michael. So that's why she was trying to recruit me."

"Although that would be reason enough, the motive driving her persuasion reaches far beyond personal concerns. The fate of humankind is at stake and Dora, though she is a royal, has the fortitude to fight the current regime."

Yanniv looked as though he had been struck.

"Let me ask you this: when the system has executed all the defenders of human rights; when the youths who wanted to remain students are all dead; when all the dissenting dreamers of a better world have been removed and you are surrounded by the cinders of destruction — think who your sole comrades will be."

Yanniv stared through the bars that were above eye level and whispered, "Their henchmen."

The Explosion 42

The increasing stench in the air drove the uneasy residents of Mu to meet in the town's central courtyard beside the well.

"The time has come. Escape through the portal is our only choice."

Grief constricted Chas's ability to speak as he referred to his livestock. "Eena, I think the horses could be a benefit."

Eena squeezed his hand as she stated the unwelcome obvious. "We have to cross the Continental Divide."

Preparations to leave ensued that day and the next. But Eena and Gavin, preoccupied with the augurs, hauled the last of the rotting fruit from the orchards to the birds. The wildness had left Phoenix but neither bird attempted a return flight to their home in the giant cypress along the river. Their human bond mates approached often to peer lovingly into the now-open eyes, and to communicate an upwelling of gratitude and love for their sensitive companions.

Cesla pulled away from Eena's prolonged grip on his neck, so as she mused aloud, she contented herself with scratching his favorite place where the neck and jaw line met. "I recall your momma's glare as I yearned to touch her chick. How adorable you were with feathers clumped randomly on stippled skin and eyes too big for your head. The first time you grew from a speck in the distance to an enormous bird responding to my call, a feeling like no other lifted me out of this world. And beyond the portal, when we soared above a boundless sea of forested mountaintops—that was freedom on steroids. Oh, Cesla, those were the glory days."

"My heart stopped the day the soldier shot at you and the feather fell into the reservoir. I willed it not to float to the shore. But it did, and the soldiers jumped in their jeep and carried it away to return with it a year later. To this day it lies somewhere in those god-awful army tents in the valley, our beloved valley.

"Remember when we airlifted the sections of the holograph emitter? Your intelligence, your leadership of the augurs, made that coordinated effort with ropes possible. Without the holographic forest to cover Three Mountains, the imperial governor riding in the plane with Nathan would have seen our village and that would have been the end of us.

"Dear, Cesla, through the years of our bond I thought I would eventually lose you to an augur mate, not that smoke spewing monster that slept through our adventures.

"You're growing restless. I'm almost finished. I must apologize for pushing you too far months ago when we saved Chase's livestock from the wolves. Before we part, I want you to know that I never would have abused your friendship again.... Here, eat this.... Because I have no better friend than you, I want to spare you any more suffering. When the vog curls its noxious fingers around this corral, hug the ground, close your eyes and go to sleep resting your head on Earth's breast for I'm sure she loves you as I do."

When the stringy papaya pulp had disappeared and only a sticky palm remained, Eena's voice broke and she could say no more, so she turned to go, but for one final, lingering moment, Cesla stretched his neck and curled it over her shoulder.

An hour later stinging eyes and the smell of rotten eggs elicited complaints from the children as for the last time the procession loaded with heavy packs followed the path away from the village and toward the stream that led up the mountain. Gavin hugged Leslie and with the promise to catch up with the group, remained behind to say his farewells to Phoenix. Though Eena dared not look back, not even a glance toward the augurs, several times Leslie turned to scan for her husband, until giant sequoias hid him from view. But, frantic about April, she pressed on toward the portal.

A hundred and fifty-seven emigrants were gasping for air by the time they reached the entrance to Three Mountains. Waves of trembling shook the ground on the Mu side as people poured through the portal.

Leslie shouted for Gavin to hurry up and doubled over in a coughing fit.

Sharing her concern, Eena offered to return for him. "Leslie, take April through. We'll meet you on the other side."

Chas, two children in tow, yelled. "Eena, the volcano could blow any second."

"Don't worry. I'll be right behind you." *Gavin, what's happened to you?*

For several seconds, as though to accommodate her as she retraced her steps, the movement underfoot ceased and calmed the final group crowding beside the portal. Expecting Gavin to be lying on the ground somewhere on the path Eena called and coughed and tried to ignore her burning lungs.

When a low rumble accompanied by a shock wave, knocked her to the ground,

a hand grabbed hers and pulled her up.

Gavin.

"Come on." He put his arm around her shoulder as she gasped for air, and pulled her forward. "We can make it."

Accompanied by a roar and peculiar screeching sounds as though metal rubbed against metal, a violent shaking threw both to the ground. They covered their noses to escape the fumes suffocating them to death.

"Just a little farther. The portal's just ahead."

It was impossible at this point to see the entire structure. But the visible stones and the exploration of their hands confirmed Eena's worst fears. The half circle of inlaid rectangular stones bordering the portal was destroyed, some stones ejected, others askew. A jagged crack, three inches wide, bisected the mountain face where the center of the doorway between worlds had been.

Gavin moved forward to stretch his hand through the portal. But solid stone resisted his palm. "We're trapped."

"So, we are to die with the augurs."

A second deafening explosion shook the ground, the mountain's seismic nod to their death sentence.

The crowd of people milled around the Three Mountains side of the portal grateful to breathe oxygenated air and for solid, unmoving earth beneath their feet. It been several minutes since the last person stepped through. Chas and Leslie stood closest to the ponderosa trunk that marked one side of the doorway between worlds, their eyes fastened on the gap beneath the arc of vines, willing the people they loved to appear.

Chas's tension grew as the interval of inaction stretched into several minutes. The mental image of Eena and Gavin overcome by fumes, lying prone on the ground spurred him to take action. "I'm going back."

Silence descended over the group as he navigated the log barrier Cosima had strewn about to obscure the portal. But a gasp marked his passage beneath the vine archway. He was still visible on the other side.

"The portal. What's happened to it?"

Dread clutched Chas's chest, his voice barely audible. "The volcano must have blown and shook the mountain. The explosion destroyed the portal."

Leslie was inconsolable. Someone reached for April, but she tightened her hold and comforting arms embraced mother and child.

After several minutes of shock, someone spoke the words they all knew must be said. "We better get moving. Those troops are gonna find us if we don't."

They briefly considered the bridge, which was the quickest way off the mountain, but also the most dangerous—with children, not an option. Down the side of the mountain offered descent well hidden by trees. They'd head for the ravine between Quartz and Blue Lake Mountains and follow the path from Three Mountains Valley to Lemon Reservoir.

Eena's cabin tucked away in the pines along the trail beckoned to Chas. "I'll catch up." Inside, evidencing a soldier's violation, the wind blew through a broken window and tossed a red-checkered café curtain. The aluminum trough where Eena had bathed and the closet emptied of her single dress and moccasins sewed by Matoskah offered mute reminders of romantic interludes that would never return. *Eena, I believed we would face down the disappearing opponent together. The still water that you equated with my nature calmed you, yet the way you blazed into dangerous situations captivated me. I basked in those sun-like rays now taken from me. Without you the path ahead looms dark and empty.*

Chas caught up with the others at the augur pilots' bunkhouse where a tree limb balanced on the roof had opened a hole in the pine tiles. Farther up the slope, their last view of Anaya's Hobbit house was the diagonal wooden planks across the front turning gray with the wear and tear of weather. Weeds had claimed the garden and gone were the chickens that used to scatter in the wake of people following the trail. After passing Anaya's house near the entrance to the rickety bridge, the emigrants began their descent.

Keys 43

Dora decided against wearing what Rolf called her 'peasant clothes for the command meeting with Scholtz.

"Jeff, Michael should sleep for the next couple of hours. I should return well before he wakes up. But just in case, there's bottle in the frig. As usual heat it to just above room temperature before you give it to him."

Dora headed out the door and up the elevator to Scholtz's office.

As usual, not one to stand on ceremony, he motioned her to sit and blurted. "The Protocol Manuals. Have you returned them to Ft. Carson?

"No."

"What do you mean 'no'.

"I mean I'm not finished culling through them.

"For what!?"

"For information, mistakes, typos. Whatever needs revision. Those are important manuals." Fortunately, with pressure building from Scholtz, Lydia had almost completed the rewrite. *And when we burn the originals, no one will ever have recourse to them again.*

The governor eyed her suspiciously. "They're fine as they are. Return them to Fort Carson immediately."

Dora knew she had promised Caellum she'd behave around Scholtz. But after a year and a half of enduring imperious directives, his tone triggered her. She stood and with an equally vehement "Yes, Sir!" almost saluted him, but restraining the urge, forced her arm down as she moved toward the door.

"Dora d'Arc!"

"Sir, I have agreed to your demand. Now, Michael needs me."

"You do not leave without my permission. Sit down." For the second time, he gestured toward the chair.

Forcing the appearance of composure, she sat.

"As Rolf's wife and a member of the royal family, you are obligated to help him."

"With what in particular?"

"To devise a plan to separate Biate from her guards."

"I have no idea how to achieve what you ask. When will she be returning?"

"She's still here. She now has a suite in the Ritz."

Dora slowed the gallop of her heart. "Governor Scholtz, Rolf and I are no match for those mechanical goons. They've been in my apartment."

"In your apartment?"

"Yes. After Michael was born, Biate tried to kidnap him."

Scholtz escalated to red-in-the-face belligerence. "Kidnap him? Why wasn't I informed of this?"

"Rolf saved the day quite magnificently. You would have been proud of him."

"I doubt it."

"Just listen." Dora described how Rolf calmed Biate, and she and her guards finally left.

But Scholtz's entire point of focus was his grandchild and he waved away the words meant to redeem his son. "That insane woman could attempt a kidnapping again. She has a suite in this building, and I believe she's there now."

Something ice-cold penetrated Dora's gut. Fortunately, Rolf or Shaun are the only two people, Jeff or myself will open the door for."

"But Rolf lives with you."

"Of course. You know what I mean." *Big mistake.*

"Henceforth, I will post a guard at your door." Right then the concerned grandfather sent for one of the bodyguards posted in his foyer and assigned him to guard Michael."

But it wasn't Scholtz's guard Dora wanted. *Caellum, Michael and I need you. Where are you? We've been apart too long. I wish you would show up today and take us away from this place — to safety.* For an instant her yearning was so strong, she imagined Caellum would be waiting, holding Michael, behind the closed door.

Charles' voice interrupted her reverie. "You, Rolf and I will devise a scheme to separate Biate from her guards. While she is in my custody,

I will force from her information on the CAI. After I have the needed codes, I will have her killed. Surely you understand my heir's kidnapping must not happen. It would make cinders of our plans."

Your grandson. A means to conquer the world. Nothing more.

As Dora left the governor's office with permission, the building trembled slightly and she recognized the effect she had noticed before: Biate's helicopter either landing or taking off from roof. Feeling relief that the mad queen was leaving the premises, Dora rode the elevator to her floor accompanied by the guard. But when they reached her apartment, the door was wide open, a key protruding from the lock.

When Dora's hysteria became gulps and gasps for air, Rolf held her away from him so that her wet eyes met his. "The governor has sent for us."

She turned to the assigned guard. "Wait inside out of sight, just in case."

When they burst into Scholtz's office, the governor, Captain Starke and Commander Feldner were bending over a long table, the surface of which was a map of Sector 10, including New Denver Airport.

Scholtz was swigging a drink when Dora and Rolf arrived. Achmed was behind them. The ice clinked in the glass as the governor slammed it on the table and shoved a paper toward them. "Read this."

"War? She's declared war?"

"Her copter left minutes before you called. "I'm deploying troops to stop them."

"The Five Hundred?"

"No doubt, on the march before this day is done."

With a long pointer, Captain Starke indicated an arced line of defense beyond Rubble Wall extending both west and east of the city boundaries. "She'd be crazy to march them through the Zone of Destruction."

"She is crazy. But like you say the valley between the foothills and ZD makes the best sense for an attack."

One thought alone surged Dora's panic. "She's taken Michael."

The jaw twitched in the enflamed features. "My heir. My, my grandson...

He turned to Captain Starke. "Provide me troops and a military transport copter." And to the presumed parents, "I'm going to get Michael."

"I'm going with you."

The shake of the governor's head rejected her resolved tone.

"You'd be a liability."

Captain Starke addressed his superior. "Sir, you could be walking into an ambush. You should remain behind your troops."

"The future ruler of Transtopia is in enemy hands. I'll take a protective force. Ten men."

"Sir, the robot force can easily shoot down your copter."

"We'll skirt the SuperRos." Scholtz turned to Achmed. "If I am shot, can you repair me?"

"Despite titanium fused bones and nanite producing inserts in your brain and spinal column to promote healing and longevity, you're mostly biological. You would need a medic."

The governor turned to his secretary. "Send a limo to fetch a surgeon in case I need one."

And to the officers, "With the SuperRo Force on the march, the number guarding Biate's palace is likely drastically reduced. This is my best chance to reach that mad woman on her own turf." Scholtz's eyes swept the room as he paused. "I have a second reason for going New Denver."

His audience waited in suspense. "I intend to find the A.I. control center, stop the march, and eliminate that silly caricature."

He called through the door. "My uniform."

When his secretary appeared with his grandfather's coat, the one with the gold braid, his back straightened as she slipped it on him.

Dora broke from Rolf's restraining hand to rush across the room to Scholtz. "Please, take me with you."

The soulless blue eyes swept Dora. "You dare to ask a second time?"

"Michael will need me."

Though she wept and begged, Scholtz stood immovable. "Get her out of here."

Rolf put his arm around Dora's shoulder and moved her from the room as Scholtz commanded Starke to deploy ten troops to accompany him.

As Dora and Rolf entered the foyer, Dr. Monroe arrived.

Within minutes the roar of the single overhauled military transport copter from Fort Carson, the CH-47F Chinook, landed with whirs and thumps on the roof. Not long after the collective hum of military vehicles moving single file on Main Street rose to the top floors. Eight troops proceeded up the stairwell followed by two more guarding the army's supreme commander.

And when the copter took off, Dora's apartment door remained open, the guard still waiting for someone: Biate, Dora, anyone to come.

Raymond didn't expect *any* visitors. But he was especially surprised to see Lieutenant Lebedev at his cell again. "I expected you'd have reached my town by now."

"The political stage has changed radically since my last visit. The capture of Caellum Nichols is now on a back burner."

Yanniv signaled the guard to let him inside the cell. When the man's echoed footsteps receded, he began his explanation. "Biate has kidnapped Michael."

Raymond silently felt into the anguish that Dora must be suffering.

"The queen took off in her copter with the abductee but left a note behind: a declaration of war.

Raymond remained motionless, every sense activated to high alert. "The Five Hundred."

"Yes, they will march toward Transtopia, possibly today." I have to return quickly to my post. If Captain Starke has discovered my absence, I'm quite sure he is infuriated."

"Why are you here and not there?"

"Your town, including your wife and child, require protection."

"Raymond ran his fingers through his hair as he contemplated the vulnerable state of Gaia's Gardens."

"They won't know the danger they are in unless you inform them."

Raymond shrugged and threw up his hands.

"I have brought this to present to the prison." The lieutenant pulled a paper from an envelope and handed it to Raymond. The official seal of the imperial governor leant credibility to the document.

"Let it be known by all men present that we are in a state of war with New Denver; that we are to be attacked by five hundred super robots. A cell of this prison retains, Raymond Muñoz, the one man with skill in Robotics sufficient to disable them before they obliterate our city. You are herewith commanded without delay to release Raymond Muñoz to the custody of Lieutenant Yanniv Lebedev."

"Wait a minute. Did the imperial governor actually write this?"

Yanniv swallowed and shook his head.

"Then who...? No. You're kidding. You of all people forged an official document? Think what you are doing. Lebedev. Do you want to die with me?"

"If that is what is required to save your extraordinary town and its defender, your wife, then I will die beside you with honor."

MP's and police had proceeded by march and motorcade, past the point where Main Street turned left into Canyon Road. Lieutenant Lebedev looked carefully up and down the street before he inserted the key in the lock of the gate built in Rubble Wall at the entrance to the ZD. "See that motorcycle on the other side? In less than twenty minutes it should carry you home."

Since the words Raymond wanted to say stuck in his throat, he grabbed Yanniv's hand and silently shook it before hurrying to the bike. He kicked the clutch, the engine roared and he sped forward. But within seconds the sound of two shots ricocheted around Rubble Wall. Hurling the bike around to face the wall, he almost lost his balance.

The pile of rubble hid the gate and Main Street and the shooters from view. *Yanniv and perhaps another soldier?*

Half expecting an ambush, he puttered back toward the wall, following the bend in the road toward the gate that hung wide open. Two bikes and two men lay on the road. Hurrying, he rushed to Lebedev, the circle of red growing on his upper chest. A grimace and a slight pulse indicated life.

He hurried toward Starkey who lay in a twisted position. No motion, no pulse. The man was dead. Raymond returned to Yanniv. "You will be tried for murder, whatever your story. I have to get you away from here. Can you sit up?"

With considerable effort and support from Raymond, Yanniv, raised his back from the concrete.

"Now, lean on me as we walk through the gate. With Lebedev almost swaying out of his grip, he locked the gate. Lowering his shoulder under Yanniv's, summoning all his strength, he lifted up to practically drag the man. "You have to help me get you to the bike."

Seeing a long bungee cord wrapped around a rack behind the seat he unwound it and held onto it. He had leaned the bike on the kickstand. But climbing on without tipping it over was going to be challenging. With Lebedev leaning against him, holding the man with one arm, their combined weight knocked it over twice before he succeeded in mounting it himself will holding onto Yanniv. Glancing at the gate he knew that any second now someone would spot the two overturned bikes and the dead captain.

"Yanniv, can you lean on my back while you lift one leg over. With grunts and groans and considerable effort the lieutenant raised his knee to the seat. Raymond reached around, precariously shaking the bike to grab Yanniv's calf and help him all the way on, as the blood spread to the bike, to his own shirt, everything.

He grabbed the bungee cord, wrapped it around Yanniv, fastened it at his stomach, released the brake and pressed on the gas. Sirens sounded behind them as he sped beyond the view of the drivers jumping out of their cars. *Oh, God, don't let them climb the wall and see us. If they follow us, we're doomed.*

Ambrosia 44

That night as Nathan tossed and turned, the specter of Charles Scholtz loomed. *Now that my closest allies, Lydia and Matoskah, have departed to return no more, I am left with you, you, who bully and threaten. You, who care nothing about my fate. For the first time I see clearly that you care about no one's fate but your own.*

Robbed of sleep by the nightmarish image of the bearlike Scholtz, Nathan fixed himself a cup of hot chocolate, and sat and stared into the emptiness that was once his home. When Matoskah, sitting cross-legged on the floor, appeared, he was surprised, but pleased the vision had replaced the nightmare. "I thought you had left never to return."

"I came to congratulate you."

"I beg your pardon."

"Well, Nathan you're a free man now."

"Meaning?"

"Wife's gone. No one to pull you away from your work."

"Don't rub it in. What are you doing with those grass stems?"

"Braiding them." Takes three strands. Male, female, progeny and a tie to make the braid strong.

"Lydia doesn't appreciate my plans for her."

"Your wife's essence blesses children. Compare this sweet grass braid with the gold braid of the uniform Scholtz wears. Two kinds, two purposes."

"What's that supposed to mean?"

"My people offer scented smoke from sweet grass braids for blessing friends. The Imperial Governor wears a gold braid to signify power over inferiors."

"What are you doing with that shell?"

"I'm lighting the end of this sweet grass to make little pile of cinders in this shell." With a flick of his hand Grandfather brushed fragrant smoke toward Nathan. "Smell that?"

Superstitious old man. "What's it for?"

"Your blessing."

Nathan felt like a child as Grandfather wafted the smoke around him and uttered prayers, which in an unknown tongue, still comforted his torn spirit.

"Grandfather, are you a spirit?"

"Yes, I've left that physical body."

"I'm sorry you died living in that teepee." *I've been reduced to conversing with an apparition.*

"We've had this discussion. The affection of people dear to me filled my camp. I possessed what I wanted."

"I miss Lydia."

"That's why I'm here."

"Thanks, but you're no substitute for her and my kids."

"I thought you might want company since your camp is empty."

"At least I have my work."

"Uh-huh. You're an excellent spy."

Something about the accolade punctured Nathan's bruised heart. "I don't know why I ever wanted so badly to be a spy. Like you, at this moment I most desire the affection of people dear to me to fill my home."

"How much does that matter to you, now that it's gone?"

"More than anything in the world."

"Good to know. Now sleep well, my friend. Tomorrow will test your resolve."

Nathan still smelled sweet grass when he woke up and saw Lydia standing over him. *Are Grandfather and my wife conspiring together?*

"Nathan, dear, I have a plan."

Still groggy, he ran his fingers through his disheveled hair and sat up.

"Here's a coffee and a homemade sweet roll, your favorite flavor, cinnamon."

Ambrosia. As he sipped, and savored the still-warm roll, his wife sat down beside him.

"I'll get right to the point. The threat of Biate's Five Hundred, the possibility of losing Gaia's Gardens, Transtopia, all power to her, commands George Scholtz's attention."

"You know about all that?"

"Yes, Dora..."

He waved away any revelations from that source.

"The Imperial Governor cannot personally oversee the implementation of SEI policies in day care centers, schools and at Ft Carson. He depends on SEI employees to enforce the planned modifications of over thirty-thousand children."

Along with the succulent dough, uneasiness wormed its way into Nathan's gut. "So where are you going with all this?"

"First you have to decide what matters most to you."

I most desire the affection of people dear to me to fill my home. Wiley old rascal, that Matoskah.

"Then you have to make a choice. The stakes will be high either way you choose. In one direction you ally yourself with the governor, in the other, with me."

How much does love filling your camp matter to you now that it's gone? More than anything in the world.

"Brace yourself for what I'm about to suggest. With a PhD in Psychology, I have the credentials to take charge of Ft. Carson."

Nathan swallowed the last bite for a swift reaction. "Well, you can forget that idea. You may have a qualifying degree but never the blessing of the Imperial Governor of Sector 10.

"No, but I have been prompted to take the position by The Royal Princess and daughter in law of the Imperial Governor, Dora d'Arc Scholtz."

That despised name.

"Nathan, Dora is permanently in my life. She has earned my great respect. Your resistance is futile. In fact if we are to continue our life together, you will have to accept that she will remain one of my foremost advisors."

Tomorrow will test your resolve.

Nathan processed wordlessly during the pause before his wife continued.

"You could be my other main advisor..."

"Lydia, you're just stroking my ego."

"Dear, I need you at first as a backup authority figure when I replace Dr. Olsen and establish my position. Then, dear, you must stay out of my way."

That fire in Lydia. It both intimidates and attracts me. "Lydia, are we really expecting another child?"

"No, dear. We will have more than enough children to care for from now on." She cupped his face in her hands. "Nathan, I have loved you because for our three offspring you have been such a loving, attentive father." Lydia lowered her hands and faced her husband not as a wife, but as a person on a mission. "At this stage of our relationship I'm counting on your help to ensure that Transtopia's 30,000 children at our childcare and education facilities receive the benefit of similar attentions."

Nathan's face hardly registered the magnitude of his wife's declaration because another concern crowded his brain. "Lydia, sounds like you will be very busy."

"We both will be. This project requires lifelong dedication."

"But will you still cook those meals for me?" Childlike wistfulness heightened the timbre of his voice.

"It depends largely on your efforts. Ease my path in designing Child Gardens filled with thriving children developing their creativity, finding their unique paths and exploring in Nature, and I promise to prepare mouthwatering roasts with cobbler, pie or chocolate mousse for dessert. And when we are alone, I will express my passionate gratitude to you."

Nathan sighed. "You know, I'm a dead man when Scholtz gets wind of this. But, oh well, until then, it'll be a very good life."

Blue Laser 45

With snowmelt springs tumbling pell-mell over boulders toward Destiny River, to accomplish an hour hike exhausted the travelers. At each swiftly coursing stream parents handed children and heavy backpacks across and steadied one another so slippery stones didn't topple them. They managed to cross two streams with minor mishaps until the one at the bottom, the deepest and fasted flowing, captured a child that slid down a bank. Those who ran after the bobbing, tumbling figure couldn't keep up and had it not been for the fallen limb that knocked her out and pinned her shirt, the stream might have carried her another mile and drowned her.

When she regained consciousness, the joy at her recovery was subdued as grief for Eena and Gavin shrouded the assembly. Silently, the emigrants hiked the stony path along the stream, leading from the mountains to the valley that housed Lemon Reservoir.

The two people remaining on the Mu side of the destroyed portal huddled together as they faced their last moments of life. Their eyes and noses burned and the dark vog hung so thick with smoke they could only see inches in front of their faces. Their lungs, in defense against the choking air, began to constrict their breathing. And as they gasped, the poisoned air seared their tearing eyes and the flesh in their throats.

Eena was wondering if the augurs were still alive when a slight hum overhead became noticeable. With seconds a lasered blue light penetrated the ground beside them. The beam widened to encompass the hunched pair but extruded the poisonous gases engulfing them. Between their coughs and gags, draughts of pure oxygen cooled their lungs, and they could see the hellish brew of gasses no longer engulfed them but swirled beyond the circumference of the beam that enclosed them. Too dumbstruck to question what was happening, they rose helplessly into the air until their dangling feet met a solid floor, and they faced an array of colored lights that spanned the silence.

We're dead. No can't be. We're still in these hacking, tortured bodies.

Someone who wasn't coughing, and must have been waiting for a lull in theirs, stepped closer. "Hello, I'm Jack Merrick."

More than the continued gasping left Eena and Gavin speechless.

"I really don't know anything other than that this ship is to take you somewhere — a destination unknown to me."

Eena's first thought was of being trapped in time forty thousand years in the past. "But this is not our time, our world. We can't remain here."

"Don't worry. You're not."

"Into which world are you to transport us?"

"To the 2038 world."

Gavin held up his hand in a 'not gonna happen' gesture. "The portal's closed. That's why we're still here."

"Doesn't affect this ship. It moves through both solid rock and time."

When Gavin and Eena introduced themselves, they were surprised Jack already knew them by name.

He spoke first to Gavin. "I believe you will want to meet your family beside a body of water called Lemon Reservoir."

"Definitely. Yes."

"As for you, Eena, does the name 'Techno City' ring a bell?"

"I've been there."

"You and a man named Caellum."

A slight nod escaped Eena's bewilderment.

"I believe you're to hook up with him first at a place called Garden of the Gods."

"His camp is near there. Someone has given you instructions."

"Yes, someone you know. Does the name 'Anaya' ring familiar?"

Eena's expression brightened.

"After Gavin joins the escapees from Mu, I'm to take you to those stone monoliths.

Eena's expression was quizzical. "I suppose you even know how to get there."

"I have no idea where the place is. I just have to psychically plug that destination into the system."

"Where are your controls?"

"The ship and I converse mentally."

"It's alive?"

"In a sense, yes."

As Eena looked around, hope surged. "If only we could bring along the augurs."

Jack stared at her.

"They're huge birds — taller than we are."

In the face of Jack's silence, she sighed. "Never mind. Just a passing thought. They survived best in their own time and space. We can't provide them an ecosystem suited to them." *Cesla*.

A doorway at the side of the craft opened.

"I just said I don't think we should bring the birds along."

"And I agree with you. I believe this is Gavin's destination."

"But, I don't want to stay in Mu."

"Oh, we're 40,000 years and an ocean away from that location."

Jack recalled Randolph grinning at him on the other side of the door as Gavin stared in shock.

"But we didn't move."

"Take a look."

An expanse of shimmering blue water reflected the sun past the shore where the ship had landed. Gavin seemed rooted to the spot.

"Lemon Reservoir." Jack's voice visibly shook his passenger from his disbelieving stare. "Now if you don't mind disembarking from my ship, I have another mission assignment. You should see your people...."

A couple of children dashed from the tree line, followed by more people, one of whom pointed the ship's direction.

"It's them."

"I see Chas." Eena turned to Jack. "May we have fifteen minutes?"

"Eena, I would like to say, 'yes.' But my impression is every minute counts for the exact timing of my next mission."

Gavin was already fast walking toward the growing crowd of people. "Gavin, you'll explain to Chas?"

"Of course." Gavin broke into a run. "Leslie!"

Eena turned to the pilot. "This ship is a mystery.

"Certainly, in the time/space we are familiar with. Listen, I'm not sure I comprehend this any better than you do. It's been explained to me that this ship blips into a subquantum realm of entanglement, of instantaneous connection."

"How?"

"With the speed of intention."

"Tell me. Where are you from?"

"I'm English. But I've flown this ship from Morocco."

Morocco... help from the world's underbelly, an ally. "I know this is an odd question, but please tell me: what color is the sand there?'

"Red."

Red sand that's far away.

"We have arrived at our destination. Please move quickly as another mission requires this ship's immediate assistance. In the morning watch for my disk.

Numb with grief for the augurs Eena leaned against a standing stone, and reviewed recent events. Burning coughs still wracked her body as she stared across the valley toward Transtopia Metro, the hub of life and drama that encompassed a fraction of the former Colorado Springs.

"What now?" Her fingers trailing the surface of the monolith, she walked around it to face the mountain. Someone was approaching. She squinted her still burning eyes. *Caellum.*

"Caellum."

"Eena?"

As she ran toward him, a sob escaped. "You are truly a sight for sore eyes."

She wept against his shoulder and he soothed the person that had led the group of youths including himself from Township to Three Mountains.

"Eena in the three years I have known you, I have never seen you cry." As her sobs subsided, he led her inside the circle of standing stones, and they sat down facing each other.

"The volcano on Mu exploded."

"Tell me about it."

"The augurs are all dead by now." Eena paused as the words caught in her throat. She filled in the details of the escape of all but herself and Gavin through the portal.

"I saw a UFO through the trees," Caellum said.

"The one that brought me here. Piloted by a man from England, Jack Merrick."

"Whoa."

Eena could hardly believe her eyes or how good it was to see Caellum. "Over a hundred and fifty people will soon be arriving. Where can they go? Where can we find lodging for so many?"

"At this point, I can't say. Such an undertaking will require considerable planning. We'll need Dora's help."

Eena brooded as she picked up a small pebble and threw it into the breeze. "It seems our efforts to liberate the workers are futile."

The firelight flickered across Caellum's shocked expression. "Eena, I can't believe I'm hearing those words from you."

"Three times, Caellum, you have jumpstarted the sovereignty movement, first in Techno City, then twice in the capital of Sector 10. You've done all you can. Twice you've been captured and now that Scholtz knows you're alive there's an active manhunt for you again. In all likelihood, without your leadership, the movement in Techno City has fizzled out also. Let's face it. The power of the Landlords is undefeatable, and we are doomed."

A sudden gust swirled around the pair, kicking dust into Eena's eyes. She gasped as her tortured eyelids squeezed shut. When her fingers failed to brush the sand away, Caellum grabbed his water bottle and poured a pool in his palm. "Eena, let me help." Dipping his fingertips in the water he washed the grains from her eyes until they blinked open.

She looked around. "I think we have a guest."

Sparks swirled toward the sky as Caellum stoked the fire. "Eena, we're already dealing with one crazy female."

'Oh?"

"Biate... her pretensions to being a queen."

"I'm referring to a crazy old man."

Caellum shot her a 'you've definitely gone nuts' look.

"Grandfather just reproved me."

"Eena...."

"You don't know that Matoskah died."

The pained look that contorted Caellum's features reminded Eena how much the native elder had meant to all who gathered at his teepee for counsel.

"His spirit haunts me. Won't let me even consider defeat."

"Eena like you, I grieve the loss of Grandfather. But I'm a realist. A dirt devil picked up that sand."

"Devilish Matoskah's more like it."

Caellum grinned and despite his skepticism, looked around for the invisible guest. "He did have his ways of penetrating our thick skulls."

"Yes, a three year old memory haunts me. I would like one small, but significant victory under our belts before we accede to landlord rule."

"I'm listening."

"After solar flash my first exposure to the resurrected schemes of the Landlords, other than the townships, was at Ft. Carson. The specter of the clones in the Gestation Chamber haunts me even more than Grandfather."

Caellum nodded. "Dora's visit to Ft. Carson so upset her, she lifted the Social Engineering Protocol Manuals."

"That took nerve."

"Says the clones raised at Ft. Carson are phase one of the SynRo Worker Project. Says, the project is a branch of the eugenics campaign initiated by the Nazis early in the twentieth century, the manuals delineate a series of childhood modifications to these clones. By means of inserts and genetic modifications they intend to produce a docile bionic worker race."

"I suspected as much."

Flickers of light from the fire caught their grim expressions.

"I'm with you. But for now, what about the group that escaped through the portal?"

"Apparently they're on their way here from Lemon Reservoir."

"Why didn't Jack bring them here?"

"The ship's too small to accommodate a hundred and fifty-plus people."

"Should we wait for them?

"No Jack said he's returning for us in the morning."

"Then what?"

"To Techno City."

A look of horror froze Caellum's features. "Whose insane idea was that?"

"Apparently, Anaya thinks we have an important rendezvous with destiny there."

"Rendezvous with the clinker's more like it."

"I trust her."

"Easy for you."

"I'm going, but you have the right to refuse. For now let's get some shut-eye.

Long after Eena's slow deep breathing signaled sleep, Caellum lay on his back, loathe to return to Techno City, watching the Constellation of Orion arc across the sky. Endlessly, night after night *you traverse a vast domain. Why must I keep returning to confinement in small rooms that bar my freedom and threaten to snuff out my life?*

The Bridge   46

The emigrants followed the shore of the reservoir until lengthening shadows forced them to establish their first campsite. Some were nervous about stopping so close, so accessible to the military stronghold in Three Mountains Valley. But many claimed exhaustion, and children whined and refused to walk any further. So they spent the first night with barely a two-hour hike separating them from the Valley where a soldier would be pacing, maintaining a vigilant night watch for the return of the people.

Chas, glad to have obliterated the image of Eena choked to death by smoke and fumes, his heart singing 'she's alive,' pulled out a map. "Tomorrow morning we should leave Lemon Reservoir behind to follow Promise Path. Within an hour we'll pass under the bridge that we chose not to cross."

Mid-morning the following day the travelers had broken camp and collected reluctant children to move on when someone spied a soldier watching them through binoculars from a promontory.

"Oh no, now the U.A. Army will be chasing after us."

"We better pick up the pace, whiney children or not."

"Past that bridge, about a mile ahead, Promise Pass turns east. Then we'll be out of sight."

Parents hoisted the youngest ones to their shoulders and tightly clasping the hands of other offspring, pulled the protestors along as fast as they could manage. When they walked under the sway bridge where Eena had saved Gavin from falling to his death, gawkers were urged to keep moving at a fast clip, but any real gain was small, because the pace so exhausted the children they had to stop long enough for their stamina to return. An hour past the rickety conveyance, someone turned to look through binoculars checking to see if they were being followed. Sure enough a soldier, no doubt with several behind him, had stepped onto the bridge.

"We're being pursued."

After another half hour, when they reached a bend where Promise Pass stretched east, the morning breeze gathered momentum until a brisk wind pushed the fleeing group along. Before the bridge disappeared the binoculars went up for one last view of the bridge. Swaying in the wind, the bridge tossed its single occupant side to side. He had almost reached the far side when a violent shake tore away two slats and the man followed the tumbling planks through the gaping hole.

The viewer gasped. "That was a long way down."

"Into a rock pile."

"Probably dead."

"We don't know that."

"I'm going back." Cosima's tone was resolute.

"Cosima, It's too dangerous. We don't want to risk the whole group for that spy."

"I have to help him."

"It'll take you half an hour to reach the man, who is probably dead."

Cosima was already headed that way. Doctor Sanchez, the only doctor in the group caught up with her and turned toward the rest. "Keep going. Depending on what we find, we'll catch up with you or not. Move along. You have children to save."

Chas spoke quietly. "I'm going too."

"Let's wait here for them. Leiani's eyes pleaded with those of her fellow travelers.

"Let's hope we're not jeopardizing a chance to escape."

Children broke free to play as adults grappled with various reactions to the dilemma that could doom their trek less than a mile beyond the slope of Quartz Mountain.

The three hurried to scramble through boulders and rock piles beneath the bridge until they found the body sprawled on the ground.

A cry escaped Cosi. "Emory!"

Dr. Sanchez took his pulse. "By some miracle, he landed between rock piles that would have mangled him badly, if not split his skull. Let's find a couple of strong branches about five feet long."

It was at best an imperfect stretcher by the time the doctor shoved the branches inside his zipped sleeping bag. Emory groaned but remained unconscious as they hoisted him onto his make shift stretcher and returned to the waiting emigrants.

By the time they caught up with the group and laid him on the ground he began to moan.

"Probably hurts all over."

"I have a willow bark tincture." Raiel pulled a bag that hung from her shoulder.

"Let's give it to him. I hope he doesn't have brain swelling from a ruptured aneurysm.

Cosima took Emory's hand. "How serious would that be?"

"He could die."

Noon the following day arrived before Emory opened his eyes.

Dr. Sanchez leaned over him. "Lucky you were almost across when you fell. A fall from the center of the bridge would have been fatal."

Cosima heard her name.

"I see two of you."

"How's your head?"

"Terrible headache."

"Were you so determined to give away our location, even after we have been driven from our home Mu?

"What do you mean?

"The volcano. It erupted. We escaped." She struggled to speak. "But Eena and Gavin didn't make it through."

His fingers wrapped around hers, but she withdrew her hand.

"Cosi, you're cold toward me."

"I trusted you."

"So you think I told the men the real location of the portal."

"What else could I think?"

"Why do you suppose I returned to Three Mountains?"

"To report for duty."

"Cosi, you told me you'd stay overnight. You were gone for over a week. Didn't it occur to you I might worry?"

"Grandfather was the weakest I have ever seen him. He was teaching me about healing herbs before..."

"He died."

"Yes, at least I think so."

"Soldiers searched the mountains, but never did find his body."

"Grandfather had his reasons."

"Cosi, I was worried the military were interrogating you."

"So, your plan wasn't to lead them to the portal?"

"Cosi, did any soldiers pass through the portal after your return?"

"I hid it."

"Good for you. And I pretended ignorance of where I had entered and led them on a wild chase looking for a possible portal. Our deadend search spanned all three mountains."

"So you came for me?"

"Went to Matoskah's camp first. The cold embers in the fire pit alarmed me. After searching for you, I went to the base for help. Then you showed up at the Captain's headquarters. You know the rest. Oh, this pain. I can't talk anymore."

Cosi put her finger over her lips and touched his and took his hand. "Shhh. Close your eyes. I'll be here beside you."

People hoisted packs and called their children to them. A last check of the bridge revealed no one spying on them, and almost as one body, the people were on the move again.

The March   47

Eyeing the baby sleeping in Jeff's arms, Biate prattled to the pilot as they approached the airport. "Well this is better than the last time I saw him. He's quiet at least." When they reached the palace entrance, she hurried inside and directed Jeff to hand Michael to Vanessa.

Jeff refused. "Ms. Dora has instructed me to guard Michael at all times."

Vanessa forestalled Biate's about-to-fly rebuttal with a smile at Jeff. "And you will remain Michael's guardian. Please follow me to the baby room."

In Biate's favorite private sitting room, a large clump of translucent sea glass plated with solid gold rested on an accent table near the entrance. A baby bed and changing table had replaced other furnishings. Biate proceeded with her next move, which was to retire to the hidden control room that only she could enter to activate the Five Hundred. In less than half an hour, the SuperRo force stood motionless in formation on the airport runway facing south.

Biate hurried to her balcony to see and hear the full effect of their battle launch. The central A.I. beamed a powerful signal as she gave the command, "Positions." The formation spread out to an evenly spaced three hundred yard breadth. At the second command in the sequence, "Ready All" a unified metallic swish, click, stomp reverberated the might of the greatest power hub in Sector 10. Then the code words: "This is an attack of war. Move out," activated the four hundred and ninety-eight strong killing machine, initiating the unstoppable siege of Transtopia Metro.

Of the force on the march, three SuperRos had a special mission as assassins. Charles Scholtz's removal from the scene would forever secure her supreme power. Enjoying her private glee, she pulled out her binoculars to watch the march until her forces were out of sight. From then on the holographic monitor revealed their exact location.

Vanessa was buttoning her blouse and Michael was happily satiated when Biate returned to the nursery. "Give the baby to its robot attendant." Then to the two guards at her heels, the only ones not on the march, "Do not remain beside me. Secure the front and rear entrances to my palace."

"Vanessa, please communicate to the cooks, the butler and all three servers that tonight the members of my court will eat our celebratory meal together. Then return to get me ready to proceed with my coronation as Empress of Sector 10. Afterword, as we feast, everyone shall see me wearing the crown jewels."

After Vanessa bathed and dressed the queen and styled her hair, Biate sent the maid away so she could return her focus to the screen that only she was privy to. But becoming bored with watching the uneventful march of an army halfway to the scene of attack, she decided to check on the adoptee.

Vanessa was nowhere to be found when Michael began to fuss. Biate hurried ahead of Jeff to pick him up. "I can quiet him. I am his mother, after all."

She picked him up, but immediately held him at an arm's length. "Ooooh, disgusting." With the command, "Change him," She thrust him toward Jeff and hurried out of the room.

Shifting back to her role as military leader, the onscreen blips alarmed her. A military transport copter was approaching her forces by air. As the onscreen object veered away from the battalion, she gave the order for the closest ranks to fire. Within seconds at the edge of the screen the helicopter dropped behind a Hwy 25 bridge before it disappeared.

It must have crashed. What if it was carrying Scholtz and he lay dead? Like magic, her main obstacle to unchallenged rule of Sector 10 would have blinked out of existence. She addressed her troops. "Maintain your ranks. March on to Transtopia."

Stocked with herbal remedies and sterilized cloths for bandages, Gaia's Gardens claim to a medical facility was a two-room building, of cob construction like the homes. The town had attracted a medic and a nurse, who were equipped to deal with daily abrasions, infections, and flus that sent people to the facility seeking help. But the chest wound of Lieutenant Yanniv Lebedev was out of their league. Nonetheless, they nodded grimly at Raymond, saying they'd do the best they could to save his life. He'd already lost a lot of blood, but between the two of them, someone would minister to him day and night without interruption.

The bell that hung on Raymond's porch post rang repeatedly and loudly until the people gathered to hear the Five Hundred were likely on the march. He advised the people living on the west side, closest to the likely march of the robots, to leave their homes for now. The entire populace agreed if the town came under attack, they'd escape into the grass and sage to the east. He asked for a couple of men to join him to head for an I-25 overpass to view the breadth of the march and ascertain if it would encompass the town.

As the people prepared, he and two others ran an eighth of a mile northwest toward the overpass. For an eerie twenty-minutes, they lay on their bellies, no robots in sight, until a light vibration induced them to put their ears to the pavement. A rhythmic thud reverberated through the concrete supports with such force, it made them nervous that it would bring down their high vantage point. Within minutes the advance line appeared stretching the width of three football fields across the valley between the dismembered freeway and the escarpments bordering the Rocky Mountains.

The robots held their gaze until an interfering thump, whir approaching from the south turned all heads toward the helicopter from the direction of Transtopia. When the clicks and metallic clanks signaled the rapid fire zings of the closest block, the helicopter swerved behind the overpass where the observers lay in peril and dropped to the ground.

Abruptly the gunfire ceased, and the ranks of Five Hundred marched past people who could not see the source of the heart-stopping rhythmic pound that shook the ground. And with the downed copter on one side and the passage of the soldiers on the other, the men on the overpass pressed their bodies against the pavement and waited for the next move.

In Biate's near manic state of glee that the royal heir was safe in her palace and Transtopia was minutes away from capitulating to her might, she returned her attention to Michael. Calling Vanessa, she returned to the nursery, where the freshly changed baby was smiling as Jeff lowered him to the palette on the floor.

"No, not the floor. Floors are dirty!" Biate grabbed Michael and swept him up, initiating squirms and grunts.

Jeff held out his hands. "I must take Michael. I am his protector."

Biate brushed him aside. "I am his mother. Michael, stop crying. Be still." When his writhing and the volume of his cries escalated, she held him away, pinning his arms to his side.

As though determined the squirming enfant would obey her command, Biate ignored the robot's rote claims. The volume of Michael's protests and Biate's insistence escalated while Jeff extended his arms inches from the baby struggling against his captor until Vanessa swept toward the scene. "I'll take him." She turned to Jeff. "Together, you and I are Michael's guardians."

The metallic arms lowered in response to the statement supporting his programmed role as Vanessa gently freed the writhing, twisting child from the queen's rigid hold. Embraced in the combination of sways, gentle touch and soothing tones that mothers employ, Michael calmed down. But by the adopted child's first smile, Biate was nowhere around, because she had lost interest.

After the final row of robots marched past the observers, the copter lifted from its hiding place to resume its flight path.

"Looks like it's headed to New Denver. Doesn't make sense."

The men hurried to Gaia's Gardens where a relieved buzz filled the town.

Raymond spoke in low tones as he helped Elise broadcast chicken feed while Gabe gathered eggs "We are by no means out of danger. When Biate's troops seize Transtopia Metro, we will be glaringly in her scopes and our relative freedom from interference will cease."

Elise gestured with the empty scoop. "Perhaps before the next, even worse regime becomes entrenched, our town needs to migrate."

"Let's check on Yanniv."

He pushed open the door for Elise to slip under his arm as she shushed Gabe. Yanniv lay unconscious, but it was a relief to see him cleaned up and bandaged.

The medic Rich responded to their unvoiced questions. "As far as I can tell the bullet missed vital organs or arteries. But I really don't know what's going on between the bandages of the entrance and exit wounds. Thankfully, his breathing, though shallow, is regular. All we can do is wait."

Hand in hand with Gabe darting between them Raymond and Elise walked the length of the town and over two streets from the apothecary to their home. From the cob houses that graced the lanes, to the greenhouses and the vegetable gardens that sustained radiant health, to fields of hemp providing rope and clothing and filling the apothecary with healing tinctures and salves, Gaia's gardens had been lovingly, thoughtfully constructed. Raymond grimaced at the prospect of leaving.

But something even worse overshadowed his spirit. He felt weary, discouraged, as though they would never escape the reach of the plague of ruthlessness that withered men's hopes and gobbled the fruitage of their dreams.

Thick Skulls   48

Framed by the gold trim of her throne, Biate held in her lap the crown that would be placed on her head on this memorable day, the day she conquered Transtopia-- on this, the day she would be crowned Empress of Sector 10. Startled by a scuffling sound she stared directly ahead at the door, on the other side of which her SuperRo guard stood. Biate's clasp on her crown tightened.

Shots, groans, a loud thud, a metallic scrape. The queen slid out of her chair to stand on the platform supporting her throne. Shouts. The door opened. A soldier lay several feet from the door. Only the foot of the downed SuperRo was visible. Holding tight to her crown, Biate descended to the main floor to edge toward the nearest door. but five soldiers burst in, guns ready, followed by a man wearing a doctor's smock and Scholtz.

"But you're supposed to be dead," the queen wailed.

"Yet, here I stand supported by flesh, blood and titanium." His voice boomed across her throne room.

Biate's lip lowered in a pout. "But my coronation was to be tonight."

"Sure, whatever you want in exchange for my grandson and access to the panel that controls your army."

"Neither of which you shall obtain. If you leave now, my army will merely be stationed in Transtopia to secure the city. If you do not, Transtopia's minutes away from obliteration."

"Seize her."

Biate swung her crown, which hit the nearest soldier with a glancing blow, and ran down a hallway.

"Pursue her but don't shoot. I want her alive."

She ran into the dining room, attempting to fling the door closed behind her. A chase ensued around the 10 ft long table until she barely escaped a soldier's lunge to grab her and slipped through the far door..

Biate rushed through the main reception hall, flung open the French doors leading to the balcony and scrambled up the waist high wall.

The wind dislodged her hair from its carefully arranged pile, and coppery snakes writhed in every direction. "If I die you will never gain access to the panel." Holding a thick tangle of vines she gestured menacingly with her grown.

Scholtz gasped at the Medusa-like image poised to leap, and to his troops ordered, "Stand back! Lower your guns." He pushed through the soldiers, all guns pointed at the floor.

"Now, Biate, this is childish. Let us resume our negotiations in a civilized manner."

She held tight to the vines winding around the wrought iron post. As he approached her, she teetered.

"Biate! Men, back away."

Scholtz adopted a soothing tone never before by anyone from Transtopia. "Biate, dear, how magnificent you will look with that crown on your head."

As though to prove the truth of Scholtz' declaration, she reached up and crowned herself with the symbol of might.

"Queen Biate, Your Majesty, I will send my men from the room. Let us share a glass of wine at that table and celebrate your victory and our alliance." And to his men, "To the next room. Move!"

Either the newly donned crown unsteadied the queen, or the fresh gust of wind racing around the building threw her off balance, or perhaps the slight gesture of intent to sip wine with the imperial governor caused Biate to teeter.

Scholtz's reach was too late. The vine loosened and she swayed as the smooth soles of her shoes slid on the painted railing, and she lost her grip on the roped vines. Scholtz yelled her name as, arms flailing, she fell.

Below a stalled shuttle bus broke her fall, and she landed with a thud, bounced and rolled off. Tumbling headfirst, her skull hit the pavement with a sickening crunch. Scholtz, for once speechless, leaned over the railing. Biate lay in a trickle of blood, the crown perched upside down several feet away.

For the first time, he noticed the SuperRo guard positioned at the rear entrance to Biate's palatial suite below the balcony. Alarmed that the sight of himself would activate the robot, he jerked his head out of the line of fire and with a shout ordered his troops to fire on the robot. But before the first shot, metallic crunches and a loud thud, followed by silence and puzzled looks, pulled him forward to view a robot crumpled near the queen.

Vanessa burst through the door to awkwardly navigate the collapsed form. "Biate!" Hurrying to the person she had known since childhood, she kneeled beside her and, tears coursing down her cheeks, clasped her hand. The queen's personal maid looked accusingly at Scholtz. "She was wounded already, and you have killed her."

Scholtz turned to Monroe. "We can't let her die. Find the stairs. Go!"

Imagining the access codes forever lost due to Biate's death, he turned his attention to the AI that controlled the robots and singled out three soldiers. "Locate the control room. Search Biate's suite. She surely would have hidden it there for easy accessibility."

As Scholtz hung over the balcony, Monroe reached Biate and placed two fingers on her carotid artery "She's alive, barely. She needs medical attention in my surgery."

Scholtz addressed the Pilot. "Start the copter. You two, get a stretcher from for the victim."

Vanessa pleaded from Biate's side. "Please let me be with her."

Scholtz's reply was curt. "There's no room for you. However, if you don't want to find yourself in a similar state to your mistress, you better point us to the control room."

An odd half smile crossed the maid's stricken face. "That location I'll never reveal."

Scholtz turned to a soldier. "Grab her." After the soldier reached the scene and secured Vanessa's forearm, Scholtz focused his stare, meant to engender bone-chilling fear, on Vanessa. "We will know before we leave, which is minutes from now, or we will leave behind your corpse."

To the soldiers collected around, he said, "Join the others in an all-out search for the control room. I'm going to get my grandson." Scholtz and his men moved from room to room until he entered a room that was obviously the nursery and saw Michael on a pallet on the floor. Jeff stood close by.

"Why is my grandson on the floor with no one in attendance but this idiot tin man?"

"Jeff responded with great dignity. "I am Michael's guardian."

Vanessa rushed in, "Ms. Dora has assigned both Jeff and myself to watch over Michael."

"The future leader of my empire? My flesh and blood, the one to restore global dominance to our line in the care of a machine?"

Though incapable of experiencing hurt feelings over the demeaning of himself, Jeff was always protective of the truth. "Michael is of the d'Arc royal line."

Though Scholtz stepped toward the baby, his head swiveled around toward Jeff. "What did you just say?"

"Michael is ....."

"Michael is what?"

Unfailingly honest and able to speak only in affirmative sentences, Jeff persisted with elucidation of the facts. "Michael is Rolf's stepson."

The governor stopped his advance toward the happily cooing baby, a stricken look on his face as though recoiling from the object on the floor.

"You mean, I've been duped by Dora d'Arc?"

"Duped is not in my syntax files. Dora d'Arc and Caellum Nichols trust me to guard their child."

"Dora d'Arc has deceived me." Resembling his predecessor, Charles the SynAnn escalated into red-faced rage. "My son Rolf helped perpetrate this lie. This baby is no closer to me than a street urchin. Scholtz' voice became quiet before words hammered between clenched teeth. "They will be imprisoned and tried for treason." He spoke to himself, for his own satisfaction. "They will never see this abomination again nor know of his whereabouts."

Suddenly, Charles Scholtz sprang forward to seize the baby, but a blow to the head penetrated his skull. He teetered and unable to turn his head to see the one who had attacked him, crumpled to the floor.

When the attacker dislodged the block of sea glass embedded in solid gold, blood gushed from the skull and as Jeff approached and Vanessa gasped, the once invincible leader lay unconscious.

The Foyer 49

Eena and Caellum stared through the door of the ship they had entered seconds before.

"So, where are we Jack?"

"Techno City. It appears we've landed on a college campus."

The passengers gasped as the surrounding wall seemed to disappear.

"Don't worry. The wall is still there. Just transparent from our point of view."

As the pair looked out, they saw a growing group of gawkers.

"I think you want to make your escape sooner rather than later."

"But where do we go?"

"Professor Neil's office is in that building."

"Will we see you again, Jack?"

The pilot shrugged. "Good possibility. For now I'm off to my next mission."

Caellum grinned. "Well thanks for the ride." Then, in his driest tone "Thrill of a lifetime."

Eena pulled on Caellum. "Let's head out. Hope to see you around, Jack."

Waving to the crowd, the pair heard their names shouted more than once

"They don't seem angry."

"Quite the opposite."

As the pair waved at the crowd and darted to Building Twenty-Two, the group covered their eyes as they watched the upward rise of the ship. For a few moments it spun as it levitated over the heads of the gawkers, before with a salutatory dip, it shot away, becoming a pinprick in the sky and disappeared.

After bounding up the stairs, the pair waited for what seemed like an eternity until the door opened to their knock.

"I don't believe it."

"We're here professor. Flesh and blood."

He hurried them inside and hugged Caellum.

"Caellum, my friend, I thought...."

Caellum grinned. "Can you believe Dora headed up my faked execution? We're parents, by the way."

"Sounds like a great story. And Eena, what brings you here?"

"You wouldn't believe my story without preparation. Heard of portals, Dr. Neil?"

The professor's chair creaked as he leaned back, the painting of the Aegean Sea to his left.

"So, since you two are here, I assume you're aware of what's happening in the Sovereignty Movement."

Eena shook her head. "Only that it's a dismal failure."

Neil sat silently for a moment. "Which of us could have predicted the events that have transpired over the past two and a half years?"

"We hoped for much more."

"Eena, in those days your spirit seemed indomitable."

She shrugged the dejection that hung like a tattered garment.

But gladness to see an old friend animated Caellum. "So, Neil, what have you been up to?"

Neil hesitated. "Like yours, my story needs a good starting place. Wait here, while I cancel my next class so we can pay someone a visit."

When Neil returned he led them outside to three bikes. "Our transportation."

They wound their way beside the city park, to the outskirts of downtown, passed a trolley picking up passengers, and pedaled through a residential district. After several streets of modest houses, two story homes with broad lawns came into view.

Caellum blanched when they reached the all-too-familiar estate with roses beneath the diamond paned bay window. But unlike his first visit, the unkempt lawn needed watering and the roses, pruning.

"Where are we?" Eena asked.

"The home of Dora's parents."

Of the three Caellum remained on his bike. "Neil, you sure I should be here?"

"I can assure you, you won't be thrown in jail again."

The front door opened, and the butler ushered them into the foyer, the reminder of the fateful day Peter d'Arc took the Sovereignty brochure.

The memory and the familiar voice calling, "Neil, that you? Get on in here," stalled Caellum's steps.

The butler opened the double doors to the den, the one where Dora had introduced him to her parents; the one with the familiar cathedral ceiling, imposing fireplace and overstuffed chairs. But Peter d'Arc was in none of them as he lay in a day bed. He looked smaller than Caellum remembered.

Neil approached the old man. "Peter, I don't believe you've met Eena, but you surely remember Caellum."

"Caellum? Alive?"

Nervousness shook Caellum to the core despite the professor's reassuring glance. When Neil chuckled and explained the execution was a hoax, Caellum held his breath.

Peter chuckled. "My daughter's been here to visit since then. Wonder why she didn't tell me."

"Neil raised an eyebrow as he straightened Peter d'Arc's pillow. "Now, Peter, do you honestly think she would risk anything happening to this guy?"

Hastening to secure his precarious situation, Caellum blurted. "We're parents, you know."

"Oh yes, I know about Michael. And yes, I know he's yours. Congratulations, Son."

Son?

"So Peter, we've all got stories to tell. Let's start with ours—yours and mine."

"I still say my daughter tricked me, when she hooked us up, Neil. Pour me a scotch. Okay, just a sip."

After Neil obliged, Peter smacked his lips and lowered the glass to the bedside table.

With eyes blearier than Caellum remembered in a face that had grown thin, the jaws slack, Peter gazed out the window as he spoke. "We faced famine you know. I feared mobs of people throwing rocks through my windows and public lynchings of myself and my wife. Dora's suggestion to support Sovereignty Gardens seemed almost as dangerous. She provided the seed and charged us, two men who know nothing about gardening, to rally the people to plant gardens on parks, roof tops, in yards—all around the city."

"Things got out of control, at least from my perspective." He looked accusingly at Neil. "Those meetings you were holding aggravated the situation."

"You know Caellum's the one to blame for those."

Traitor. Caellum frowned at Neil.

The man that had sentenced Caellum to death looked from Neil to Caellum. "So how'd you meet?"

"In the city park Caellum shamed and hounded me until I agreed to help seed infiltrators. So, go on with your account."

Dora's Mother, dressed in exercise cloths, poked her head in and after polite greetings and a kiss on her husband's cheek, glided away.

"Loves her exercise classes. The flower shop manager offers the weekly workout routine." Peter reached toward a stack of leather bound books on the table that served as his nightstand. "Get that top one for me, would you, Neil?"

"Ten years ago, the d'Arcs were one of the wealthiest families in the world. Trillionaires, we owned corporate conglomerates, central banks, and vast swaths of continents. But we hid our wealth behind our public charities. When you're riding high like that, you don't think you can ever go down."

He held the book in the air and shook it. "When you have such vast power the greatest aphrodisiac is more power. Convinced we were gods, by divine right we controlled the planet."

"It's all in here." He thumbed through the thick pages with brittle edges. "This ancient volume records cyclic cosmic events recurring over thousands, tens of thousands, hundreds of thousands, even millions of year time spans. We knew Solar Flash was coming. We knew it was a Cosmic housecleaning of the extortion, bribery, usury and lies that kept corporate heads and elected officials kneeling at Baal's altar.

The scepter waved over our careers offered a choice: For defection: ruin, family deaths even, or for obeisance to the landlords and our corporate appendages, or increased power and wealth by oppressing humanity. Meanwhile, our games of smoke and mirrors kept most people's eyes straight ahead and feet to the grindstone.

"We were gods after all. We were determined to outwit some vast awareness, which though willing to let humanity struggle, issues a universal honing signal, triggering the prodigal sons' and daughters' return to their high estate. Often cyclic events, like Solar Flash, appear on the surface to be disasters, but they actually set the stage for humanity's fresh start."

Peter let the volume fall to his lap as his head dropped to his pillow. When Neil approached he waved him away. For several minutes his audience waited as he closed his eyes. The clouds outside shifted, so that the sun's rays shown on Peter's face.

Neil moved to pull the drapes.

"Leave them open. The warmth feels good." Peter breathed deeply, then sat up again. "That Source, the spark of all life, even included my kind in its sweep, that is, if we didn't take great strides to secure our self-serving power over others. We shuddered at the thought of transformation. We spent trillions building vast networks of underground tunnels and cities to outwit and outlive the Cosmic clock. When right on schedule our Solar System intersected that cosmic cloud, we even did our best to prevent the proliferation of children with DNA activated for unimpeded communication with Source."

Neil's voice coaxed Peter to continue.

"It all began with Dora bringing all that seed and forcing you and me to get together."

Neil leaned against the window. "Although Peter insisted I keep quiet concerning his efforts on behalf of the gardening project, I credited him for park and vacant land donations from the start. The governor even had warehouses raided for soil amendments.

"So what effect did this bring on your head, Peter?"

"It was all those people crowding my door."

"Breaking windows?"

Peter eyed Neil. "You know what happened."

"When the gardens were flourishing, people started delivering baskets of produce, flowers and thank you cards at the door."

A wry smiled twisted Neil's lips. "You old rascal. Appears to me Solar Flash zapped you good. It switched on your DNA and got the better of the old Tyrant of Techno City."

Refusing to be duped by the cards and flower scenario, Eena leaned forward. "That's all very nice. I'm glad the people gave you accolades for helping feed them and incidentally saving your own skin. But the townships? The Sovereignty Movement? Have they strewn pretty flowers over the grave of their chance for freedom and dignity?"

Neil addressed Peter. "At this point our voices won't suffice. Eena needs to hear the truth from the people. Think we should call a meeting?

"Yes, a large one."

"In the College Auditorium perhaps?"

"Good idea."

"But where do we stay overnight?"

"Plenty of room here."

"No, thanks."

"There's a couple of visiting students' rooms in the dorm. You can spend the night there."

Caellum and Eena both felt more comfortable to be sitting in Neil's office.

"At three o'clock in the afternoon the student body and whoever else, will gather in the Performance Hall. But first I know a couple who may like to meet with you to tell you what's happening in the Sovereignty Moment."

Neil went to his door, motioned toward the hallway, and introduced Margaret and Dan.

Margaret spoke first, addressing Caellum. "When you were jailed, we continued to spread the word, especially among the student body. Your presence gave us courage. But when you were hauled to Transtopia, we began to lose heart and argue among ourselves. We lost hope. I won't deny the newsreels of your execution at local theaters crushed our spirits."

"Two factions of Sovereignty Seekers rose up. Those dedicated to peaceful infiltration of managerial positions and consequent insertion of rights and privileges, and those strategizing to attack SEI officials where it hurt most, their homes, with homemade bombs and other weapons to wipe out the SEI. The attacks of the main gang brought marshal law on our heads. Strict curfews, soldiers patrolling our homes, demanding passes everywhere we went. Techno City became a prison camp for a couple of months.

Dan took over. "The threat of famine and the urgency to plant gardens pulled our movement together. Changed the focus of the whole town. Governor d'Arc sent accomplished gardeners to the townships.

"Groomed to rely on forced labor, the SEI left the project to us. Their dependence on our success caused a subtle role shift.

"This self-important SEI approaches to chide me for spending too much time away from work. I say, 'Okay, I'll return to be your office servant. But when people like me return to business as usual, who will haul the dirt, or run the tillers, or plant and water the seeds to feed your families this spring?'

"I liked speaking up to those sagging jowls accustomed to lingering at tables over five course meals. Approaching famine and the Sovereignty Gardens project restored our look-them-in-the-eye confidence. In fact, we spoke as more than their equals. Their fate was in our hands.

"The garden project also won over the opposition gangs. They figured out real fast they better join us or starve.

"Caellum, you've become a folk hero. Eena, we remember you well and quote you often. Your return plus the about-face of Governor General d'Arc had signaled the beginning of the end of landlord rule. I'm confident a tour of the townships by you two and Neil and the governor will help promote a major power-shift."

Neil joined Caellum and Eena back stage. "In both the balcony and main auditorium, there's standing room only, and that's almost gone. Look for Peter and me on the far right of the front row."

For another quarter of an hour the heads of the Sovereignty Movement addressed the packed auditorium. Robust applause greeted the conclusion of the final speech.

When the applause died down and before Caellum and Eena walked on stage, silence settled in the assembly. As though the hall had emptied, not even the creek of a chair violated the stillness.

When Eena and Caellum stepped through the curtain, only the rustle of bodies shifting from seated to standing greeted them. To signify appreciation for the people's hard-won victory, the pair stood at the center of the stage and solemnly bowed low and deep, their hands pressed palm to palm over their hearts. The moment of silence held until a thunderous release in the hall reverberated the people's response—joy to be re-united and free at last.

Regrouping 50

Dora's hands shook as she returned the blood-speckled ornament to its stand. She grabbed up Michael, and said to Jeff, "Get Michael's things," and to Vanessa, "Yes, you and your baby are welcome to join us," and to the soldier who appeared at the door, "Governor Scholtz needs immediate medical attention. Get Dr. Monroe."

The control room. They needed to find it. Maybe they could even halt the march of the Five Hundred. She directed the remaining soldiers to make a sweeping search of the premises. But the search yielded no room with a control panel — nothing.

Dora called for Dr. Monroe. In the presence of the soldiers, she explained the imperial governor had fallen and the collision of his head with the vase had left the gushing wound. When Scholtz had been carried away on a stretcher, she commanded the soldiers to file onto the copter, which now served as a medevac flight for the wounded royals.

As they lifted off, her thoughts flew ahead, conjuring the image of Transtopia occupied by Super Robots.

Anxious to reach the outskirts of Transtopia, Dora planned to veer away from the robot entry point and land near the Garden of the Gods, if the city looked occupied, or worse under a bloody siege. No telling what they would find. She looked anxiously ahead for a glimpse of the marching mechanical soldiers, which by now would certainly challenge, and probably mow down the military and civil police before wreaking havoc in the city.

Minutes later, the pilot's exclamation penetrated her reverie. "What's that shining expanse reflecting sunlight?"

Seated in the cockpit Dora leaned forward, unable to make sense of the valley strewn with clumps of shining aluminum. It couldn't be. But it was. Four hundred and ninety-eight robots lay crumpled, yet evenly spaced from one another as though they had fallen simultaneously while marching in formation.

The copter reached the line of defense of the MPs and city police of Transtopia. The fallen SuperRos were just beyond their line of visibility.

"Hand me the radio.... The march from New Denver has been halted. I repeat. The SuperRo threat to Transtopia is no more."

Dora, Rolf, Shaun and Adair stood around Dr. Monroe's desk.

"So you want to understand what halted the SuperRos." The doctor opened his fist to reveal a small rectangular metal object. "This is the computer module that directed the SuperRos."

"So you must have found the control room and extracted it"

"No."

"But where did that come from, and what makes you think this tiny device directed the SuperRos."

"The first clue was the robot guard that went down moments after Biate's head hit the pavement. And when we flew over the field of deactivated robots I suspected they went down the same time."

"So where was this computer chip?"

"Imbedded in Biate's brain."

"But the Central Artificial Intelligence? Have you located that?"

"Yes."

"Where?"

"The interface was between Biate's brain and this module."

"Wait a minute. You're saying she was the central AI?"

"Precisely. The blow to her head instantly deactivated the entire force."

Thanks to Raymond's testimony, which backed up Lieutenant Lebedev's, the homicidal shoot out on the motorcycles had been ruled 'self-defense' in Lebedev's favor. When he was sufficiently healed, Dora promoted him to 'captain' and invited several people and the entire military force to the award ceremony.

"Lieutenant Yanniv Lebedev, I employ the temporary executive powers vested in me as supreme head of the military police, to promote you to the rank of Captain Yanniv Lebedev." She pinned the bars on his collar and stepped back to face him. "I trust that the military forces of Sector 10 will be in good hands under your leadership."

In his quiet understated way, the captain clicked his heels and saluted his superior officer, the one who had served him tea.

The Manuals   51

Chimed notes floated from the balcony, and sunlight streamed through an open window toward the child nestled between his parents. As Michael cooed happily and attempted to grab his toes, Dora mused about the past and days to come. *Do I have the right to feel such joy, such a degree of happiness based on the two royal leaders losing their minds?* When Caellum stirred, she waited patiently for his eyes to open. He rolled on his side, pulling Michael toward him, and with a full heart, the mother watched father and son with tiny fists enclosed in big ones make cooing sounds together. Dora sighed — a heartfilled, reluctant sigh. *If only we could linger and extend these precious moments.*

"We'd better get up. The reading of the Sector 10 Constitution begins in an hour and a half."

"What a spoil sport you are," Caellum teased as a tiny finger explored his nose.

Dora swung her legs over the side of the bed. "And I'm sorry to say, the entire week will be like this. Meeting today, wedding tomorrow and the surprise visit to Doctor Olsen the day after that."

"Okay, okay," he said. "We'll be waiting for your return." Two-year-old habits were difficult to break, even if they entailed hiding in the shadows to evade capture in a bustling world.

"Caellum, you don't have to hide out anymore."

He looked taken aback, and shook his head. "Hard to believe I can walk the streets of Transtopia unimpeded, and with the president."

"The transitional president requests your presence at the reading of the constitution."

"Well, since the president's so good-looking, how can I refuse?"

By the time the meeting for the reading of the new constitution convened, the students had been released from jail and all of them, including those still employed at Onmatson Farm, were reinstated in college. The semester was nearing its end, but they would spend the summer catching up. Meanwhile, every single one was present for this momentous occasion.

The old music hall, including main floor, balcony and wall space, was filled to capacity. The audience, the majority of whom voted for the delegates, was buzzing about the momentous proceedings. To signify the central and leading roles of those formerly designated 'workers,' the royals and former Three Mountains leaders of the Sovereignty Movement scattered themselves in seats on the outskirts of the vast circular hall. In hushed tones, at the door to the hall, Dora had emphatically insisted former SEI personnel not gather as an antagonistic block. Only the students sat together, a youthful, enthusiastic group, who knew as well as anyone the importance of a free and open society.

The Sector 10 Constitution signified a change of leadership, governed not by privilege but by principle. Now it would be up to a new governing body composed of the 'common' people to hash out declarations, amendments and laws in support of the spirit of the new constitution. Throughout the coming months, candidates for the presidency of the new republic would be giving speeches, debating and making promises as contenders for such roles do.

From the stage where Dora would introduce the delegates, she glanced toward Scholtz and Biate seated side by side in their wheelchairs. Vanessa attended Biate, who wore the jeweled crown she had intended to sit atop her head the day of her coronation. When someone took offense, those nearby audibly defended her with "Mentally, she's a child," "Think of her as playing dress-up" and "Harmless."

Scholtz appeared to be staring at the new flag and Dora who stood beside it. Though only disjointed memories of his former role as imperial governor had resurfaced, a significant measure of his old personality often leant force to his demands and momentarily unhinged his listeners.

After Dora's opening address, the introductions and reading of the constitution were met with a standing ovation. Throughout the four-hour meeting, Scholtz and the former Social Engineering minions had the good sense to restrain themselves while the wave of the future obliterated the oppression of yesterday's stronghold.

Strong posts supported Cedarhenge and Titus as he leaned against the fragrant wood. Toying with a blade of grass, he faced Adair, the woman who, with motherly faithfulness had supported his convalescence for a month. Dora, who wanted to be present for this step in the young man's rehabilitation, remained in the background, at the table covered with pieces of colored glass, mostly brown, for the repair of the great tree that had been shattered.

Titus cocked his head as he asked Adair, "So you made that stained glass picture, the one I shot?"

"With help from friends."

"I don't understand why you're so nice to me."

"Listen."

The wind that caressed the trio in Cedarhenge smelled of pinesap and spring flowers and played the chimes that hung from the partial roof. Deftly, the gusts reverberated crescendoed runs and tinkling diminuendos. A particularly strong blast resounded two octaves of notes playing simultaneously.

Adair opened her eyes. "Did you feel that?"

The youth nodded. "Nice sounds."

"Those tones play not only chimes, but us."

Titus shot her an "Are you crazy?" look.

"Our DNA."

"What do those sounds have to do with DNA?"

"Our DNA resolves to sound and light frequencies."

"Okay."

"It codes who we are."

"Like our eye and skin color, height—things like that?"

"Yes, and also our character. Life experience alters DNA."

"You sure about that?"

"I'm an artist, but I'm also a scientist."

"You've lost me."

"It's a matter of frequencies. The DNA of a person who intentionally destroys a thing of beauty vibrates at one level."

"You're referring to the day I shot a hole in the tree."

"Yes. But raised DNA harmonics correlate with incremental shifts from destroyers to creators."

"Raised harmonics?"

"Yes. Like being tuned by a chimed melody."

"So, you're saying I'm no longer the person who shattered that glass tree?"

"Don't ask me. Ask yourself."

"How would I know?"

"One indicator would be helping me restore the mural."

"I know nothing about stained glass."

"I suspect you're a quick learner. The pattern's over there." She gestured toward the table where Dora was sorting bits of glass by color. To the side of the table a paper pattern indicated the knothole section of the Douglas fir trunk.

"So, you said you and others watched me shoot this mural."

"Uh-huh."

"From where? You just disappeared."

"From the center of this structure. On that mound supporting the etched glass Triskelion."

"But that's impossible."

"Then how did I recognize you on the mountainside?"

Titus stared at Adair, his expression blank.

She continued her explanation. "Our raised our harmonics buoyed us."

"There was a group?"

"Yes, a terrified one."

"What do you mean by 'buoyed us?'"

"Lifted us out of harm's way."

Titus frowned. "You're not making sense."

"We had help, I admit."

In answer to Titus's confused stare, Adair continued. "Years ago, I located Cedarhenge here because I had discovered the portal to another world on that central mound."

Abruptly Titus approached the triskelion symbol mounted on the marble pedestal. He circled the top of the mound.

"I see that you still see me."

Adair laughed. "It's a dimensional shift. Takes effort to raise your harmonics to that extent."

"So how did you disappear?"

"With concentrated heart energy."

"Enough to make you invisible?"

"Enough to lift us out of harm's way."

"Meaning, us soldiers?"

"Meaning, a system that would imprison and execute innocent citizens."

"Adair, I don't understand any of this, and my brain's too tired to think about it."

As Adair motioned Titus to the table, Dora smiled and handed him a dark brown piece of glass intended to initiate repair of the shattered trunk of the Douglas fir. "Then think about where to place this tile."

Cedarhenge provided an ideal outdoor cathedral for Cosima and Emory to say their vows. Emory's gaze told Cosima all she wanted to know about the effect of soft white deerskin gracefully accenting her shape and her face framed with white flowers wound through shining chestnut waves.

At the conclusion of the ceremony, an accommodating gust played the chimes, and sunlight glinted on the repaired knothole of the Douglas fir. The guests rose from chairs loaned by the Garden of the Gods Inn, and when the orchestra played the first dance, Leon, who had given away the bride, danced the father-daughter dance with her.

Rolf, looking strikingly handsome as he stood beside Alexi, studied Dora with a hooded sideways glance. "So I suppose this has given you an idea."

She assumed an offended look. "Rolf, can it be at this wedding of our friends, you are asking me for a divorce?"

Rolf nodded toward Caellum, who carried Michael as he visited with the guests. "I don't think *he'll* object."

With a mischievous glint in her eye, Dora whispered into Rolf's ear. "But what would a divorce decree say?"

"Whatever you say will be fine. Alexi, you help her."

Several minutes later, expletives from Charles Scholtz's wheel chair echoed around the clearing.

Rolf's voice rang strong and commanding. "Sign here," and with a disgruntled pout, his SynAnn dad, now more like his son's son, grabbed the pen. In less than a minute Rolf was carrying the paper to Dora. "Here it is: the retraction of the former document by the SynAnn who signed our marriage certificate. You are now a free woman."

"And you an equally free man." Dora smiled suggestively.

The thespian who had grown used to being Dora's husband faced her with a melodramatic pout. "I must ask you. Will you still serve me Rita's superb home cooking, and take me on hair-raising car rides?"

"Certainly. On one condition."

"Yes?"

He handed Dora the signed paper, and she waved it overhead to catch Caellum's attention. Planting a kiss on Rolf's cheek, she replied, "I'll expect Alexi to join us."

Alarm was written on Dr. Olsen's face as he leaned back in his chair to survey the delegation that had crowded into his office. The presence of Dora, the temporary president, Captain Lebedev and Eena, the half-breed who said she wouldn't miss this for the world, added to his sense of something not good about to happen. Lydia looked down at the floor like a demur wife, as though indicating her husband should take the lead.

Nathan signaled with his finger for a man standing outside the office door to deposit a plastic bin on Olsen's desk. "Doctor, I know you have anxiously awaited the return of these manuals. I want you to know the imperial governor, now deposed, credits you with faithfully carrying out the mandates of these SEI Protocol Manuals for three years. And the new Social Facilitation Agency, of which I am the head, mandates you to continue the precise execution of the upgraded codes delineated in these revised volumes."

Apparent relief relaxed Doctor Olsen's jaw.

Nathan glanced at Lydia, glad her advice was effective as he removed one volume at a time for Doctor Olsen to place on the shelf — the red spines arranged precisely in a straight row.

Discarding her demure façade, Lydia addressed the doctor pointedly, not taking her eyes from his. "As Nathan Talbot, Chief Inspector of the newly established Social Facilitation Agency has indicated, we return these manuals to your care with major revisions. These eight hundred pages will require time and careful study in order for you to ingest the new rules and regulations."

Nathan broke in. "You look concerned. Don't worry. Dr. Lydia Abelt" — he gestured toward his wife — "inserted the updated policies in collaboration with the daughter of Peter d'Arc, Governor General of Sector 10, Dora d'Arc, who is the interim president. Henceforth, Dr. Abelt, the professional best equipped to ensure staff compliance for this phase will head up the project."

Ignoring Olsen's shocked expression, Lydia added, "The demanding requirements of the updated policies necessitates staff re-education and internships under my direction. Some staff will naturally be reluctant to release old behaviors. We will replace them with personnel endowed with natural enthusiasm for enlightened child guidance. Any questions?"

After Olsen's dazed headshake, Lydia continued. "As a model for childcare and education throughout Sector 10, this facility will undergo major renovations. Huge, demanding tasks face you and me, Doctor Olsen. During your internship and after you finish thoroughly ingesting the manuals, I will depend on you to be my right arm throughout the momentous transformations at this facility. Doctor, I believe Fort Carson's equipment includes a bulldozer. Am I correct?"

Though Olsen nodded, he avoided eye contact.

"Your first task is to locate it and an operator. Beginning Monday morning, we will bulldoze three acres of asphalt adjacent to the childcare rooms. After loaders and plows distribute sand and soil, we'll hire professional landscapers to build a sandbox and plant trees and other greenery. You will hire carpenters to install French doors to open from each classroom to the outside gardens, which will include tricycle paths, swings and climbing apparatus.

"Are you with me?" Lydia faced down the glazed stare while waiting on his hesitantly spoken 'yes.' "Which brings me to an important question. When is the due date for extracting the current batch of clones from the chambers?"

"Give me a moment, please. I... I have to look at my calendar." Olsen's hands shook as he flipped through the pages. "One week from today."

Lydia beamed. "Excellent, as that is to be the final extraction from that lab." She leaned forward, palms of her hands squarely planted on Olsen's desk. She wanted to impact her assistant with her determination and his good fortune. "After those babies are remanded to the loving care that is rightfully theirs, you will order and oversee that lab's complete, down-to-the-last-screw, dismantling.

"Yes, Dr. Abelt."

"Oh, and one more thing. I'm sure we don't want any reminders lying around of our close brush with losing our humanity to mindless cyborgs. Are there any incinerators at this facility?"

Of everyone standing in Dr. Olsen's office, Eena struggled the most to manage her emotions. For her, the monitored heartbeats in the dimly lit lab had resounded in the background of the sovereignty seekers' endeavors for three years—three long, hard years of struggle. Years in which augurs patrolled the skies over Three Mountains, and rovers seized control of the community. Years in which Caellum faced execution, and an army of super robots marched toward Transtopia. Years of dashed hopes and discouraging setbacks. And through it all, she had worried that she would fail the babies at Fort Carson, and humanity would be doomed in the end.

Suddenly, she was no longer standing in Dr. Olsen's office. The sun-drenched waters of a blue lake shimmered just below, where Ama', midwife of multitudes of children, and Grandfather wearing the Journey of Man pendant stood on either side of her. The soft leather of the beaded moccasins caressed her feet as she gazed at Grandfather. Hunkering on the ground he placed a smoldering nest of grass and twigs under piled sticks, and his breath excited embers to ignite sparks that blazed into red hot flames around and over a carefully placed log.

Ama' took Eena's arm in the crook of her elbow. "Lightning simply zaps a branch and starts a fire," she mused.

Grandfather, looking younger again, smiled with his eyes. "It takes understanding and persistence for us two-leggeds to ignite a fire."

"Likewise, some births test the understanding and persistence of midwives."

Eena remembered Ama's words: "Dora will help you birth a new world." Rare tears filled Eena's eyes. "I'm so happy to see both of you." Her breath caught in her throat. "But being with you makes me realize how I miss my forest home, my beloved Three Mountains."

"And why must you miss them?" queried Grandfather with an eagle perched overhead, as Mato with her new cubs passed behind him.

Why would the old man ask such a question?

Ama' must have read her thoughts. "My daughter, the soldiers have returned to Durango. Three Mountains Valley awaits your return."

Grandfather broke in. "That new president cleared them out. She's got spunk."

Eena couldn't wait to tell Chas. Perhaps others, maybe Leslie and Gavin, would also want to return.

"Grandfather, will I see you again?"

"Probably. You and Nathan need a kick in the pants sometimes."

That was *not* the answer she expected.

The old eyes peered at her. "Do you want to lodge enmity in your mountain home?"

Her sigh was not heavy. It was exasperated, like Gavin's reponses to Grandfather's quirky ways.

"My daughter, when you welcome the one you have despised into your home, your home will welcome you."

"I should have known you'd have another assignment for me." She looked from the blue waters that washed over the crashed plane to Matoskah's clear brown eyes. "Because I have learned from you, Grandfather, because *you* befriended Nathan, I too will befriend the 'disappearing opponent.'"

When she looked up from staring at the moccasins made by Grandfather, he and Ama' were gone, and everyone in Olsen's office was filing out the door. Eager to hurry to Chas and share the good news, she rushed forward to first grab Nathan's arm and thank him. And surprisingly, he thanked her back — Nathan, the opponent who had disappeared.

Thoughts of returning home winged sadness over her heart. How she'd miss Cesla and flights over Three Mountains. *Augurs. So, this is the future you augured. Good name for you, giant birds of Mu. I wish you could know my gratitude, my treasured memories of you, for between your great wings I have soared over mountaintops, patrolled the skies of two worlds and experienced the return of freedom to this one — all that from a sublime vantage point: the augur's view.*

EPILOGUE

With a rush of emotion Eena greeted Anaya for the first time in over a year, and moving forward to embrace her, exclaimed, "I thought I'd never see you again."

"Though I returned to Erath, I never abandoned you."

Gavin also embraced Anaya and shook hands with Jack who was standing close by.

"You two know each other?"

"We conspired together to remove you from the final submergence of the island."

Eena grinned at Jack. "Glad you found us."

As they stood on a balcony admiring the planted fields in one direction, Eena noted the terraformed forest in another and not far from that a jungle.

"Come with me." Anaya's enigmatic smile accompanied her invitation to ride the elevator to below ground level where a tube-like car parked at the entrance to a tunnel awaited them. "There's another terraformed area I want to show you." After a quick passage through the tunnel, the door slid open, and an elevator took them up to a balcony overlooking yet another ecosystem. At first, they had to shield their eyes from the bright light outside. But as their gaze followed the tall grass in the distance, giant cypress trees became visible. "Like our other terraformed ecosystems, this terrain covers about a million acres. Remember the river that ran through the city? Branches of that river meander through this land."

Eena recalled standing on a balcony similar to this one two years ago after the amazing surgical skills of the Erathans brought her from the brink of death. "When we stood overlooking the jungle, I heard an elephant trumpet and the roar of a lion. I also recall the scarlet bird resembling a firebird that flew over the canopy."

"And what do you hear now?"

Eena and Gavin stood still, side by side.

They shook their heads. "Nothing."

"Let's be quiet and feel it."

As their eyes adjusted to the glare, a strange, yet familiar sensation vibrated in their chests.

"Hey, look there's a bird landing in that grove of short trees."

"Fruit trees."

Eena's eyes widened and blinked her amazement. "Anaya, I feel and hear it. The rumble coo."

The shock on Gavin's face rivaled Eena's. "How? Have these augurs always been here?"

"The recent arrivals were a challenging cargo for Jack."

Gavin turned to Jack. "Your mission with no time to lose."

"After beaming them up one at a time, I had to put up a force field between myself and them. Otherwise, a huge one, mean as bloody hell, would have sliced me to mincemeat."

Gavin groaned. "Phoenix."

Awe rang in Eena's voice. "Thank you, Jack." And to Anaya, "So, your people saved them from extinction."

"None of the creatures from Zoological Garden Earth have actually gone extinct. Besides an all-encompassing DNA bank, terraformed ecosystems preserve some creatures, like those augurs, for instance."

With their eyes adjusted to the light, Eena and Gavin counted fifteen augurs, the number they had moved to Chas's corral. Like a moat surrounding the grove of mango and papaya trees, shades of blue-green shifted and glinted in the light. While some twelve-foot wingspans descended into the golden sea of savannah grasses, others carried satiated sky travelers to the cypress groves lining the river. Huge limbs invited the birds to perch in contentment and bask in clear skies with breathable air.

Palpable excitement quickened Eena's and Gavin's breath as they walked through the gate opened by Anaya. "That path leads to the fields beyond. I have put up a force field to protect you from predators."

Their eyes were glued to the augurs, the creatures that had helped Sector 10 win its freedom, that had been beloved companions for almost three years, the ones they assumed had died forty-thousand years ago during a volcanic eruption. The visitors' legs remained locked.

Anaya cocked her head. "Well?"

Spontaneous grins spread over Eena and Gavin's faces as they entered the path and psychically called Cesla and Phoenix. Two augurs rose from the golden waves, and sunlight glinted on turquoise and teal wings at the approach of an unexpected but most welcome reunion.

The hexagonal stargate enclosing seven glowing circles loomed huge, as did Jack's hesitation. Although his dreams of breathtaking speeds at the helm of a spaceship had receded to the stuff of boyhood, he wasn't ready to portal to the vastness of space. He paused to muse, to consider the invitation.

First, my thanks to you, Randolph Ring. Not that I totally understand our connection, and how you came forward in time to send that odd, scribbled note. You told me to follow the instructions on that paper and I would reach the Blue Star Center for Research and Development. I did, and soon after, as I stuffed my face with muffins, you pointed the way to soul-satisfying possibilities — to future missions — to the recent one that saved the lives of two people fighting for human sovereignty.

But, Randolph, regarding my next mission assignment, it's not so easy to pilot this ship through that stargate; it's not so easy knowing I may never return to this planet; it's not so easy to face the vast unknown. I know. You'd hold your mug and say, "It's not meant to be 'so easy.'"

Anaya, the Erathan, picked up where you left off, Randolph. She mentioned some place called Tall-ah Earth. Said my next assignment would land me there. "Prepare yourself to meet the 'Oids,'" she said.

"Oids?"

"Avesoids, Caninoids, Pantheroids, Humanoids and so on. The 'oids' are ad infinitum in the cosmos."

I groaned.

"You'll interact with seven races — all but the humanoids, alien to you."

"Like the seven circles glowing within the border of the stargate, the hexagon."

"Precisely. All interconnected, like the oids in the next adventure — that is, if you decide to engage the stargate."

I don't say anything, because I haven't decided anything.

"Brace yourself. It will be scary at times. But you'll have backup to help you navigate dangerous situations."

I have to admit I was about to back out of my next mission before it began, when Anaya told me about the abductees.

"Abductees?"

"A young woman and a group of Apisoids, also known as Bee People. As we speak, an artificial planet called the 'Dark Planet' holds them captive in its interior."

I also have to admit I'm a sucker for rescuing beautiful maidens. And the Apisoids remind me of the levitating bee in Randolph's explanation of levitating spaceships.

When the glowing pulse of the stargate accelerated, Jack jerked himself back to the present. Anaya had said stargates can close abruptly. In which case he could be waiting indefinitely for the next opportunity. No telling what would happen to the woman and Apisoids prior to a delayed rescue.

He asked himself if he'd gone crazy to even consider the Dark Planet for his next destination. How to get there; what to do when he arrived; how he would succeed as a one-man rescue team—he had no idea. But Randolph insisted his craft was intelligent, and Anaya said it would take him where he needed to go and help him accomplish what he needed to do.

Jack recalled how he reached Blue Star Center for Research and Development. In the middle of the Moroccan desert he boarded that small craft without any idea how to fly it to Randolph's center. Written on the note inside were the words "Just intend it."

Since that worked, Jack guessed he'd intend to reach the Dark Planet. Then he'd intend to rescue the maiden and Bee People. Apparently, next stop for intended arrival would be Tall-ah Earth.

So, in a huge leap of faith, Jack first engaged the responsive consciousness that was his vessel, and then himself. "Okay, prepare for a rendezvous with the Dark Planet and its captives." In the style of Captain Piccard, Jack said, "Engage," and the stargate disappeared and total darkness surrounded him except for distant stars, and he was all alone. At least he *thought* he was all alone....

THE END

ABOUT THE AUTHOR

In seventh grade, Mrs. Trader inspired me both as a writer and a teacher. In her class, I learned I loved to write and that my classmates liked to hear my stories. Her spirited students engaged in dramatic performances, hands-on projects, and lively discussions—nothing like the poor subdued souls across the hall, managed by the teacher with long green eyes. So Mrs. Trader was my model when I started a school and set aside my writing—that is, until it dawned on me that tribes of children have loved learning by listening to stories for thousands of years. So I wrote about a million words that speak to head and heart, which I am still reading to my child listeners. But now I'm writing stories, my second million words, to speak to the heads and hearts of adult readers and listeners, and hoping my classmates will like them.

For more, please visit me online at:
Website: www.NewEarthChronicles.net
Facebook: Victoria.Lehrer22
Twitter: @VickiDJ22

MORE FROM EVOLVED PUBLISHING

We offer great books across multiple genres, featuring high-quality editing (which we believe is second-to-none) and fantastic covers.

As a hybrid small press, your support as loyal readers is so important to us, and we have strived, with tireless dedication and sheer determination, to deliver on the promise of our motto:
QUALITY IS PRIORITY #1!

Please check out all of our great books,
which you can find at this link:
www.EvolvedPub.com/Catalog/

Thank you!

Printed in the USA
CPSIA information can be obtained
at www.ICGtesting.com
LVHW040258200324
774875LV00006B/576